# Loving Jordan
## An Ache of Desire
## M/M Romance Trilogy

by

## Andrea Dalling

Published by
### Artesian Well Publishing
www.ArtWellPub.com

This steamy gay romance bundle is intended for a **mature** audience. It contains scenes of groping, fumbling, wet kisses, angst, and two-man showers.

I0524853

Loving Jordan
© 2016 Andrea Dalling
ISBN 978-1942198062

Published in the United States of America
First edition, February 2016

# Table of Contents

# Book 1: Seducing Jordan

# Chapter 1

*2008*

Jordan Callahan braced against the dashboard, the SUV lurching as Rick Ferguson pulled hard on the steering wheel to navigate around the hairpin curve. His heart slammed into his ribcage and beat double.

His frantic breathing steadied as Rick regained control. "Slow down, shithead."

"Sorry."

Typical Rick, pushing the boundaries until they pushed back. Maybe it hadn't been a big risk when they were playing on the monkey bars in first grade. These mountain roads were less forgiving.

Rick's silence and the tightness at the corners of his mouth showed his consternation. Jordan chewed his lip to keep from smiling. He couldn't stay angry when Rick knew he'd screwed up.

He clenched his fist to hold back the urge to clutch his friend's hand. The longing washed over him to stroke the tension from Rick's body, fingers exploring the arcs of solid muscle. He leaned forward, forearms on his thighs to hide the rising bulge in his crotch.

A lump gathered in his throat. Would this be the last weekend he and Rick spent together? College started in two weeks—new places, new people, new priorities. What would happen to their childhood friendship now that they'd grown up?

He sat back and gazed over the rolling Pocono Mountains. Green slopes rose above the haze cloaking the valley in the August afternoon. The SUV's motor chattered, climbing toward the campground. Not like they'd be roughing it—Rick had rented a nice place, he said, for this last trip together before they left for campuses in different states.

The truck pulled into the driveway in front of the cabin, grinding gravel under tires. The cedar siding made the A-frame look like part of the landscape, bushy conifers softening its lines.

He hopped out of the SUV. From the ridge, the campground sprawled below them: tennis courts, hiking trails, a lake for kayaking. Plenty of activities to distract him from the decadent things he wanted to do to Rick's body. *Right?*

Rick came and stood by him, patting his back. The warm sensation sent shivers through him.

"What do you think of the view?" Rick asked.

"Beautiful."

He wasn't talking just about the scenery. He pretended not to notice the shine in Rick's brown eyes, or the way the breeze tousled his wavy dark hair. A smile brought Rick's face to life. He burned to kiss that mouth, to nibble the cleft of his chin.

"Cyn doesn't mind you going away this weekend?" Jordan asked. Cynthia Darlington, the most popular girl in school, had been Rick's girlfriend for three years.

"Cyn and I aren't a couple anymore. I mean, we're still sort of dating, but we agreed to see other people."

"And that includes me?"

Rick's cheeks flushed crimson. "I didn't mean it like that."

*Of course he didn't. What a fucking stupid thing to say.*

"Just kidding."

Smiling, Rick punched his arm, and Jordan pushed him away. The awkward moment passed. Jordan would have to control himself better this weekend. If he said out loud the things he felt, he could lose Rick forever.

Rick popped the hatch so they could get their gear. The tension in his stomach wound into a knot. In a few minutes, Jordan would know what he had in mind for the weekend. He couldn't hide it once they got inside the cabin.

He stole a glance at his friend. Jordan had lost the bulk from weight training during football season, but a summer job at his uncle's landscaping business had given him a lean, hard physique. His toned body would get him noticed when he arrived on Princeton's campus in two weeks.

Hot fingers gripped his heart. Jordan hadn't had many opportunities to date in their semi-rural hometown, since none of their other classmates was *out*. The thought of strange men cruising him, only interested in a blow job, raised the bile in his throat.

Jordan leaned inside to pull out his bag, offering a view of hard, round glutes and thick thighs. He swallowed and adjusted his jean shorts.

Jordan slid his duffle over his shoulder, the slanting light of the afternoon sun kissing his blond hair. He was tan from working outside. The darkness of his skin made his eyes shine even bluer. No wonder all the girls at school had lamented he was gay.

Rick retrieved his bag and a small cooler, then led the way along the wood-chip path toward the cabin. It was cleaner here, away from the city. Pine spiced the air. The hills of eastern Pennsylvania stretched for miles below them, filling him with a sense of freedom, like standing on top of the world.

But the next moment, an image of Cynthia encroached on his mind, and anxiety bit his gut. Agreeing to see other people hadn't silenced the voice that told him to escape that trap. Why was he staying with her at all?

Maybe his feelings for Cyn were as good as it got. In the three years they'd been together, he'd never been tempted to cheat on her. Other girls didn't cross his mind. Was that love?

"The view of the lake from here is fantastic." Jordan's voice broke through his worry. Water shone like silver in the valley below. "I see why you chose this cabin instead of our usual one."

He nodded. He and Jordan had been to this campground a few times since they'd gotten their licenses. They'd been in Boy Scouts together as kids, but Jordy wasn't welcome after he came out. Rick had quit in protest, even though he was well on the way to Eagle Scout. Anger throbbed in his chest. Jordan was an all-star running back headed to Princeton, yet he wasn't good enough for that stupid organization. What a bunch of turds.

They reached the door, and he fumbled for the key. The view wasn't the reason he'd chosen a different cabin. Jordan would see that soon enough. Still, he wasn't ready to give up the charade. He clung to the last moments of normalcy between them. "This place has a bigger kitchen, too." He tried to sound natural, but his fingers trembled as he slid the key into the front door.

Jordan followed him inside and let out a whistle. "You're not kidding."

He shut the door, and his eyes scanned the open space. Off to the right, the black granite countertops of the modern kitchen reflected the shine of the overhead light. To the left was a sitting room with an overstuffed sectional and a big-screen TV. Dominating the room was the king-sized bed on the far wall, the white bedspread contrasting with the dark walnut headboard. How would he explain, when Jordan realized the cabin didn't have another bedroom?

He dumped his luggage at the foot of the bed, then took Jordan's duffle and set it beside his own bag. Apprehension surged through his belly. He wasn't ready for this conversation. What if he was wrong about Jordan's feelings for him?

"We should get some groceries," he blurted, "then, uh, maybe some sandwiches for dinner." He needed to get them out of the cabin.

"It's only four o'clock."

"Right, but, you know how long it takes me to pick out the perfect variety of potato chips."

Jordan arched his brows, then shrugged. "Okay."

Jordan leaned over the shopping cart at the Acme, pressing the heel of his hand into his forehead. The muscles around his eyes were tight, forming a dull ache. The disco music playing through the speakers overhead didn't help.

It wasn't just the potato chips this time. Rick lingered over every selection…cookies, soda, cereal. They'd been in the store almost an hour, and they had four items in the cart.

"Ooh, pancake mix," Rick said. "Maybe we should have that instead of cereal."

He clenched his jaw. "I will fucking kill you."

"Why?" Rick scowled.

"It took you fifteen minutes to decide on Frosted Flakes."

Rick set the pancake mix into the cart. He took out the box of cereal and slid it onto a shelf at random. "We'll need eggs and milk, too."

Jordan massaged his temples, to stop his head from exploding.

He followed Rick to the back of the store where the milk was. "What do you think?" Rick asked. "Whole, two percent, one percent, skim—"

"Just pick one."

"Gallon, half-gallon, quart—"

Jordan grabbed a half-gallon of two percent and dropped it into the cart. "We're done here." He pushed the cart toward the far corner to get the eggs.

"Jordy, are you mad at me?"

He clenched his fists and glared. Rick's eyes were large, his mouth frowning. He looked upset. Jordan looked away, his anger softening against his will.

Rick pulled at the hem of Jordan's T-shirt. "Don't be mad. I know I'm a pain in the ass sometimes, but I want this to be a good weekend. I spent a lot of time planning this trip. After we leave for college, I don't know when we'll be able to hang out again."

His heart swelled and hurt his chest. He wanted to kiss that sweet, stupid face, thread his fingers through that wavy hair. The heat from Rick's body washed over him. *Fuck.* He was so screwed.

Rick patted his back. "See, I knew you weren't mad."

A jolt of electricity shot straight to his cock. He swallowed hard, getting a grip on the shakiness that had taken over his insides. His neck and cheeks warmed, and his breath deepened. Surely Rick could tell the effect he was having. Yet he didn't pull away. He met Jordan's gaze. Rick's brown eyes darkened, his pupils dilating.

Jordan stepped back and forced a grin. "Want to get some sandwiches at the deli?"

"How about burgers instead?"

They stepped into the burger joint, one of Rick's favorites because it wasn't a chain. It was popular among the locals, and tourists flocked there, too. The place wasn't crowded yet because it was early. The staff all wore cowboy hats, and the corny Western theme was reinforced with appliqués of saddles and horses spattered across the wood-paneled walls. The aroma of frying beef and melting cheese made his stomach rumble.

He laid his hand on Jordan's shoulder. "Know what you want?"

Jordan stepped back. "Usual, I guess. Burger, fries, Mountain Dew."

He swallowed. "Yeah, me too, except I think I'll get a Coke." Why had Jordy pulled away like that? He looked like he was in heaven when Rick touched him back at the grocery store. A crimson blush had covered his cheeks, making him look sweet and vulnerable. Rick wanted to wrap protective arms around him, tell him everything would be okay. Whatever Jordan wanted, Rick would give him. He didn't have to be afraid of his feelings anymore.

A group of younger teens rushed inside, giggling. They crowded toward the counter. A big kid bumped into Rick's back, pushing him into Jordan. Their chests brushed together, and he grabbed Jordan's arm to steady himself.

"Sorry," the kid said.

"S'okay," he replied, still holding on to Jordan. When he'd fallen into him, he'd felt a bulge in Jordan's shorts. He looked over. Jordan's eyes were wide, his lips parted. Rick's body tingled, wanting to kiss that waiting mouth. He was getting to Jordan. Maybe tonight would work out okay after all.

He let his hand linger, hoping Jordy would get the hint. But there were too many people crammed into the place now to risk looking like they were a couple. Rural Pennsylvania wasn't known for its open-mindedness.

Pulling back his hand, he missed the warmth of Jordan's skin, the softness of the fine hair on Jordan's arm. He could never get enough of him, that beautiful face and body, the flashing of his eyes when he was mad, the sound of his laugh when he was happy.

Rick had never felt that way about Cyn. Pretty and so sweet, she delighted in taking care of him. Kissing her turned him on. Yet he had never ached for her like he did Jordan.

They got to the front of the line and ordered their meals. They carried their trays to a two-person booth by the window, with a view of the sun glimmering over the mountains. His watch read six o'clock. They had almost two hours of daylight left.

In the small booth, their knees rubbed together. "Want to sit somewhere else?" he asked.

"Don't think there is anywhere else."

Rick looked around. The group of teens had claimed the last two tables. "S'okay," he said. "I don't mind being close to you."

Jordan's eyes widened. He pulled back, his body shrinking.

Warmth crept up his torso toward his face. Man, he was making a fool of himself! Jordan must think he had lost his mind.

He slid his Coke back and forth across the tabletop. He leaned down and took a sip. Anything to avoid Jordan's eyes.

Finally, he looked up. He needn't have worried. Jordan was staring out the window.

"Pretty here," Rick said.

"Remember the last time we went camping with Boy Scouts? We hiked down to the lake and caught tadpoles and crayfish." The lines of Jordan's jaw hardened. "Do you ever miss it? I mean, feel like you gave up something because of me?"

Jordan's words shot through his heart. Had Jordy been carrying that burden all these years? "I didn't quit because of you. I quit because of them. All that time I'd worked hard to follow their rules, to win their approval, only to find out their approval wasn't worth having.

They made me feel dirty. I'd let them become part of my identity, but I never really knew who they were. It was like finding out they were part of the KKK."

A soft smile lit Jordan's features. "I wouldn't go that far."

"That's how it felt." He shuffled in his seat and clutched his fist in his hand.

"I miss doing stuff like that with you. I mean, we still hang out. But since you started dating Cyn..." Jordan shook his head. "Not like things would have stayed the same between us anyway. We were kids then."

"I miss it, too." He combed his fingers through his hair. "In high school...I'm starting to realize how many choices I made because of peer pressure or whatever, the things people expected. I know I was a jerk, shutting you out sometimes." He rocked, trying to regain control of his emotions. The words he had to say burned his throat. "I was afraid people would say I was gay. So I started going with Cyn." He scraped the wax off the paper cup with his thumbnail. "I wish I'd been a better friend to you."

Jordy's lips moved, but no sound came out. He leaned forward. "I don't remember it that way. You had my back."

His chest lightened, and a smile broke out across his lips. "Buds forever."

Jordan bumped Rick's outstretched fist.

"Want to walk down to the lake when we get back?" Rick asked. "We still have time before dark."

"Sure."

He suppressed a grin. The lake was a pretty spot, romantic even. A walk there would buy him more time so he could introduce his intentions gradually.

# Chapter 2

Jordan led the way down the woodland path toward the lake. Cardinals fluttered overhead and chickadees sang their nasal call. In the shade, it was ten degrees cooler and a pleasant walk, as long as he remained shirtless.

He was glad to be in front. If he'd had a view of Rick's ass the whole way down, he'd have lost his mind. He was in his sexual prime without a boyfriend in sight. He hoped Princeton would change that.

Were his fantasies about Rick getting in the way of a real relationship? It wasn't as if he had options, not without traveling to a larger town. He didn't know of any underage gay clubs. Was there such a thing? How did gay teens meet each other?

The lake came into view. Hugged by a mix of pine, spruce, and hardwoods, it stretched to the horizon and beyond. Sailboats, jet skis, and other watercraft dotted the surface, spreading lines of white across the blue.

He clambered over rocks to a patch of sand, Rick following behind. Their sneakers gently sank into the soft earth. The lowering sun cast a sheen of golden light across the water.

"I love the peacefulness of this place," he said.

"Me too." Rick laid his hand on his shoulder.

A tingling pulsed through his body. He pulled away. Why was Rick always touching him? He didn't touch straight guys like that. Did Rick think it was okay, because Jordan was gay? Wasn't that all the more reason for Rick *not* to touch him? Straight guys always worried that people would think they were gay. So why was Rick so open about his affection?

If it had been any other close friend, he wouldn't have minded. But Rick was his dream guy. Every touch reawakened the hope that somehow, they could be together. Now that Rick and Cyn had agreed to see other people, that hope was even stronger. Even though he knew it could never happen.

Two more weeks. Then he and Rick would be apart for two months until the mid-semester break. They'd never been apart that long since they met in first grade. It would be good to have the space to figure out who he was without his best friend.

Rick looked out over the lake, then at the back of Jordan's head. That was the second time in an hour Jordan had shrunk from his touch. What did it mean? If he'd read Jordan's signals wrong, it was going to be a long, uncomfortable weekend.

"Jordy, is something wrong?"

Jordan turned, his eyes wide. "Why would something be wrong?"

"You're acting like you don't want to be here with me."

Jordan scuffed his shoe against the sand. "We're starting a new phase of our life, and we don't know what that means for us. Will we still be friends a year from now?"

"Of course we will. I love you, buddy. College won't change that."

Jordan's lips quivered, and he looked away.

That flicker of emotion renewed his hope. He stood beside Jordan. "Other than my family, you've been the one constant in my life. We're not kids anymore—this friendship can become whatever we want. We're not limited by other people's rules."

Jordan looked at him with confusion in his eyes. This wasn't going well. Jordan wasn't getting his hints. "What do you want our friendship to be?" Rick asked.

"It doesn't matter what I want," Jordan said. "I'll go to Princeton, make gay Ivy League friends and lead a gay Ivy League life, whatever that means. You'll go to Penn State, make jock friends and lead a jock life. Our worlds will never meet."

"Who says I'll make jock friends? My parents and I agreed that football would be too much of a distraction for me my first semester of college—and I would never have made the Penn State team anyway. Maybe I'll make gay friends and you'll make jock friends. Those Ivy League gays might be too gay for you."

Jordan chuckled. "You may be right. Which sucks, because I'd like to lose my virginity some time this decade."

"Maybe the right person is closer than you think."

Jordan smirked. "You mean I might get paired up with a hot, gay roommate?"

"Your problem won't be finding guys, but fighting them off." He swallowed. "Promise me you'll be careful."

"I know about condoms, if that's what you mean."

"Not just that. Guys taking advantage of you." His chest heaved. "You're fucking gorgeous. Some guy who can't seduce you might decide to take what he wants. It would kill me if someone hurt you like that because I wasn't there to protect you."

Jordan squeezed his shoulder. "I'll be careful. I won't go out alone, I won't go anywhere with a strange guy—"

"Don't believe the first guy who tells you he loves you. In fact, don't believe any guy who tells you that. If they want sex, they'll tell you anything."

Jordan grinned. "Is that what you did with Cyn?"

He scanned the sky. The clouds were edged with pink. "I thought I loved Cyn. I wanted to. By the time we finally slept together, we'd already started growing apart. At fifteen, we were perfect for each other. At eighteen—"

*At eighteen, I started fantasizing about you. And I don't know what the hell that means.*

He grabbed Jordan's forearm and pulled him to his chest. "You need anything, I'm there. I don't care if I have to drive four hours in the middle of the night. I don't care if I miss midterms or finals. Nothing's more important to me than you."

Jordan looked at him with wide eyes, then nodded. "That goes both ways."

He wanted to kiss him, to taste that hot mouth. But not here. Not where some homophobe with a gun might see them. Hunters used these cabins, too.

He let go of Jordan's arm. "It'll be dark soon. We should get back."

They headed off in the direction of the trail. They climbed a steep hill, but Rick stopped when they reached the summit. Trees closed around them. With half an hour of daylight left, the shade was heavy.

He cleared the debris from the path with his foot. "I know that people grow apart when they go to college, but I don't want that to happen to us. We've got too much history. You mean more to me than even Cyn does."

"Dude, what is up with you? My mom isn't this clingy."

His stomach twisted. This was getting worse and worse.

"Hey." Jordan squeezed his arm. "If something's bothering you, you can talk to me. About anything."

He was past talking. He wanted Jordan with a ferocious mix of love and sex and possession. This secret had burned too long and was about to burst out of him. He needed Jordan naked, soon, before his self-control left him.

"Let's just get back to the cabin."

# Chapter 3

Hot and sticky after the walk, Jordan got another bottle of water out of the cooler. He twisted off the top with a snap. The cool liquid slid down his throat.

He took off his tee, balled it up, and tossed it into a corner. "I need to wash up."

Rick nodded but didn't speak.

Jordan looked around the bathroom. The double vanity was painted black and topped with Carrara marble. Brushed nickel fixtures and porcelain tile floors continued the sense of opulence. Despite the spa-like feel, he couldn't relax. Something was going on with Rick. It was more than just going off to college—he seemed spooked, as if their friendship was at stake somehow.

He stepped into the two-person shower. Like the rest of the cabin, it seemed designed for a romantic rendezvous. He quickly soaped up and rinsed off. Wrapping himself in a thick, sage-green towel, he luxuriated in the softness.

Thoughts of Rick left his skin sensitized with desire. The towel dragged across hard nipples, sending heat into his cock. He breathed deeply to calm himself. In two more weeks, the three years of temptation would be behind him. He dabbed himself lightly, then dried his hair. He stepped back into his shorts.

As he exited the bathroom, Rick went inside, arm glancing his as he stepped through the doorway. He swallowed to suppress a moan. Rick closed the door, but Jordan's eyes lingered after him. The sound rushing water in the shower conjured images of Rick naked and slick with soap, hands cleansing those hard pecs and firm glutes.

He flopped onto the bed, staring at the ceiling. How would he get through this weekend without losing his mind? Or worse, doing something stupid? The intensity in Rick's eyes at the lake...like Rick wanted to kiss him, but that was insane. He was projecting his own feelings. He had to stop before he lost control.

The latch sounded on the bathroom door. He didn't let his eyes wander over Rick's nude form as he put on his briefs and shorts.

Rick flopped onto the bed next to him. They lay in silence for a while, both flat on their backs. When they were boys, they used to lie like this on the grass in the backyard and look at the clouds—or at night, the stars. Sometimes they'd talk, but other times they'd just watch, the silence comfortable between them.

"This is nice," Rick said, "being here with you."

"Yeah." He looked over and smiled, but Rick didn't meet his gaze. His heart rate accelerated. This felt *too* nice. He froze, his eyes scanning the cabin. Where was the second bedroom?

"Sometimes I think about you." Rick's hand brushed against his. "Do you think about me?"

His breath stilled. *What the hell?*

Rick's fingers intertwined with his. "Sometimes when I'm with Cyn, I imagine it's you underneath me. Do you fantasize about me like that?"

*Holy mother fuck.* Rick thought about him *that* way? This couldn't...Rick couldn't...But Rick's hand was squeezing his. That was real. And now the silence was stretching on too long. He had to speak, couldn't leave Rick hanging, even though blood was rushing from his head like he might faint.

His throat was so dry he could barely get the words out. "All the time."

"Do you want it to be more than a fantasy?"

His heart pummeled his chest as if a 300-pound linebacker were running toward him. Adrenaline pulsed into his arms and legs.

He hurried into the kitchen. His trembling hands pulled the groceries out of the bags, sticking them into cabinets at random. A bag of chips slipped from his fingers and hit the floor. "Shit." That would make Rick mad. He didn't like broken chips.

Except Rick didn't get mad. He walked up behind him and laid warm hands on his shoulders.

His breath hitched and his body stilled. *This isn't happening. I want this so bad I'm imagining things.*

Rick pushed aside Jordan's hair and kissed his neck. His skin caught fire. Lips soft as suede caressed his flesh. The flick of a tongue sent blood rushing, engorging his penis. Hips pressed against him, erection molding into the cleft of his ass. "Want me?"

He tried to speak, but no sound escaped. He'd forgotten how to breathe. Rick squeezed the bulge in Jordan's pants, and he gasped.

*More, please.* His body trembled with need. He rubbed against the hard shaft pressing into him.

Rick let out a throaty growl. "Bed."

He wasn't sure whether it was a question or an order, but he wasn't about to refuse.

Cradling Jordan's hand in his own, Rick led him to the bed. He hadn't seen this gentle side of Rick since they were little boys, before the testosterone kicked in. Tenderness swelled his heart, followed by fear. Frantic thoughts pushed through the haze of lust. What if Rick hated this?

*Damn it.* Why couldn't his brain have kept silent? His heart and body ached for this. But he couldn't give up Rick's friendship. He'd rather stop this thing now than lose Rick forever.

Standing at the side of the bed, he pulled his hand free. "Are you sure about this?"

Rick nodded tentatively, as if hovering at the edge of the ocean with only his toes testing the waves.

"That's not very convincing."

"I'm scared." Rick's voice was taut. "This changes everything. But I love you, and I trust you."

He wanted to sink into Rick's arms, to revel in those sweet words. But he didn't dare. Where was this was coming from? Love? Idle curiosity? *He can't be in love with me. I couldn't survive that much happiness.*

"What about Cyn?"

"The last few months, whenever I've been with Cyn, I've fantasized about you. I need to know if this is who I am."

His knees nearly buckled. Tears threatened his eyes. "You can't do this. You can't suddenly decide…and just expect me…"

Rick took his hand. "I can't stop thinking about you. I don't know what it means, but I need to find out."

The glide of a thumb across his palm left him weak with desire. Lips pressed to his shoulder. A shiver shot through him. Rick's mouth traveled along his collarbone to his neck.

"You like it when I touch you."

Jordan massaged his brow. "That doesn't mean I'm ready—"

"We've been friends since we were six years old. We're attracted to each other. Why shouldn't we—"

"Because you like girls! Because we've never been on a date!"

Rick slid his hands into the pockets of his shorts. "You can set the pace. If you're not ready for sex—"

"Is that why you brought me here? To a cabin with a king-sized bed?" The realization washed over him like a cold rain. "There's no second bedroom, is there."

"I can sleep on the couch, if that's what you want."

"How long have you been planning this?"

Rick shrugged. "About a month. I've been thinking about it a lot longer. I didn't know how else to tell you."

He stared. "We hang out every day. You couldn't have just *said* something?"

Rick lowered his eyes and shuffled his feet. "I wanted to make it special."

*Fucking idiot.* "You can't use me like that, experiment to see if you're gay."

"I'm not saying I fantasize about men. I fantasize about *you*. The dimple in your chin when you smile." Rick cupped Jordan's cheek in his hand. "The way the sunlight turns your hair to gold. When you look at me, I feel this sudden dip in my stomach. I've got a huge crush on you. I need to know what that means."

He paced. Rick followed after him. "If you don't want to, I understand. It won't change our friendship either way."

"You think you can fuck me, and go back to being just friends."

Rick looked away, then murmured, "I don't know."

"Well, I can't." He swallowed hard. "You're thinking about the sex, not after. It will change things between us, and maybe not in a good way."

"I'm willing to risk it."

"I'm not." He took Rick's hands. "I love you too much to lose your friendship. What if one of us doesn't like it? What if one of us wants more from the relationship than the other?"

"What if we decide this is what we want for the rest of our lives? Are you willing to miss out on that? Because I'm not. Getting closer will only make me love you more."

He trembled. Rick was luring him in, and he didn't want to fight it.

"Look," Rick said, "I'm the one taking the bigger risk here. Until a few months ago, I thought I was straight. My whole identity is on the line. But touching you…holding you…it felt right. More right than anything I've done with Cyn. Maybe this is who I am. I need to know."

He couldn't stop his tears. His cheeks burned with shame at his weakness. He rushed out of the cabin.

The darkness and warm air engulfed him. He dried his eyes and looked up at the stars, but he couldn't bring them into focus. The door behind him creaked. He lurched forward, gravel crunching under his feet.

Rick jogged up and grabbed his arm. "I'm sorry. I didn't mean to freak you out."

"After all these years being friends, how can you manipulate me like this? You want to use me to see if you like cock?"

"Keep your voice down. You don't know what kind of crazies might be out here."

Jordan crossed his arms and bit his cheek to contain his fury.

"I screwed up, okay?" Rick said in a low voice. "I see how you look at me sometimes, and I thought if you were attracted to me, maybe you would want to...But if that's not how you feel, I'll sleep on the couch. Tomorrow, we'll pretend this never happened. Please, Jordy."

"You're an asshole."

Rick pulled his shoulders in tight and shrugged. "Maybe. But we're still friends, aren't we? You said you wanted us to stay friends."

Jordan strode back inside. The door squeaked, and Rick's footsteps followed him. He didn't turn around.

"Do you want me to take you home?"

Rick's voice was tight. He was obviously hurting. Well, that's what he deserved, ambushing him like that. Just expecting him to fuck Rick because he offered. Like he was that desperate.

Did he want to go home? *Shit*. He loved Rick too much to leave things hanging between them. He wanted to work this out, repair the damage.

He turned. The sight of Rick took his breath away. Downturned mouth, brooding eyes, pale cheeks—he had never seen Rick so sad. And those bulging biceps, those steely abs made him want to kiss the pain away.

"Stop looking at me like that," Rick said.

"Like what?"

"Like you want to fuck me."

He bit his lip. "Sorry."

"If both of us want the same thing, why are you fighting it?"

"Because you're not my boyfriend."

Rick scowled. "Would you feel better if I asked you to go steady?"

"Don't be a prick. This isn't a joke."

Slowly, Rick approached. Jordan closed his eyes, fighting the yearning Rick's nearness brought.

"I'm more than a boyfriend," Rick murmured in his ear. "We've shared our entire childhood. Don't turn me down because you think I don't love you enough. No man loves you more than I do."

His throat swelled and his hands trembled. He couldn't open his eyes. He'd lose his will to resist if he saw the desire in Rick's face.

A hand swept down his arm, and a strangled moan pushed through his lips. A velvet mouth caressed his neck. His knees buckled.

"I—" He couldn't form the words.

Rick's hands gripped his waist. "We'll take it as slow as you want. If you're not ready for sex, that's okay. It's enough to know how good it feels to hold you. That answers the big question. I'm bi. And that doesn't freak me out. I thought it would, but it doesn't. Because it's you. My oldest friend. The person who knows me best in the world."

He met Rick's eyes. They were soft and filled with deep affection. Warmth suffused Jordan's body.

"Tell me what you want, Jordy. I feel like I'll die if I can't kiss you."

"We can't do this."

"We can." Rick nibbled his earlobe. "Say yes."

Rick's tongue outlined the spiral of his ear. The thing he wanted most in the world was his, if only he'd claim it. Suddenly, he didn't care about the future, only about the moment, about Rick's arms cradling him, Rick's mouth warming his cheek with tender kisses.

"Yes." The word escaped as a plea. Rick moved in so close that his breath touched Jordan's lips. Callused fingertips brushed his cheek. He closed his eyes, not wanting Rick to see the depth of his need. A firm hand gripped the back of his neck and their mouths crashed together.

# Chapter 4

Rick kissed Jordan greedily, his tongue invading every crevice to savor the taste. He wasn't sweet like Cynthia. He was spicy and masculine. Their teeth scraped together as he nibbled Jordan's lips.

Hands on his hips pulled his pelvis against Jordan's. A hard cock pressed into him, and he rubbed his own against it. Desire and relief poured over him. This was what he'd been missing with Cyn.

The glide of skin on skin intoxicated him, hard pecs against his chest, thick arms encompassing him. Strong hands squeezing his ass.

He grazed his teeth along Jordan's neck, licking away the salt and finding the earthy taste beneath. He sucked, but not so much as to leave a mark. That would be hard to explain when they got home.

He slid his tongue across Jordan's clavicle. Jordan groaned and ground his pelvis into him. He nuzzled the soft blond hair on Jordan's pecs, then found a nipple and bit. Jordan cried out, a breathy yelp thick with lust.

The sound kicked open something in his chest, a happy satisfaction mingled with desire. They had been friends so long, they just fit together, reading each other like words on a page. He liked being rough, and Jordan seemed to like it, too. That was good. He intended to be a whole lot rougher.

Jordan tore into Rick's fly. Lips warmed the flesh of his neck while a firm hand massaged him though his briefs. The heat of desire rose from his center. Fingers cradled his balls, the touch whisper-soft. A groan rumbled in his throat.

"If I touch you," Jordan said, "promise you won't hate me."

"Could never hate you." He kissed Jordan's temple, wanting to protect him from the slightest pain. "Want it so bad."

Jordan's hand slid under the waistband. He palmed the shaft and skimmed his thumb along the cap.

A rush of pleasure turned his vision dark. He tugged Jordan's hair, drawing his head back, then covered his mouth with his own. Jordan returned the kiss, still pumping Rick's cock. Despite his being a virgin, his touch was firm and sure.

"Good." Rick's voice was strangled. Desire dulled his senses, all except the feel of Jordan's hand on him. Some part of his brain told him he should reciprocate, wanted to. But he was intoxicated with kissing Jordan's mouth, palms sweeping the broad stretch of skin and muscle on his back.

Jordan pulled away, breathing hard. "Need you." He sank to his knees.

*Oh fuck.* Excitement burned through him as Jordan tugged down his shorts. This wasn't how he'd envisioned it, but he sure as hell wasn't going to complain. He cupped Jordan's shoulders in his hands.

As Jordan lowered the shorts and briefs to mid-thigh, the cool air hit his hot cock painfully. Jordan slicked the precum over the head. "Do you want me to do this?" His voice was thick with uncertainty. Eyes gazed up at him.

Affection stirred Rick's heart. "Jordy." He laced his fingers through his friend's hair.

A tongue circled the tip of his penis. Tightness gripped his diaphragm so he could barely catch his breath. Lips slid down his shaft.

He snapped his head back, desire rumbling through him. *Fucking amazing.* He tightened his grip on Jordan's hair. He didn't have to fantasize, because this was sweet fantasy come to life.

In his downward gaze, the sight of his cock sliding between Jordan's lips hurled him toward orgasm. The suction of Jordan's mouth stole his will. He hadn't wanted to come like this, but now it was all he wanted. His mouth formed words to encourage his friend, but the sound escaped as grunts. A constriction in his shaft gave its warning. "Now!" he gasped, shaking as hot fluid shot through him.

Jordan kept sucking until Rick fell to his knees. He wrapped his arms around him and pressed his forehead into Jordan's neck. A warm glow of happiness pumped through him.

"Was that what you wanted?" Jordan asked.

He pulled back and looked into Jordan's eyes. They were soft, unsure, vulnerable. Love surged through his chest. He murmured in Jordan's ear, "I want everything. I want *you.*"

He pulled Jordan into a kiss, tasting his own bitter essence. Jordan sucked his lips and painted them with his tongue. His body turned greedy, wanting to possess him, become one with him. "I've never felt like this before," he said. "Wasn't sure I could."

Jordan's Adam's apple bobbed, and his eyes shone.

He shucked off his shorts as he rose to his feet. Jordan joined him. Rick glided his hand across Jordan's chest and down to the lean torso. His body tingled at the sight and feel of Jordan's hard, muscled form, the ridge of soft blond hair leading south from Jordan's belly button.

Desire quivered in his stomach. "Your turn." He unzipped Jordan's jean shorts, not knowing what he was going to do next, but knowing he had to get his hands on that cock. He'd seen it plenty of times when they showered after a football game, but lately he'd been imagining running his fist down the thick shaft, satin skin covering hot steel.

The erection popped out of Jordan's briefs as he lowered them to the floor. Damn, it was beautiful—thick and rosy purple, elegantly cut. He slid the back of his fingers down the length.

"Mmm," Jordan murmured. Between lingering kisses, Jordan undressed and got into bed.

Practical matters filled Rick's mind. He hunted down a box of tissues in the bathroom and put it on the nightstand. In his shaving kit he found the bottle of lube. He left the condoms inside—didn't want to freak Jordy out. But he intended to use them before the weekend was over.

He sucked in his cheeks imagining it—Jordan bent over for him, taking him in that most intimate of ways. He'd never wanted a man like that before, but he wanted Jordan.

Lust swirling through him, he joined Jordan on the bed, the covers pulled down to their ankles. Jordan's cock bobbed playfully.

*So fucking hot.*

"Want me to jerk you off?"

Jordan nodded, eyes closed.

He smiled. He got the lube and squeezed it onto his hand. "This will be cold." Jordan sucked in his breath, but the rhythm of Rick's palm quickly warmed the lube.

Jordan's tongue flicked out and licked his lips. That vulnerable expression tugged at him, and the impulse to give Jordan pleasure sizzled under his skin. The cock in his hands was hot and responsive, putting Jordy totally in his power. With his thumb, he stroked the seam between Jordy's balls. That earned him a sweet moan. He leaned down and kissed a pink nipple.

Jordan whimpered. "Yeah."

He bit the hard nub and increased the pressure on Jordan's cock. Each stroke caught Jordan's entire length, from tip to root, in a spiral motion. He spread the precum along the slit. Jordy cried out. His cock quivered just before cum shot out over his belly and chest.

Rick kissed him, teasing his tongue and sucking his lips. Jordan was pliant in his arms. He grabbed the box of tissues and cleaned Jordan up, enjoying the look of bliss etched into his lover's features.

*Lover.* He lay back, Jordan's head nestled on his chest, and settled into a contentment he'd never known.

Jordan listened to Rick's heartbeat, lulled by the soft touch of fingers combing through his hair. Happiness swelled his chest until it ached. This was literally a dream come true—but like any dream, it couldn't last. In two weeks, they'd be starting college in towns four hours apart.

This wasn't a beginning. This was goodbye.

Tears gathered in the corners of his eyes. The two of them had been friends since they played light sabers during recess in first grade. He had known leaving Rick would be hard. Now, it was unimaginable.

A wave of grief rolled over him. He couldn't hold back his tears, even though Rick would hate him for being such a woman. He rose from Rick's embrace and headed into the bathroom, leaning against the vanity to steady himself.

Rick followed, wrapping his arms around him from behind, chest pressed to Jordan's back. He didn't say anything—just waited while Jordan spent his emotions.

Finally, Rick murmured in his ear, "Are you sorry?"

The question fired through his mind, and his stomach clenched like a child's fist clinging to a favorite toy. He turned to look into Rick's dark eyes. "I wouldn't trade this for anything. Even though it'll hurt like hell when you leave."

"You don't know what a gift you've given me. When I'm with you, I feel joy."

A thrill suffused his chest. Maybe there was a chance for them, even if only a slim one. "You don't feel weird? I sucked your cock."

"And it was fan-fucking-tastic."

He grinned. "All forty-five seconds of it."

Rick punched his arm.

"Do you always go off that fast?"

"Not with Cyn. I have to listen to her complain about her sore jaw…" He rubbed his palms over his face. "Shit. I have to break up with her."

"You already agreed to see other people. That's one foot in the grave."

"I know. But we've been together so long—it's a habit."

"Like me loving you."

In the sticky nighttime air, Jordan bounced the volleyball, trying to shut off his brain. He couldn't believe he'd told Rick he loved him. Stupid. And Rick's only response had been a kiss.

Beneath the lights, the green of the volleyball court shone against the darkness. He and Rick, shirtless in the heat, had attracted a couple of spectators, girls in their early teens. He avoided eye contact. No point making them think he might be interested.

He looked across the net at Rick. His eyes glared, his lips pressed into a thin line, but Rick knew better than to hurry him. It would only slow him down.

His quiet patience had been a tempering force to Rick's impulsiveness their whole lives. In elementary school, Rick had been the kid the teachers had to shush at assemblies, had to scold for running through the halls. His humor and kind heart had kept him from getting into too much trouble even though he constantly pushed the boundaries. Plus, he'd been a cute kid, big brown puppy-dog eyes and an always smiling face. It was impossible to stay mad at him.

Jordan tossed the ball into the air and shot it over the net. Rick took two steps back and got under it, sending it back with powerful ease. Jordan jumped and smacked it back with one fist. Rick spiked it, but it hit the net and landed on his own side.

"Shit."

"That's what you get for showing off." He took the ball Rick handed him. "We've talked about this," he said, imitating the condescending tone of their old Little

League coach. "Use your skills. Don't make a spectacle of yourself to impress the other boys."

"Fuck you."

Jordan served again, and Rick hit the ball hard. It landed on the line. "Nineteen all," Rick said.

Jordan tossed him the ball. Rick served, and he returned it, but barely. Rick spiked it at the net. Jordan shook his head and swore.

"Game point." Rick served, and the ball bounced right past Jordan before he could react. "Take that, fucker."

He squinted, but elation rose in his chest. Rick's eyes shone, his mouth pulled into a wide smile. His muscled body glistened like a Roman gladiator's. Jordan fought the urge to kiss him. That wouldn't do here under the spotlights with those girls watching.

He and Rick picked up their shirts and left the volleyball in the bin. They followed the moonlit path back to their cabin. Rick brushed an arm against his as they walked, casually, like it was unintentional. The crotch of his shorts grew tight.

The night breeze cooled his sweat-slicked skin. He wanted to get Rick into bed, lick his body clean. He might not have Rick's heart yet, but if fucking him into oblivion was the way to win it, he was sure as hell going to try.

As the screen door slammed shut behind them, Rick said, "I'm starved." He took the peach cobbler from the fridge and stuck it into the oven. Jordan went into the bathroom to wash up, and Rick joined him at the other sink.

With their washcloths hung on the rod to dry, Rick grabbed Jordan's ass and pulled him in for a kiss, mouth hot and greedy. He relaxed against Rick, sliding a hand behind his neck, holding him close.

Rick's lips trailed down Jordan's neck to a pointed nipple, then over to his armpit. He licked and sucked. "Love the smell of you."

He didn't think he could get any harder, but those words did it. Who knew armpits could be so erotic? Rick's tongue on him was tantalizing yet so gentle, he wanted to cry.

*Don't say you love him. Tell him you want to fuck him. No, not that. He might think you mean…*

The oven dinged. "Shit." Rick pulled away. "Don't want that to burn."

He panted, body quivering with want. Rick sure as hell was no romantic. He followed Rick to the kitchen, frustrated desire clenching his jaw and curling his stomach.

Rick scooped the dessert into bowls, wisps of steam rising. The fragrance of peaches woke the hunger that Rick's kisses had lulled into slumber.

Jordan poured two tall glasses of milk and set them on the café table in the breakfast nook. He turned on the Phillies game on the big-screen TV.

Rick brought over the cobbler, and they sat to eat their dessert. It was touted as home style, but it didn't taste that way—probably used shortening instead of butter. Rick's mom's peach cobbler was renowned in their neighborhood, and he and Rick could devour one in a single sitting. The oversweet store-bought version couldn't compare.

He leaned forward for his glass of milk, and his knee brushed against Rick's. He gritted his teeth to fight the thickening in his groin. After years of denying himself from indulging those feelings, he didn't have to do that anymore.

Rick wiped the stray juice from the side of his mouth with a napkin. Jordan wished he could lick it off instead. Four hours ago, he thought he'd never have a chance with Rick. Now, the thought of leaving him hurt like an auger drilling into his heart.

"So are you gay or bi or what?"

Rick chewed, then took a sip of milk. "Bi, I guess."

"You still like girls?"

"Sure."

"So when you get to college, you're going to date women, and make them just as unhappy as you've made Cyn."

Rick's brow pinched together. "What's your problem?"

The doughy pastry sat like a wooden block in his stomach. "You're leaving me."

"You're leaving me, too."

He tapped his foot. "Except you don't want a long-distance relationship. You want to date girls."

"I'm just coming off a three-year relationship. Fuck, Jordy. I'm eighteen years old. I'd like to date for a while without a commitment. Is that so much to ask?"

He finished off his milk. "I can't compete with girls."

Rick grinned and skimmed his fingers along Jordan's hand. "They can't compete with you, either."

The teasing left his stomach hollow. Picturing Rick with someone else opened the gash in his heart wider.

"Jordy, please. I'm not rejecting you. This is about me. I've got stuff to figure out. Like whether I'm really gay, or just gay for you."

"That's a ridiculous expression, used by guys in denial about their sexuality."

"I don't think that's true. You love who you love."

His head hammered. There was no chance of the two of them leaving this cabin with Rick as his boyfriend. If he tried to push Rick into something he wasn't ready for, it would destroy their friendship. Then he'd have nothing.

"Do you love me?" He bit his cheek. He couldn't believe those words had left his mouth.

Apprehension darkened Rick's eyes. "As a friend, sure. As a lover...too soon to say, I guess."

He hated sounding needy. His heart was involved, and Rick's wasn't. "You're using me. You're confused about your sexuality, and you're using me to figure it out."

Rick reddened. He sat back, arms crossing his chest. "This isn't about sex. If I'd understood what these feelings meant, I'd have broken up with Cyn for you months ago."

He swallowed. Rick moved his chair close and took his hand. "I'm here because I want to be with you. I don't know about the future, but right now, today, I want you more than I've ever wanted anyone."

He was tempted to throw himself at Rick's feet, lay his head in his lap, listen to those sweet words wash over him. Yet the ache in his chest wouldn't go away. He didn't want today from Rick. He wanted forever.

"I realize the timing sucks," Rick continued. "I'm nowhere near ready to be open about my sexuality. I just found out today that I actually like guys...or at least, I like you." Rick kissed his hand. "If you were anyone else, I couldn't have trusted you enough to do this. You're my oldest friend. I would die for you. You said yourself, you're glad we did it, even though it hurts."

"Does it hurt you?"

"Of course. But the chance to be with you is worth it."

He wasn't sure he believed that. Maybe Rick had a crush, but Jordan was in love. Not the same thing.

He rose and placed the dishes in the sink. He flopped onto the couch in front of the TV.

Rick joined him, leaving a space between them. "I wish you weren't mad at me."

"I'm not mad."

"You said you weren't sorry, but I think you are."

"No. I wouldn't trade today for anything. But as soon as you get to Penn State, you'll forget about me and fuck every pretty girl you meet. I'll have to fuck an awful lot of guys to forget about you."

Rick grabbed his arm. "That's not you, Jordy. Promise you won't sleep around. A broken heart is no excuse for risking a potentially fatal disease."

"Straight people can get HIV too, you know."

"Don't give me that shit. I was faithful to Cyn for three years."

"And now you're free. To fuck every girl—or guy—who catches your notice. You were captain of the football team, commencement speaker, most likely to succeed. You don't think you'll be Mr. Popularity in college, too?"

"There are forty-five thousand people on the Penn State main campus. I won't make a ripple." Rick stroked Jordan's fingers. "Why are we fighting?"

"Because I just got you and I'm already losing you."

"We'll see each other on breaks." Rick sidled next to him and pulled him close. "Until then, we should make the most of the time we have."

He nodded.

Rick turned off the TV. "This game sucks." He kissed Jordan's mouth, tasting of peach syrup. His lips followed the line of Jordan's jaw to his ear.

Rick cocked his head toward the bed and stood. Jordan followed suit. He had forty-eight hours to own Rick, and he intended to make the most of them.

They made their way to the bed and stripped quickly, eagerly. Rick wanted to show Jordan this wasn't a fling, even if he wasn't ready for commitment. They were still growing, still discovering themselves—he'd learned that much from dating Cyn. It had nothing to do with his feelings for Jordan.

They lay on the bed kissing. He ran his hand along Jordan's bicep, muscle thick and firm. Jordan's body fitted perfectly to his, cocks sliding together in delicious friction. How could anyone call this unnatural? It felt like the most natural thing in the world, the most pure. He had loved Cyn, but he'd never been struck by this desire to shelter and care for her, to put her needs before his own, like he did with Jordy.

Jordan rolled him onto his back. Lips caressed and explored his neck, his nipples, his abdomen. He writhed in pleasure, combing his fingers through Jordan's hair. *Mine*, his brain shouted. The possessiveness pulled him taut like strings of a bass guitar, but he pushed the worry aside to lose himself in his lover's touch.

Jordan moved his way upward and captured his mouth. He moaned, lips humming against Jordan's, body relaxed and pliant. *Forever*, his brain said.

A boyish grin spread across Jordan's face. He clenched Rick's wrists and pressed them down on either side of his head. Legs captured him like a vise so he couldn't kick free.

"Say you're my bitch."

A jerk of his arms didn't loosen the tight grip. "You've got that backwards."

Jordan kissed him, then bit his lower lip. "Say it."

He couldn't get leverage against the mattress—the box spring just sank beneath him. He and Jordan were well-matched for strength, so if he could get out from under Jordan, he could escape.

"I want you, Jordy."

"Say it. Or maybe I should make you suck me instead." Jordan slid up Rick's body until he straddled his chest. Jordan's cock bobbed inches from his chin. His stomach clenched. Jordan wouldn't really force him. Still, his breath grew heavy and adrenaline pumped through his system.

He grabbed Jordan's arms and flipped him onto his back. Jordan tried to wrestle back control but he held him off. They grappled with each other, arms interlaced, muscles straining, fingers gliding across sensitized skin. He kissed Jordan hard, and Jordan's body stilled as their tongues swirled together.

He lay on his side with his elbow underneath him and stroked Jordan's cock.

"Nice," Jordan said.

He picked up a small black bag from the floor and set it on the bed between them. Fingers trembled as he unzipped it. Jordy would probably laugh at him, but…

"I brought some things—you know, if you want to try them." One by one, he tossed them onto the mattress: cock rings, butt plugs in two sizes, a blue silicone anal vibrator.

Jordan's eyes widened, the pupils dark. He shook his head. "What do you think I'm into?"

"Nothing." He shrugged. "Aren't you a virgin?"

Jordan picked up the larger of the two butt plugs. "Well…yeah."

"So I thought we could learn about this stuff together."

Jordy smiled. "You want this shoved up your ass?"

His face warmed. "No, but I thought you might. You know, to get you ready."

Jordan stared. "You think because I'm gay I automatically…"

"No. Like I said, only if you want it. No pressure."

"You mean like you didn't pressure Cynthia?"

A tingling in the back of his neck rose into his cheeks.

Jordan grinned. "Yeah. She told me. At least now, I understand why."

"We never did it that way, Cyn and me. She turned me down flat."

"Well, sure, if you came at her with this butt plug."

He swallowed, his mouth dry. "I didn't. I bought it for you."

Jordan laughed. "You're a fucking idiot."

He blinked, and his throat thickened. He'd planned everything out, anticipating what Jordan might want, yet somehow, he'd screwed it up. Like he always did.

Rick's forehead wrinkled, and his lips turned downward. Jordan's stomach tightened, like a drawstring was pulling it closed. Regret flooded over him. Rick acted nonchalant, but he was more sensitive than he let on. Sometimes Jordan forgot that.

He found Rick's lips. They were soft and willing, and he sucked them tenderly. "You don't understand seduction."

Rick's eyebrows arched. "You got on your knees for me, and I didn't even ask."

He bit his cheek. His fantasies had always started with him sucking Rick off. It was nonthreatening, something Rick could do with a girl. Except Jordan would be more eager, more willing.

The supple skin had felt good on his tongue, but he hadn't quite been ready for the mouthful of cum. That would take some getting used to. Still, there was so much more he wanted to try. Take Rick deeper into his throat. Suckle his balls. Lick his taint until he writhed and begged.

He picked up the vibrator. How would that toy feel inside him, massaging his prostate? He didn't want silicone. He wanted Rick.

He almost tossed the vibrator back into Rick's bag as a reject, but it was less intimidating than the butt plugs or Rick's cock. He switched it on and it hummed through his fingers. Then, he switched it off again and tossed it onto the bed.

Rick had taken control, planning everything from the cabin to the cock rings, without consulting him. Rick just assumed he was a bottom—that because Rick was a natural leader, Jordan would follow in the bedroom.

He lay back, gritting his teeth. "Any chance you might get down on your knees for *me?*"

Rick's jaw hardened. "I don't think I'm ready."

"So as long as you're the one doing the penetrating, you're okay with it. But to be penetrated—that would make you gay."

"You've had years to adjust. This is new to me. It's going to take a while to get used to the idea of sucking cock."

"It feels great."

"Then be my guest—I could go again."

His chest hollowed out, but Rick smiled and kissed his cheek. "Lie on your stomach," Rick said.

"Why?"

"Just do it."

He rolled over and wrapped his arms around the pillow. If Rick tried to fuck him, he would have to hurt him. Instead, butterfly kisses at the nape of his neck slowly followed his spine down the length of his back. Annoyance seeped out, limbs turning to liquid. Each kiss sent sparks through his body. His thickening cock pressed into his belly. He would never have imagined that something so gentle could be so erotic.

The kisses stopped at the cleft of his ass. The next moment, cold lube pressed at his hole.

"What do you think—"

"Shh," Rick soothed. "I won't hurt you. Relax."

A fingertip penetrated him. He clutched his pillow and curled his toes. The slick massage sent tingles into his cock, but…Rick's finger was in his ass. The fact of it was weird. With anyone else, he would have been humiliated, but he trusted Rick. There was no part of himself he couldn't bare to him.

Rick pushed deeper inside. The in-and-out motion was pure bliss, stretching and massaging his sensitive tissues. He groaned in pleasure. Rick picked up the pace and went deeper. Jordan gasped. "More. Please."

A second finger joined the first, increasing the stretch. Jordan hugged the pillow tighter and clenched his eyes shut. He couldn't find the breath to speak. The ecstasy Rick gave him left him helpless. *Damn.* He was Rick's bitch.

Rick rubbed Jordan's ass cheek. "I want to try the vibrator, to make sure I'm hitting your prostate."

"Okay."

Rick's fingers left him, and a sense of emptiness washed over him. He wanted Rick's touch, not some toy. Still, the idea intrigued him, so he didn't argue.

The flick of the lube cap opening and closing was followed by the low hum of the vibrator. The buzzing tickled his entrance, and the soft silicone slipped inside.

A shiver spread through his body, followed by a pleasure so intense he could hardly keep his body from bucking. He struggled to lie still so the vibrator wouldn't hurt him.

"How's that?" Rick asked as he slid the toy deeper.

Incoherent murmurs exited Jordan's lips. He reached for his cock and fisted it.

"Let me do that." Rick's warm, callused hand grabbed the engorged penis.

"So fucking good." The dual massage of his prostate and his cock took him to heights he'd never imagined, and he soon fell over the precipice. A guttural cry escaped his throat. Rick pumped him dry, then turned off the vibrator.

He lay on his stomach, ignoring the pool of cum beneath his belly. Breathing deeply, he tried to come down from the high, but he was utterly immobile. Rick took the vibrator into the bathroom, and the sound of running water reached Jordan's ears.

Rick returned and set the vibrator on the nightstand. With a wet washcloth, he cleaned up Jordan's body, then the puddle on the bed sheet. After dropping the washcloth on the floor, Rick lay facing him. "You like that?"

"Fan-fucking-tastic." He swirled his finger around Rick's nipple. "Want me to return the favor?"

Rick's eyes widened, then his brow furrowed, like he was considering the idea. "Maybe later."

He kissed a trail across Rick's abs as he reached for the lube. He squeezed some out and warmed it in his hand, then palmed Rick's cock. Rick's eyes closed as a low moan rasped in his throat.

He pushed Rick's thighs apart and settled between his legs. He accompanied the slow strokes with teasing kisses on his balls. Rick's murmurs of pleasure encouraged him. His tongue swirled along the sensitive area behind the sac. How would Rick react if he rimmed him? Better not chance it yet.

He suckled each ball while pumping the shaft. Rick thrust into his palm, but Jordan slowed the pace, wanting to draw out the pleasure.

"More," Rick cried, his voice low and breathless.

He kissed his thigh. "Beg for it."

"Please, Jordy, need it so bad."

He quickened his pace. Rick's body arched as hot cum spilled over his hand. "So good," Rick mewled over and over. Jordan smiled at the power he had over his friend.

He cleaned up, then curled beside him. He tugged Rick's lips with his own. Rick deepened the kiss, rolling him onto his back.

Jordan lay on his pillow and drew Rick into his arms. "Tell me you're my bitch."

"I'm your bitch." Rick lay his head on Jordan's chest, then smiled up at him. "Tell me you're mine."

"I am *so* your bitch."

# Chapter 5

Rick lay in the darkness, the gentle rise and fall of Jordan's breath the only sound. He reached for him, then pulled back. Better not to wake him.

Rick threaded his fingers through his hair, straightening the curls. He'd really done it, confronted the obsession that had taken hold of him.

*Now what?*

He should feel different, shouldn't he? Like he'd undergone some shift. But he didn't—this encounter with Jordan just felt like an extension of their friendship.

The same was true when he'd had sex with Cyn the first time. Losing their virginity together was...well, fun. Cyn was so beautiful. Long dark hair flowing over soft curves. Body smooth and yielding under his hands. After three years together, it seemed like a logical progression, not a major event. Nothing really changed. Except...once he slept with her, his curiosity was satisfied. Every time with her was less and less exciting.

That's when he'd started thinking about Jordan.

Would he get bored with Jordan, too? Fear clawed at his gut. *That can't happen.* His love for Jordy was so different from what he had felt for Cyn. It was almost as if the roles were reversed. Cyn was his buddy, someone he liked hanging out with, joking with—being able to kiss her and fuck her was nice, but it was a bonus.

Jordan was his heart. He didn't care that Rick was impulsive and sometimes a goofball, didn't stay mad when he screwed up. Just loved him. When he saw himself through Jordy's eyes, he liked what he saw.

Sometimes he'd watch Jordy's hands move as he talked, long fingers, broad palms. Even his nails were beautiful, always neat, not like most guys. And something stirred in Rick when he looked at those hands, making his breath hitch and his senses heighten. Like everything in the world but Jordy slipped away.

His throat thickened and his jaw grew tight. He got out of bed and walked to the window. In the light of the full moon, the outline of the trees was visible. If only he never had to leave this place.

His love for Jordan built to an ache in his chest and split him open. The feelings that had been lurking…he finally understood what they were. He was in love with a man. What the fuck was he going to do?

If they weren't leaving for college in two weeks, he could pursue the relationship. As it was, that wasn't realistic. Their friends who'd graduated the year before, the couples who'd tried to stay together long distance, had all broken up by now. That's just how it went.

He couldn't picture himself with another man. Jordy was the only one he'd ever wanted. Could he go back to dating girls after this?

What choice did he have?

Time and distance would make Jordan part of his past. He'd meet a girl he could fall in love with, get married, have a family. Nice and normal. And he'd chalk this experience up to curiosity, a teenage obsession.

Pain gripped his chest. He'd worried about other men hurting Jordan, when he was using Jordan himself. It didn't matter if he was acting out of love. This was the last thing Jordan needed. It would have been better to let Jordan go off to Princeton never knowing how he felt, where Jordan would have found a nice guy who wanted to be with him openly, who wasn't praying that no one would ever find out what they'd done together. Instead, he had given Jordan hope—hope that would leave Jordan pining for him instead of eagerly starting a new life.

Acid burned his stomach. He had to make this right. Not that he could, without turning back time. He'd have to do the next best thing.

Jordan woke with a start, gray shapes unfamiliar around him. The brightening sky through the window reminded him where he was. The cabin. Rick. He couldn't hold back a grin.

He reached for Rick but the bed was empty. Probably in the bathroom. Minutes ticked by, and Rick didn't return. He sat up and let his eyes adjust to the dim light. Rick lay on the couch, asleep with a thin blanket pulled over him.

His throat tightened. Only one reason Rick would do that—he'd changed his mind, sickened by what they'd done together. Tears came hot and sudden, followed by wracking sobs. Jordan tried to be silent, not wanting Rick to see his shame. Pain seared through him. He was so stupid to think this could turn out any other way.

He gasped for breath, his chest so tight he could scarcely force his lungs to expand. Bare feet pattered against the floorboards. The bed springs squeaked, and Rick's arms encompassed him.

"Shh, Jordy, don't cry. I'm a fucking idiot. You're tearing my heart out."

Rage shot through him, restoring his senses. "Get away from me, asshole."

Rick pulled back. "I was trying to do the right thing. If I acted like I didn't care for you, it would be easier for you to forget me."

He sat up and whacked him with a pillow. "You're a shithead."

Rick nodded. In the early morning sun, tears glistened on his cheek.

That vulnerable expression struck him in the gut. The last time he'd seen Rick cry was in second grade, when a fourth grader knocked him down on the playground. Even their freshman year, when Rick broke his nose in a baseball game, he didn't cry.

"This weekend was a mistake," Rick said. "I brought you here to satisfy my curiosity, and I didn't think how it would affect you. Last night I was going on about how I love you and would never hurt you, but that's exactly what I've done. I've been so selfish."

"Still a shithead."

"I'm not denying it. I screwed up. I've never been able to see beyond my own happiness. What you said about me making Cyn unhappy…it's true. She's spent three years trying to be a good girlfriend, and what do I do? I pressure her to go down on me, when I won't return the favor. Just like I've been doing with you."

He clutched his temples. Rick had the emotional intelligence of a twelve-year-old, but he was sweet and loyal and the best friend Jordan had ever had. Despite his anger, he hated seeing Rick in pain. "You haven't pressured me to do anything. I made a choice."

Rick wiped his tears away. "I don't know why Cyn put up with me for so long. Things have been falling apart between us since last summer. I destroy everything I touch, Jordy, just like I'm destroying us now."

*When the fuck did Rick turn into a drama queen?*

Should he point out the obvious—that Rick didn't want to go down on his girlfriend because he was gay—or let him continue believing he was bisexual? In the state Rick was in, he couldn't handle any more life-altering revelations.

"You're not destroying us. You're confused. Discovering your sexuality can be traumatic, especially when you've been in denial."

"I haven't been in denial. I just…I assumed I was straight, and that the things I felt were normal for straight men. Checking out other guy's butts in the locker room. Wanting to touch my guy friends the way women touch their girlfriends, even though it was taboo. It was only a few months ago I realized that most straight men aren't like that."

"You were right about one thing. You are a fucking idiot."

"Yes, but I'm your fucking idiot." Rick lay down with his head on the pillow.

He reclined by Rick's side. "I need to know how you feel about me."

"I love you."

"You mean as a friend."

"Jordy, we are way beyond friends. You swallowed my cum. I had my fingers in your ass. Men don't do that with their friends."

"So what are we, then?"

"We're lovers."

He nodded. He could live with that. He was still pissed, but he accepted that Rick was doing his best in a stressful situation. "Don't ever fucking lie to me again, or I will pummel your ass. And I don't mean in a good way."

"I didn't lie, exactly," Rick said.

"I can take it if you want to be with women, and if you don't want a long-distance relationship. But not if you pretend that what happened between us yesterday wasn't real. It wasn't just sex. We made love. I know that's a girly thing to say, but it's true."

Rick cupped his cheek, hand soft and warm. His brown puppy dog eyes turned soft and liquid. "I'm sorry I hurt you."

"It's too early to have this conversation. You're a shithead. I'm going back to sleep."

The next time Jordan woke, Rick's eyes were on him from the other side of the bed. Rick smiled.

"How long have you been awake?" he asked.

"A while."

"Then what are you doing way over there?" He drew Rick close, cradling Rick's head on his chest.

"I feel awful," Rick said. "When I woke up earlier and heard you crying—"

"Forget about it."

"I should have told you what I was hoping for this weekend. I should have given you a choice."

"I could have turned you down. I'm exactly where I want to be."

Rick looked up at him, his expression soft and pleading. Jordan leaned down and kissed him. Contrition and absolution flowed between them, cleansing them both. He didn't want to be mad at Rick anymore. Holding Rick in his arms this way spread warmth and contentment through his chest.

The kiss slowed, and Rick pulled away. "It's after eight. Want to take a shower together?"

His cock gave a thumbs-up to that idea.

# Chapter 6

Rick stood under the hot water, letting it relax the knots in his muscles from sleeping on the couch. The pain served him right.

Jordan picked up the bar of soap and spread the suds over Rick's chest and arms. "Beautiful," Jordan said. "I can't believe I get to touch you like this."

He kissed him. "You're the beautiful one. Blond-haired, blue-eyed Adonis. Like out of a painting."

Jordan smiled. He finished cleansing Rick, paying special attention to his balls and his crack. The sensual strokes lit a soft glow in his veins.

He took the soap and ran it over Jordan's arms, tracing the curve of his biceps. Next came shoulders, clavicle, pecs, abs. The feel of them tugged his desire. He stroked each pink nipple until it stiffened under his touch and Jordan shuddered.

Kneeling, he washed Jordan's muscled legs. Excitement writhed in his stomach. He soaped up Jordan's balls and his penis, and then rinsed them clean.

He kissed the tip of Jordan's cock, sweet with just a hint of saltiness at the slit. Curiosity drove him on, and he spiraled his tongue around the head. The soft feel of it sent a tickle of pleasure through his belly. Jordan let out a deep moan, and the supple flesh turned rigid.

He stood and ran his lips along Jordan's neck and ear. "Turn around."

Wordlessly, Jordan turned to face the marble. Rick washed Jordan's back, hands gliding over ropes of muscle. He cleansed his ass, from the hard glutes to the tender hole. He splashed water over him until the last trace of suds was gone. Then, he knelt.

Hands squeezing Jordan's ass cheeks, he parted them so the pucker of his entrance was visible. His tongue tentatively flicked over it, waking Jordan's musky scent. He had fantasized about this. Cyn had turned him down, but he wanted Jordan more.

He circled the hole with his tongue. Jordan groaned, then took in a sharp breath. Rick pressed his tongue inside, relishing the texture, as smooth as jelly. He couldn't break through the tight ring of muscle, but he pushed as far as he could go, and Jordan writhed against him.

Humbled to be allowed this intimacy, he licked and stroked, flicking his tongue inside, parting Jordan's body. His lover's murmurs encouraged him.

The water cooled. He stood and turned off the faucet. "To be continued," he whispered in Jordan's ear.

They dried each other off, then walked hand in hand to the bed. They lay on top of the sheets. Jordan tongued Rick's ear. "Want me to suck you?"

His balls tightened, but it wasn't Jordan's mouth he wanted. "I've got something else in mind. Lie on your stomach."

Jordan obeyed. He took out the bottle of lube. He coated his cock, then spread the remainder on Jordan's crack.

Jordan inhaled. "Rick—"

"I won't go inside, I promise." He caressed Jordan's backside. "Pull your knees underneath you."

Jordan lay crouched, and Rick positioned himself behind. He slid his erection between Jordan's cheeks, squeezing them together until they provided the perfect friction. Pleasure rippled through him. "How's that feel?"

"Nice. Just…be careful."

He angled himself so he could massage Jordan's hole without slipping inside. Tension built in his cock—he loved having Jordy bent over for him. He sucked in his breath, aching to possess him utterly. The throbbing in his cock told him he was on the brink. Yet the restraint of holding back his desire to enter Jordan was making it impossible for him to relax enough to let go.

He flopped onto his back.

"What's wrong?"

"Temptation's too strong."

Jordan nodded. He rose and headed into the bathroom. He came back with a wet washcloth, cleaning the lube from Rick's cock and his own ass. Dropping the washcloth on the floor, he lay next to him.

On his back, Jordan looked over at Rick, at his soft, handsome features lit by the morning sun.

Rick reclined on his arm and stroked Jordan's cheek. "So beautiful. I want to fuck you, you know."

His stomach clenched. Rick had shown him how pleasurable anal play could be, but he wasn't sure he was ready.

Rick kissed him deeply. "I don't want you losing your virginity to the first guy in college who's nice to you. With that face and that body, you'll have every gay man in New Jersey after you. I want to make sure your virgin ass gets the love and respect it deserves."

He laughed. "You're full of shit."

"I'm serious!" Rick sat up and leaned against the headboard. "Okay, I admit, this is a major fantasy of mine. But it's a fantasy because I want you, not the other way around."

"You wanted Cyn that way, too."

"No, I wanted you, and Cyn was a substitute."

His throat tightened, and tears threatened to overwhelm him. He breathed deeply until he regained control.

Rick groaned. "I am so screwed."

"Why?"

"Because I'm falling in love with you, you queer."

"Seriously, you need to work on your seduction technique."

"Tell me you're willing to try," Rick said. "If you hate it, we'll stop."

"You're missing my point!"

"No, you're missing mine. You can't tell me I don't mean more to you than some guy you'll date a couple of times. I'll take care of you, Jordy. You can count on me forever, even if we're not a couple."

He drew his knees up to his chest. "I'll think about it."

Rick drew him close and kissed him. "Sorry I freaked you out."

"I guess I should be flattered you're obsessed with my ass. But Rick, it's kind of a big deal."

"I know. It's just…that's what I fantasize about." He nuzzled Jordan's ear, suckling his neck and shoulder. "Tell me about your fantasies."

Jordan stroked Rick's cheek. "This is basically it. You, me, a cabin in the woods…"

"I want details."

Jordan looked down, his fingers teasing the hair on Rick's chest. "We're sitting together, watching the game or something. You say that since I'm gay, that must mean I like to suck cock, and do I want to suck your cock? You whip it out—"

"That's so cheesy, except it's totally something I would do."

Jordan smiled. "I go down on you, and we sixty-nine each other for a while. Then…" Jordan turned silent, and his face flushed.

"Jordy, half an hour ago, I had my tongue in your ass. You can tell me anything."

"You bend me over, and we don't have any lube, so you use spit. It hurts at first, but then it starts to feel good. You tell me how much you like it, how happy I make you."

He stroked Jordan's cheek, honored that he'd shared that confidence with him.

"I'll be so gentle. I don't want to hurt you."

"I'm not afraid of it hurting. I'm afraid I'll like it."

"It's probably a good thing if you like it."

"No, because it means I'm a bottom," Jordan said.

"Do you ever fantasize about being on top?"

"I imagine it. I wonder what it would be like, but it doesn't get me off."

"So why do you care if you're a bottom?"

"Being gay already means I'm a second-class citizen," Jordan said. "Being a bottom…to some people's thinking, that makes me submissive. Like I have less power in the relationship."

He ran his finger along Jordan's back. "Do you think I have more power?"

"Obviously." Jordan glared. "I'm in love with you. You don't feel the same about me."

"I'm not less attached to you than you are to me. It doesn't matter what words you use to describe it— you're part of me. Making you happy gives me joy."

"I wouldn't pretend I didn't care for you, like you did to me."

Pain gripped his heart. "You would if you thought it would make me happier in the long run."

"I'd never think dishonesty would make you happier."

"Maybe. But that's a difference in how we think, not how we feel for each other. I may have been wrong, but I did what I thought was best for you."

Jordan frowned, but the caress of Rick's thumb on his lips drew a smile. Rick covered Jordan's mouth with slow, tender kisses. "How do you want me to make you come?"

A grin spread over Jordan's face. "I want to get on top, like you did to me. I want to rub against your ass, see how it feels to be on that side of the fantasy."

His insides shrank. He bit his lip.

A cloud darkened Jordan's features. "Never mind."

He lifted Jordan's chin and met his eyes. "Stop assuming that if I hesitate, the answer is no. This is new to me. The idea of being that vulnerable…"

Jordan rose and went into the kitchen. He got out a mixing bowl and a box of pancake mix.

He walked up behind Jordan. "Come back to bed."

"The only way I'll come back to bed is if you bend over it."

He swallowed. "Okay."

Jordan leaned his head toward the bed. "Then go."

He started forward. A hard slap made his ass clench.

"Faster, bitch."

Shame heated his face. If he wanted Jordan to bottom for him, then he would have to do this. Assume that vulnerable posture, to show he didn't regard himself as the dominant one in the relationship.

When they reached the bed, Jordan grabbed him and grazed his neck with his teeth. He traced Rick's ear with his tongue. "You know what to do."

A tight band gripped his stomach. He would be at Jordan's mercy.

Closing his eyes against the fear, he bent at the waist and rested with his elbows on the bed. Jordan leaned over him and clamped his mouth on Rick's shoulder. Jordan's erection pressed against his ass. His body wanted to flee, but he breathed until the impulse passed.

Jordan guided his arms out in front of him and held his hands flat on the bed. He grabbed the lube and slicked it on Rick's crack. The slippery fingers, so gentle and loving, warred with a sense of violation. Words like "no homo" and "exit only" ping-ponged around in his head. So much bullshit was attached to this part of a man's anatomy—men were afraid to enjoy their own bodies, even with women. He wouldn't buy into that. He exhaled, relaxed his muscles, and forced conscious thought from his mind. Instead, he focused on Jordan's touch.

Jordan positioned his cock and squeezed Rick's cheeks together. "Good, babe."

That hard, thick rod rubbed against him. The friction heated his skin. Once Jordan got into a rhythm, he leaned over and rained kisses on Rick's back. The tenderness of the gesture coiled a knot in his belly. He wanted to stroke his penis but it was crushed into the mattress. With no avenue for relief, the ache grew.

"Jordy!"

"Your ass is so hot. I could fuck you all day."

He concentrated on the sensation of Jordan's cock massaging his hole. It was decadent and terrifying. He didn't *want* to like it, but he did—a lot. The idea of allowing himself to be penetrated that way floated around his mind. He'd never fantasized about it, but he would now. He couldn't really consider it yet. Wasn't willing to take that big a step.

*I like girls*, he told himself, even while the feel of Jordan's erection left him aching for release. He pictured himself fucking Jordan, his cock sinking deep inside Jordan's lithe, muscular body. He would be so gentle with him, like Jordy was being now.

The strokes grew faster. "I'm close, babe," Jordy said. "Can I come on you?"

"Yeah." He squeezed out the word through clenched teeth.

Jordan cried out, and hot cum spurted onto his back. He wanted Jordy to rub it into his skin so his lover's pleasure would be a part of him. Jordan's pleasure was more important than his own. He'd never felt that way with Cynthia. He'd felt guilty about not going down on her, but not enough to actually do it. He didn't like the taste of her. But licking Jordan's cock in the shower, the salty sweetness of him…he'd never tire of that.

Jordan picked up the cold washcloth from the floor and wiped the cum off his back. Jordan lay on the bed, his cock spent and glistening.

He crawled up beside him. "Good?"

"Your ass is perfect. Hard muscle, with just enough padding. I could pound it all day." Jordan kissed him. "Want me to suck you off?"

Excitement rose in his stomach. He closed his eyes and moaned in assent.

Jordan drew Rick into an embrace, cupping his ass. He reclined on one elbow and ran his lips along Rick's ear, his shoulder, his chest, taking special care with the red points of his nipples. Alternating between them, he licked and sucked, grazing them with his teeth until Rick's cock jerked.

He trailed his fingers along Rick's erection. "Can you control yourself?"

The wary expression in Rick's eyes told him Rick wanted to say yes but the real answer was no.

He rifled through the nightstand drawer full of sex toys. He found a couple of cock rings. One was clear and knobbed, the other purple with a built-in vibrator. He grinned. The last thing Rick needed was a vibrator.

He picked up the clear cock ring and worked it down Rick's shaft until it was seated just above the balls.

"What's that for?" Rick asked.

"Staying power. You didn't know that when you bought it?"

"It was in a sale bin. It didn't come with instructions."

He circled the head of Rick's penis with his fingertip. "This is just foreplay. I don't want you to come."

"Okay." Worry crossed Rick's features.

He tongued the salty tip, dipping into the slit. Rick moaned.

"You have no self-control."

"You take it away." Rick feathered his hands through Jordan's hair.

He covered the head with his mouth and applied the slightest suction. He pulled back and mentally counted to ten. Then, he sucked the tip again.

"Jordy, you're killing me."

"You need to learn self-control. I can't make you my bitch unless you've got self-control." He took the whole shaft into his mouth in a quick motion. Rick cried out.

Jordan laughed. "You're so easy."

"Suck me. Please."

He slid up the bed and faced him. "Suck me first."

Hurt and confusion twisted Rick's features.

He grinned and kissed him. "Kidding. I wouldn't ask you to do anything you're not comfortable with. But damn it, I don't want to be just a fuck buddy who gets you off." He gently massaged Rick's bulging erection. "Can we take our time? Please?"

"I'll try."

He slid down the bed and swirled his tongue over the head, then spiraled down. Slowly, he took in the length. The tip pressed against his soft palate. He smiled at the sound of Rick's gasp.

With rhythmic strokes of lips and tongue, he teased his lover, squeezing the cock ring whenever Rick got too close to the edge. Rick moaned, pumping his hips, until finally Jordan pulled off the cock ring and took Rick as deeply as he could. Rick's cum shot into his mouth and he quickly swallowed to keep from gagging. He now understood the sore jaw phenomenon, but the joy of giving Rick pleasure made it worth it.

He lay with his head on Rick's chest, listening to his heartbeat slow back to normal. He'd never been closer to anyone. As tentative as the situation was, he couldn't imagine trusting anyone more. Wanting anyone more.

The bottom fell out of his stomach. Could he give Rick what he'd asked for? The alternative was some guy he'd known a few months, groping hurriedly in a dorm room—his desire threaded with fear, not knowing if the guy would stop if it hurt too much.

Rick would be slow and careful. He'd put Jordan first. The truth was, he wanted this as much as Rick did. There was no point in waiting.

He took Rick's hand and kissed his palm. "Tonight."

"Tonight, what?"

"You can fuck me. But you're going to have to wine and dine me first." He grinned.

Rick bit his lip. "I don't want to pressure you."

"You're not. As sappy as it sounds, I want you to be my first."

Rick kissed him. "Only if you're sure."

"I'm sure." Even as he spoke the words, apprehension swirled in his stomach. If he gave himself to Rick so intimately, how could he ever let him go?

Rick stroked Jordan's arms, wanting to stay in bed forever. He tried not to get his hopes up about tonight, knowing Jordy might change his mind. Just holding him like this gave him a pleasure he'd never known before.

The sexual play between them was surprisingly natural. He had worried it would be weird or awkward, but it wasn't. Jordan seemed utterly relaxed about their games—Jordan, who had always known he was gay. He was at peace with his sexual identity. Rick didn't know what to think about his own. After all, he'd never been attracted to any man except Jordan, but he'd been attracted to lots of girls.

"What do you think it means that you're the only guy I'm attracted to?"

Jordan squeezed his hand, then rose and headed to the kitchen. He cracked a couple of eggs into a mixing bowl. "Do you want to go kayaking this morning?"

"Sure." His eyes followed Jordan. Why had the question made him run? His face was hidden—like he was deliberately keeping his back to him.

Jordan added the milk and the pancake mix. Rick got up and approached him, wrapping his arms around Jordan's waist, his front to Jordan's back. "What's wrong?"

"You're a shithead." Jordan whisked the batter, then ladled it into the hot skillet. The butter sizzled.

"Why?"

"I don't go around lusting after other guys either, you prick. You're the only one I want. Does that mean I'm not really gay? No. It means I'm in love with you."

Jordan flipped the pancakes.

He pressed his cheek to Jordan's temple, nuzzling the soft blond hair, breathing the scent of shampoo and musk. His teeth nibbled Jordy's ear, tasting the soft sweetness.

"Please stop," Jordan said, his voice thick. He slid the pancakes onto a plate, then spread a new layer of butter onto the pan.

Rick pulled away. His jaw tightened. "You want me to say it?"

Jordan poured two pools of batter into the skillet.

He grasped Jordan's arm and turned him around. "I'm in love with you. If I've learned anything the past twenty-four hours, I've learned that."

Jordan's eyes glistened. "If I don't watch these pancakes, they'll burn." He turned away.

Rick hesitated a moment, then retrieved some clothes from his bag. He slid on his briefs. The ache in his chest deepened each second. He slipped a gray T-shirt over his head and zipped up his denim shorts.

He got out the maple syrup and some silverware, setting them on the table.

"Can you watch these pancakes while I get dressed?" Jordan asked.

"Okay."

Jordan didn't make eye contact while he went to his duffle and rifled through it to find his clothes. Rick watched the pancakes until they bubbled, then flipped them.

When the pancakes finished cooking, he slid them onto a plate. He set the food on the table. Jordan, now dressed in a blue tee and khaki shorts, got out the milk and two glasses. Rick stood facing him, and Jordan finally met his eyes.

"Don't tell me you love me again, okay? I can't take it."

"But it's true."

"It doesn't change anything."

He kissed him hard, but tightness gathered in his throat. Jordan was right. Talking about love would only make it harder when they had to say goodbye.

# Chapter 7

The kayak glided through the lake, silent. Jordan, in front, watched for hawks and herons. On shore, the leaves of the dogwoods already showed a red blush.

The sun approached the apex of the cloudless sky. The breeze touched his skin, cooling him. He drew the oar through the water, pulling hard, driving them forward. The physical exertion helped block his thoughts.

He pictured himself at Princeton, at a gay club, trying to meet someone who wasn't desperate for company and acceptance. He knew he was good looking, fodder for predators. And he wouldn't have Rick watching out for him anymore.

This shouldn't be so hard. He'd been in love with Rick on some level for as long as he'd known him. He'd realized in tenth grade that it wasn't just friendship. He was used to this dull ache, wanting something he could never have. Except now, maybe he could have it after all.

What if he transferred to Penn State? They had a good architecture program, and it would save his uncle a butt-load of money. Would it really matter, in the long run, if he didn't get an Ivy League education? Would it matter more if he gave up Rick without a fight?

Rick was nowhere near ready to relinquish his illusion that he could have a wife and kids and a perfect suburban life. Rick, the most popular kid in high school, was not going to begin his college career by coming out as a queer. Jordan's tug on him was physical and emotional, but the intellectual part of him would be harder to reach. Rick could rationalize his way out of anything.

He'd always been like that, mentally manipulating inconvenient facts. He could talk his way out of detention, talk the coach into believing he hadn't really been late for practice. He was so persuasive that he came to believe his own bullshit. Jordan was the only one who saw through it.

He wasn't about to transfer based on a hope. It could be months—years even—before Rick accepted the truth about his sexuality. He couldn't hang around pining after him. He needed to live his own life. Being away from Rick—forming an identity without him—would be good for him. They would see each other on breaks, maintain that bond of friendship, and if Rick came around, he would be there.

Or not. Maybe he would meet someone else, a man who filled his heart with something other than the pain of unrequited love. He didn't want to give Rick up. But he might not have a choice.

The stretch ached in his arms and abdomen from pulling the oars. He was ready to go back to shore, and he knew Rick was, too. But Rick would never admit being tired. He'd wait for Jordan to say something first, or else he'd do something stupid, like—

"Tree stump!" Jordan yelled. "Turn left." He paddled hard with his oar on the right side of the kayak, but they kept heading straight for the stump.

"Right side!" Jordan called.

"You said left."

"I said *turn* left."

They grazed the stump, and water rushed in.

"Sorry," Rick said.

"Asshole." His blood pulsed, heating him, and he ground his teeth. Now they had no choice but to head to shore. This was typical Rick—making a boneheaded move without thinking through the consequences. He could have overturned the kayak. Rick was always taking chances, and putting Jordan at risk in the process.

"Guess we have to go back to shore now," Jordan said.

"Are you mad?"

"Just paddle."

"Okay." Rick didn't argue, just exhaled a deep sigh.

The sad sound melted Jordan's anger. He loved Rick too much to let him feel bad.

After beaching the kayak, they handed the oars and life vests over to the attendant at the rental kiosk. They headed to the little outdoor shower situated between the beach and the parking lot. Jordan took off his tee. Wearing only his swim trunks, he got under the water, letting it flow over his hair and body, washing away the sweat. The bracing water chased away the heat of the August sun.

He stepped out, and Rick took his turn under the shower. Jordan shook off the water droplets. He turned to Rick, who looked good enough to lick, water caressing his hard pecs. Still, he wasn't letting him off that easily.

"You hit that stump on purpose."

Rick splashed him, grinning. "You said left."

He smacked Rick's ass hard. Rick's vanity, his refusal to admit weakness, was oddly endearing. It was part of the bond between them.

He dried off and put on his tee. Rick did the same. Jordan couldn't stop looking at him, tall and slim, shoulders broad and strong.

His heart twisted. "You're my best friend."

"Always." Rick fist-bumped him.

For now, it was okay, the not knowing. As long as they were friends, they would figure it out.

At lunchtime, they pulled into a sandwich shop they'd been to once before. As they strolled across the asphalt parking lot, Rick's forehead wrinkled. Mulling over the events of the past twenty-four hours, Jordan guessed. Like he'd been doing. A lot to absorb, but even more so for Rick. He reached out and squeezed Rick's hand. Rick turned his way and smiled. His heart ballooned, secure that Rick's feelings hadn't waned.

They entered the shop. He massaged Rick's fingers.

A white-haired man in a plaid shirt approached. "I'm sorry, but this is a Christian establishment. We don't serve your kind here."

The corners of Rick's eyes crinkled. He stepped toward the man. "What kind would that be? Star athletes? College students?"

"You know what I mean, goddamn it." The man's voice rose. "This here's private property. Get your faggot asses outta here 'fore I call the police."

"Did you learn that language in church?" Rick asked. "You took the Lord's name in vain. Haven't you heard of the Ten Commandments?"

"I already told you twice, faggot. You're trespassing."

Jordan glanced around the room at the faces of the other patrons, some flushed with eyes averted, others pale and staring. He took Rick's hand. "Let's go, babe. He's the one losing a sale." To the customers, he said, "Sorry to have disturbed your meal." As he and Rick walked out, he said to the proprietor, "God bless you, sir."

As soon as the door closed with a jingle behind them, Rick was on his smartphone, walking and keying at the same time. He guessed what Rick was doing. He pulled out his own phone and opened the Yelp app.

He and Rick had been through these scenes a couple of times before, but with Jordan alone as the target. Once when they were juniors, they'd passed a couple of freshman in the hall at high school and heard the word "Faggot." Rick had turned instantly.

"What did you say?"

He was inches from the freshmen, in their faces, the school's starting quarterback staring down two kids who weren't shaving yet. "You owe my friend an apology."

Jordan tried to scowl, but the expressions on the kids' faces were comical. They looked like they were ready to piss themselves.

One of them murmured, "Sorry."

"I didn't hear you," Rick said.

"Sorry," the kid said, louder.

"Apology accepted." Jordan offered his hand, and the kid shook it limply. He and Rick turned and walked away, laughing and joking like nothing had happened.

He slid his phone back into his pocket. He'd played good cop to Rick's bad cop for as long as he could remember. Once he left for college, he would have to fill both roles. His instinct was to avoid a confrontation. But if he was pushed, he'd stand up for himself. Rick had taught him that.

A young woman exited the restaurant and came running up to them, a man following slowly behind. "I'm sorry that happened." She pushed a strand of long, chestnut hair behind her ear. "We canceled our order and left. I won't give my business to an asshole like that."

"Thanks," he said. "Appreciate the support."

Her companion caught up, a thick, tatted arm flexing as he slid on his sunglasses. "Sorry, dudes, that was not cool, what he did."

Rick smirked. "That's okay. I just gave him a one-star review on Yelp for losing his temper and swearing at customers."

"Good idea." The woman smiled and took out her smartphone.

# Chapter 8

Rick remembered another sandwich place a half mile away. It was mostly a general store, but it had a few tables, and the food was good. He pulled into the parking lot and got out of the car. As he and Jordan headed toward the entrance, he took Jordan's hand.

Jordan paled. "Are you sure—"

"I won't let some asshole change my choices."

Jordan smiled and squeezed his hand.

The woman at the register rose from the stool where she sat. Her short, wispy hair was streaked black and white. She wore square glasses on her round face. "How can I help you boys?"

"Still serving lunch?" he asked.

"The kitchen's open another ten minutes."

He looked over at Jordan, whose eyes were scanning the menu board. "See anything you like, babe?"

"I don't want anything fancy. Roast beef with provolone on a hoagie roll," Jordan said to the woman.

"And I'll have a ham and Swiss on rye. Unseeded if you've got it."

"Sure thing." The woman disappeared into the kitchen.

"That wasn't too painful," Rick said.

"Still, we should pick our battles. No point being reckless."

He nodded. He was a hypocrite, insisting on being open about Jordan with strangers, but terrified anyone at home would find out. How would it change people's perceptions of him? It wasn't just people like that asshole at the café. How would his buddies on the football team react? What would his parents think?

And Cyn. She'd be crushed. They weren't even officially broken up. If she found out that not only had he been with someone else, but it had been Jordan…No. He had to protect her from that. After everything they'd been to each other, everything she'd put up with from him, he owed her more than that.

The woman emerged from the kitchen. "Can I get you boys some drinks? The iced tea is fresh brewed."

"Sounds good," he said.

The woman filled the Styrofoam cups. She set them on the counter and pressed on the lids. "You two make a cute couple."

"The guy at Mountain Grill didn't think so," Jordan said.

She chuckled. "Don't let Morton bother you. He's the unhappiest man I ever met, and wants everyone else to be as miserable as he is."

"Any more like him around here?" Jordan asked.

"A few. If you're looking for a nice gay-friendly restaurant, try Mia Kristina's. Mia's the cook, Kristina's the manager…and yes, they're a couple."

"Lesbians in rural Pennsylvania," Jordan said. "Who'd have imagined?"

"It's a resort town," the woman said. "We get lots of artistic types around here."

Jordan turned to him. "Are you an artistic type?"

He grinned. "I'm going to major in business."

Jordan laid his hand on his. "Then I could open a design firm, and you could run the business end. Just like Mia and Kristina."

The idea made him ridiculously happy. He could picture them at thirty, working together, free to make their own choices with no one to answer to. Could this be his future?

They found a table. The woman brought their sandwiches and headed back to the register. Jordan reached over and brushed his arm. "Thanks for not freaking out at the diner."

"I'm not ashamed of being with you. It's just...complicated."

"This is new to you. I get that."

He massaged the heel of his hand. "If I told my parents I'm bi, how do you think they'd react?"

Jordan shrugged. "Hard to say. They've always been cool with me, but I'm not their son. I mean, it's not like they'd kick you out or anything, but..."

"It's not what they expect of me."

"They'd get over it."

"Yeah." He shook his head. "The kids at school..."

"We're not at school anymore. The people we considered friends—we'll never see half of them again."

"They'd laugh if they knew. They'd think less of me."

"Welcome to my world."

He rubbed his temples, fighting off a headache. "How do you deal with it?"

"I have no choice. But you do."

Did he? He shook his head. He and Jordan fit in a way he and Cyn never had—that wasn't a choice.

He didn't like where these thoughts were leading. He couldn't base his entire sexual identity on these two experiences. He'd been attracted to girls since third grade, and to Jordy for six months. Something didn't make sense. He wasn't about to abandon everything he'd believed about himself until he figured this out.

It was ridiculous, thinking he had to work this out now. He knew what Jordan wanted, but this wasn't just about Jordan. If he made a commitment before he was ready, it would only be a matter of time before he rebelled against it, hurting Jordan even more.

"I'm sorry I can't be what you want."

"Maybe you can, in time. And if not, we'll always have this weekend."

"Is that enough for you?"

Jordan shrugged. "I'm not going to pressure you, and I'm not going to beg. I can get over you if I have to. I just don't want to."

He didn't want to, either. But if a straight lifestyle was still an option for him, he wasn't ready to give that up.

After they finished eating, Rick went out to put gas in the car. Jordan wandered up and down the aisles. Cereal, granola bars, cookies, crackers. Bread, peanut butter, jelly. Was there a health and beauty aisle? Bumblebees buzzed in his stomach.

"Can I help you find something?" the owner asked, coming toward him from the other end of the aisle. His cheeks grew hot.

"Condoms?" she suggested.

Was his embarrassment that obvious? "No, um, enemas." He couldn't look at her as he said it. They weren't necessary, but he didn't want to risk grossing Rick out. He'd seen a video about it online, how you should pour out half the medicated liquid and replace it with distilled water to avoid cramping.

"Right back here," she said, and he followed her to the far corner. "Don't be shy. I get gay couples in here all the time." She handed him a box. "Will this do?"

*Apparently, you know better than me, lady.* "Uh, yeah, this is fine."

Her eyes softened. "This is new to you, isn't it."

He looked away.

"This guy you're with…do you trust him?"

He looked at her, tears burning the corners of his eyes. "With my life."

She nodded. "Trust is what matters most. Even more than love. Love can steer you wrong, make you ignore that voice in the back of your head, or that feeling in your gut that tells you something isn't right. But if you've got trust, that's half the battle."

He nodded and made his purchase. Walking to the parking lot, he thought about all the reasons he was making this choice. Doing it for love wouldn't be enough, as long as Rick wasn't able to commit to him. But doing it for trust—for all the times Rick had looked out for him, stood up for him, taken care of him—that was reason enough. Not for their romance, but for their bromance.

Rick stood at the pump, sun baking the concrete. The odor of gasoline swirled around him. He half expected the heat to ignite the fumes.

Traffic dribbled past, not like the tight lines of cars on the main drag at the Jersey shore. He liked the beach, but the mountains were quieter, more peaceful.

A red Ford Focus drove into the lot. Two girls got out, late teens, one in a bikini top with cutoff jeans, the other in a swim tank with a white mesh cover-up. The driver, the one in the bikini, looked over and gave him a smile. High cheekbones, pretty eyes, dark hair halfway to her waist. He smiled back, not flirting, just being civilized.

The two girls headed toward the entrance, chatting and laughing. The girl in the tank was slender, the other more voluptuous. His mind wandered to the idea of fucking them, the way it had been trained to. Bikini girl was more his type. He pictured the big, firm boobs in his hands, her legs open and waiting for him.

His dick wilted. Just like it had with Cyn the last few times. He liked looking at pretty girls, but lately, looking was all he wanted to do.

Maybe he was making too much of it. The atmosphere at the gas station wasn't exactly conducive to a stiffy. The pump halted, and he stuck the nozzle back into place. As he pulled the receipt from the slot, Jordy exited the store, tall and tan, gait masculine but graceful.

Rick's cock pressed into his fly, the metal rough even through his briefs.

*That's what you want*, his brain said. He brushed it off. Of course he got horny looking at Jordan. It was operant conditioning, like Pavlov's dogs. He was getting

sex from Jordan, so seeing Jordan made him hard.
Simple as that.

# Chapter 9

When they arrived at Mia Kristina's that evening, a hostess with a streak of blue in her black hair greeted them. "Table 7," she said to the waiter next to her. Rick eyed the slim blond, about his age. The guy picked up two menus, giving him the once-over, gaze lingering on his package before he turned and said, "This way."

His face heated. Something about a guy checking him out was incredibly sexy. Not that he was interested—the guy wasn't muscular like Jordan, more what he supposed would be called a twink. Still, he was hot in his own way, and Rick's stomach tickled at the attention.

As they sat, the waiter said, "I'm Aidan, and I'll be your server tonight. Let me tell you about our specials..." He rested his hand on the back of Rick's chair. He sucked in his cheeks, and Jordan raised his brows, the hint of a grin on his lips.

He tried to listen to the specials, but the language part of his brain had switched off in favor of the horny part of his brain. The nerve endings in his skin were hyper-aware of the closeness of the waiter, heat radiating from his body.

"What can I get you to drink?" Aidan asked. He met Rick's eyes. "Besides a tall glass of water."

Jordan said in a louder-than-normal voice. "Iced tea for me."

Aidan gave him a quick glance, then turned his gaze back to Rick.

"What other soft drinks have you got? A fancy place like this—I bet you've got something special to offer."

Aidan licked his lips. "Raspberry lemonade?"

Rick's eyes swept over him. "Delicious. I'll have some of that."

Aidan blushed and headed toward the kitchen.

Jordan let out a laugh.

He gave him his most intimidating glare. "What?"

"You're not just gay for me, apparently. You're gay for that waiter, too."

"He's not my type. Too fem."

"You have a type?"

His cheeks warmed. "Shut up."

"I don't mind, babe. Flirt all you want, as long as you don't touch."

"We'll get better service if he thinks I'm into him. Which I'm not."

"S'okay." With a sexy half-smile, Jordan leaned in and said in Rick's ear, "We could invite him for a threesome. Maybe *he'd* suck my cock."

He pulled away, the words slicing through him. Was Jordy mad that he hadn't gone down on him? After all, he kept asking for it. And he'd promised to fulfill *Rick's* fantasy…

"Babe, I'm kidding." Jordan slid his chair closer and murmured, "I mean, I don't get why you're comfortable rimming me, yet not sucking me. But if that's where you are, I'm fine with it."

"If that were true, you wouldn't have said it that way."

Jordan stared at the salt shaker like it was the most interesting thing in the room. "Okay, yeah, I want it. But you're clearly not ready to go there." Jordan looked up, eyes wide, then said softly, "You're afraid someone will call you a cocksucker, and it'll be true."

He jerked back, mind rushing, a pit forming in his stomach. Yeah, the idea bothered him. How fucking shallow could he get? This thing between him and Jordy was private. Why should he care what other people thought?

Jordan stroked his arm from the shoulder to the elbow. "S'okay. You're going through a lot. It's taken me years to adjust, and you're trying to do it all in one weekend." Jordan's eyes gleamed in the candlelight, the love in them clear for anyone to see.

His stomach pulled taut. Being with Jordan felt natural. The disapproving look from the guy at the next table didn't. Heat burned his cheeks, and he pulled away. Jordan stiffened.

"Don't be mad," he murmured.

"I'm not. I understand." Jordan's voice was cold.

He breathed deep to loosen the tightness in his chest. Loving Jordan was the most liberating, exciting experience of his life. Nothing had ever made him feel more like a man. But the world wouldn't see it that way. If their friends from school ever found out...Captain of the football team turned queer. Could he live with that? That emasculating perception following him everywhere he went for the rest of his life?

His eyes met Jordan's. He wanted to grab him and kiss him hard. Reassure him that he was the most important thing in Rick's life. But was he? Rick's self-image was on the line.

He hadn't thought through what this weekend would mean for him. He'd wanted to get Jordy into bed. He hadn't expected to fall in love. But how could he not? He'd loved Jordy for twelve years. In the past six months, the attraction had grown into an obsession. Of course sex with him would send Rick over the edge. He couldn't undo it. Leaving Jordy now would be heartbreak.

Obviously, they'd be physically separated. But if they got together one weekend a month, agreed to be exclusive...That might work. He could drive to Princeton. No one at Penn State would have to know he had a boyfriend. But how could he ask Jordan to be faithful to him when he was living a lie—when he was unwilling to face the discrimination that came with coming out?

"I need some air." He rushed from the building. Outside, he sucked in breaths like a man pulled from a sinking ship.

He hurried to a little stream that ran next to the parking lot. Sobs threatened to overwhelm him. He loved Jordy, but he couldn't adopt this lifestyle. It wasn't who he was.

Cynthia's face flashed in front of him. He doubled over in pain. The idea of kissing her, even touching her, nauseated him. Sex had made their relationship worse, not better.

What did that mean? Was he gay? Was he kidding himself about liking girls?

He looked down along the ridge, a deep ravine cutting through rock. Part of him wished the earth could swallow him up. How could anyone think people *chose* to be gay? Why would anyone choose this—to be ostracized by family and friends, to be faced with the hateful stares of strangers?

Footsteps sounded on the pavement. He turned. Jordan approached, his features wide with fear. "I'm sorry."

"You didn't do anything."

"I should have told you no," Jordan said. "I'm no good for you."

"You're the best thing that ever happened to me." Sobs shook him. Jordan's arms encompassed him. "How can you stand it? Knowing people will hate you, no matter what you do?"

"I've always had you to watch out for me."

He blinked, and a thrill tickled his gut. He wasn't in this alone. He was used to protecting Jordan, but maybe it was time to let Jordan be the strong one. Time for him to admit he needed help.

"I don't know if I can do this. I should never have brought you here—started something I couldn't finish."

Jordan took his hand and caressed his palm. Without looking up, he said, "If all we ever have is this weekend, it's enough. If this is goodbye, it's a hell of a way to go out."

"I don't want it to be goodbye." He wiped the wet tears from his cheeks. "But I don't know what else it *can* be. I couldn't stand it if we weren't friends anymore. How can I be with you and not touch you? I can't go back."

"Of course you can." Jordan's eyes were wide, his face pale yet calm. "You'll go away to college, make new friends, get immersed in your classes…and this weekend will become part of our past together. When we see each other over the semester break, these feelings won't be fresh, the pain of separation won't be fresh. We'll have some perspective. And we'll be better equipped to figure out what our relationship should be." Jordan's expression cracked, and his own tears fell.

"You already know what you want," Rick said.

"Yes. But it's not what you want."

"Maybe it could be."

A fragile smile crossed Jordan's face. "Then you've got time to figure it out. At Christmastime, if you decide to embrace your life as a gay man, we'll announce to the world that we're a couple. If not, we'll be friends. We'll always be friends."

"Friends with benefits?"

"No. I won't be your fuck buddy. I want love. If you can't give me that…well, you have until Christmas to decide."

"You're giving me an ultimatum?"

"I'm giving you time. I'll be faithful to you until the spring semester starts. After that, I move on."

Rick gazed at the pink horizon, the sun blazing in its last throes of life. His heart thumped against his chest. It was too much too fast. He wanted a future that included marriage and kids. He'd never envisioned anything else. Could he have that with Jordan?

All summer, when he'd talked to Cyn about whether they should see other people, he'd imagined what it would be like to be free. He liked the idea of dating—something he'd never really done.

He wasn't ready to be in love with Jordan. A semester apart would be good for them. As much as it hurt to think about, the space would relieve the pressure.

"Maybe it's too soon to talk about being faithful," he said. "Cyn and I did that, and look where it got us. Jordy, we're eighteen. College is a time to explore. Can't we date each other, but date other people too? I don't mean sleeping with anyone else. Just…figuring out if this is forever." He took Jordan's hand. "You've never dated anyone. Don't you want to try that?"

"You think the only reason I love you is because I haven't dated someone else?"

He slid his hands into his pockets. "Won't you always wonder?"

"I guess being in love is different for you than it is for me."

"That's not fair. Look at this rationally."

"Love isn't rational. If you can't commit to me for one semester—"

"I didn't say I can't. I have no idea what will happen at Penn State once I get immersed in that city of people. Maybe I'll be miserable without you. Part of me will. Is it so much to ask, to hold on to you, but to try new things, too?"

"You swear you won't sleep with anyone else?"

"I swear."

"You understand what this means. I could meet a guy, someone who's out, who wants to be with me openly. You're willing to take that chance?"

"You need to date other guys. If we end up together, I want it to be because you chose me."

"People date because they're trying to find the right person. I already found you. I don't need to keep looking."

Rick shrugged. "Maybe. I mean, I think we could be happy together. I need to be sure. And to be sure, I need to see other people."

"Girls, you mean."

"If I'm attracted to them, yeah. If I'm attracted to another guy, maybe I'd like to explore what that's about, too."

Jordan shook his head. "If you had to choose between being straight and being with me, you'd choose being straight."

He combed his fingers through his hair. "Until I figure out who I am, I'm not ready to be in a committed relationship with anyone. I don't want to give you up. But I also don't want to feel guilty for experimenting with someone else. How do I know whether I want to be with girls, unless I try? How do I know if I'm attracted to other guys? I'm not talking about sex—just kissing and stuff. Is that so awful? Don't you want that, too?"

Jordan stared at him, struggling for words. *Don't be needy.* He didn't want someone else. He wanted Rick.

What if Rick was right? Maybe Jordan should date other guys—just casually—to make sure Rick was The One.

Open relationships were lame, but at least it was a relationship. Twenty-four hours ago, he would have given *anything* for a chance with Rick. Now he had it. Was he going to throw it away because it wasn't all he wanted?

He squeezed Rick's hand. "If that's what you want…I can live with that. I mean, as long as you're questioning, it's not really fair to ask for a commitment."

Rick's body relaxed. He threw his arms around him.

He kissed Rick's cheek. "We should get back inside before they give our table away." He took Rick's hand and led him into the restaurant.

# Chapter 10

Back at the cabin, they watched the Phillies game for a while with Jordan curled into Rick's arms. Rick glanced over at him and the wave hit, the sheer beauty of Jordan. He leaned in for a kiss, and Jordan's mouth plundered him. They tore into each other's clothes. He raised his body over Jordan's and rubbed their erections together. "So good, babe. I could come like this."

"That wasn't the plan." Jordan ran his tongue across Rick's lips.

"You're sure?"

He shrugged. "Nervous. But I want it."

In the lamplight, Jordan's golden hair glowed against his tan skin. Looking at him, Rick didn't care about tomorrow or next week or next year. Life was lived in the moment, and if you thought too much about the future, you missed out on today. Right now, the most beautiful man he knew was underneath him, hot and ready.

Longing blossomed in his chest, not just physical desire, but a spiritual need to become one with Jordan. He wanted to be tender, to reassure Jordan that he was cherished. It wasn't just Jordan's body he wanted. It was all of him.

He was a better man because of Jordan. The desire for Jordan's respect had tamed his natural selfishness, made him work at compassion. He hated to think who he'd be if Jordan hadn't come into his life.

"You're my best friend," Rick said. "My lover. Maybe my future. This means everything to me."

Jordan's eyes turned to liquid. "Me, too."

Jordan headed into the bathroom. He stripped out of his clothes and used the enema he'd stashed under the vanity. It felt weird, but he didn't want to take any chances. He wanted to convince Rick that sex with him was better than it could be with a girl.

The idea of giving himself to Rick this way made his body shiver with excitement. He'd read a lot about it, and felt confident he could do it without much pain, as long as they went slow. He trusted Rick to do this right, putting Jordan's needs first.

In the shower, the hot water ran down, relaxing his muscles. To combat his apprehension, he shuffled through the fantasies he'd had of Rick fucking him. His favorite was in the limo after prom. Desire pumped through his veins.

He soaped and rinsed, then dried himself, barely sweeping the towel against his erection. It wouldn't take much to send him over the edge. No matter what happened, Rick loved him. That much he knew for sure.

Hair dry, he wrapped the towel around his waist. He ran hot water over a couple of washcloths for later. Was that OCD, or a nervous virgin thing? Or maybe it was a retired Boy Scout thing: he wanted to be prepared. The irony amused him.

He stepped out of the bathroom to find Rick standing naked and glaring at him. "You locked the door."

"I needed my privacy." He kissed him. Rick smiled and bobbed his erection. He took Rick's hand and led him to the bed.

Under the covers, Rick held Jordan close. He smelled like soap and clean skin. Rick could tell Jordan was working to make himself as appealing as possible, which was ironic. He was as attracted to Jordan when he was sweaty after a game and yelling at him for being an asshole, as he was when Jordan was like this: fresh, sweet, and curled into Rick's arms.

Light from the setting sun bathed Jordan in an orange glow. A happy sigh forced itself from Rick's chest. His cock was eager, but he wanted to draw out the pleasure, make this the best experience of Jordan's life.

He tugged his lover's lips with his own, nuzzled him, ran a hand over hard nipples. Blood rushed, heating his skin. In the falling darkness, the room took on a dream-like quality. "You're a fantasy come to life."

Jordan nibbled his earlobe. "Tell me your fantasy. I told you mine."

His mouth grew dry. Somehow, talking about sex was more difficult than doing it. Raw, like he was laying his soul bare.

"Um…in the empty locker room, after practice. You come out of the shower glistening with your hair wet. I dry you off, touching your body through the towel."

"Mmm. Hot."

He moved over him, brushing his lips with his own. "We kiss, and our cocks rub together, like this." He pressed his pelvis against him, evoking a soft moan. "You get on all fours on the bench between the lockers. I enter you slowly, and your ass clamps down on me so hard I can barely breathe. And you want it. You beg to be mine."

Jordan stroked Rick's cheek and ran his thumb along his lips. "I do want it. To feel you inside me. To give you pleasure." Lips touched his temple, soft as a moth's wings. "Let's make your fantasy come true."

He forced himself to swallow. The ferocity of his desire curled into a ball in his gut, ready to spring.

Jordan grazed his tongue along Rick's chest. His hands wandered over Rick's back, then slid down to his ass. Heat gathered in his cock, engorging and tightening him. He let go of the worries holding him back, ready to fulfill the longings he'd harbored since his first stirrings of desire for Rick had told him he was gay.

He pressed his lips to Rick's earlobe. "Fuck me."

"You sure you're ready?"

He got on top and straddled him, ravishing his mouth with hot kisses. Rick rolled him onto his back, massaging his erection with his own.

His balls stiffened. This is how he wanted to be. Underneath Rick. For the rest of his life.

He thrust his pelvis forward, grinding their cocks together. Pleasure rippled over him. He needed more, urgently.

Rick nuzzled the hair in Jordan's armpit, flicking his tongue along the edge, then nipping the sensitive skin. Jordan groaned. The sensations spread through his body, heating him.

"I love the way you smell," Rick said. "It reminds me of all the times we've spent hanging out, being best friends."

He trembled. The depth of Rick's love overwhelmed him.

Rick moved lower and lapped at his nipples. "Mine," Rick murmured. "Every part of you." His eyes darkened. "Say it."

He swallowed against the dryness in his throat. "I'm yours."

A wave of freedom washed over him. Only by giving himself utterly to Rick could he become fully himself, releasing his fears and indulging his desires.

"I brought some massage oil," Rick said, "to help you relax. Lie on your stomach."

He rolled over while Rick rifled through the drawer of the nightstand. Rick's sweetness surprised him. He'd put a lot of thought into this weekend—into how he could take care of Jordan.

Rick opened the bottle of oil and rubbed some into his hands, releasing the scent of sandalwood. He straddled Jordan's waist.

Strong hands worked his shoulders. He moaned. A sense of release washed over him as his muscles softened.

The hands moved downward, massaging his back and his glutes. His breathing slowed. Rick's touch soothed him, keeping him on the edge of sleep. The tender pressure moved down to his legs, then his feet. No one had ever massaged his feet before, freeing the tension in his arches. The feeling of relaxation was almost better than orgasm.

Rick finished by stroking his arms and hands. Jordan intertwined their fingers. "So amazing. Thank you."

"I like making you feel good." Rick kissed his lips. "I need to get this oil off my hands. Be right back."

Jordan closed his eyes. Water gurgled in the sink. Soon, feet padded back into the room and the bed springs squeaked. Rick's body warmed him.

Teeth nibbled his ear. "I want to give you pleasure, Jordy," Rick breathed. "If anything hurts, we'll stop. You don't need to worry about disappointing me."

Lying on his side, he kissed Rick's mouth. He fisted their erections, loving the feel of Rick's silken skin against him. His mouth suckled Rick's lips.

"Need you," Rick said, his breath heavy.

"Get the lube." He lay on his back with his knees bent and his feet flat on the mattress.

Rick smiled and retrieved the tube. He kissed his way down Jordan's cock. Ripples of pleasure shot through Jordan's belly. Moans escaped his lips.

The hot, wet mouth caressed the seam of Jordan's sac. He closed his eyes, thrilling to the sensations. Rick lifted his ass and ringed the hole with his tongue.

The nerve endings came to life. He writhed. Rick's velvet tongue worked the tender tissue, leaving him desperate for more.

His cock hungered for touch. He resisted the urge, wanting to save all his desire for when Rick entered him. His breath grew ragged, the movement of Rick's mouth filling him with bliss. Grabbing a pillow, he clutched it to his chest, trying to quell the ache. He needed Rick inside him.

"Can't wait. Want you now."

Rick sat back. Jordan rolled onto his stomach, pulling his knees up to his chest.

Rick groaned, then squeezed Jordan's ass. "So hot. Want you."

"Do it."

"Hell, Jordy."

He closed his eyes, and a luxury of decadence built in his chest. This was the rawest, most sensual thing he had ever done. He anticipated how it would feel, Rick sinking inside him, opening him with his thick heat.

Cold lube made his breath hitch. A finger slipped inside, pumping and relaxing the solid muscle. He wanted more, much more. He pushed back as far as he could go, taking Rick's finger up to the knuckle.

A second digit joined the first, twisting and stretching. The deep, intense sensations pushed thought from his mind. "Hot."

"So hot, babe." Rick kissed the small of his back.

Love washed over him at the tender display of affection, even as Rick thrust hard inside him. The pressure on his prostate made him shudder.

A third finger entered him. "Fuck, yeah!" He pushed back, increasing the penetration. Rick wrapped his free arm around Jordan's waist, giving him leverage to establish a firm rhythm.

The fingers fucked him hard and deep. "You want it?" Rick's voice was stretched taut.

Trembling with desire, he struggled for words. "Need it."

The fingers left him. The ripping of a foil wrapper quickened his breath. Blood engorged him. This wasn't a fantasy. This was happening. He focused on Rick, the tenderness of his touch, the thickness of that hot cock.

Rick's erection caressed his hole. An involuntary whimper escaped his throat.

"You okay?"

"Go." He needed Rick inside him before fear overwhelmed his lust.

A slight pressure teased his nerve endings, increasing his desire. It stretched but didn't open him. "Mmm," he moaned, urging Rick forward.

The pressure released, then came harder. He wanted this, was desperate for it. With the next thrust, he exhaled and relaxed, and the tight circle of muscle parted. The hard shaft slid inside, the pain-pleasure splitting him in two.

Rick growled. "Fuck, Jordy!"

"Stay still," he pleaded, the new sensations overwhelming him.

Rick stopped. "Am I hurting you? Should I pull out?"

"Just stay like that. Let me get used to it." He breathed. As his muscles adjusted, the pain eased. He loved the sense of fullness. *Rick's cock is inside me.* Happy tears sprang to his eyes. "Go."

Rick moved slowly. "That okay?"

"Good."

"You don't have to do this if it hurts." Rick's voice shook.

"Good, babe. Want more."

Rick lengthened his strokes and hit Jordan's prostate, an irritation at first but quickly turning into a hard knot of longing. Rick's arm encircled his waist, and his free hand caressed his spine. "Perfect," Rick moaned.

He tried to focus on his breathing instead of his galloping heart. The sense of violation crept into his consciousness but he pushed it down. He fought to relax his muscles. "Lower."

"Like this?" Rick angled down, increasing the pressure on the prostate.

Warmth spread from his core to his cock. "That's it." His nipples hardened. He stroked his erection, spreading the precum over the head.

Rick picked up the bottle of lube and squeezed some onto Jordan's hand. The slick sensation combined with the pleasure in his prostate. "So good, babe."

"You have no idea." Rick's voice was rough. Jordan loved that he had that effect on him.

Pressure built inside him. He wanted to wait until Rick finished, but he couldn't stop it. The orgasm barreled over him. His ass clenched, and the next moment Rick's body shuddered.

Rick slipped out and collapsed against Jordan's back, encircling his waist with his arms. He kissed his neck and shoulders, soft lips with a hint of stubbled cheek. "My Jordy."

He turned and lay on his back. The bright, adoring look in Rick's eyes filled his chest with happiness unlike any other.

Rick wrapped the condom in a handful of tissues and tossed it into the trashcan. He sank onto the bed, and Jordan ran a hand down Rick's back. He could still feel the pressure of Rick inside him. It ached, but not in a bad way.

Rick lay beside him, a big stupid grin on his face.

Jordan chuckled. "Proud of yourself?"

"You make me happy."

Tightness gripped his throat. "Was it what you expected?"

"So much better. The way you gave yourself to me, trusted me with your body…it was beautiful. You're beautiful." Rick kissed him, wet tongues swirling, teeth grazing, hard bodies pressing together, sucking, licking, enjoying each other's maleness.

Rick pulled him close, so that Jordan's head rested on his chest. "I'm sorry if I hurt you."

"You didn't hurt me. It was uncomfortable at first, but it got better."

"Still think you're a bottom?"

"Definitely."

Rick kissed him. "You liked it?"

"Best orgasm I ever had."

Rick wrapped him in his arms. "I'm glad. I wouldn't want to do it if you didn't like it."

They lay in silence a while. "Say it," Jordan murmured.

Rick leaned toward him and scowled. "That I'm your bitch?"

"No. The thing I told you not to say."

Rick's fingers caressed Jordan's hair. "I'm in love with you."

His tears dropped onto Rick's chest. "I love you, too."

"You're mine, Jordy. Mine."

# Chapter 11

Jordan woke at the first light of dawn. This time, when he reached for Rick, he found him. He snuggled against him, head on his pillow, and slid a fingertip down Rick's arm.

How long would it be before he had this feeling again, waking up to the warmth of a man beside him? Months, at least. Would the man be Rick? Would Rick be able to give up the persona of the popular kid, tough but with a sense of humor, a charismatic leader that everyone loved to be around?

But then, Jordan had been popular, too. His looks didn't hurt. All the girls wanted to turn him. He liked girls—a lot, actually—just not *that* way. And even though he was open about his orientation, whenever he gave a girl a little extra attention, invariably she hoped it meant something more.

As for the guys—well, he could kick most of their asses. And he made sure he had his posse with him: Rick at a minimum, usually another friend of theirs as well, pitcher on the baseball team, slim but strong. No one would have been stupid enough to challenge the three of them, not even a group of four or five. They were the elite.

Being gay didn't mean being a social outcast—not anymore. Most kids didn't care. Of course, in their small Pennsylvania town, there were plenty of Bible-thumping assholes who condemned homosexuality even as they cheated on their spouses and coveted their neighbor's sports car.

He ran his hand down Rick's body and found his morning erection. Rick grunted and Jordan smiled. Rick opened his eyes.

Jordan kissed him. "A hard man is good to find."

Rick rolled on top of him, cock firm against Jordan's.

He kissed his neck. "I want to use the vibrator on you."

Rick's eyes widened. "I'm not sure—"

"You don't know what you're missing. And I want you to know. It's important to me."

"It's not my fantasy."

"Aren't you curious?"

Rick shrugged.

Jordan rolled his eyes. "Then what do you *want* to do?"

Rick gave him a sly smile.

"No chance, big boy. My ass needs a rest."

Rick continued pressing against him, dicks sliding together.

Jordan's balls tightened. "Anything you want that we haven't already done?"

"Not really."

"Are you totally against the vibrator?"

Rick rolled off him. "No, I just…"

"Think it's gay."

"Maybe. I know it's not, but I don't think most straight couples do this stuff."

"They don't know what they're missing. I'm serious, Rick. I want to do this for you."

Jordan got out of the shower, and Rick laid a towel over his shoulders. He squeezed the wetness out of Jordan's hair, then patted down his back. Turning the towel over, he rubbed Jordan's arms and chest and perfect abs. He leaned in and kissed him while ministering to Jordan's cock and his hard, round ass. He finished with Jordan's legs and feet, noticing the elegant shape of Jordan's toes.

They kissed again, and Jordan led him to the bed. He couldn't believe Jordan had talked him into this. He really had no interest in the vibrator, but Jordy thought he'd like it, so what the hell.

He lay on the bed face down.

"You have no idea how beautiful your ass is." Jordan tongued his neck, gradually kissing his way down his body. Teeth clamped onto his ass cheek, and his body bucked. The pleasure-pain shot lightning into his cock.

Two large, warm hands spread his cheeks. He trembled to think of Jordy looking at him that way. A wet tongue flicked his hole. His toes clenched at the sensation, in lust and fear. Fear that he liked it so much, and that maybe he *wanted* to be penetrated that way.

He clutched the pillow beneath him. It was stupid to feel shame at Jordy's eyes on him, or embarrassment at the pleasure of his touch. He had done this to Jordy and loved every second. Jordy hadn't felt ashamed.

Cold lube made his hole constrict. His breath quick and shallow, he clenched his toes, steeling himself. A slick finger entered him. The sensation teased his delicate tissues, arousing him further.

"Relax, babe. You're tight." Jordan's sweet lips rained kisses on his butt cheeks. "The vibrator won't hurt. It might feel weird at first. Once it hits your prostate, you'll be on the ceiling."

"Okay."

"Do you like what I'm doing?"

"S'nice."

"Can you handle more?"

"Okay." He exhaled.

Jordan chuckled. "You're mighty agreeable."

"Don't make fun of me."

"Sorry. It's unlike you. You don't have to be scared. I'll take care of you."

He buried his face in his arms. He forced his apprehension from his mind and concentrated on Jordy's hand working him open.

"Am I hitting your prostate?"

"Not sure." He focused on a sort of swelling that might feel good if Jordy stroked it more.

"I'll try a second finger. If you don't like it, tell me."

The cold lube and the increased stretch made him clench. He let his muscles go soft. The pressure hit his prostate, sending ripples of pleasure through his core. He pumped back against Jordy's hand.

"You like that?"

"Yeah."

Jordan's fingers twisted inside him, and he shuddered. His cock stiffened. A thought raced through his mind of Jordan fucking him. His heart jackhammered his ribs.

"Ready for the vibrator?"

"Okay."

With the fingers still inside him, the sound of buzzing startled him. Jordan must have grabbed it with his other hand. The tip invaded him, and only then did Jordan pull his fingers out.

The tremors on his prostate made him gasp. He never dreamed it could feel that good. Sparks fired behind his eyes.

Jordan increased the pace, but not too fast. Semen dribbled out of him. "Jordy…damn."

"Told you." Jordan's teeth teased his ass cheek.

The pulsing built the tension in his gut. He wanted to stroke himself, but he was lying flat and couldn't reach.

"Want to come like this?"

"Can you touch my cock?"

Fingers caressed his balls, then reached down and grabbed him. His body shook as the orgasm wrenched from him, cries harsh and guttural.

The vibrator switched off. Jordan ran his hand over Rick's back until he calmed.

He closed his eyes and floated, the energy wrung from him. Light kisses teased his arms and shoulders. *Bliss.*

Rick followed Jordan into the bathroom, cleaning himself up while Jordan washed the vibrator with a cloth. He kissed Jordan's neck and stroked his ass. He breathed the scent of shampoo and aroused male, sharper than the feminine scent he was used to with Cynthia. Everything about Cyn was sweet and nice, but it didn't inspire the carnal longing he felt with Jordan.

Jordan had fulfilled all his fantasies, yet he ached for more. He wanted to give Jordan his fantasies, too. Could he go down on Jordan? He remembered how the head of Jordan's penis had felt against his lips, how much he'd wanted to take it in his mouth.

He was terrified that Jordan would come that way. The other things he had done with Jordan were things he could have done with a woman. Sucking off another man would be different.

A slow inhale opened his lungs and forced the tension from his gut. He could finish Jordan off with his hand, right? He loved rubbing him, feeling the cum shoot out of his body.

He led Jordy back to the bed. "Your turn."

They lay facing one another. He kissed his way down Jordan's body, sucking nipples, licking abs. He kissed the trail of fuzz on Jordan's stomach, then circled his tongue around his shaft. Jordan gave him a sweet moan in return.

The heat from Jordan's cock teased Rick's lips. Damn, he wanted it. Tentatively, he suckled the tip, and Jordy writhed. He kissed down to the balls, spitting out a hair. Strange it didn't bother him. He took the balls into his mouth one at a time, and that didn't bother him, either. He loved the way they fit into his mouth, the rough texture of the skin against his tongue. The sweet, earthy taste stoked his desire. It wasn't gay sex that made him uncomfortable. It was the thought of being gay.

He was a fucking hypocrite. All this time, he'd been telling Jordan there was no shame in it, yet Rick felt shame. He was allowing himself to be affected by idiots. Who cared what they thought? The haters were the ones who should be ashamed.

He hooded the cock with his mouth. Jordy let out a deep moan. It hit him that Jordan had never had a blow job before, and he wanted to make it memorable. He sucked him in a long stroke, making him squirm. That show of Jordan's pleasure tickled his chest.

Relaxing his throat, he swallowed him down. He gagged and tried again, sliding his mouth slowly from tip to root.

"So good!" Jordan cried.

He licked around the head again. With his hand, he pumped Jordy's cock while sucking hard. He'd never fantasized about this, but he was sure as hell enjoying it.

He took Jordy deeper with each stroke, learning how far he could go without gagging. The sound of Jordy's moans drove him on.

"Need to stop, babe," Jordy cried.

He kissed his way up Jordan's body while continuing to work that pretty cock. "Come for me."

Jordan trembled, soft moans forming his mouth into an O.

His chest warmed at the look of pleasure on Jordan's face. He squeezed and rubbed, then jacked him in fast strokes. Jordan gasped, and Rick pumped the cum from his lover's body, continuing until he was spent.

He wiped his hand on the sheet and drew Jordan against him. Their lips mingled in soft kisses.

"Amazing," Jordan murmured.

"For me, too."

"You didn't hate it?"

"Love your body." His finger grazed Jordan's chest. "I thought sucking you would make me feel like a queer, but I just feel like I love you."

"Do you think I'm a queer?"

"I think you're perfect," he said. "Always have."

"I think you're perfect for me."

He intertwined their fingers, then kissed Jordan's palm.

They lay warm together. His gut tore open. Would they ever be together like this again? He drew a ragged breath and swallowed his sobs, but he couldn't keep a tear from falling. Jordan rose up on one elbow and kissed him long, slow, and deep.

"I've never been this happy," Rick said, "or this sad."

Jordan nodded. "It's getting late. Want some breakfast?"

"Um, yeah." He sat up while Jordan dressed. He hated when Jordan turned to activity to stave off the emotions between them. He needed to talk about it, but he sensed Jordan couldn't.

Jordan wanted them to be together. Rick's sadness was his own creation. Of course Jordan couldn't talk about it. What could either of them say?

"I need to figure out what life as an openly gay man would mean for me," he said.

"I know."

"If I come out, there's no going back."

"You don't need to explain. You're where I was three years ago."

He scrubbed his face with his hands. He had thought, junior year, that he was in love with Cynthia. If he could feel that way again about a woman, would that be enough? What if no woman ever compared with Jordan?

What if, by the time he figured it out, Jordan had moved on with someone else?

Jordan had warned him that might happen. As long as he refused to commit to monogamy, Jordan was free to look elsewhere. Who was he kidding? A guy like Jordan—sweet and gorgeous and smart—would have no trouble finding a man willing to give him what he wasn't.

Jordan looked over from the skillet where the pancakes sizzled, to the bed where Rick sat, fully dressed, staring at the cherry floor. He had no idea what his friend was thinking, but clearly something was occupying his mind.

Their weekend was nearing its finale. Impossible to say how it would end. The glow of sex was still warm in their veins, but the expression on Rick's face said his mind had moved on to other things.

Jordan couldn't worry about that. As much as he wanted a commitment from Rick, he wouldn't allow himself to pine away for him. He needed to put himself first. Rick had a long journey ahead of him, discovering and coming to terms with his sexual identity. Jordan would support him as a friend, but he wouldn't be his on-again, off-again boyfriend, available when it was convenient.

He knew who he was and what he wanted. Yeah, he wanted Rick, but more importantly, he wanted monogamy. Not random hookups. Not blow jobs in the bushes. A meaningful relationship with someone he could have a future with.

He was still a Boy Scout at heart.

He put the pancakes on the table, then went and sat by Rick. "Breakfast is ready."

Rick took his hand. "You're leaving me."

He kissed his cheek. "We're leaving each other."

"No. I'll never leave you. You're my best friend, and maybe you could be my future. But we're in different places. You need more from this relationship than I do. If I can't commit, you'll move on."

"We agreed we wouldn't sleep with other people–"

"But you'll date guys who can give you things I can't, and you'll want that."

"And you'll date women."

"What if I don't?"

He fought the heat rising from his gut. Where was Rick going with this? "You said you needed to date other people to figure out your sexuality. And you wanted me to date other people to have that experience."

"Yeah, but I'm an idiot. You were right. You date to find the right person, and when you find the right person, you stop dating."

His chest rumbled with soft laughter. "Boy, you liked that vibrator more than I expected."

Rick's brow furrowed, his eyes darkening and turning liquid. "I'm serious. If being with you makes me happy, then what else do I need to know?"

He kissed him. "Your identity, babe."

"Does it matter whether I'm gay or bi, when I'm in love with you?"

An ache gripped his temples. Rick was offering him the one thing he wanted most in the world. Could he risk accepting it? In the best of circumstances, love came with no guarantees. But especially not when you were eighteen and living in different states and one of you was questioning his sexuality.

The odds were against them. And yet…sometimes people married their high school sweethearts, and it worked out. If Rick was willing to try, then Jordan was, too.

He squeezed Rick's hands. "So, no dating other people?"

"Just you and me. I want to be your boyfriend."

The words untied the careful knot he had kept on his emotions. Joy washed over him. Ragged breaths sputtered into his chest until he pulled in a deep gulp of air, opening his lungs.

He swallowed down the knot in his throat. "Are you coming out?" His voice was soft and strained.

Rick bit his lower lip. "Are you asking me to?"

"Not if you're not ready."

"This is still new to me."

"I know." Jordan kissed him. "What are you going to tell Cyn?"

"That it's over. She doesn't need to know why. She'll assume it's because of college, and that's reason enough."

"You're over her?"

"I'll never be over her. She was my first love."

Jordan shook his head. "No—I was. Since first grade."

Rick kissed him slow and tender. "You'll always be mine, Jordy. Nothing can break the bond between us."

He rested his head on Rick's shoulder and looked out the window at the rolling hills. The friendship and love and sex between them weren't separate things but one. The future that stretched before them was uncertain but exciting. Jordan was content to live one day at a time. For now, he had everything he wanted.

# THE END

# Book 2: Tempting Jordan

# Chapter 1

*2013*

Jordan Callahan strolled through the hotel lobby, the sounds of conversation reverberating off the brass and granite surfaces. Walking by a mirror, he unbuttoned his cobalt blazer, opting for a more casual look to go with his sun-bleached jeans. The ring of his cell phone raised the tension in his neck. He only used that tone with one number.

He tapped the phone on. "I told you not to call me again."

"Jordy, hear me out." Damon's voice sounded as desperate as an out-of-luck gambler's.

"Do I have to change my number? I don't give second chances to cheaters."

He ended the call with an unfulfilling click of the off button. His ex's smooth baritone awakened the old desire—and the humiliation of catching him with another man. Pain wrenched his stomach. He sank into a couch near the bar. That was three boyfriends in a row who'd slept around.

He drew his arms to his chest and laid his head on his hands, straight blond hair falling over his eyes. He had to be more careful, take more time to get to know a man before giving his heart. He looked for the good in people, but too often they didn't deserve it.

He headed to the bar, which was open to the lobby, the cushioned barstools upholstered in sage-green leather. "The best scotch you've got. Neat."

"ID?" the bartender asked as she dried a glass and hung it overhead.

Jordan showed his license, used to being carded. He was twenty-three but looked younger—which was ironic, because at fifteen he could have passed for eighteen. When he came out, the other kids didn't give him much trouble because he could kick their asses.

Jordan sipped his scotch. He had planned to take it easy at the reunion tonight, enjoy the company without the swim of alcohol to dull his senses. Thoughts of Damon made his heart ache. One drink would make the pain bearable.

A man walked up beside him. "Versace?"

"From their fall line." Jordan gazed at the man, taking in the green eyes and chiseled jaw. The navy blazer and pinstripe shirt said he was traveling on business.

"Frank," the man said, offering his hand.

"Jordan."

"You here alone?" Frank asked.

"For the moment. I'm joining friends, but I've got some time to kill."

"Maybe we could kill it together."

"Sure." Jordan glanced at the TV behind the bartender, where the Sixers pregame show played. "Not sure what that announcer is so excited about. The team hasn't won a game all season—why would tonight be any different?" He grinned.

"I don't really follow Philadelphia basketball. You a fan?"

"Football's my game. Could have played for Princeton—" Jordan broke off. A familiar form headed away from the front desk. "Excuse me *one* minute." He took a few steps across the lobby and called, "Rick!"

His old friend turned. When his eyes met Jordan's, he flashed a smile, wide and bright enough for a toothpaste ad. His strong jaw was more defined than ever, and his curly dark hair was neat and trimmed, showing none of its unruliness from their high school days.

A flush of desire rippled through Jordan. Rick had maintained his athletic build, broad shoulders and thick arms. Jordan told himself to let it go. He'd been in love with Rick since he was fifteen, but Rick didn't— couldn't—reciprocate.

Rick approached and offered a masculine hug, complete with back clap. Jordan breathed the familiar scent of musk and peppermint Altoids.

"Anyone else with you?" Rick asked.

"Not yet."

"I need to shower and change. Should I meet you at the bar, or at the banquet?"

"Banquet," Jordan said. "Just thought I'd get a drink first."

"Okay. See you in an hour."

Jordan headed back to the bar, where Frank was still waiting. Jordan sipped his drink, letting the smooth, smoky liquid sit on his tongue a moment before he swallowed it. He savored the long burn as it slid down his throat.

"So what brings you to Chestnut Grove?" Frank asked.

"Class reunion. You?"

"Customer visit. Home is Atlanta."

"I'm in Allentown, a couple of hours north."

"So that guy you were talking to…he's, uh, a friend?"

Jordan nodded. "A bunch of us decided to come stag tonight."

It had been Jordan's idea, when his breakup with Damon coincided with Rick's breakup with Jessica. No point in bringing a casual date to a high school reunion.

Jordan sipped his scotch again. He felt the other man looking at him, perhaps for signs of encouragement. He supposed it could be dicey, if you didn't know whether the man you were trying to pick up was gay. Jordan was accustomed to being approached rather than doing the approaching.

But Jordan wasn't looking for a hook-up. Sex with a stranger wouldn't fill the emptiness in his heart. "Look, Frank, I don't want to waste your time. I'm just coming off a breakup…"

The man brushed his thumb against Jordan's. "I understand. No pressure. I'm here alone, and I could use the company. Looks like you could, too."

Jordan rotated his glass. "They always cheat."

"They must be crazy. A guy who looks like you…"

"That's the problem. They're attracted to what's on the outside. They're less concerned about what's on the inside." He swallowed the thickening in his throat. Only one man had ever loved him for himself, and Jordan had let him get away.

Rick slicked some gel into his hair and turned on the blow dryer. The cheap hotel model burned hot but was stingy with the air flow. He combed his fingers through his dark curls to style them.

He'd hated leaving Jordan alone at the bar with that guy. The way the man eyed him, he was clearly looking for a hook-up. Jordy deserved better. Rick might not have much say over Jordan's life anymore, but tonight at least, he could rescue him from that scumbag.

He turned off the dryer and dressed quickly. The navy sport coat over pressed khakis struck a balance between dressy and casual.

He was headed out the door when his cell rang. A customer. His shoulders tensed. He'd finally convinced his boss to transfer him out of that shithole of a dead coal town, so he had to be especially attentive to his new clients. He answered the woman's questions with as much patience as he could, watching the second hand on his Tommy Hilfiger watch tick by.

When he finally got off the phone, it was time to head to the reunion. He walked by the bar, where Jordan was still drinking with that man.

Rick grasped Jordan's shoulder. "Ready, man?"

"Soon as I finish my drink."

"How many've you had?"

"This's only my second. Stop mothering me."

Rick held out his hand to Jordan's companion. "Rick Ferguson."

"Frank."

"What do you do, Frank? Got a business card on you?"

"Sure." Frank fumbled through his jacket pocket and handed him one.

Rick looked at it and grinned. "Oh, sure, the fast food place. Aren't they closed on Sundays, because it's the Lord's day?"

"Um…yeah…"

"They know you're gay?"

"Rick," Jordan warned.

Frank paled. "I don't see how it's any of their business."

"It's not, of course. But if you were to hurt my pal Jordy, I would hate for them to find out about your lifestyle."

"Ignore him," Jordan said to Frank, then turned to Rick. "We're just having a couple of drinks. Back off."

Rick slapped Jordan on the back. "See you in the ballroom in a few." He headed through the lobby and down the corridor.

He thought about the last few guys Jordan had dated and how they had broken his heart. Then, he remembered that Jordan had once told him Damon's parents didn't know he was gay. A smile broke over Rick's face. He opened the Facebook app on his smartphone, went to Damon's timeline, and posted, "Congratulations on coming out, dude! You've been in the closet too long!"

With a smug smile, Rick headed for the ballroom.

# Chapter 2

The ballroom, large and open with tables at the entrance and a dance floor in the back, sported balloons and bouquets in their school colors, blue and yellow. Rick looked around, eyes adjusting to the dim light, and started to make out faces. A stream of old friends stepped forward to shake his hand. He chatted with them absently, scanning the room for his ex, Cynthia Darlington, prettiest girl he'd ever met.

He couldn't believe he hadn't seen her since the day they left for college. Longing filled his chest and made his arms ache. Facebook kept them in touch, but it was no substitute for face-to-face. He missed her, missed how easy things had been with her. Missed how she understood him, and he could tell her anything.

But there was one thing he couldn't tell her, not even now. It would break her heart.

Conversation lulled as heads turned. Rick's turned with them. She stood in the doorway wearing a short black dress, her body slender, a great rack well-proportioned to her body. Any straight man would want a piece of that, and Rick had had it.

Shoulder-length black hair, curled at the ends, framed her face and bounced as she walked. Rick strode forward and captured Cynthia in his arms.

He kissed her, and it felt like the most natural thing in the world. Soft, sweet, and so gorgeous, dark eyes looking up at him. "Damn, it's good to see you," he said. "You look great."

"You too." She squeezed his hands. "I've missed you."

"Then why'd you stay away so long?"

She shrugged. "Family moved to Connecticut. You could have come to see me at Columbia."

"I was dating Amanda then, and she would have cut off my balls if I'd gone to New York to visit my ex." He led her to a table, but they continued to stand. "So, big-time author. What's that like?"

"Not big-time, exactly. But with the money I'm making indie publishing, I was able to quit the advertising job to write novels full-time."

"That's great. I know it's what you always wanted."

"What about you? You're in sales?"

"Yeah, telecommunications systems," Rick said. "It's not exciting, but the good news is I finally got the transfer to Allentown I wanted. Jordy and I will be living in the same town again."

She touched his arm. "I'm happy things have worked out. You guys were practically joined at the hip in high school."

*Not at the hip.* The memories hit, Jordan's body hard beneath him. He cleared his throat and swallowed, fighting back a reaction that might give him away. *Cyn can never know.*

"It was tough," Rick said, "in college, when he spent summers at school so he could finish his bachelor's early and get his master's. Then I ended up in the Poconos, and Jordan in the Lehigh Valley…"

She nodded, eyes soft.

"I know it sounds stupid," he continued, "but the separation has been hard. We text each other a hundred times a day, but it's not the same. Until college, I'd never gone two weeks without seeing him." *Yeah, that's smooth. Straight guys always talk about their friends that way.*

"He's coming tonight, right?" Cyn asked.

*He is if I have something to say about it.* "Yeah, he's here, at the bar. Having a drink with some loser. Said he'd be by in a few minutes."

"He's picking up a guy already? The night hasn't started yet."

"Not picking up a guy," Rick said. "Having a drink. Jordy doesn't sleep around. He's just been depressed since Damon cheated on him."

"Attention from random guys in bars isn't the answer."

"No, it's not." *But my lips on his cock might be.*

Rick pushed down the urge, knowing it would be hours before he and Jordan could be alone. It was the first time in years they'd both been single at the same time—the first chance to rekindle the flame that had sparked all those summers ago, before they left for college.

Rick hadn't been with a man since, and the desire nagged like an itch he couldn't reach. He'd dated three beautiful women since he and Cyn had broken up—three smart, caring, devoted women—but all those relationships had fallen apart. Rick couldn't deny the truth about himself anymore. Hell, he didn't want to. All he wanted was Jordan.

"Hey, loser."

Rick turned. *Trent Weber.* One of his best friends from high school. He and Trent got together about once a month when visiting their hometown. Trent was working on a Ph.D. in chemistry at the University of Delaware, so he didn't have a lot of free time. But he made time for Rick.

Trent greeted Cyn with a long hug, and Rick looked around. *Where the fuck is Jordan?* Rick didn't like it—Jordan vulnerable, that guy Frank on the road and horny. Jordan with two scotches in him by eight o'clock. Maybe three by now.

He excused himself to his friends and strode out to the bar in the lobby. He spotted Jordan just where he'd left him, glass now empty, still talking to that fucking vulture. He sidled up to him, close enough to smell his peppery body wash. His cock took notice, but he pictured his mom with her hand inside a Thanksgiving turkey, pulling out the giblets. That did the trick.

"Cyn's here," Rick said to Jordan.

A smile broke over Jordan's face. "Frank, it's been great talking to you. Have a safe trip back to Atlanta."

With a brief handshake, the encounter was over. Rick whistled a low sigh of relief.

As they walked the long corridor to the ballroom, he squeezed Jordan's shoulder. "No more creeps at bars."

"We were just talking—"

"Fucking promise me." Rick halted, and Jordan stopped to face him, eyes downcast.

"Fine. I'm just looking for company—"

"And they're looking for a blow job," Rick said in low tones. "I don't want some lowlife taking advantage of you, or worse."

Jordan arched his brows. "Jealous?"

Rick didn't ease his hard stare.

Jordan's muscles slackened, and cold anticipation formed a lump in his stomach. *Rick isn't really jealous?*

But the feral look in Rick's eyes said he was.

The hand on his shoulder nudged him toward the ballroom. Did Rick want him? Was that why he'd agreed to come stag?

Rick's fingers idly tapped the small of Jordan's back as they walked. The whisper of contact was odd and possessive, and it sent Jordan's blood surging to all the wrong places. He shouldn't have had that second scotch. He was relaxed and horny, especially with Rick so close, when he needed to keep his wits about him. Rick would never forgive him if he let something slip about their past together in front of their high school friends.

The tapping continued, revving his nerves into high gear. His fly pressed painfully against his flesh. He turned to Rick. "Will you stop touching me?"

Rick's easy smile fled. "Why?"

He grabbed the collar of Rick's shirt and said in his ear, "Because, you dumb shit, you're making me hard."

Rick raised his brows and smirked. They moved forward again. The tapping slowed but didn't stop.

Now he was sporting wood in earnest. Was Rick sending a message, or being his normal asshole self? He wanted to talk to him alone, but suddenly they were surrounded by once-familiar faces, now oddly transformed, in a dimly lit room with a DJ blaring dance music from 2008. He caught sight of Cyn, and for a moment all other thoughts fell away. She looked prettier than he'd ever seen her, and if he were straight, he'd be trying to get inside that dress. Instead, he contented himself with a bear hug.

She stood with an arm around him while he shook Trent's hand. "I haven't seen you since you graduated from Penn," Trent said. "What was that, six months ago?"

"You sound like my mom."

"No," Rick said. "If he sounded like your mom, he would have added something about me being a dumbass."

"You are a dumbass," Jordan said. Rick punched his arm.

They gathered around a table but didn't sit. Rick set a bottle of water in front of Jordan. Apparently, Rick didn't want him getting drunk. Which was good, really, because this was the first time he'd been out lately without Damon at his side. How pathetic was that? Three months, and he hadn't been out with friends?

It had been too easy to immerse himself in work. As an intern, he was still proving himself, and the architects in the firm were impressed by the long hours he was willing to put in. Jordan didn't mind hard work. He loved the job, and had ambitions to start his own firm one day. But he needed a social life. With Rick moving to Allentown...

*Fuck.* What did that mean? What did Rick want from him? If it was just friendship, Jordan needed to find a boyfriend quick, or he'd end up making a fool of himself, offering something Rick didn't want. Well, didn't want anymore. There was a time when he'd wanted it badly enough.

Rick was bi. He'd made it clear he wanted to be with girls. His family had expectations, and he wasn't going to let them down. Not even for Jordan. Not while women were an option for him.

*Hell, that hurt.* It had been so long since he'd let himself think of Rick that way, but those old memories rushed back, Rick calling the first semester of college, saying he'd slipped. Hadn't cheated, exactly, but had gone further than they'd agreed when they decided to date other people, too. And Jordan had ended it, because they were eighteen and apart and monogamy was impractical. By the time Jordan realized he'd made a horrible mistake, Rick was with Amanda.

Jordan sucked down the remains of his water bottle. Bernadette Holt strolled over with Max Martinov in tow. Which was just like high school, except geeky little Max had grown up and founded a billion-dollar tech company, with some help from his dad. He'd been featured in *GQ* or something—tall, blond, and hard-bodied, no trace of the boy he'd been. And Bernie had matured into her height, nearly six feet, mostly legs, her long, red hair halfway down her back.

She avoided Trent's glance. The two had dated in high school, but Trent had been secretly pining away for Cyn. Jordan knew it, and Cyn and Bernie probably did, too. Rick was clueless. It would have pissed him off that his good friend Trent had wanted to be inside his girlfriend, but then, Rick had wanted to be inside Jordan. So Rick had no right to complain.

Cyn and Bernie, on the other hand...

Guys were such dicks to women. At least gay men could be dicks to each other, which was more fair. But Jordan was tired of the lies and the bullshit.

"Stop thinking about Damon," Rick said, and Jordan smiled. He and Rick had been friends so long, they could almost read each other's thoughts.

"This is a party," Rick continued. "You're supposed to be having fun. Cyn is here. You love Cyn."

She sidled up next to him and slipped her arms around him. "You want me to kick his ass for you?"

It was an old joke, petite Cyn threatening to beat up people for her three jock friends. But it showed the loyalty they felt for one another. She took care of them emotionally, and they would have jumped in front of a bus for her.

"I hear Carlos Ramirez is gay," Bernie said.

Jordan turned to her. "What?"

"I'm trying to get you laid. Best way to put a cheater out of your mind."

"Carlos has a date."

"Lesbo. Look at those shoes."

Max took her hand and patted it. "Good to see you're as politically correct as ever."

"*Lesbo* isn't a slur."

"It kind of is," Jordan said, "unless you're actually a lesbian."

"I'm pansexual," Bernadette said with a grin. "I'll fuck anything."

"Obviously," Rick said. "You fucked Trent."

Bernie gaped at Trent in mock horror. "You told!" She wobbled her martini glass, then looked at Max. "Why are you just standing there? My drink is empty."

He took the glass. "Dirty martini?"

"Congratulations. You remembered from ten minutes ago. Hop to it, dweeb."

"Yes, ma'am." He smiled and sauntered off.

"Bernie," Cyn scolded in a whisper. "He's worth 800 million dollars. You can't talk to him like that anymore."

"Why not?" Bernie asked in her raspy voice. "He likes it."

"He's grown up since high school," Jordan said.

"You noticed, too?" Bernie asked.

"Hard not to. Nordic jaw, ice-blue eyes…"

"Don't think he plays for your team, though. Carlos, on the other hand—"

Max stepped up and handed her a martini. "For you, milady."

"Such a good boy." She patted his cheek. Then, her eyes widened. "Is that Lynne Rubinstein? Hey, Ruby!" she called.

She headed off without looking back. Max followed like a puppy. A six-foot, four-inch, Viking god of a puppy.

But Max, gorgeous as he was, wasn't Jordan's type. Every man he'd dated had been tall, dark, and handsome.

Like Rick.

*Damn it.* He'd never realized that before.

While Cyn and Trent went to get some food, Jordan looked sideways at Rick, unsure what to say. Things had never been awkward between them, not in the seventeen years they'd been friends. Even after he and Rick had broken their romantic ties, they'd stayed close, their unspoken longing a shared grief.

Now, Jordan had no idea what Rick wanted from him.

Truth was, he'd been hoping to hook up with Rick tonight. That was why he'd suggested the four friends come stag. Were Rick's thoughts heading in the same direction? From the way he was acting...

*Fuck.* He hadn't thought this through. It was like the summer before college all over again, Rick looking for sex, Jordan looking for love. He was setting himself up for heartbreak. Hadn't he had enough of that with Damon?

He wasn't a dumb kid anymore. If Rick wanted sex tonight, Jordan wouldn't say no. But that's where it would end. He wasn't getting involved with men who weren't out. Not again, not ever.

"Look at Gianelli over there," Rick said, startling Jordan from his thoughts, "losing his hair already. Poor bastard."

"Like father, like son."

"Bodes well for me, then."

"Yeah, your dad's still got a full head of hair." The old dull ache came into sharp relief, Jordan's sadness at never knowing his father.

Rick squeezed his shoulder. "Neither of your grandfathers lost their hair, right?"

He shrugged. "My mom's dad died pretty young. Barely fifty."

"I'm sorry. I know it hasn't been easy for you." Rick's soft brown eyes gazed at him. Their warmth telescoped into him, enveloping him in the comfort of Rick's friendship. Rick had always been able to ease his pain and doubts with a simple *I love you, man* look. For all his posturing, Rick was the most loyal, loving friend he had.

And if that was all he could ever be, it was enough.

But that didn't stop Jordan from wanting more.

No, he couldn't think that way. Wouldn't. This stupid high school crush would end tonight.

♥ ♥ ♥

Cyn and Trent rejoined them with plates of hors d'oeuvres to share. It wasn't exactly gourmet fare, Jordan thought—standard finger food, though the mini crab cakes were good—but Chestnut Grove wasn't known for its upscale dining. Or upscale anything. No wonder he and his friends had scattered after college.

They had barely finished eating when Bernadette wandered over and pulled Rick aside. He came back to the table where the rest of them stood, and put his arm around Cyn. "We're going bowling."

She stared at him. "Who's going bowling?"

"We are. The four of us. With Bernie and Max. Ruby and her date are coming, too."

"Why?"

"Grudge match."

Cyn's baffled expression lingered. Jordan suppressed a laugh.

"This is so juvenile." She turned to Trent. "You're not doing this, are you?"

"Of course he's doing it," Rick said.

Trent shrugged. "It'll be fun."

"I can't bowl in this dress!"

Jordan squeezed her arm. "You'll look hot bowling in that dress."

"If Bernie can do it, you can," Rick said.

Outnumbered, Cyn shook her head and sighed.

They went to their rooms to get their coats, and Jordan wondered for a moment if Cyn would come back. But she did, still in her dress and heels, no longer protesting.

This pattern was typical of Rick and Cyn's relationship. He'd come up with some impulsive idea and drag her along. She complained but went anyway. Jordan had asked her about it once, worried Rick was taking advantage of her.

She said she was so much of an introvert, her natural inclination was to say no to social opportunities. Rick pulled her out of her shell. It took her a while to adjust to his suggestions, but she always had fun. As much as she minded it at the time, she didn't regret it afterward.

They piled into the car, following their old habits, Trent riding shotgun because of his long legs. Except Jordan had caught up to the rest of the guys in height now, so he was jammed in behind Rick. "Move up the seat, asshole."

"I need room for my legs to drive."

"You can give me a few inches."

"Is that a proposition?" Rick asked

"Fuck you." Jordan tried not to laugh but couldn't help it. He would've said more if Cyn hadn't been in the car.

Rick moved the seat forward so Jordan could at least fit his feet on the floor. Fortunately, the bowling alley was only half a mile away.

Chestnut Grove Lanes hadn't changed much in the five years since high school. The lights were still harsh, the carpet had grown even thinner, and the stale odor of cigarettes lingered, even though the place had been non-smoking for as long as Jordan could remember.

They found two lanes side by side, Rick's team at one and Bernie's at the other. By the fifth frame, Max was the clear leader. He shrugged it off. "My house has a bowling alley. It's not my fault—it came that way. The rhythm helps me think when I'm designing a new game app."

"You're still designing?" Cyn asked. "Don't you have lackeys for that?"

"The day I can't design anymore is the day I sell the business. I do it for love. I mean, I don't do the coding. But I've always got one or two ideas in development."

"Me, too. I'm writing a novel in my head right now about a woman whose lame ex-boyfriend makes her go bowling when she could be dancing."

"I didn't make you do anything," Rick said. "You came along willingly."

"Will you shut the fuck up," Trent said. "I'm trying to bowl."

Jordan smirked. The dynamic between Rick and Trent was the same as in high school. They were stereotypical jocks, at least in their posturing, always trying to out-testosterone each other. Cyn thought it was fucking stupid (her exact words), but Jordan understood, sort of. That constant pressure to be strong, to be a man—which often translated into *prove you're not gay*.

When it came to physical strength, Jordan could hold his own with either of them. But he could never have passed for straight. He'd come out at fifteen because some of the kids had started calling him queer. Might as well be open about it.

But Rick? No one had suspected. Not even Jordan, not until the moment Rick had made a move on him that weekend at the cabin. And he'd been so into it, not just the sex, but wanting to hold his hand when they were out together.

Jordan's chest hurt thinking about it, like he'd just run five miles. He wanted that life. But Rick didn't. He couldn't give up the persona he'd spent a lifetime building.

Jordan took his turn bowling, then looked over to see Rick watching him. Rick didn't smile or look away, just kept up the dark, smoldering gaze. There was want in it, need even, and if Rick wasn't careful, others would notice, too. But Rick *wanting* him and *acting* on it were two different things. For an impulsive guy, he had self-control when it counted.

Jordan slumped down onto the seat next to Cyn. She turned to him and searched his face. "What's wrong?"

"Being here…it reminds me of how simple things were in high school. I mean, in lot of ways, things were harder, especially the pressure to fit in—"

Cyn took his hand. "You and I were never going to fit in."

She was right. Being the only openly gay guy in his class had made him conspicuous, and not in a good way—if there even *was* a good way to be conspicuous as a teenager. And Cyn, for her it was just as bad. Her dad had been CEO of the town's largest employer. Her family was in a different social sphere from all their classmates—and they never let her forget it, even if she was voted homecoming queen.

He shrugged. "We did okay. We weren't outcasts or anything."

"We were different."

"We're still different. It just matters less now."

Cyn nodded, but her wistful expression remained.

Jordan tried not to think about it, how hard those teenage years had been, especially when most of his childhood had been happy and carefree. Sure, money was tight, but his uncle—his dad's brother—made sure

Jordan and his mom were okay. His grandparents all lived nearby. As hard as it was for his mom, being a single mother, they had a strong safety net.

Then hormones and middle school happened, and people noticed that Jordan wasn't like other boys.

It wasn't that Jordan resented his sexuality. He was comfortable in his own skin. The problem was that most guys his age weren't into monogamy like he was. In that sense, being with a woman might be easier. But he'd never been attracted to a woman—and let's face it, if he were going to be attracted to a woman, Cyn would be it. She didn't raise his interest that way even a little.

He stretched and stood. "Maybe I'll get a beer. This match is too boring to watch sober."

"No beer." Rick sauntered back from bowling a spare and stopped him mid-stride.

"Excuse me?"

"You're thinking about Damon. No beer."

"I'm not—"

Rick grabbed his shoulder and pulled him aside. "He's an asshole. You deserve better."

"It's not just Damon." He swallowed the knot in his throat. Men let him down. Every. Single. Time.

"Jordy," Rick murmured, in a voice thick with longing that turned Jordan inside out.

"Don't. Not here. I won't be able to keep it together."

"We'll talk later."

"Yeah." Jordan wondered how he was still standing, with his legs turned to water. He wanted to sink into Rick's arms—hell, he wanted to push him against the wall and grind into him until they both came hard and fast. But they were in a stupid bowling alley and Cyn was there and nothing like that was possible.

Rick's words reverberated in his mind. *Later.* Was that an invitation? Because it sure as hell sounded like one.

Rick pulled away, body shaking. What would happen if he kissed Jordan now, with everyone watching?

He wanted it, maybe more than he'd ever wanted anything. But he couldn't in front of Cyn. How could he possibly explain it to her? *I've always been gay, but I didn't know it until I slept with you.*

Well, that wasn't exactly true. He'd thought he was bi until about a year ago, when things with Jessica started to deteriorate. His dick left the relationship months before he found the courage to end it with her. He'd hung on because Jess was great, and Jordan was with Damon. But when he got the phone call from Jordy, barely able to speak after he'd walked in on Damon sucking off another guy, Rick knew that his life as a straight man was over.

He just had no fucking idea what his life as a gay man would be.

Jordan was still the only person who knew. Rick wanted to be out, but the thought of his mother's disappointment stung. He didn't want to make some big pronouncement about his orientation. The gay label felt wrong on him, like a borrowed shirt too tight in the shoulders, constricting his movements.

The only thing that felt right was the memory of Jordan in his arms, their bodies discovering each other, their hearts open and free.

He wanted to feel that way again.

Suddenly, bowling seemed like a lame idea. He was eager to wrap up and get back to the hotel.

Until Bernie bowled two strikes, and his adrenaline kicked up again.

"Take that, Ferguson," she taunted.

"Take this, Holt." He thrust his pelvis toward her.

"Not enough meat there to tempt me. Cyn gave me the details."

"I don't know what she told you, but she didn't tell you *that*. You could dislocate your jaw trying to take it all."

"Richard Ferguson," Cyn's voice said as she walked up behind him. "You're a vile human being. I don't know how I put up with you for three years."

He turned. "Bernie doesn't mind." He took Cyn in his arms. "She's not sensitive like you."

"That's right," Bernadette said. "I've got a bigger dick than any of you. I just don't have it with me right now."

"Too much information!" Cyn looked up at Rick. "Can we get out of here?"

"One more frame, sweetheart." He kissed her chastely, more out of habit than anything. She felt good in his arms, comfortable, but the orange-cinnamon scent of her roused no hint of desire.

He let her go, glancing at Jordan's tight, round ass as he picked up the bowling ball. His fingers ached to sink into Jordy's sweet flesh. One more hour and they could say good night to their friends. Then, the real party could begin.

# Chapter 3

Jordan sat in the car, simmering. What was up with Rick and Cyn? They might as well have been making out at the bowling alley. Was Rick looking to hook up with her again?

Maybe it was for the best. Sleeping with Rick would only remind him of what he was missing. After five years, he was over the pain. No point reawakening it.

Okay, that was a lie. He was still in love with Rick and probably always would be. But he was over the breakup, over the bitter longing for what they'd shared.

The awful thing was, without the distance of college, they might have made the relationship work the first time. Too many temptations at Princeton. It seemed like every gay man on campus had hit on him at least once. Even though he wasn't looking for casual sex, it felt good to attract that kind of attention.

And he worried that if Rick was the only man he ever dated, he might look back on his life one day and wonder. Not with regret, exactly, but with curiosity. Jordan wanted to know what it was like to go on a date, maybe kiss a little, enjoy that frisson of attraction. And why not? It wasn't like he and Rick were engaged.

It seemed fine at first. Rick needed no convincing about the dating-other-people-but-no-sex part. That's what Rick had wanted all along. They were young and needed to experiment, he'd said. He only agreed to monogamy because that's what Jordan wanted.

Unfortunately, they hadn't been explicit enough about the "no sex" part. Rick, with his hetero-centric worldview, had taken it to mean no penetration. While Jordan was battling to keep it in his pants with a hot and very persuasive junior, Rick was casually getting off with some girl. Jordan wasn't sure whether he was more hurt by Rick's lack of real effort at sexual fidelity, or the fact that he'd gone back to dating women.

Angry, he'd convinced himself that Rick was too immature and impulsive for a relationship. And maybe Jordan was partly influenced by the fact that he really wanted to get naked with that junior. But before too many weeks had passed, he realized how stupid he was acting. Rick had been faithful to Cyn for three years, and the junior was already getting naked with someone else.

He called Rick to apologize, saying he made a mistake in ending their romance. But by then, Rick and that girl, Amanda, had become exclusive. Rick wasn't going to give up on that, he said, when Jordan couldn't make up his mind *what* he wanted.

Jordan felt like he'd been pushed off a pier into a cold lake. He was so accustomed to Rick being an asshole—he was shocked to realize *he* had been the asshole this time. He had dumped Rick when someone else came along, then tried to get him back when it didn't work out.

Except, that's not how it had felt from the inside. He and Rick couldn't be together, not physically. He wasn't sure what that meant for them, and he was trying to figure it out.

He hadn't expected that one impulsive decision to end things between them forever.

Rick brought the car to a stop, jerking him back to reality. They stepped out into the cold fall air. Beneath the lights of the dark parking lot, Rick gave him a broad smile. But he couldn't return it, not with his stomach woven into knots.

Back in the ballroom, Rick got a plate of food for Cyn and made her eat it. Jordan rocked in his chair, thinking he would lose his mind watching the two of them and their easy rhythm together. But he didn't want to interfere, because Cyn needed to eat. It wasn't like she'd ever had a disorder, but while she was very careful not to eat too much, she wasn't nearly as vigilant about eating too little.

He got up and went to the bar. His drinks from earlier in the night were out of his system, so he ordered another scotch. The bitter liquid couldn't ease the jealousy and regret in his chest, but it *could* quiet the swirl of thoughts in his mind.

Rick approached. "What are you doing over here alone?"

"I needed another drink."

Rick's eyes said he disagreed, but he made no comment. "So you got a drink. Why didn't you come back to the table?"

*Because being close to you shreds my insides.*

"Cyn looks great, doesn't she?" Jordan said in lieu of a reply.

Rick beamed. "More beautiful than ever. Didn't realize how much I'd missed her until tonight."

Jordan nodded slowly, jaw tight. "Are you going to ask her out?"

Rick's happy expression shattered. His brow furrowed, and his lips thinned. "Why would I do that? You know why I broke up with her."

Jordan shrugged. "College."

Rick glared, eyes darkening, then grabbed Jordan's arm. He dragged him out into the hallway and led him into the empty business center. They sat in the chairs in front of the computers, the room's only light source.

"You *know* why I broke up with Cyn. That hasn't changed."

Jordan bit his lip, all the unsaid words wanting to come out. But what good would it do to rehash the past? They'd moved on. And just because Damon had broken his heart, that was no reason to think rushing into Rick's arms would be a good idea. Not that Rick wanted him that way.

"Jordy, you're the one who ended things between us."

He looked up, the intensity in Rick's voice echoed in Rick's gaze.

"That's not how I remember it."

Rick took Jordan's hand, brushing a thumb across his palm. "I told you from the beginning, you weren't ready for a committed relationship, even though you *thought* you were. But when you called and said you wanted to see other people, it was like a knife slicing me open."

"I said *see* other people, not sleep with them."

"I didn't sleep with Amanda!" Rick's face twisted. "We were just kissing. And the next thing I knew, her hand was in my pants, and that was all it took. You know I had no self-control back then…And after that happened, I had to return the favor. It was the gentlemanly thing to do. But I didn't sleep with her."

"You wanted to be with girls."

"I didn't pursue her. She was into me."

"That's the way it always is with you. You hook up with whoever's convenient."

Rick shrugged. "I suppose. The only person I ever pursued was you."

He exhaled a sharp breath. He wished he could argue it away, but it was true. No man had ever wanted him the way Rick had that weekend they spent together before they left for college.

It seemed like a lifetime ago, but it was part of them, their history. And now, with them sitting a breath apart, it felt very much like their present. Like despite the years, nothing had changed.

"What happened with you and Jessica?" Jordan's voice was low and faltering.

"Jess was a huge mistake. It was my senior year at Penn State, and I wanted to focus on graduating and getting a job. And then Sandusky happened."

Jordan rocked in his chair. Rick hadn't played football in college, mainly because he didn't want his grades to suffer. But the entire campus had been rocked by the allegations of child abuse and a subsequent cover-up.

Rick continued, "I was active in the LGBTA center, and people talked, even when I reminded them that the *A* stood for ally. It didn't feel safe, with ignorant assholes talking like pedophilia and homosexuality were the same thing. And Jess, we were good friends, and I thought that's all we were until she kissed me." He sucked in his cheeks. "It was easy to use her as a shield."

The frown on his lips looked so sad, Jordan wished he could kiss the corner of his mouth and wipe the expression away. But anyone might pass by and see.

Rick's voice was low and strained. "It was just for a few months, until we graduated. I took a job in Scranton, and her family was a hundred miles away in Reading, so I thought that would be the end of it. Until she showed up at my crappy little apartment in that shithole town, and said she'd gotten a job at a call center there. We could be together—wasn't that great?"

Jordan let out a soft, ironic laugh. So typical of Rick's life.

"You were stupid in love with Damon at the time. And Jess was one of my best friends, so I figured, what the hell? She moved to *Scranton* for me. I should at least try to make it work."

"Scranton's not that bad."

"You've never lived there." Rick gave him a teasing smile. "Anyway, with so much change, Jess was comfortable. Easy. But she wasn't what I wanted, and my dick kept reminding me of that. It got so bad, I was using condoms even though she was on the Pill, in case I went soft and had to fake it."

Jordan blinked. *Did he just say what I think he did?* "You faked orgasms with her?"

"I'm not proud of it."

Jordan hadn't thought Rick could be more of an asshole, but this raised the game to a whole new level. "You don't think she knew?"

"I can be pretty convincing."

Jordan could only glare. "You're so fucking vain that you'd rather *fake an orgasm* with a woman than admit to yourself you're gay."

"I'm bi. I've already told you that."

"If you can't stay hard with a woman, then the bisexual train has left the station. You are on the line to Dudeville." Jordan shook his head. "Why am I even friends with you? You are the biggest asshole I know."

Rick shrugged. "You like assholes."

He narrowed his eyes and smirked. "And I seem to recall that you're obsessed with them."

Rick held out a key card. "After Cyn leaves the party, come to my room. I'm in three-fifteen."

A shot of adrenaline sped up his heart. He took a calming breath. He couldn't let Rick see how the offer affected him.

His brain struggled to form thoughts. Could he be reading the situation wrong? Was he just assuming Rick wanted to hook up?

He inhaled, long and slow, to calm his racing pulse. *He isn't offering you the future. It's one night.*

He pocketed the key. "Just to talk."

Rick smirked. "If you say so."

He wasn't surprised Rick didn't believe him. His own heart didn't believe him, either. Tonight might be his last shot with Rick, and damned if he would let that slip away.

Rick stepped up to the bar and ordered a bottle of water, handing the bartender a ten and dropping the change into the jar. Rick's job didn't pay that great, but he didn't have a lot of expenses either, and being generous to people who worked for tips was easy enough to do. In this hick town, they got stiffed all too often.

Across the ballroom, Cyn and Trent were dancing, and Jordan was standing near Bernie and her crowd, but not really joining in their conversation. Rick drank down a good third of the bottle, not sure where the night was headed. Jordan wanted him but didn't trust him. The one thing he and Jordan had always had was trust, and somehow, he'd managed to screw that up.

Had their breakup in college been Rick's fault? Hell, it hadn't even felt like a breakup. More like a break while they were physically apart, an acknowledgement that they weren't ready for monogamy. Dating other people seemed a reasonable solution as long as they weren't in a position to make a lifelong commitment.

Now that they were both done with their education, they could finally start up their relationship again. That was reasonable, wasn't it? Why was Jordan acting so negative about it?

He sipped the water, letting the clean taste sit on his tongue, the cool liquid clearing his mind. Okay, he and Jordy would talk. Maybe that's what they needed, anyway. Figure out what dating would mean for them. Was Rick ready to date openly? He'd be in a new town, so he didn't have to worry about shocking anyone—he didn't know anyone. And Allentown was far enough from his parents that he wouldn't have to come out to them right away.

His parents loved Jordan, and had treated him like a son ever since the two of them had become inseparable when they were little boys. But this was different. Rick dating a man would be a shock.

How stupid was he? He'd had five years to prepare them, but instead he'd acted like a coward, pretending he was a hundred percent straight. If he'd told them he was bi during his junior year in college, after he and Amanda broke up, things would be easier now.

No point dwelling on that. He couldn't change the past. But he could move forward with the life he wanted, the life he was meant to have. He would tell his family at some point, but not right away. Give his mom a chance to adjust gradually, as he stopped dating and brought Jordan to family events instead. His sister would realize the truth and start dropping hints. And eventually, he'd confirm it.

No big drama. He smiled at the thought.

He walked over to the little group where Jordan stood, Bernie's raucous laughter slicing the air. He caught the tail end of a conversation between Jordan and Max.

"Strange that no one's called me a faggot tonight," Max said.

Jordan chuckled. "It is. You were called fag in high school more than me."

"Ironic, since I'm actually straight."

"You sure? It would be a big win for my team."

"Sorry." Max beamed and clapped Jordan's arm.

Rick thought back to those days, and the ribbing he'd given Max, mainly because he was a little guy and a total geek. But he'd never bullied him the way some kids did—in fact, Rick had once pulled a guy off Max when things threatened to get violent. Grabbed the guy by the shirt and forced him back against the lockers, warning him what would happen if he didn't keep his fists to himself. Jordan and Trent had hovered close by to reinforce the point, while Cyn wrapped her arms around Max to calm him.

And now, six years later, Max was a couple of inches taller than Rick and had made a fortune. The bastard.

Rick squeezed Max's shoulder. "So, wuss, you still have the photos of Princess Leia you used to keep in your locker?"

Max laughed. "I've grown up since then. You apparently haven't." His muscles flexed beneath Rick's hand as Max patted him on the back.

Rick's dick took notice. *What the hell?* He'd never thought of Max as anything but a dork—but since he'd grown a foot and his shoulders had filled out, he was now exactly Rick's type. Tall and blond and gorgeous. *Shit.* He could happily have gone a whole lifetime without thinking of Max that way.

Not that he wanted to do anything about it. It was easier to come to terms with the idea of being gay for Jordan, than of being gay, period. But yeah, that little wry smile the guy was giving him, and the scent of his citrus cologne, made his stomach tighten a little while a zing of excitement shot lower. Max was hot, and it was impossible not to notice, with the guy so close.

Cyn walked up to them, Trent a few feet behind, and said, "I'm calling it a night. See you tomorrow at breakfast?"

"I'll be there," Rick said, warm affection for her swelling his heart. "And *you'd* better be, too. No changing your mind and sleeping in."

She smiled and hugged him. He felt the pressure of her hip against his semi-erect cock. *Damn it.* She raised her brows, and he grinned. May as well let her think he was hard for her, and not Max Martinov, of all the seven billion people on earth.

He drew her close again and kissed her mouth, an incredible sense of relief washing over him. He had missed her like crazy, and was only just starting to realize it. High school had been the best time of his life, and she had been a big part of the reason why. He would always love Cyn, even if he didn't feel attracted to her anymore.

She said goodbye to the rest of the crowd and ambled toward the door, hips swaying. She had a pretty ass, but it didn't do the things to him that the sight of Jordan's ass did.

He looked at Jordan sideways, and his stomach curled up into a ball. This was it. After five years apart, this was their moment.

Trent walked up. "I should head out, too. Got to call my lab partner, see how things are going. We've got some experiments running over the weekend, and the outcome is critical to my research."

"Yeah, okay, I'll probably just, um, watch the end of the Sixers game or something."

While Trent chatted with Bernie on the way out, Rick turned to Jordan and said to him, in a voice loud enough for the others to hear, "Want to watch the game in my room?"

"Sure," Jordan said with a smile. "I just need to change first."

They headed for the elevators and stepped inside, but they weren't alone. Otherwise, Rick didn't think he could have stopped himself from backing Jordan against the wall of the car and devouring that sweet mouth.

# Chapter 4

Rick sucked in a breath and looked around the room. He took the condoms and lube from his shaving kit and put them into the top drawer of the nightstand. In the bathroom, he found a box of tissues and placed it next to the bed.

His heart raced. He rifled through his suitcase and pulled out a T-shirt and knit pajama pants. He changed quickly, glancing at the door. Should he turn on the TV, keep up the charade? No, he'd made his intentions clear. Jordan's suggestion that they come stag had seemed like an invitation. His demeanor that night hadn't contradicted that assessment.

The click of a key card entering the lock brought a thrill to Rick's chest. The door opened, and there stood Jordan, a white T-shirt clinging to his pecs. Gray sweatpants, flared at the ankle, were slung low on his hips. Rick stared, and Jordan gave him a sultry smile as he closed the door.

Jordan approached, eyes glued to Rick. He stopped with their bodies just inches apart, then lifted his T-shirt off over his head, revealing firm biceps and contoured abs. He tossed the T-shirt into the corner. "Is it hot in here, or is it me?"

Rick's balls tightened at the heat coming off Jordy, the sharp scent of his arousal. He licked his lips. "Definitely you."

He couldn't look away from those gorgeous eyes, blue like an autumn sky. High cheekbones and a dimpled chin, golden-blond hair long enough to fall across his eyes and skim the nape of his neck.

His gaze traveled down Jordan's torso to the V of muscles pointing from his abs to his groin. He slid his fingers beneath the waistband of Jordan's sweats and circled around his body, soft skin over muscle, the depression at the small of his back inviting Rick to slide his hands lower.

He'd imagined this moment. Now that it was here, he didn't want to rush it. He pulled Jordan in. Air rumbled in Jordan's throat, and his lips parted, capturing Rick's.

Velvet tongues flicked together. Rick explored every crevice of Jordan's mouth, sucking and nibbling. It had been so long since a kiss had excited him like this—not since the last time he'd been with Jordan.

He nuzzled him, then swept eager lips across the line of his jaw and downward. "Could kiss you forever," he murmured into the curve of Jordan's neck.

Jordan pulled off Rick's T-shirt and attacked his nipples, teasing and twisting and sucking. Heat spread from Rick's groin outward, his veins pulsing with want.

Despite the fire inside him, Rick wanted to take this slow, to savor every inch of Jordan's body. He noted how it had changed since they were eighteen, shoulders broader, torso longer. The sculpted muscles could only have come from working with a personal trainer. Jordan wasn't bulky but finely toned, as if he were carved from marble.

As if he were made for Rick.

He caressed Jordan's face, and Jordan laid his cheek on Rick's palm. That vulnerable gesture undid him. The walls of protection around Rick's heart split open. His fingers combed through Jordan's hair, soft as corn silk. He trailed kisses along Jordan's neck. "Missed you."

A whimper caught in Jordan's throat. "I remember everything." His voice was barely more than a whisper caressing the silence. "The way you taste. The way it felt to be underneath you. When I close my eyes, all my lovers look like you."

Rick kissed Jordan's cheek tenderly, relishing the feel of stubble on his lips. "I was born to love you. I know that now."

They pressed together, devouring each other with hot kisses. Their cocks pressed into each other with nothing more than thin cotton between them. An explosion of fireworks shot off behind Rick's closed eyelids. He grabbed the fabric and pushed it down until he felt Jordan's skin, soft as suede, against his own. He fisted both their cocks, and Jordan gasped.

With a hand on Jordan's perfect round ass, Rick danced him toward the nightstand and pulled out the lube. Still grinding against the cock in his fist, he squeezed out a couple of drops of the slippery stuff, then slicked it down the two dueling shafts.

Jordan moaned and sucked on Rick's neck. "Gonna come if you keep this up."

"Do it, babe. Come for me. Love that sweet look you get on your face when you shoot."

"You like it? Want this with me?" Jordan's voice was strangled, his breath labored.

He nibbled Jordan's ear. "Love it with you."

The sudden tightening in his shaft told him he was close. He locked his knees and grabbed Jordan's ass before shooting his load over Jordan's chest. Jordan came a moment later, his sticky liquid a trail of heat from Rick's stomach to his nipple.

Rick ground his chest into Jordan, mingling their seed, gluing their bodies together. With fingers gripping Jordan's hair, he kissed him frantically. The odor of man-sweat and semen filled his nostrils. He didn't know when anything had smelled so good.

Coming down from the high, he looked into Jordan's blue eyes. "Perfect." It was all he could say, a word murmured low.

"Happy," Jordan replied.

After a quick shower, they lay in the bed together, clean and naked. Jordan tried laying his head on Rick's chest, but he couldn't stop grazing his lips over Rick's skin. When was the last time he had felt joy like this? This time with Rick was even sweeter than the last, because now he knew how it felt to have his heart broken. How it felt to be used. That was something Rick would never do to him.

Rick's hands ran down the length of Jordan's back. "I'm glad Damon cheated on you. Otherwise, you wouldn't be with me now."

Jordan squeezed his hand. "In that case, I'm glad, too."

"I had almost convinced myself that our time together at the cabin hadn't been everything I remembered. That I'd built it up in my head to be something more than it was. This feels right, Jordy."

Jordan answered with a soft kiss. He had thought being with Rick would release the tension that had built between them over the past five years. He hadn't been prepared for this rush of emotion. He felt like a teenager again, aching for his first love, knowing they had no future.

He settled into Rick's arms, wishing he could live inside the fantasy: endless stretches of days before them, the companionship easy, the sex both urgent and tender. It would hurt like hell when the weekend ended, when Rick went back to his straight life.

Rick kissed Jordan's fingertips. "In another week, we'll be living in the same city again. Won't it be great?"

The words felt like a punch in the chest. How could Jordan be in close proximity to Rick, and remain just friends? He remembered how it had been when they were in college. On breaks, whenever they were alone together, they struggled to keep their hands off each other. It didn't matter if one of them was in a committed relationship with someone else. Call it attraction, desire, love—this thing between them made the rest of the world disappear. Jordan had decided to spend his summers away from Rick, taking classes so he could finish his architecture degree in three years before getting his master's. He was sure the time apart had been the only thing that had saved their friendship.

"Allentown's a big city." Jordan gulped. "It's not like when we were kids and lived two blocks apart."

"You don't want me to live near you?"

He cupped Rick's cheek in his palm. "My terms haven't changed. What happened tonight—we both needed this, coming off bad breakups. Needed to be with someone we can trust. But the fact remains, I'm an openly gay man, and you're—well, I don't know what you are. A closeted bisexual, I guess."

"Do we have to put a name on it?" Rick's voice was soft and pleading. "For tonight at least, can't we just be two people in love?"

*Say it again. Tell me you love me.*

Jordan had thought, after five years, he'd be stronger than this—that Rick wouldn't be able to steal his will. But nothing had changed. He was clay in Rick's warm hands. Worse, that was what he wanted to be, molding himself to Rick's needs and desires.

Jordan looked into Rick's eyes, wide with uncertainty, and kissed him to ease his apprehension. Yes, that's what they would be tonight. Two people in love.

He clutched Rick to him, bodies grinding. Rick's heavy length awakened his desire.

"I've got to ask, babe," Rick said, "have you been tested?"

"Yeah, after Damon and I split up. I'm good."

"Thank God." Rick suckled Jordan's fingertips. "If that asshole had made you sick—"

"I'm always safe."

"I got tested after Jess and I broke up. Not that I didn't trust her, but I wanted to tell you for sure."

Jordan kissed him. "You got tested for me?"

"Of course." Rick nuzzled Jordan's neck, kissing and nipping. He made his way down to his clavicle, then the soft peaks of nipples that hardened under Rick's ministrations. Jordan moaned.

His mouth traveled over Jordan's stomach to the tip of his cock. Jordan gasped as Rick's tongue circled the head, teasing and flicking the slit. He kissed down the shaft and sucked on his balls one at a time. Deep pleasure settled over Jordan, rooting him to the mattress.

Cupping Jordan's ass, Rick lifted and opened him. Jordan hungrily rose toward him, nothing hidden between them.

Rick rimmed him, mouth exploring the sensitive tissues. Jordan writhed at the too-tender sensation, all his barriers breaking down. He wove his fingers through Rick's hair. "Yes. Just like that."

As Rick's tongue continued to probe, Jordan's muscles softened. A palm encircled Jordan's erection. He fucked Rick's hand, a low rumbling in his throat, his body needy and pliant.

"I want to make love to you, babe." Rick's tone was soft and undemanding. "Will you let me?"

*Damn it.* How long had it been since a man had asked to make love to him, rather than to fuck him? It had never happened with Damon, he was sure of that.

Three months ago, when he had first imagined this night, he thought it would be about two friends reconnecting, getting each other out of their systems. Instead, Rick was talking about love and Jordan's body was saying *hell yes*. Love was what he wanted from Rick, but he knew better than to believe he could have it.

"Think about it," Rick said. "I'm going to brush my teeth."

Jordan watched him walk into the bathroom. Rick was sweet to think of brushing his teeth before kissing him again after rimming him. Typical Rick, always watching out for him.

Jordan sighed. He hadn't had sex in three months, and he missed it. He wanted Rick inside him, even if Rick was clumsy and it hurt. His body craved the closeness of the man he loved possessing his entire being.

Rick emerged from the bathroom carrying a wet washcloth and a folded bath towel. He dropped the cloth onto the nightstand and slid the towel under Jordan's ass.

Rick got onto the bed and showered him with kisses. "No pressure. Want to make you happy. You deserve a man who appreciates what he has in you."

Jordan's stomach tightened. "When was the last time you..."

"I haven't been with any man but you, if that's what you're asking."

Jordan swallowed down the sudden emotion. He didn't know why, but that meant something, as if Rick was being true to him.

"I know you're used to guys with more experience," Rick said, "but I'll be careful. Just tell me what you want, what you like."

Rick kissed his stomach and swallowed his cock in a swift movement. Jordan cried out and thrust his hips off the bed. Heat pooled in his groin. His attempts to speak escaped as incoherent syllables.

What Rick lacked in technique, he made up for in enthusiasm. He licked and sucked with abandon. Jordan remembered how hesitant Rick had been to blow him the last time they were together. There was no hint of that now. He was going at it like Jordan's cock was the best damn thing he'd ever tasted.

Jordan switched positions so he could sixty-nine him. Rick's cock jumped in response. Jordan kissed the head, then took it in his mouth. He slid his tongue around it, licking the slit and savoring the salty taste.

He tackled the task, sure he could give a better blow job than any of those sweet, pretty girls Rick liked to date. He bet none of them had ever gotten on her knees for a man. When Jordan was done, Rick would be the one on his knees, begging for more.

He knew he wouldn't be able to take the entire length, but he relaxed his throat and fit as much as he could. Deep, long strokes, while his fingers massaged the seam of Rick's scrotum.

"Jordy…so good." Rick sounded breathless, his throat tight. His voice told Jordan he was deeply aroused, might come with a few hard, quick strokes. But Jordan wanted to prolong the pleasure. His lips caressed the length of the shaft, burning with its heat. He pushed his knuckle into the dimple behind the ball sac. He dipped his finger into his saliva, then circled the rim of Rick's hole.

"Yes…oh fuck, yes."

Jordan smiled around Rick's cock, pleased that Rick was so malleable, so receptive to his touch. He breathed the musky scent of him, the sharpness of his arousal.

Rick's ministrations found a new urgency, sudden suction stealing Jordan's breath. Watching his shaft slide between Rick's lips threatened his self-control.

"Wait," he cried. "Fuck me."

Rick fought the trembling in his chest. Desire pulsed through him, but he didn't want Jordan to do anything he would regret. "You sure?"

A soft, strangled plea erupted from Jordan's throat. "Need you inside me."

Rick planted a few kisses on the head, then grabbed Jordan's hand and pulled him into a sitting position. He sat up and nuzzled the tender flesh of Jordan's neck. "So hot. Want you so bad." He reached into the nightstand drawer, fumbling for the condoms and lube.

"Rick—" Jordan broke off.

"What?"

"Never mind."

He threaded his fingers with Jordan's and massaged his palm. His balls ached, and his stomach tightened with desire to be inside Jordy. He'd fantasized about it every night for five years. But if Jordy was having doubts, he couldn't go through with it. "Tell me."

"I've never barebacked with anyone. But with you, I'd like to."

Rick's body shuddered. *Fuck, that sounds hot.* His unsheathed cock filling Jordan, moving inside him. Every muscle of his body wanted this, to be one with Jordan, no latex between them.

"I can't." He forced the words from his lips. "I haven't earned that privilege yet."

"I trust you."

Rick kissed him, suckling and nipping at his lips. "It's not just trust. It's commitment. We don't know where this is headed."

"The other guys I've been with," Jordan said, his voice thin and strained, "they didn't care about what was best for me. You do."

Rick brushed his finger against the stubble on Jordan's chin. "You're my best friend. That's why things are so good between us." He squeezed Jordan's cock. "Why I need you so bad."

Jordan kissed him. "Fuck me. Please." He lay on his back, knees bent with his feet flat on the mattress.

Rick eyed him with a twinge of apprehension. "Like that?"

"Face to face."

Rick grinned. In the dim light, Jordan looked sweet and vulnerable. The contours of hard muscle were lax, receptive. Rick flipped up the cap of the lube with one hand while stroking Jordan's chest with the other. He flicked a nipple, and it grew rigid beneath his touch.

He lay on his side and kissed Jordan's belly, then rubbed a well-lubed finger over his hole. Jordan let out a soft moan. Rick couldn't get enough of the blissful sound, knowing he was giving Jordy pleasure.

With a hint of pressure, Rick pushed a finger inside, gliding easily with the help of the thick liquid. "Tell me if I hurt you."

Jordan combed his fingers through Rick's hair. "So good, babe."

He kissed Jordan's thigh as he worked him open, loving the feel of the slick tissue and the grip of muscle. Jordan pushed toward him, each soft intake of breath heightening Rick's desire.

"Ready?" he murmured.

"Mmm."

Rick rolled on a condom and lubed it. Supporting his weight on one arm, he lined himself up with Jordan's body. He leaned forward, and heat engulfed him. The urge to shove deep shot through his muscles, but he gritted his teeth and pressed forward by millimeters. A groan rumbled in Jordan's throat.

"You okay?"

"So fucking good. More."

Panting heavily, Rick moved in and out until his balls slapped Jordan's ass. A grunt tore through his lungs. Jordan shuddered, hand gripping him.

Rick pulled out in a long, slow draw, seeking his lover's prostate. "That's it," Jordan groaned. The sound sent ripples of happiness through Rick's heart. He pushed in again, pressing his torso to Jordan's, undulating against his cock. Jordan's moans grew louder.

Sweat slicked their bodies as their pace quickened. Rick fought the rushing sensations. He stilled, buried deep inside Jordan, to calm the frantic beating of his heart.

Jordan shrank away. "Keep moving," he pleaded.

Rick pulled back. "Sorry, didn't mean to hurt you." He kissed him, then entered gently and found a rhythm, tightening against his release until Jordy shouted and warm cum spurted onto his belly.

His own orgasm rocketed through his body, flooding him with heat. He kissed Jordan hungrily, like a predator capturing its long-elusive prey. A sob threatened to rise from his throat but he swallowed it down.

The hot, wet swirling of tongues stopped the words of love that begged to be spoken. He couldn't freak Jordy out that way. The breakup with Damon was too fresh.

Rick cleaned them up, then lay on his stomach with his head on Jordan's chest. This was where he wanted to be—in Jordy's arms, now and for the rest of his life. But it was too soon to say the words aloud.

Jordan lay on his back, stroking the waves of Rick's hair. Splayed open, his heart gushed like a jagged wound. He had thought he could hook up with Rick, then return to being friends. He should have known his heart would always find its way back to the man he'd loved since he was fifteen.

*Stupid, stupid, stupid.* The first time they'd gotten together, distance was only one obstacle. Rick was bi, and girls were an option for him. A normal life, instead of disappointing his parents and facing the irrational hatred being gay sometimes evoked. How could Jordan fault him for wanting to avoid that hardship?

So now here they were, five years later, the heat between them still burning, yet they were no closer to being a couple than they'd ever been. Rick had said it himself—this wasn't a commitment. They were friends. Best friends, but Jordan had no reason to think they could ever be more. He couldn't risk getting attached.

*Too late.*

His hand grazed the length of Rick's back, skin smooth and warm. He knew he should go, sleep in his own bed, but the press of Rick's body was too much of a temptation. He would let himself enjoy these few hours in Rick's embrace before plunging into the icy waters of reality.

A reality where Rick was straight in everyone's eyes but his.

# Chapter 5

The next morning, Rick woke to an empty bed. A note from Jordan on the nightstand read, *Went to my room to shower. Call me for breakfast.*

Rick stared at the note. After the night they'd had, he'd expected Jordan would want to linger in bed, maybe take advantage of their morning erections. An ache settled on Rick's heart.

This wasn't a simple case of Jordan wanting to shower in his own room. He'd rather share a toothbrush than sneak out on a lover. Something was bothering him, though Rick didn't know what. He knew it wasn't good, though.

His mind lingered on that moment when he'd been fucking Jordan, and Jordan had pulled away. He'd hurt him—maybe more than Jordy had let on?

He raked his fingers through his hair. He'd wanted so much to give Jordan pleasure, and he'd screwed it up. Now Jordy didn't want to be with him. Was that it?

He paced the room, wondering how to make it up to him. He'd do anything. Bottom for him, even. If he knew how it felt, then he'd have a better idea of what to do, and not to do. The thought of it strangled his gut, but he'd do it.

He pushed aside the impulse to call Jordan. He had to think, get his head straight.

In the shower, the chorus of *want Jordy, want him so bad* overwhelmed any attempts at rational thought. The emotions settled once he was dressed. He summoned the calm logic that had served him on the football field. If he could keep his mind clear with four defensive linesmen bearing down to sack him, he could handle a conversation with his best friend.

He dialed Jordan's cell number. "Hey, I'm ready for breakfast. Do we need to, um, talk first?"

"Let's talk after. Cyn and Trent are expecting us."

"I missed you this morning."

Silence. "Yeah."

"Jordy, are we okay?" Sudden, hot tears streamed down Rick's face. He couldn't lose Jordan. Not now, after all these years, when they were finally so close to being together.

"Yeah, I mean…Being with you affected me more than I expected. I needed some space."

"It affected me, too. Last night was the best night of my life."

A little gasp, barely audible through the phone, teased a smile out of Rick. It was the same sound he made during sex, when Rick's mouth found his cock.

In a strained voice, Jordan said, "It was the best night of my life, too."

Rick closed his eyes, relief pouring over him. "See you downstairs, then. Love you, babe."

"You, too."

In the lobby, Jordan looked for his friends. He spotted Cyn and Trent at a table, and was about to head over when a hand touched his shoulder.

"Hey." A big, stupid grin spread across Rick's face, and the sight of it made Jordan deliriously happy.

"Hey yourself." He matched his friend's smile.

A breath away, Rick murmured, "Wish I could kiss you."

"Then do it." Jordan didn't know where the steely tone that entered his voice had come from. Maybe it was muscle memory, after eighteen months of Damon jerking him around, fucking him in private but never kissing him in public.

"It's not that simple."

"You're right. What was I thinking?"

Jordan headed into the dining area and got a cup of the dark roast coffee, softening it with half and half. Rick followed, but Jordan didn't meet his eye. *I am such an idiot.* How many times would he give his heart to a man who wasn't out before he learned?

He piled his plate with scrambled eggs, sausage, hashed browns, and fruit salad. Rick shot him glances from the waffle maker station, but Jordan slid into a chair across from Cyn and Trent. "Morning."

"Sleep well?" Cyn asked.

"Um, yeah." That was a lie. He'd slept great for four hours, until he'd woken up in Rick's arms and realized he had to go. Had to get out of that warm bed that felt like heaven, and go back to his real life.

Rick sat beside him, brushing his knee against him. The contact shot heat straight to Jordan's cock. His body wasn't helping his resolve. He and Rick needed boundaries. They couldn't just fuck nonstop, as if the world outside them didn't exist. At some point, Rick would meet a girl—one he could settle down with and have kids. That would be the end for him and Jordan. Rick wouldn't be one of those married guys who fucked men on the side. When he made a commitment, he meant it.

"I, um, need some juice." Jordan went and put some ice in a cup, then poured himself an orange juice. He drank it down quickly, then poured more, hoping the cold liquid would clear the fever in his brain.

Sitting down again, he moved his chair farther from Rick's, to prevent any contact. The dawning emotions in Rick's eyes—from surprise to pain to anger—showed he knew what Jordan was doing. They were like a couple of teenage girls, but that's how it was when you weren't out. You couldn't say what you meant, so you had to pantomime it.

Cyn and Trent chatted away, but Jordan could only half listen. Cyn was in a pissy mood, which didn't surprise him. Half the eyes in the room were on her. She hated being the center of attention, but she couldn't help it. Her dark beauty, her controlled posture, her confident speech all drew notice. She'd inherited the charisma of her CEO father, and she'd matured into it since high school.

Jordan tried to soothe her, but that only made her angrier. Rick took her hand across the table and managed to calm her down. Jordan eyed their interlaced fingers, jealousy creeping over him, a rush of adrenaline urging him into action. But he clamped his jaw shut and held his muscles in place.

Cyn and Rick getting back together was not outside the realm of possibility. Their interactions were so easy, it was as if no time had passed. After three years together, they understood each other's nuances. Rick knew exactly what to say to make her smile.

Her eyes turned softly to Rick's. "I think everyone expected us to hook up last night."

An affectionate smile broke across his face. "As hot as you looked in that dress, I'm surprised I restrained myself."

"You looked pretty hot yourself. Even better than in high school, and you were the best-looking thing I'd ever seen when we first met."

"That was a long time ago."

"Yeah, it was. We've both got good lives now, right?"

Rick shrugged. "Job is going well. I'm happy about the transfer—I'll be out of the mountains before winter sets in."

She leaned her head to one side. "You don't sound happy."

Rick's glance skated to Jordan, then back to Cyn. "Dating is hard, you know? You think you've got it all figured out, then love kicks you in the gut."

"I heard your breakup with Jessica was pretty bad."

He arched his brows. "Yeah. Totally my fault."

"You gonna give us the details?" Trent asked.

"Not much to tell. She was expecting a proposal. I broke up with her instead. She deserved better."

"You can't help it," Jordan said. "You're so desirable, everyone you date wants to marry you." The venom in his words startled even himself.

"I didn't mean to mislead her."

"You never do. Your natural charm deceives people into thinking you really care."

"I *did* care about Jess. I just wasn't in love with her."

"And it took you a year and a half to figure that out."

Rick's eyes turned to granite. "Yeah, I guess it did." He stood and said, "Excuse me," then headed toward the men's room.

Jordan's phone beeped a minute later, and he checked the text: *We need to talk*

He keyed his reply: *Your room after breakfast*

He pocketed his phone. A minute later, Rick returned to the table.

They didn't speak again, but instead quickly finished their meal. Alone in the elevator, Rick pinned him against the wall. Before Jordan could resist, Rick kissed him hard and deep. The tension in Jordan's body broke down. He welcomed the invading tongue, stroking it with his own.

Rick broke the kiss. "Stop being a prick and talk to me."

The elevator dinged Rick's floor, and they quickly walked to the room. The tension in Rick's body was high, but the kiss had eased it some. Despite the sniping, Jordan was still hot for his kisses, so that was something.

The lock accepted Rick's key card with a whirl and a click. He closed the door behind them, then sat on the bed. Jordan joined him.

Rick grabbed his hand. "You gonna tell me what's wrong, or do I have to fuck it out of you?"

With a sigh, Jordan pulled his hand away. Rick's stomach crashed.

"I thought I was over you," Jordan said. "I thought last night we could hook up for old times' sake, then move on with our lives." He buried his face in his hands. "I'm not over you. And I'm tired of being another broken heart you leave behind."

Rick cradled him in his arms. "Who said anything about leaving?"

"You did. Five years ago, when you said we couldn't get back together because you'd committed to Amanda. What you really meant was that you were choosing women over me. And that's what you've been doing ever since. Yet I'm such a stupid shit that when you drop a little honey on my tongue, I think you're offering the whole honeycomb."

"Jordy, I don't know what I'm offering. Every time I've been inside a woman, I've imagined she was you. I don't think that means I'm bi. I think it means I'm gay."

Jordan scrubbed his face with his palms. "As tempting as it is for me to be with you while you figure it out, I'm not going to do that to myself. What you said about Jessica deserving better? Yeah, I deserve better, too. I won't be a hole for you to fill while you decide whether you're straight or gay or somewhere in between."

"That's not fair." Rick's eyes darkened. "You talk about me leaving—but you're the one who walked out this morning, instead of talking about what was bothering you."

Jordan stroked Rick's hand. "I didn't mean for you to feel rejected when I left."

"Of course I felt rejected. I was completely vulnerable with you. I sucked your cock. That may seem normal to you, but I've done it twice in my life." Rick swallowed hard to calm himself, to fight off the threatening tears. "You're used to guys with more experience, but I'll get better. Give me time to get to know your body, what you like. I want to give you pleasure."

Jordan clasped his hands and kissed him. "Last night was fantastic. The hottest sex of my life. But Rick, we've talked about this. I can't be your fuck buddy. I'm not saying I regret it. After all the men who've used me, it meant a lot to be in your arms, to know you love me for *me*, not just for sex. But we can't make it a regular thing. It would be too easy for me to fall in love, to get hurt."

"I won't hurt you. I'd cut off my arm first—"

"I swore after Damon that I wouldn't date anyone again who isn't out. If you can't commit to being gay, then you can't commit to me."

Rick pressed his fingers to his temples. Jordan was right. All last night at the reunion, he'd been coming on to Jordan in secret, unwilling for anyone else to know he wanted him. He'd had the perfect opportunity to come out to his friends, and it hadn't even crossed his mind. And just this morning, when Jordan challenged him to kiss him in the lobby, Rick had balked at the idea.

Jordan didn't deserve to be someone's dirty secret. He was the most open, loving man Rick knew. He deserved someone who would shout his love. Rick was too much of a coward even to tell Cyn and Trent.

Jordan's fingers skimmed Rick's back. "Your friendship means everything to me. So we need rules. I'm not saying sex is off the table…but we can't let it become a habit." His hand dropped. "It's just too good between us. When I'm with you, I want so much more."

"So do I." Rick kissed him, thrusting deep into his mouth. He laid Jordan down on the bed and rolled on top of him, their cocks rubbing together through denim. Jordan's frantic mewling pushed Rick forward. He reached for Jordan's fly, but Jordan pulled away.

"I can't." Jordan stood.

"I want a relationship!"

Jordan turned to stone. After a few ragged breaths, he said, "When you're ready to come out, give me a call."

Jordan stood outside the closed door to Rick's room holding the handle. Three deep breaths didn't stop the spinning in his head. *Relationship.* The word made him want to pound on the door, to fall back into Rick's arms.

It wasn't the first time he'd heard that word from Rick. But a semester apart had weakened his resolve. Too many pretty girls at Penn State. Too many homophobic assholes.

As a kid, Rick had been too easily influenced—by his peers, by adults, by anyone he liked or respected. Half their time together was spent with Jordan trying to talk Rick out of a reckless idea some joker had put into his head. But he wasn't a thrill-seeker. At the heart of it, his impulses grew out of a deep attachment to others, a desire to shine. And the concept of moderation seemed to elude him.

Rick's mother complicated the situation. He could do no wrong in her eyes. Every time he and Jordan got into trouble, she blamed Jordan. It happened often enough that when they were nine, Jordan's mom threatened to stop letting them play together. She was sick of the stupid shit Rick pulled, and more so his mother's inability to hold him accountable. Jordan's mom found that going to Rick's father was the way to handle the situation. Rick idolized his dad, and with a word, he could keep him in line. In retrospect, his mother's easy acceptance and his father's tough love had been a good combination to fuel Rick's character. He was the most loving, loyal friend Jordan could imagine.

But coming out to those parents—shattering his mother's perfect image of him, and maybe letting his father's down—wouldn't be easy for Rick. Of course he was paralyzed. Their good opinion meant everything to him.

Jordan knew lots of guys who'd had a rough time coming out because they'd had a shaky relationship with their parents to begin with. But how much worse was it when you had a great relationship with them? Rick had more to lose than any of those other guys. His family was his bedrock. If he lost that, his identity—his sense of self—would be smashed to pieces.

Was it wrong for Jordan to make this ultimatum?

He loved Rick and didn't want to hurt him. But he had to be true to himself first. He was done sneaking around, pretending to be friends with guys he was dating. It made him feel shitty about himself. He couldn't do it again, not even for Rick.

He laid his head against the door, wanting to curl up into a ball in his bed until the ache went away. What made him think it ever would? Eight years of longing, and he hadn't found anyone who could make the pain subside. He wanted a drink, but it was ten in the morning. Bars weren't even open yet.

No, he'd have to deal with this pain on his own. He thought about the guy from the bar the night before, but a random fuck would only make things worse. Maybe the guy would be willing to suck him off. Guys were always offering to suck him off. Figured a little taste of him was better than nothing.

*Get a grip.* He didn't want a blow job. He wanted Rick. Rick's sweet lips around his cock, learning his body like he'd said. The guy was twenty feet away and miserable, wanting the same thing. *Knock on the door. Ask him to blow you. Hell, tell him you want to fuck him. Your cock in his ass will prove he's gay.*

Jordan steeled himself against the temptation. He hurried toward the elevator, thankfully finding it empty so no one could see the tenting in his jeans. The thought of Rick spread wide for him, open and vulnerable, had lit a new fire inside him. Not that Rick would ever go for it, but he hadn't topped since before Damon, and he was hungry for it.

Inside his room, he freed his aching cock. He thrust into the tunnel of his fist, imagining it was Rick—hot, tight, and well-lubed.

Rick rattled around his room. The persistent, cold rain made outdoor activities unappealing, and besides, there wasn't much to do in this town. He'd texted Trent, but Trent never responded.

Rick could head down to the lobby to see if he could find someone he knew, kill time shooting the shit. But what good would that do? Ignoring his situation wouldn't get him past it. He needed to think, to plan his next move.

His talk with Jordan hadn't gone right. Jordan acted like the choices were straightforward, but Rick's thoughts were all jumbled. He felt something opening inside him, or trying to. The only way he could figure it out was to talk with Jordan.

Jordan had made his boundaries clear. Could Rick blame him? Everything Jordan had said was true. Except...not.

He had let Jordan take control of the situation. That was a mistake. Rick should have started talking first. If he had, what would he have said? That he loved Jordan, wanted to be with him no matter what the cost. Sneaking around together might be fun, but it didn't have to be forever. They could play it by ear, see where things led. Instead, Jordan had given an ultimatum. And it was fair, Rick couldn't argue that. But if Rick had taken control, things could have gone a different way.

Now, Rick's choice was clear. If he wanted Jordan, he would have to come out. The thought of telling people he was gay, when he didn't feel gay, was weird to him. The only thing gay about him was wanting to fuck Jordan every time he got within ten feet of him. Wanting to put a ring on his finger and spend the rest of his life with him.

Rick didn't go to gay bars or watch gay porn or listen to Bette Midler. He had never been attracted to another man, just Jordy. Well, that wasn't *quite* true. He'd felt a jolt of attraction to Max the night before (ew). If he was honest with himself, there had been that twink at the LGBTA center at college—he'd come close to asking him out for pizza a couple of times, but didn't dare because he was afraid of where it might lead.

And, sick bastard that he was, he'd sometimes fantasized about inviting Jess's brother Aidan to join them for a three-way. Aidan was a bit swishy for his tastes, but he sure would look pretty sucking Rick's cock. He was more attracted to Aidan than he'd ever been to Jessica.

Rick grabbed his key and jogged down the hallway to the stairs. He ran down them, then back up a couple of times, until his breath came fast and heavy. He leaned over, hands braced above his knees.

*I. AM. TOTALLY. GAY.*

*Well, shit.*

He stumbled back to his room and flopped onto the bed. He had the answer he needed, even if it wasn't the answer he wanted.

Jordan spread a cool washcloth over his face to clear his head. He was proud of himself for turning down Rick's offer of sex, but his heart and body still ached for the man.

To distract himself, he checked Facebook on his iPad. He had a private message from Damon the previous night. He was about to delete it without reading but his curiosity got the better of him.

*Dude, WTF? That asshole Rick Ferguson tried to out me on Facebook. Fortunately I hid the message from my timeline before my parents saw. I blocked him, but if he tries anything like that again, tell him I'll report him to Facebook for bullying.*

Jordan grinned and wrote back,

*Dude, it's not bullying if it's fucking true. You drink jizz like it's Kool-Aid. Man up and tell your parents you're gay before someone else does, you closet case.*

Jordan clicked Send, then laughed out loud. He'd have to say something to Rick. Outing people was not cool. You never knew what their situation was, what coming out would cost them. But Damon? Half his friends knew, and two of his sisters. The way his mother had looked at Jordan, it was clear she suspected they were more than friends.

Damon was a coward, that was all. He wanted it both ways—same as he had in their relationship. Wanted to keep Jordan for himself but to sleep around, too.

*Fuck him.*

Jordan realized that the heaviness he had felt over Damon was gone. It had been replaced by Rick's love, and the dream that maybe there could be more between them. He wouldn't let himself hope. Still, despite the clouds and cold rain, the sun was glimmering in his heart.

# Chapter 6

Rick entered the lobby to find Jordan, Cyn, and Trent waiting. A rush of surprise and longing hit him at the sight of Jordy, long and lean and fuckable in tight jeans and a white button-down shirt open at the neck, showing tan skin and a gold chain. Rick wanted to lick the hollow of that gorgeous throat. Knowing he couldn't felt like a cement block crushing his chest.

He summoned up his hallmark cheerfulness and greeted his friends. Kissing Cyn's cheek, with her softness and her sweet perfume, made his dick shrivel. His mind flooded with all the reasons he couldn't be with women anymore. He'd tried so hard, being with them when he didn't want to be, that now the thought of it repulsed him. If he'd ever actually been bi, he wasn't anymore. His body, his whole being, cried out for Jordan.

"Hey," he said, looking into those blue eyes that had shone with desire for him just twelve hours before, but now were hard and wary. "You're still coming. I wasn't sure you would."

"If you don't want me to, that's fine." Jordan strode toward the elevators.

Rick hurried after him and grabbed his arm. The touch ratcheted up his desire, but he forced it down. "Sorry, that came out wrong. Of course I want you there." His voice dropped to a whisper. "Please, Jordy."

The guarded look on Jordan's face dissolved, and for a moment, the want from the night before flickered across it. "Okay." They walked back to join Cyn and Trent.

"What is up with you two?" Trent asked.

"Nothing." Rick's tone sliced the air, sharper than he'd intended. He had to keep it together. His emotions were getting the better of him, and it showed.

"You guys are fighting," Cyn said. "You never fight."

"We have a difference of opinion."

"Guys, it doesn't matter," Jordan said. "Can we just go? You know how Rick's mom gets when people are late."

A smile broke across Cyn's face. "Some things never change, I guess."

They piled into Rick's car, Trent riding shotgun, Jordan in the back with Cyn. Rick was hurt at first, but then realized Jordan was being smart. No way Rick could keep his hands off him if they were riding side-by-side in the car. It wouldn't even be intentional, necessarily, just a brush of fingers against denim that could give it all away.

But was that so bad? Maybe coming out to Cyn and Trent was exactly what he needed to do. It would show Jordan he was serious.

As the familiar streets gave way to quiet country roads, his mind played out how his friends might react to the news. Trent was difficult to call. He might be open and supportive, or he might back off, quietly letting the friendship drop. Rick gave him a quick glance as Trent rattled on about the Eagles. Typical guy talk, but he showed a real incisiveness for the game. Trent was a smart, easy-going, no-bullshit kind of guy. Their history together had created a bond Rick didn't want to lose.

Cyn was easier to peg. In the reflection of the rearview mirror, she was whispering with Jordan, their bodies wrapped together as well as they could be while seatbelts restrained them. Anyone who didn't know better would have thought they were lovers. Jordan understood Cyn in a way Rick never had, how her feminine mind worked, always searching for ripples of conflict to resolve. He could only imagine what the two were talking about, but he knew Jordan wouldn't reveal Rick's secret.

Cyn would be pissed. Rick had been a selfish kid when they were together, and pleasing her sexually hadn't been his top priority. Not that he didn't try. He just couldn't figure out how the female body worked. One day she'd love it when he kissed her nipples, the next day she'd scream in pain. *Fuck that shit.* He just hadn't been interested enough to work through it. And every time he put his cock inside Cyn, he'd wondered what it would be like to put it inside Jordy.

Yeah, when it came to playing for the straight team, he was a prime candidate for least valuable player. And especially with Cyn, whom he'd been with the longest, and who deserved the most from him. She'd been an amazing, loving, supportive girlfriend for three years. All the women he'd dated had been amazing. And he'd tried to make them happy. But the whole time, he'd been in love with Jordan. He couldn't shake those feelings, and he was fucking sick of trying.

They reached his parents' house, a four-bedroom colonial built in the 1970s, sitting on a one-acre lot. Surrounded by housing developments interspersed with farmland, it was close to everything yet its own little oasis, a big yard where kids could run and play and grow. His childhood had been idyllic, the neighborhood kids gathering in his driveway to shoot hoops or to regroup after riding their bikes. His mom always had lemonade and home-baked praline cookies waiting for them when they got tired. Rick had been the leader of the pack, the hub of activity, the school's golden boy. No one had expected him to grow up to be a queer.

Rick got out of the car and gazed at the white-painted house with the blue shutters back-dropped against the gray November sky. His love for the home where he'd spent so many happy years washed over him, and he wondered if it could ever be that way again. Whether he could still have that security if he told his folks he was gay. He knew they loved him, but his mom had one definition of a happy, successful life: marriage, kids, and enough money to get by.

Family was everything to her. Could she be persuaded to view Rick and Jordan as a family? What if they adopted a baby—would she consider it her grandchild and love it as her own flesh and blood? Or would the child always feel second-best?

Rick's heart twisted and his stomach roiled as he led his friends to the front door and rang the bell. No time to agonize over it now. No, time to paste on a happy face so his mom didn't analyze every aspect of his life for trouble. Was he eating enough protein, getting enough sleep? Probably drinking too much beer, because young men always did. She hoped he was dating again, but being safe.

Yes, she would say those words. Because every mom should remind her twenty-three-year-old son of the importance of condom use at every possible opportunity.

His sister Kat opened the door, long dark hair flowing down a fluffy pink sweater. Damn, she was a pretty sight, a smiling college senior, and one more reminder of all the things he loved about home.

He hugged her, warmth bursting his heart, and twirled her around. "I didn't know you'd be here."

"An hour-and-a-half drive from Lehigh for the chance to see Cyn? Totally worth it." The two women hugged with little squeals of delight, followed by a torrent of words too quick for him to follow. Kat carted Cyn off to the kitchen where their mother would surely be waiting.

His dad sauntered up from his workshop in the basement. He hugged Rick and shook his friends' hands, and when they greeted him as Mr. F., he said it was about time they started calling him Steve.

Rick had the kind of relationship with his dad that other kids dreamed of. It had taken Rick years to understand this, that his idea of normal was something special and elusive for most young men. His dad was mentor and friend, demanding when Rick needed a kick in the butt, wise when he needed advice, loving always in a quiet, unobtrusive way.

A lump thickened Rick's throat. He needed his dad's advice now, but didn't know how to ask for it. "I've got this friend..." wouldn't work. He couldn't lie to his dad. They didn't have that kind of relationship, and besides, his dad would see through him. But he couldn't share his secret and ask his dad to keep it from his mom. She would be so hurt, and would never forgive either of them. His parents functioned as a unit, always had, even when they vehemently disagreed.

He supposed he should be grateful. Their united front had kept him from getting his ass whipped more than once, because his mom insisted that corporal punishment was ineffective and cruel. The heat of his dad's anger, the weight of his disappointment, and the attending loss of privileges had kept Rick on the right path. His dad had made a man of him, and Rick respected him for it.

His dad looked solid and strong, arms bulging in a flannel shirt over a plain white tee. In his late forties, he still worked out every day and had the appearance of a younger man, despite the gray running through his hair and the laugh lines on his face.

Rousing from his thoughts, Rick realized he'd better go say hi to his mom before she came looking for him. He found her in the kitchen directing the action, coordinating the delivery of the food from the stove and oven and fridge into the dining room, Kat and Cyn her ever-cheerful minions. They had all learned long ago the importance of never showing a hint of imperfection around his mom.

"There you are!" She hugged him tightly, smelling of lavender. Her golden-brown hair brushed his cheek, her ribs sharp in her thin frame. "Look at you! I think you've bulked up since the last time I saw you. I hope you're not spending too much time at the gym. You need a social life, too. No point in looking good if you never date. What happened to your hair? You didn't go to one of those places in the mall, did you? They don't know what they're doing."

"Hey, Mrs. F.," Jordan greeted her, sparing Rick any further inspection.

"Jordy! I swear, you get handsomer every day." She hugged him. "Are things still good at the architecture firm?"

"I'm still mostly assisting, but I've got a couple of my own clients now. I have to get everything approved by a senior architect, but overall, it's good."

"That's wonderful. I'm sure they'll want to make you a partner before long."

"I'm thinking about starting my own business once I've got some experience."

"That's risky, isn't it? And you'd have to worry about bookkeeping, which I'm sure would bore you to tears, you're such a creative soul."

"You're right, Mrs. F., business is hard."

Rick eyed Kat, who bit back a laugh. That gentle way of humoring their mom was one more reason for Rick to love Jordan.

His mom greeted Trent with a flutter as she poured the drinks. Rick had long since given up on telling her she should relax, they could get their own drinks, and it would be easier all around. Instead, she catered to everyone: water for Kat and Jordan, iced tea for Rick, his dad, and Trent, Diet Pepsi for Cyn. ("Are you sure you don't want Diet Coke? It's no trouble to open a new case.")

They said grace before the meal, as always. As a teen, Rick was embarrassed by the ritual, but now he thought it was kind of nice. A constant reminder that God was working in their lives. Rick believed in God, believed God had made him gay and there was no sin in it. His parents' church had been performing commitment ceremonies for years. Now, with gay marriage legal in Maryland—a little over an hour away—he supposed there was less call for that. What would he and Jordy do? Wait until marriage was legal in Pennsylvania? Elope across the border? Maybe by the time they were ready, the laws would all have worked themselves out. The only thing he was sure of was that Jordy was his soul mate, and he wanted to spend the rest of his life with him.

He wished he were sitting next to Jordan, so he could stroke his knee under the tablecloth. Maybe he'd even risk grabbing his crotch. Wow, that would be stupid. Why did he have these reckless impulses? He'd had them ever since he was a kid. It had taken a lot to learn to keep them in check (part of the reason his dad had threatened to beat his ass so many times, despite his mom's protests), and his lust for Jordan made him feel as out-of-control as he had at ten. Even with his mom to his left with one chair between them, all he could think about was bending Jordy over her beautifully appointed cherry table and ramming his ass until he came all over the linens.

"I hope the chicken's not dry." His mom's voice interrupted his fantasy. "I had to keep it in the oven to stay warm. It was ready at noon. I thought you'd be here in time for us to sit down at the table by then."

And there it was. The little jab to remind him that no matter how hard he tried, it would never be enough. They'd gotten there early, he thought, but he must have misunderstood what she meant by lunch at noon. Guilt rose in the pit of his stomach, even though he knew how crazy it was to live ruled by a clock. It was the reason he'd left his hometown, moved far enough away that his mom couldn't expect him to come to dinner every Sunday. With her, there was no good enough, and he couldn't meet her impossibly high standards.

He heard laughter around him, his dad telling stories, and Trent too. Rick tried to follow along, but he could hardly breathe for the weight pressing on his lungs. This might be the last happy meal he spent in this house. If he came out, everything could change. Who at this table would he still have left?

If it was only Jordan, would that be enough for him? Could he give up everyone else if that's what it took to live openly as a gay man?

He couldn't be happy without Jordan. The past five years had taught him that. But he couldn't be happy without his family, either. Maybe happiness wasn't in the cards for him. Whichever hand he played, he lost.

"Rick, honey, are you sick? You're not eating. I made my chicken parmesan because it's your favorite."

He looked up into his mom's solicitous face. *What an asshole I am.* She'd spent his whole childhood reading his face, his looks, his moans, for signs of illness or unhappiness, so she could fix it. And here he was resenting her for what came naturally to her.

He wanted her to tell him it would all be okay, but maybe she couldn't do that. Maybe it would never be okay again.

"I guess I'm not that hungry."

"It's too dry. You don't like it when it's dry."

*Shit.* What she'd said before—she hadn't been berating him for being late. She'd been worried he wouldn't like the meal she'd made for him and his friends.

"No, it's great. Free breakfast at the hotel. We ate kind of late because we were up partying last night."

"Oh, I see."

He furrowed his brow. What did she see?

"Don't worry," Cyn said to his mom, "none of us drank that much. Although I did have a second glass of wine, which is a splurge for me."

Cyn to the rescue. She had a way with his mom. If he'd been straight, he'd have married that girl. It was clear to him now—he'd always been gay. He'd been happy to have sex with women because teenage boys aren't particular about where they stick their dick, as long as they get to stick it someplace. As much affection as he felt for Cyn, he'd never been in love with her.

He'd wasted so much time, caused so much heartache trying to be someone he wasn't meant to be. He'd never understood the concept of finding yourself, never really thought about it enough to care, but maybe he should have. A week in a monastery was sounding pretty good to him right now. Silence to cleanse his mind, quiet the voices.

The scraping of a chair against the hardwoods roused him. He looked over at his mother standing at the head of the table, eyes wide, jaw firm. "Ricky, come with me. I'm taking you to the urgent care center."

He drew his brow. "Mom, I'm fine."

"You've barely touched your food, and I haven't seen you this pale since you had that stomach flu in sixth grade."

"I'm not sick."

"It's just stress, Mrs. F.," Jordan said. "The move, changing jobs…it's a lot to deal with."

"Plus, he and Jordy are fighting," Cyn said.

"Cyn, everything is fine." He hoped no one could hear the panic in his voice.

"Bullshit."

Jordan expelled a soft laugh. "Rick and I will work it out. We always do."

He looked up into those beautiful eyes, like a midday sky, and wondered how Jordy could look so calm when everything was falling apart. What if they couldn't get through it this time? What if he lost Jordan not only as lover, but as a friend, too?"

Jordan tossed his napkin onto the tabletop and rose. He strolled over to the Rick and grabbed his arm. "Come with me."

Rick stood, unsure what was happening, but not caring if it meant being close to Jordy.

Jordan led him across the foyer into the den and closed the door. With the lights off, and the north-facing room dim, Jordan ran his hands down Rick's arms. Rick gave a soft moan at the contact.

"Your whole body is choked with worry, babe. Let it go. I meant what I said. We'll work it out."

Rick, his stomach in knots, couldn't find the words to speak.

Jordan stepped in and their bodies brushed together. Lips grazed his in soft, gentle kisses. "I'll always take care of you. I'll never leave you."

Rick keened, then swallowed the sound. "Let's go upstairs."

"No, shithead, we're not going up to your room to get off with all these people down here in the dining room."

"Need it."

"No, you don't. You need to trust me. Everywhere you look, you see a brick wall. You need perspective. Things are not as bad as they seem right now. We'll find a way through this. And no matter what, we'll always be friends. We made it through our last breakup—"

"I don't want to break up!" The sound came out as a soft whine. "Please, Jordy, I love you. Tell me I'm what you want."

"Of course you're what I want." Jordan cupped Rick's cheeks and kissed his forehead. "We will find a way."

He kissed Jordan hard, and the tension in his body unwound a little. Even though he was still enrobed in black despair, if he just held on, Jordan would lead him into the light.

After lunch, the men gathered in the den to watch football. The room was cozy, a quiet place for them to get away from female ears for a while.

"Penn State?" his dad suggested.

"Let's watch Princeton," Rick said.

His dad gave him a warning look, but turned on the Princeton game anyway. "You need to get over it, Ricky. Holding a grudge doesn't hurt anyone but you."

That was easy for his father to say. He hadn't been a student at Penn State when the scandal broke. He didn't see the riots, the police on horseback, or the drunken, homophobic assholes who put football first and blamed the gay community for the acts of a pedophile.

Rick had dreamed of playing on the Penn State football team as a kid. Even after that dream had died, he went to Penn State anyway to be part of that culture. The school had let him down, just like the Boy Scouts had let him down when they kicked Jordan out for being gay.

"The Princeton team is good this year," Jordan said. "They're seven and one. Don't you want to see them kick Yale's ass?"

"Kat may be going to law school at Yale," Rick's dad said.

Rick shook his head. "She's just saying that to drive you and mom crazy. She'll never go to New England—she hates snow."

Sprawled out on the couch next to Trent, he tried to get into the game. Princeton was good for an Ivy League conference school, but Rick was used to watching Big Ten games.

"Jordy, why didn't you play football at Princeton?" his dad asked. "You were as good as any of these guys."

"Because I wanted to finish a four-year architecture degree in three years. And there was another reason, too, let me see if I can remember...oh yeah, I'm openly gay, and I didn't want to get my ass kicked."

Rick's dad raised his brows. "You think that would have been a problem there?"

"Don't know. Didn't want to find out." The recliner squeaked as he leaned back. "I'm not an activist. I just want to live my life without people interfering with me. Football wasn't important enough for me to take a stand."

Rick wanted to take Jordan into his arms, to kiss the hurt expression from his face. He hated that Jordan faced that kind of discrimination. Or at least, that he faced it alone. Somehow, it would be easier if they faced it together. Like, if discrimination was the price of being with the person you loved, it was worth paying. But if you had to face it alone, it was just mindless hate.

Rick's dad nodded. "The last time I saw you, it was right after you and Damon split up. Things okay with you?"

Jordan smiled. "They're good, Mr. F. He taught me who *not* to trust, and that's a lesson worth learning. I'm over him."

"Glad to hear it. Seeing anyone else?"

A faint blush rose in Jordan's cheeks. "The guy I'm interested in, um, he isn't out. He's bi, and his last relationship was with a woman, so...Even though the chemistry is great between us, I don't want to rush into anything. I'm tired of getting my heart broken."

A weight settled on Rick's chest. It killed him to hear Jordan talk about him like that, as if he weren't committed.

Rick's father shifted in his chair. "It must be complicated, being in your situation. Dating is tough enough for straight couples."

"The worst is guys who are closeted, who have wives or girlfriends. It's not even a one-night stand they're looking for—it's ten minutes in a restroom or an alley. I understand that it must be hell for them, pretending to be something they're not. But that's no kind of life."

Rick squirmed, knowing Jordan's words were aimed at him.

"Not to mention how dangerous it is," Rick's father said. "I'm glad you're looking for someone you can settle down with, Jordy. I used to worry that you'd be out there, playing the field in that kind of environment. It must be tempting for young men, when sex is so available, not to get caught up in it."

Trent leaned forward. "Sex is pretty available for straight guys, too, these days, Mr. Ferguson."

"So you mean I need to worry about you too, Trent?"

"No, I'm...I'm seeing someone."

Rick startled. "You are?"

"Yeah, I mean, it's new, so it's too soon to talk about. But it's got potential."

Rick's father turned to his son. "What about you? Are you playing the field since you and Jessica broke up?"

"No. I don't sleep with someone unless I want a relationship. And I'm always safe."

"Glad to hear it," his father said, though his brow creased.

Rick raised his eyes to Jordan. Jordan's gaze was fixed on him. He gave a little smile and looked away.

"C'mon, Rick," Trent said, "I think your Dad is disappointed. Aren't you going to regale us like you usually do, with stories of all the women throwing themselves at you?"

Rick glared at him. "You mean women like your mom?"

Trent smirked but said nothing.

Rick had a feeling he'd pay for that later.

At half-time, they went into the kitchen for dessert. The women were sitting around the table drinking coffee. For the first time maybe ever, Rick envied the fact that women could have a heartfelt conversation rather than trading insults the way guys did. His competitive nature was strong, but today he barely had the energy.

Before he could cut a slice of pie, Kat took his hand and led him back into the now-empty den, closing the door behind them. She sat on the couch. "Spill."

"What?" He sank into the thick cushion beside her. This room was his dad's retreat, the only masculine space in the house. All dark wood and leather, it had none of his mom's frills.

"You know what. You and Jordy. And don't fucking lie to me. I can tell when you're lying."

He scrubbed his face with his hand. "It's personal, okay?"

"You need to talk." Her hands, soft and warm, clutched his. "I'm your sister. You can tell me anything."

"If I could tell anyone, I would tell you." His chest deflated. "It's not just about me."

"It's because you're moving to Allentown, isn't it."

"What?"

"You think you and Jordy can just go back to hanging out all the time like you did when you were kids, and he doesn't want that. Because he's in love with you."

Rick sucked in a breath and bit his lips.

"Ha, I knew it!"

"Kat, that's not it."

"But I'm close."

He rolled his eyes.

She squeezed his hands. "Be careful not to break his heart."

"I am the last person in the world who would break Jordan's heart." He rose and paced.

"You wouldn't do it on purpose. But like I said, he's in love with you. Now that you're both single, maybe part of him can't help hoping..."

A rush of panic gripped his heart. If Kat talked about this with his dad—who now knew Jordan was involved with a closeted bisexual—Kat would figure it out. Shit!

He combed his fingers through the hair on the back of his head. He needed a timeline, a schedule for coming out. And a plan for damage control if the truth was discovered before he was ready. His mom would need to be prepared.

"Jordy is a grown man," he finally said. "He can take care of himself."

He flopped back onto the couch, and they sat in silence a while, Kat letting him process his thoughts without pushing him. Finally, he said, "You ever notice that no matter what I do, Mom thinks I'm perfect?"

She chuckled "Did I ever *notice*? You have no idea what it was like growing up in your shadow." In a mocking voice, she said, "'Why can't you be more outgoing, like your brother? He can make friends anywhere. You could, too, if you'd take your nose out of that book.'"

"Well, you know what I heard from Dad. 'Your sister's teachers never call about *her* behavior. You need to buckle down and take school more seriously.'"

She leaned her head on his shoulder, and he put his arm around her.

"I don't know why Dad could see I was such a screw-up, and Mom never did."

"You weren't a screw-up. You were a boy. You questioned authority, pushed the limits. I wish I'd had your courage."

"You were smart enough to choose your battles. You've always stood up for what you believed in."

She squeezed his hand. "Ricky, be honest with me. Why are you so sad?"

His chest collapsed, and his eyes stung. "What d'you suppose will happen when Mom realizes I'm not perfect?"

"She never will. She's an expert at revising history so nothing is ever your fault."

A lump blocked his throat so he could barely swallow. *Tell her. Tell Kat.* The little voice in his head sang a low chorus. How would she react? He knew he could trust her to keep his secret from their parents until he was ready, but was that fair to her?

He shook his head. "I don't think so. One of these days, Mom is going to see me for who I am, and she won't love me the same way anymore."

"Okay, that is fucked up." She jumped out of the couch. "What did you do? Are you selling drugs or something?"

He scowled. "Why would you think that?"

"I don't know. You've been living in Scranton for the past year and a half."

He rose and shoved his hands into his pockets. "It's Scranton, not South Philly."

"Don't you always say there's nothing to do in Scranton but get high?"

"I don't think I ever said that."

"Maybe I'm extrapolating."

"You've got a wild imagination."

She laughed. "Not as wild as Cyn's. Have you read her books? There's all kinds of weird sex stuff in them."

He drew his brow. "What kind of stuff?"

"Nothing she did with you." She looked at him sideways, a mocking grin on her face.

"How would you know?" he asked.

"Because she told me."

His jaw fell open and heat rushed to his cheeks. "And you *let* her?"

She shrugged. "I was sixteen. I was desperate for any information on sex I could get."

Rick shook his head, wondering when his quiet little sister had turned into this shameless woman. "Then it's fortunate we didn't do anything that would corrupt your impressionable mind."

"I've seen hotter stuff on network television."

"Are you disappointed?"

"No, but in retrospect, I think maybe Cyn was. Seriously, her books are hot."

He chuckled and looked away.

She took his hand again. "What Jordy said earlier about the stress of moving…If that's all that's bothering you, fine. But if there's something more, and you decide you're ready to open up, *call me.*"

Jordan looked up as Kat walked into the open family room, where the men had reconvened in favor of the larger-screen TV. His stomach had been clamped in a vise while she was with Rick in the den, behind closed doors. What had he told her? Jordan hoped—but didn't dare hope—that he had told her the truth. If he had, she had a great poker face.

"Penn State?" she asked. "No wonder Rick decided to go back into the kitchen with Mom and Cyn." She flopped onto the couch with Trent.

"I tried to get your Dad to put the Princeton game back on," Jordan said, searching her eyes.

"Princeton sucks."

He bristled, sitting up straighter. "They're seven and one!"

"Lost to Lehigh."

"By one point."

Kat's gaze swept over him. "You're cute when you're angry."

His shoulders tightened in frustration. "I'm not angry."

"You sure you don't want to give girls a try?"

He threw a pillow at her. "Stop sexually harassing me."

"Just think how much easier your life would be if you were straight."

*As if I haven't thought that a million times.* "You're right, Kat, thanks for opening my eyes. You've ungayed me."

She gave a little sigh and glanced at Trent. "What about you? Wanna go make out?"

"Oh, I'm your second choice? After the gay man?"

"My second choice of all the men *here,* at least."

"Glad I rank ahead of your dad and your brother."

She pouted and turned to her father. "Daddy, I can't find any cute boys who will play with me."

"Good. Be quiet and watch the game." He picked up the remote and turned up the volume.

She sat back, relaxing into the couch, softly teasing Trent from time to time. But no significant looks at Jordan. His heart slowly drooped into his stomach.

Rick had made his choice, and it wasn't Jordan.

Rick strode back into the now-deserted den. He couldn't believe his dad had put the fucking Penn State game on. Was it so hard to respect Rick's opinion about that?

And his mom wasn't much better. While he had sat to eat dessert, she had suggested he and Cyn should start dating again. *With Cyn right there.* He thought he had handled the situation okay, suggesting Cyn wasn't interested in him anymore, which he didn't think she was. But what if she had been? Shouldn't his mom at least have checked with him before potentially getting Cyn's hopes up?

Rick looked through the picture window at a flock of crows rising from the spent cornfield across the road. His father ambled in through the open doorway. "Everything okay?"

"Fine."

His dad closed the door. "I wasn't just being polite."

"Mom overreacted earlier."

"This have something to do with Jessica?"

"A little. And like Jordy said, the move."

His dad nodded slowly, then rested a hand on Rick's shoulder. "Are you two really fighting?"

Rick shook his head. "Not fighting. Difference of opinion. We'll work it out."

"You two keep saying that. I wonder if you're trying to convince yourselves."

He exhaled a thin stream of air to clear his head. "It's tough right now. I'm trying to keep my perspective."

"And what about Jordy? Does he seem okay to you?"

Rick shrugged. "I guess."

"He was such a happy kid. Carefree. I don't see that in him anymore."

"I see it sometimes." Rick's face heated. He walked away so his father wouldn't see his blush. But he understood what his father meant. Most of the time, Jordan had a haunted look behind his eyes, like he carried around a deep hurt that couldn't heal. Maybe that was why Rick loved watching the expression on Jordy's face when he came. It was pure happiness.

Rick heard the shuffling of his father's feet and looked over at him.

"You remember when the Boy Scouts kicked him out?" his dad asked.

"How could I forget?"

"He seemed to take it well, like it was inevitable. He knew what coming out would mean. But he was different after that."

"Maybe it had more to do with coming out."

Rick's father shook his head. "I wonder sometimes…the message the Scouts sent. Not just to Jordy, but to the other boys, too. Whether any of them might have been gay or questioning. And seeing what happened to Jordy made them think it wasn't safe to come out."

Rick's stomach collapsed like the air had been punched out of him. He paced to keep his father from seeing his emotions. Memories swirled around him, the shock and betrayal he had felt. Scouting had been like a second home to both of them. And for the organization to turn on Jordy when he most needed their support—Rick had felt like he couldn't trust anyone anymore. Even his father, who had fought to get Jordy reinstated.

Had Rick suspected, even then, that he himself might be gay? He couldn't remember feeling that way. But maybe, subconsciously—and he had suppressed those feelings, because he knew he wouldn't be accepted.

"Love is conditional," he murmured. "That's the message, right? And some parents of gay kids, they do the same thing."

His dad put his hand on his shoulder. "There are no conditions in this house."

He snickered and shook his head. "Try telling Mom that."

His dad pulled his hand away. "Richard Steven."

He looked up at him, too exhausted to care if his dad was pissed.

"Your mother has sacrificed for you. She devoted her life to caring for you and Kat."

"Trying to mold us into what she wanted us to be."

"To mold you into responsible adults. Up until now, I thought she'd done a pretty good job. What the fuck is wrong with you?"

He glared, meeting his father's eyes, sick of feeling he would never be good enough to meet his parents' expectations. "It isn't *me* she loves. It's some ideal I can never live up to. And I'm so damn tired of trying. I can't be the man she wants me to be. I can't."

"Your mother and I only want you to be happy. Whatever that means for you."

"She was trying to set me up with Cyn earlier."

"Of course she was. She loves Cyn."

"But I don't!" He couldn't keep the rage out of his voice. "And I don't love Jess, either. I tried, because that's what I thought I was supposed to do. I can't keep pretending to be this person you want me to be. And I can't keep living with this fear of disappointing you. It's killing me, Dad."

His father's eyes widened. Strong arms drew him into a hug. Rick tried to pull away, but his dad wouldn't let him. Finally, he stopped trying, and allowed himself to accept the comfort his father offered.

"You always were a dumb shit," his father said. "Coming to all the wrong conclusions, believing the worst. You have no idea how it feels to be a parent. I never knew what love was until the first time I held you in my arms. I never knew what fear was until the first time you got sick."

His dad released him. "You and Kat are your mother's entire world. She used to watch you in your crib and wonder what kind of man you'd be. It turns out, you're kind of lazy. I never met anyone who would work harder to get out of working than you. But we discovered early on that if we set the bar high, you tried to reach it. You took it as a personal challenge. You wanted to prove yourself. So we just kept raising the bar."

He walked to the window, his face set in shadow. "We were never the ones who were disappointed in you, Rick. You were disappointed in yourself. Whenever you failed at something, you changed your tactics and tried again." He stopped and stared. "Is that what you did with Jessica? You kept trying to get it right, even though the relationship was wrong?"

Rick shrugged.

"That won't work, son. Love only works if you find the right person."

"What if the right person for me is wrong for everyone else?"

"What do you mean, wrong for everyone else? Is she a terrorist or something?"

Rick chuckled. "Contrary to what you and Kat seem to think, Scranton is not a hotbed of criminal activity."

"Is there a woman you're afraid to tell your mom and me about?"

"No. There's no woman."

"You're being cryptic. You're never cryptic unless you're hiding something. Your sister's the cryptic one. I never know what the fuck she's talking about. Unless she's coming on to your friends to make me crazy."

He raised his brows. "Did it work?"

"Of course. But I can't let her know that. Why do you think she does that?"

"On one level, she's actually in love with Jordan, and is pissed off that he's not interested. On another, she's glad he's gay because gay men are safe."

His dad nodded. "You figured this out?"

"She told me."

"I should have known." His dad pulled him into a hug again. "I realize you're a man now, and you don't need your old dad anymore. But Ricky, I will always be here for you. I'll love you no matter what. And believe it or not, I may have some words of wisdom I can offer."

Rick tried to smile. He knew his father was sincere. But his father didn't know the truth, and the harm it could do to their family.

But Rick couldn't keep lying—not to himself, and not to anyone else. He was a gay man. He was in love with Jordan. And he would be with Jordan, whatever it took.

# Chapter 7

Sweat crawled down Rick's neck and dripped off his eyebrows. After twenty minutes running on the treadmill under the dull fluorescent lights of the hotel's exercise room, his legs burned. He lowered the incline and deepened his breaths until the feeling passed.

He had wanted to talk to Jordan when they got back to the hotel, but Jordan said Rick needed time alone to think. That was bullshit. Rick's head was clear.

The talk with his dad had helped. He would come out—after the holidays. His mom was already under stress, with the extended family coming. She didn't need a life-changing announcement on top of it.

When he *did* tell her, what would he say? How could he convince her that, after dating women all this time, he wanted to be with Jordan for the rest of his life? She wouldn't believe him. She would think it was a phase. She might even think it was just a sex thing, and try to talk to him about it.

*Fuck.*

Had anyone's life ever been this messed up?

Okay, so maybe, compared to all the problems in the world, this wasn't the worst. It wasn't like he was still a kid who couldn't support himself if his parents kicked him out. They couldn't repossess his college education. Materially, he would be fine.

And anyway, his parents wouldn't disown him. They'd accept his orientation eventually, though he wasn't sure his mom would ever recover from the disappointment.

What about his friends? A bunch of people from his high school class were still hanging out at the hotel. If he came out to them, he'd go from *Most Likely to Succeed* to *Most Likely to Suck Seed*.

Damn it. That was totally not wrong. Even if he hadn't, technically, done that yet.

He didn't like the idea of people laughing at him. Jordan was right about one thing—Rick was vain. He hadn't realized that about himself until Jordan said it. Jordan was confident in himself and his sexuality no matter what people thought. Rick cared very much about what people thought, and his confidence over the course of the past two days had crumbled into rubble.

The first time he and Jordan had gotten together, Jordan had accused him of thinking only about the sex, not the aftermath. And damned if he hadn't done that again. He was so used to improvising, he didn't think about step two until he'd completed step one. The sex was step one.

Mission accomplished. What next?

His mom kept pushing her heterosexual agenda on him. He should have known that if he took Cyn to see her, she would try to set them up. Why was she so eager for him to settle down?

The ironic thing was, he wanted to settle down, maybe even have kids in a few years. Just not with a woman. Could his mom accept that? Was it really so different from her dreams for him?

He shouldn't care what his mom thought. He was a grown man.

His dad would be more accepting, but would he think less of him? And Kat—Kat would give him such shit. Every text message he got from her for the rest of his life would include an attached photo of two guys fucking. Along with her speculation about whether he and Jordan might enjoy that position.

Which, come to think of it, might not actually be an argument against coming out.

Damn it, this was stupid. Hanging out alone wasn't going to accomplish anything. He needed to talk to Jordy.

He wrapped up his workout, then showered in his room. He jogged down the stairs to the floor below and knocked on Jordan's door. No answer. He knitted his brow, looking at his watch. Still an hour before dinner. He wasn't going to hang out in his room all that time.

He trotted down to the lobby and wandered into the restaurant, vaguely looking for someone he knew at the bar. His senses went on alert when he heard Jordan's voice.

"Look, Frank, I'm flattered—"

"Don't be shy. We could have fun together."

Rick bounded over to the barstools where they sat and inserted himself between them, facing off with Frank. "Look, asshole, the guy said no."

Jordan's hand grabbed his arm. "Back off. I've got this."

Rick pulled his arm away, his gaze never leaving Frank's face.

Frank's eyes darkened and he blinked, holding up his hands. "Look, I don't want any trouble."

"Sorry," Jordan said, pushing Rick away. "My friend overreacts sometimes."

"What the fuck are you apologizing for?" Rick felt the bartender's eyes on him. Okay, so he'd said that louder than he meant to. He breathed, trying to slow the adrenaline coursing through him, but it was no use. His heart raced at double speed.

Jordan squeezed his shoulder and said in his ear, "Let's grab a table so you can calm down."

The blue depths of Jordan's eyes calmed him. Rick exhaled. "Yeah, um, okay."

Jordan shook Frank's hand. "It was great meeting you. Have a safe flight back to Atlanta."

"Thanks." Frank looked like he wanted to say something more but thought better of it. He didn't react when Rick and Jordan sauntered over to a table in the corner, half hidden from view.

Jordan stopped the cocktail waitress and ordered two drafts. Then, he sat at the small round table across from Rick. "That was uncalled for. Frank wasn't being aggressive."

"He wanted to fuck you."

"Half the gay men I meet want to fuck me. Very few have had the privilege."

Rick grabbed the bottle of ketchup and flicked the top open and closed. "This is messed up, Jordy."

"I understand that you're going through something right now, something life-changing. I will be there for you as your friend. I can't be more than that until you figure out what you want."

"I know what I want."

"You want the easy part, not the hard part."

Rick sat back and glared at him. He didn't want to avoid the hard part. He just didn't want to go through it all at once. "Can't you give me time?"

"Sure. You've got three months. I won't date anyone else. And then, you either come out or I move on."

Rick smiled. "And we can be together until then?"

Jordan stared. "No. Not until you come out."

"Why not?"

"Because this isn't a casual thing anymore. We're talking about commitment, and I can't commit to you while you're in the closet."

"I've been waiting for you so long—"

"You have not been waiting for me. You've been fucking women."

Rick scraped his fingernail across the tabletop. "It's not the same."

"Look, I get that you've been unhappy. You need to figure out who you are for yourself, not for me. I can't be the reason you decide you're gay."

"You said yourself, last night—"

"It isn't enough for me to say it. You need to believe it in your heart, and accept it. As long as you're questioning—"

"I'm not. I know who I am now. I'm a gay man. I'm not afraid to say that."

"Then what *are* you afraid of? Your parents have always supported me. You think they won't do the same for you?"

Rick stared at his hands, unable to envision his parents' reaction. All he could see was darkness. They'd be disappointed. That's all he knew for sure.

Tears stung his eyes, which was stupid. He'd been so happy last night with Jordy, and today he was miserable. Why couldn't they just love each other? Why did he have to make some big public announcement?

Jordan's warm hand touched his. He tried to steady himself, but it all felt impossible. He didn't want to change who he was on the outside because of what he felt on the inside. His private life should be private.

"Ricky?"

He looked up to see concern in Jordan's eyes, but he couldn't speak. The room was closing in on him, crushing the air from his chest. There was no way out. He couldn't have the life he wanted with Jordan without giving up the life he had.

Coming out meant risking everything.

The people who'd looked up to him, who'd envied him in high school, would now laugh behind his back. Or to his face, which would be worse. He couldn't be like Jordy, who figured people who couldn't accept his orientation weren't worth having in his life. Rick cultivated relationships and knew how to put them to use. All those connections he'd built...lost.

And what about his clients? If they found out he was gay, it would affect his ability to do his job. He would lose sales. Some people would stand up on their screwed-up interpretation of the Bible and say they wouldn't do business with a sodomite.

He was already starting from nothing, building a new client base in a new town. He didn't need another obstacle in his way.

He swallowed hard and looked at Jordan. "How can you ask me to choose between you and everything else in my life?"

Jordan rocked back and forth, then gripped the edge of the table. "You act like coming out will be the worst thing that ever happens to you, when it might be the best. For the first time, you'll be leading an authentic life. Don't you want that?"

"I want to be with you, and for everything else to be the same."

Jordan looked at him hard, then sat forward. "What's the worst thing that ever happened to you?"

He shrugged. "I guess… when I was eight, and my grandfather died."

Jordan nodded. "And next to that?"

He bit his cheek and scrunched his brow. "When you got kicked out of scouting."

"That didn't happen to you. It happened to me."

"But I quit, too. I thought they stood for something, and it was all a lie."

Jordy sat back and crossed his legs, eyeing Rick narrowly. "You know the worst thing that ever happened to me?"

Rick nodded and said softly, "Your dad."

"Yeah. And even though my mom is a nurse, she struggled to put food on the table and pay for childcare on one income. Half the clothes I wore in elementary school were things you had grown out of. Kids made fun of me in middle school because they suspected I was gay. Meanwhile, you were more popular with the girls than Justin Timberlake, your dad had a six figure income, and your mom made pot roasts and baked cupcakes every weekend."

"Jordy, I know you've had a hard life—"

"My point is, you've had an easy one. You've never struggled, so you never learned that even though bad things happen, you'll survive. Things will get better."

"I've struggled. Remember in ninth grade, when I was getting Cs in geometry—"

"Rick. My dad's fighter jet was shot down over Baghdad in Desert Storm. My mom was a widow at twenty-four. Compared to that, coming out was easy. The reason it's so hard for you is because you don't know what hard is."

Dark rage built in his chest. Jordan knew him better than anyone, knew how much he was asking of Rick. So maybe he *had* had an easy life. But shouldn't he be able to come out on his own timetable, rather than Jordan's? Why was Jordan making him choose?

"I can't do this. It's an impossible choice." He shook and struggled not to start bawling like a kid.

Jordan rose and pulled him to his feet. "Let's go to my room to talk."

Rick let him lead, his decision-making skills used up for the day. And maybe, if he got Jordan alone, he could change his mind about a few things.

Jordan dead-bolted the door while Rick collapsed onto the bed. Jordan kicked off his shoes and joined him. He lay on his back, and Rick snuggled against his chest. His fingers combed through Rick's soft, dark curls. "Tell me what you need."

"You. Naked."

Jordan chuckled. "As your friend, I would do anything for you. But I can't be your lover. Not until you work your shit out."

"Why can't we be together while I'm working my shit out?"

"I'm tired of hiding."

"I'm not Damon," Rick said. "I would never treat you like he did."

"At your parents' house today, I couldn't lean against you on the couch. I couldn't hold your hand. I had to keep a safe distance, and I hate that. If I'm going to be your boyfriend, I want to be open about it."

"It's only for a little while," Rick said.

"If it's only a little while, then waiting for sex isn't so much to ask."

"Don't you like sex with me?"

Jordan kissed his temple. "There's nothing I like more."

"You don't act like it."

"I'm pretty sure you had me begging at some point last night."

"We could rub off together," Rick suggested. "No penetration."

"Still counts as sex."

"Phone sex?"

Jordan shook his head. "I'll consider it."

Rick pulled out his cell, and Jordan's phone rang.

Jordan grinned. "Not if we're in the same room."

"You're no fun." Rick ended the call and pocketed his phone. He rolled onto his side and looked hard into Jordan's eyes. "I'm in love with you."

Jordan's throat closed. His eyes misted, and he swallowed hard to regain control. "I'm in love with you, too." He couldn't speak above a whisper.

"But you don't want to fuck me all the time."

"I've always had more self-control that you."

Rick scowled. "I waited two and a half years to have sex with Cyn, and I never pressured her once."

"Maybe being gay had something to do with that?"

"I didn't know I was gay then."

"Did you get hard from kissing her?"

Rick shrugged. "A little."

"Do you get hard from kissing me?"

Rick pursed his lips. "I see your point."

"You're desperate for sex because it's been unsatisfying for you until now."

Rick's eyes turned hollow. "And meanwhile, you've been having great sex with other men."

"It's never been as good with anyone else." He brushed his lips against Rick's, the touch as soft as a feather.

"Please don't cut me off completely. I need the contact."

He traced Rick's jaw line with his fingertip. "You had plenty of opportunities today—you could have come out to your dad or Trent or Kat. You chose not to. Whatever fears are in your head, you put them before me."

"Jordy, don't you get it? I don't *feel* gay. I feel just like I did in high school, when I was captain of the football team dating the prettiest girl in class. People looked up to me. They wanted to *be* me."

"And nobody ever wanted to be me, right? The loser queer kid wearing hand-me-downs, raised by a single mom?"

"What the fuck are you talking about? You were an all-star running back. Girls hung all over you. Being gay just made you more interesting."

Jordan smiled and ran a finger along Rick's chest. "And you don't think it will make you more interesting?"

"It's been part of your identity since you were fifteen. It's never been part of mine."

"I'm not asking you to advertise it. I just don't want to have to hide it. Especially not from the people closest to us. Did you see how worried your mom was today? And both of us were making excuses to explain away what was wrong."

"But it wasn't a lie."

"It's only part of the story, and not even the biggest part. Did that feel good to you? Deceiving your family?"

Rick's eyes fell. "The truth would hurt them."

"Don't you dare. That was Damon's excuse. It's bullshit."

"What if I tell Trent, and he doesn't want to be friends with me anymore?"

"Do you think that's going to happen?" Jordan asked.

"It could."

"Only if he was never really your friend. If he cares anything about you, he'll have your back. Because that's what friends do."

"Maybe he's not really my friend. Maybe nobody is. They like the public image." Rick licked his lips. "You're the only person who really knows me. The only one who loves me for me."

"You don't think your parents love you? Or Kat?"

"This isn't what they'd choose for me."

"They don't get to choose. And for that matter, neither do you. You were born gay."

"I'm not sure about that. Maybe sleeping with women turned me gay."

Jordan shook his head. "That may be the dumbest thing I've ever heard."

"It's like operant conditioning. By sleeping with them when I didn't want to, I created an aversion."

"Dude, if you didn't want to sleep with them, you already *had* an aversion. Because you're gay."

"I didn't always hate sex with women."

"Did you ever like it?"

Rick shrugged. "It was okay. When I was with Cyn—"

"You were fantasizing about me. Isn't that what you told me?"

"Yeah, but, I never lost an erection with her."

"Rick. If your definition of good sex is not losing an erection, you've set a low bar."

"Cyn is amazing."

"Yes. She is. And even though I can see that, I have no desire to sleep with her."

"But I did," Rick insisted. "Don't you get it? If I was gay back then, I was using her. I wasted three years of her life."

The distress in his voice pulled at Jordan's heart. He stroked Rick's curls. "Sexuality can be a complicated thing. If you don't feel comfortable putting a name on it, that's fine. But I'm not willing to hide in the shadows of your life. You don't have to tell everyone at once. If you want to be with me, you have to tell at least one person. And not a stranger, either. Someone close. You have to be willing to put something on the line."

"It's not fair for you to make a demand like that."

"It's not a demand. It's a condition. You take the first step toward coming out, and I'll take the first step toward a relationship. That's fair, isn't it?"

Rick pulled him close. "If I tell one person, then we can fuck?"

"For now." He nibbled his ear. "If I didn't know you better, I'd think you were using me for sex."

"But you do know me. And sex between us has never been just about sex."

Jordan kissed him. "No, it hasn't. And I hope you tell someone soon, because I can't wait to fuck you."

Rick grinned, but then his eyes widened. "You don't mean—"

"Yes, I *do* mean. I'm not pressuring you. It's not a deal-breaker, but it's something I want."

"Fuck, Jordy, it's not like I didn't have enough to think about."

"What, you didn't think that would come up eventually?"

"Eventually, yes. But today?" Rick said.

"I was kind of hoping it would be extra incentive. Fantasizing about what it would be like to feel me inside you…"

Rick moaned and pulled him in for a kiss. The press of their bodies together, hands and mouths exploring, was pure bliss.

Jordan pulled away, determined to avoid temptation. "Are we good now?"

"We are amazing."

Jordan smiled and forced himself to stand. "You have to go. Think about setting a timeline for when we can date openly."

Rick rose. "When did you get so bossy?"

"You need structure, or you'll bounce all over the place. Go."

Rick eyed the tenting in Jordan's jeans. "You don't really want me to go."

"No, I don't. Which is why you have to."

Rick grinned and gave him a brief kiss on the cheek before quietly making his exit. Jordan took a cold shower before dressing for dinner.

At the restaurant, Rick sat at the glass-topped square table across from Trent, with Cyn and Jordan on either side. Being close to Jordan but unable to touch him was like ants crawling over his skin. He set his jaw and breathed.

To distract himself, he looked around the dining room. Rich shades of russet and gold dominated the walls and linens, warming the black wood. Dim overheads and candlelight added romance. The cozy, upscale ambience created a sense of intimacy.

They placed their orders, and a tense silence fell. *Tell them*, the voice in his head said. The lie of omission loomed over them. He couldn't relax, and neither could Jordan, while they had to choose their words carefully to avoid letting something slip.

The truth would hurt Cyn, and he didn't want to do that. But was the lie worse? She wouldn't want him protecting her. She'd always been strong and independent, even when she was scared and alone at fifteen, in a new school where everyone was predisposed to hate her.

The whole town knew that when her dad was brought in as CEO to save ElyraCon, it would mean layoffs. Concerned for her safety, her parents had kept her out of school for a week when they happened. Rick had offered to stop by every day while she was supposedly home with the flu, in case she had questions about the lessons she missed. She was aloof and contained, but his light-hearted humor drew her out. After five days, he took a chance and kissed her. And her whole body responded, molding to his. He could have kissed her forever.

Cyn's voice broke through the silence. "Jordy, you look so sad. Boy troubles?"

The corner of Jordan's mouth quirked up. "Not exactly."

Trent said, "He's seeing someone who's not out."

Cyn shook her head. "I can't imagine living that way, pretending to be something you're not."

"Maybe he's not pretending." Rick sipped his scotch to quiet the trembling inside. "Orientation is a spectrum. Why should he change his whole identity to conform with some false binary definition?"

"So you think I should date him," Jordan said, eyes a stormy blue-gray, "even though he's in the closet?"

"You have to do what's right for you," Rick said, "and he has to do what's right for him."

"In which case, they both lose," Cyn protested. "Relationships require compromise. Even I know that."

Rick felt the cut at his heart. When he had dated Cyn, the give-and-take had gone in one direction: she gave, and he took.

"I'm sorry." His voice was low and gravelly.

She wrinkled her brow. "For what?"

"For taking you for granted, all those years we were together."

"Rick." She grabbed his hand. "You were wonderful to me. I trusted you completely, and you never took advantage of that. You looked out for my best interest. And even when things started falling apart senior year, you never lied to me. You never went behind my back."

"I should've taken better care of you."

"You took excellent care of me."

Jordan chuckled. "I think he's talking about sex."

Trent downed his beer, his face flushed.

Cyn sat back and pursed her lips. "You always took care of me that way, too."

"I didn't do everything."

"Maybe not all the time." Her eyes widened. "Do you think other guys do it all the time? They don't."

"I bugged you to do stuff you didn't want to—"

"You didn't bug me. You asked. And when I said no, that was the end of it. In three years of dating, you never pressured me. Not once."

He shook his head. "Cyn, I was there. I know things weren't great between us."

"We were young. We were learning. You always made it about me, as much as it was about you. That's pretty rare, at least in my experience."

"Then you've dated a lot of jerks, Cyn." Trent's voice was strained with suppressed emotion. Rick wasn't sure what to make of it.

"Apparently, I have too." Jordan sipped his drink.

"We already knew that." Rick bumped his shoulder against Jordan's.

"Maybe that's my destiny. Dating guys who care less about me than I do about them."

Flames shot through Rick's chest and up to his face. He couldn't take this, Jordy thinking he wasn't committed. He had to do something—something irrevocable, to prove he was sincere. "Excuse me."

He rushed through the crowded restaurant and out the door. Key in hand, he pushed the button and his car lights blinked. He sat inside, catching his breath and gathering his thoughts.

He had to come out. It was the only way.

Could he tell Cyn and Trent? A chill snaked down his spine. Not Cyn. Couldn't let on that he'd been fantasizing about Jordy when he was with her. She deserved better.

Maybe he could pull Trent aside, take him to the bar when they got back to the hotel, spill the truth over a couple of beers.

The thought made him miserable. Trent would hate having that conversation with him. And he didn't want Trent to be the first person he came out to. It should be family.

The one person in the world who had loved him all his life, and would never, ever judge him.

Through tears, he could barely find her number in the contact list on his phone. His stomach somersaulted while it rang. But when she answered, it was the sweetest sound he had ever heard.

"Kat," he said, his voice strangled.

"Ricky. You okay?"

He sensed her panic. He didn't want her to be afraid. "Yeah, I'm fine. I just...I need to talk to you."

"Shit. I knew something was wrong today."

"Not wrong, exactly. Kat, you...you'll love me no matter what, right?"

"Oh, hell, what did you do? Are you in trouble?"

"No, I told you, everything's fine."

"You don't sound *fine*. Do not fucking lie to me."

He shivered from the cold. Dumb to leave his coat inside. "It's not a bad thing. It's just a weird thing. I'm...I'm in love."

Kat paused. "Is she married or something?"

"No. Nothing like that. But it's not..." He took a deep breath and held it before saying, "It's not a she."

Silence.

*Just say the words—I'm gay.* But he couldn't. They didn't seem real to him. His identity hadn't changed. He felt the same as he always had.

"It's Jordy," he said. "I'm in love with Jordy."

A burst of laughter broke through the line. "Motherfucker. You scared me half to death."

"I'm not joking."

"I get that." A low chuckle rumbled through the phone. "So you and Jordy. Are you guys...I mean, have you..."

"Don't freak out, okay? It feels right with him. Natural. Like that's how it's supposed to be."

"So...what about women? Are you still interested in women?"

"I've never been in love with a woman. I tried. Broke Jess's heart trying. I can't do it anymore. Want to be with Jordy."

"Are you two a couple?"

"He wants me to come out. Says he won't get involved with closet cases anymore."

"Are you ready for that?"

Bile burned in his throat. "I hate thinking how Mom and Dad will react."

"They'll be fine. They love Jordy. This...this is *good* news, Ricky."

"You think?"

"It'll take some getting used to..." Her giggle sounded like music. "I bet you guys are cute together. Maybe, if you want to have kids one day, I could donate my eggs, and you could use Jordy's sperm, so it would be almost like your own baby."

His jaw trembled, and his throat shut. He swallowed hard. "You're jumping ten years ahead, as usual."

"Think about it. It would be cool."

"You're really okay with this—you don't care that I'm gay?"

"It's weird hearing you say it, but no, why should I care? I want you to be happy."

"Don't say anything to Mom and Dad, though. I want to wait until after Christmas."

"Coward."

His chest contracted. Was she right? "You know how Mom is about Christmas. I don't want to spoil her holiday."

"Ricky, I get that you need time to adjust. I won't pressure you. As long as you don't have some dumb idea they're going to disown you."

"Not exactly."

"Well. You ever start freaking out about this again, call me, I'll talk you down. I love you. No matter what."

The soothing sweetness of her words washed over him.

After ending the call, he sat in the car a minute and breathed. Then, he texted to Jordan, *Called Kat, told her I'm gay.* Because he wasn't ready to say that in front of Cyn and Trent.

He got out and ambled back toward the entrance. Jordan stepped out of the doorway, then spotted him and rushed toward him.

Jordan led him into the shadows and kissed him, mouths pressed hard together, lips soft and tender. "Can't believe you did that for me."

"I'm glad I did."

"How'd she take it?"

"She offered us her eggs in case we ever want to have a baby."

Jordan laughed so hard he folded in half.

"What's so funny?"

"You've been so worried about how your family would react. Ironic, isn't it?"

"Save your laughter until I tell my mom."

Back inside the restaurant, Jordan's head swam, his dizzying emotions dulling his perceptions. He barely tasted the food or noticed the glow of the candlelight. Rick was committed to him, and nothing else mattered.

He tried not to wish that Rick would tell Cyn and Trent—there would be time for that later. Jordan understood Rick's worries about how Cyn would react. Although, when he glanced across the table, Cyn seemed to be focused on Trent, in an intense way that looked like more than friendship.

Was that what Trent had meant earlier, when he said he was seeing someone new? Had he and Cyn hooked up?

Rick's leg brushed against Jordan's, interrupting his thoughts. He looked over, wondering if he could get away with holding Rick's hand under the table. Somehow, hiding their relationship seemed different now, like the secrecy was exciting rather than burdensome. Rick wasn't ashamed of him. He didn't have to fear that anymore.

Rick offered Cyn a bite of his lobster, which would have made Jordan jealous an hour earlier, but now seemed sweet. Their high school romance had been nothing more than two kids trying to figure out how relationships worked. She was no threat to Jordan. He realized that now.

Trent, on the other hand, wore a dark expression. Clearly he still felt threatened by Rick and Cyn's past together. Cyn seemed to notice, too, and her playful expression disappeared.

"You okay?" Rick asked her, concern in his voice.

Trent's arm slid around her shoulders possessively. "You don't have to worry about her. I've got this. Cyn's with me now."

She paled, and Rick's face flushed. The poor guy had apparently never suspected what Jordan had known: that Trent had wanted Cyn for as long as Rick was dating her, and only his loyalty to Rick stopped him from making a move.

Rick grew rigid, as if steeling himself for combat. Jordan touched his shoulder to remind him they all had moved on. That seemed to soothe him—the tension in his jaw eased. His eyes were still sharp as granite, but his agitation quieted.

Trent coaxed a smile out of Cynthia, and her face radiated happiness. "You should have seen yourself today," she said to Rick, "when your mom was trying to set us up. You had that deer-in-the-headlights look, like any move you made would be the wrong one. You didn't want to encourage her, but you didn't want to hurt my feelings, either. Maybe I should have put you out of your misery and told you about Trent and me."

"Why didn't you?"

"Because it's new, and I didn't want to freak you out. Didn't want you thinking something happened between us in high school, when it didn't."

Rick's brow furrowed. "Yeah, I can see how you might worry about that."

Jordan realized that Rick, too, seemed to recognize the parallels to their own situation. But apparently it wasn't enough to persuade him to reveal the truth.

Jordan's jaw tensed. *Be patient. He's taken the most important step.*

Surreptitiously, he slid his hand across Rick's thigh. The corners of Rick's mouth pulled up. A flush of happiness warmed Jordan's body. Forever was in his grasp.

# Chapter 8

After dinner, they parted ways with Cyn and Trent in the hotel lobby. Jordan's thoughts swirled, euphoria building inside him. He battled the urge to press Rick into the nearest solid surface and stake his claim with fierce kisses. *He's mine. For good this time.*

As they rode the elevator, he was aware of each breath he took, now labored. His chest pounded with the pumping of his heart. He couldn't meet Rick's eye, afraid that acknowledging the change between them would undo it somehow. It didn't seem real yet.

He followed Rick to his room, electricity stringing them together even though they weren't touching as they hurried down the corridor. As soon as Jordan closed the door behind them, Rick pinned him to the wall.

Their mouths clamped together, and Rick ground into Jordan's pelvis. Jordan moaned, the sound rumbling through his throat, his mouth too busy kissing to breathe.

Rick's hand moved downward and found Jordan's erection, now throbbing. Every nerve in his body came to life. He gripped the back of Rick's neck with one hand, deepening the kiss.

Unbuttoning Rick's shirt, he stroked his chest. His pecs were hard, topped with soft, dark hair. Jordan liked the masculine feel of an unwaxed chest. He teased the nipples, and Rick groaned.

Burying his face in Rick's neck, he breathed the earthy scent, so familiar. A scent that said security and loyalty and love. His heart jumped, the joy washing over him again. Rick was his now.

With nimble fingers, he unbuckled Rick's belt and opened his fly. Rick's hands fisted Jordan's hair. "Hell, Jordy."

The guttural sound of his voice was rough but laced with affection. Rick's tongue outlined the spiral of Jordan's ear. Decadent sparks of sensation fed his need. Sliding his hand inside Rick's briefs, he let out an involuntary moan. His cock was beautiful, of average girth but long and elegant like Rick's fingers. He ached to feel it inside him.

Rick thrust into the contact, hand squeezing Jordan through his clothes. "Want..." he murmured. He nipped Jordan's neck. "You. Naked."

They stripped off their clothes, mouths still fully engaged in kissing. Rick's warm body covered him, wall solid behind him. With one long arm, Rick reached through the open doorway into the bathroom and retrieved his shaving kit. Unzipping it, he pulled out a condom and a travel sized bottle of lube.

Jordan sucked Rick's neck as Rick set the kit back inside the bathroom. "Always prepared," Jordan said. "What a good Boy Scout."

"I'm a terrible Boy Scout." Rick turned him to face the wall. The bottle of lube clicked open and closed. A slick finger found his hole and pressed inside.

Jordan huffed out a breath, then gasped as Rick hit his gland. A second finger joined the first, and he rode them hard. "Please." He couldn't find words. Fortunately, Rick didn't seem to need them. A rustle of foil, a quick thrust, and Rick was inside him.

He keened, the fullness driving out thought and fear and doubt. His awareness shrank to the man he loved, the only man he'd ever really wanted, riding him with a rhythm perfectly in tune with his own. He wanted to call his name, to encourage him, to beg for more, but all he could do was move, meet Rick stroke for stroke, to keep that delicious friction *right there*. His thoughts weren't words anymore, just sounds and color. Everything was red, red, red, glowing hard and hot and crackling in his ears.

A roar and a gasp, and Rick's body was shuddering all around him, arms encircling him and holding him tight. Rick quieted and kissed the back of Jordan's neck, then pulled out, tossing the condom into the trash.

Jordan's mind cleared, but his body was still hot and desperate. Rick turned him around to face him. He ran a thumb up Jordan's shaft, and Jordan groaned.

"What are we going to do with this?" Rick quirked a smile, then dropped to his knees.

Jordan gasped. A shiver jetted up his spine. Thick, uncontrolled breaths heaved his chest.

Rick's tongue dipped into the slit, and Jordan pounded a fist against the wall. Oh, hell, that whisper of touch constricted his balls and made the hair at the back of his neck stand on end. Next came a gentle circling of his cap, followed by teasing kisses along the shaft.

He whimpered, and Rick got the hint, taking him into his mouth, enveloping him in heat. He tried not to pump into him, but this fantasy-come-to-life eroded his control.

"Oh, babe...that's it...so good."

Rick pumped his fingers into Jordan's well-lubed ass. He took his cock deep and swallowed. Jordan swore under his breath, wanting more. Was Rick ready for this? "Close."

Rick pulled back. "Do it." Rick went back to work, tongue teasing, cheeks hollowing.

Hell, that was hot. He clutched Rick's face, guiding him. His old desire of fucking Rick's mouth came back to him. With two hard thrusts he exploded, every muscle convulsing, every cell of his brain lighting up. Rick kept on going, swallowing it all.

Lightheaded, Jordan leaned against the wall, panting as Rick kissed his way up Jordan's body. Jordan pulled him close and their mouths crashed together. Tasting himself on Rick's tongue was like nothing he'd ever experienced before, because it was Rick and they were in love and he'd wanted this for so long.

With his palms pressed to Jordan's chest, Rick nuzzled his ear. "Beautiful."

Jordan sucked in his cheeks. "You didn't mind?"

Rick stepped into the bathroom and washed his hands. Grabbing a towel, he grinned. "I could get used to doing that every day for the rest of my life."

Relief and happiness bloomed in his chest and rose into his throat.

Hand in hand, they made their way to the bed and lay in silence, bodies intertwined. Rick rained tender kisses. Jordan could barely move, sex and contentment leaving him weak.

"Is it just me," Rick asked, "or was that the best sex ever?"

"Best ever," Jordan said, eyelids heavy.

"I'm serious." Rick stroked his cheek. "Sex with you is so far beyond anything I've experienced before. Is it us? Or do you have mind-blowing sex with every man you're with?"

Jordan forced himself awake. "It's us, babe. You read me so well. And I know I can trust you."

A huge grin spread over Rick's face. "A lifetime fucking you wouldn't be enough."

"You're such a romantic."

He sucked in his lips. "Should I stop talking so much about the fucking?"

"No. I understand what you mean. You're not just talking about the sex part. You mean the entire experience."

"Sex and love are the same when I'm with you."

"I know." Jordan pulled him into a deep kiss.

"Do you feel it too?" Rick asked.

"I don't think I experience it exactly the way you do. I spent a lot of years being in love with you before I ever got to have sex with you. So I can feel the love without the intense need for sex you seem to have. But I can't have sex without feeling the love."

Rick nodded. "I have to ask you something, and I don't want you to get mad or feel like you have to say yes."

"I can't promise not to get mad if you ask something stupid, but I don't think I've ever had trouble saying no to you."

Rick bit his lip. "I want to move in with you."

"You mean while you look for a place?"

Rick shook his head. "I mean permanently. If that's what you want."

Jordan's lips parted, and he breathed to steady himself. That level of commitment was beyond what he expected. Not just dating, but building a future together. Of course it was what he wanted.

But to move so fast, to risk failure at this level...What if it didn't work out?

Jordan sat against the headboard. He had come to this reunion just hoping to hook up with Rick. Instead, Rick wanted a relationship, and Jordan didn't know what to make of it.

He combed his hands through his hair. His dream had come true, and now it was no longer his to control.

*Rick could be my boyfriend. I could come home to him every night. We could go to little bed-and-breakfasts on the weekends, maybe even get married someday.*

All that had been fantasy a few hours earlier. And fantasy didn't include things like arguing over money or kids or household chores. This would be a hard road for them, because relationships were hard and gay relationships were harder. But if the tradeoff was waking up to Rick every morning, coming home to his kisses every night...Jordan could do that. It was worth the risk.

"Never mind," Rick murmured, sitting up beside him without looking at him. "It's too soon. You're not ready. I understand. I'm not mad at you."

The tremble in Rick's voice broke Jordan's heart. Rick had handed him his heart, and he'd let it lie there bleeding while he figured out how to say yes to the only thing in life he really wanted.

Jordan took his hand. "The two of us, living together...it's what I want more than anything."

"Yeah?" Rick drew him into a bear hug. "Why didn't you just say so?" The sound of Rick's ragged breathing told him he'd given him a scare.

"If we do this thing," Jordan said, "we need to approach it like any other relationship. We can't just assume it's going to work out because of our history."

"I'm committed to making you happy. I realize how lucky I am to have you, especially after I made you wait so long. I can be what you need. No one could love you more than me, Jordy."

For all his surface arrogance, Rick was ridiculously humble and unselfconscious underneath the façade. That quality had endeared him to Jordan even while they were boys. It was the reason Jordan had never been able to fall out of love with him.

Jordan grinned, then slid his finger along Rick's jaw line. "I can't get enough of this handsome face, or that manly hairy chest of yours, or that firm, apple ass. You're my dream guy, Rick. Sleeping or waking, I dream of you."

Kisses rained down on his lips. "Mine," Rick murmured.

"Yours."

Lying flat on his back, feeling the soft friction of Rick's body, Jordan wondered if the feeling of happiness was real. Could it be this easy? The two of them in love, becoming a couple? But of course it wouldn't be easy. Rick would have to go through the trauma of coming out, which would be a huge surprise to his parents. He'd had a girl on his arm since he was fifteen.

Jordan squirmed and Rick pulled away. "What's wrong?" Rick asked.

"Are you sure you can commit to this? What if you meet a woman who can give you the straight life you've always wanted?"

Rick's dark eyes flashed. "I never wanted a straight life. I wanted you. And I didn't know how to get that without disappointing everyone around me. Now, I just don't give a shit. Let them be disappointed. This is my life, and I need to live it. They don't get to do that for me."

Jordan drew him close, and Rick laid his head on Jordan's shoulder.

"We'll get through this together, okay?" Jordan said.

"Yeah."

"You hate the idea of being gay."

Rick shrugged. "Gay isn't a lifestyle. It's being with the man I love. Maybe people won't be okay with that at first—some people will never be okay with it. But they don't matter. All that matters is us."

Rick woke the next morning and wrapped his arm around Jordan's waist. Jordan rolled away and shoved a pillow between them.

Rick scowled. He got up and took a piss, then brushed his teeth. When he got back to the bed, he knelt on the floor by Jordy's side and brushed a fingertip along his cheek.

"Hey. What's wrong? "

"You're a shithead."

"As a general statement, I'd have to agree. Did you mean something specific?"

"You're the most impulsive person I know."

Rick narrowed his eyes. "I've spent five years considering this decision, and I've learned that nothing else comes close to you. I don't think that's impulsive."

The tension left Jordan's face, but sadness replaced it. "This is happening so fast," he said. "How can I trust it?"

He slid into bed and kissed Jordan's mouth, long and slow. "Because you can trust me." He combed his fingers through Jordan's soft blond hair. "I wouldn't commit to you unless I was sure. I wouldn't hurt you that way."

"You're ready to come out?"

"Yes." Rick squeezed him. "Hell yes."

Jordan smiled, but his smile didn't last.

Rick ran his hand down his lover's arm, intertwining his fingers with Jordy's. His lips teased Jordan's neck, then slid along his collarbone to his shoulder. He nibbled the tender flesh of Jordan's armpit, breathing his musk.

Jordan's masculine scent fired electricity straight to Rick's cock. He wanted this man, wanted to wake next to him every morning. Nothing matched the pleasure of sleeping in Jordan's bed, their bodies entangled, expressing the deep love that existed between them. Joy settled in his stomach. For the first time in his life, he felt free.

But worry still lined Jordan's features. Rick pressed his mouth to those soft lips. The kiss deepened, tongues exploring. Running his hand down the long torso, he caressed Jordan's body, but he remained tense.

"What can I do to reassure you?" He sucked Jordan's ear.

Jordan propped himself up on his arm. He stroked Rick's chest, massaging his nipples. Finding Rick's cock, he teased it with a light touch.

Desire rippled through Rick's body. He eased onto his back, one knee bent. He took Jordan's free hand and slid his mouth over Jordan's index finger, massaging it with his tongue.

Jordan smiled and pulled his finger out, then ran the slick digit around Rick's hole. He pushed inside and pumped. Rick moaned.

Jordan kissed his way down Rick's body. He slipped his hands underneath Rick's ass and lifted it. His tongue circled the rim, then pushed inside.

Rick pulled back and turned over to give Jordan better access. Jordan licked and circled and thrust. It was so erotic, so intimate. A finger pushed inside, opening him. He felt the pressure on his prostate. Shivers crawled up his back. Jordan's touch was gentle but insistent.

His finger still working, Jordan slid upward and kissed Rick's shoulder. He said in his ear, "Want you."

"Want you, too."

Jordan slid his finger deep inside. "Want you *here*."

Rick tensed. *Fuck.* He should have seen that coming.

"Relax," Jordan said in his ear. "I want to give you pleasure—show you how good it can be. Make you mine in every way."

Rick swallowed. He'd always expected to do this for Jordan—let him penetrate him. Just not so soon. He wasn't sure he was ready.

"I'll talk you through it," Jordan said. "If it hurts, we'll stop."

Rick pulled away, breaking the contact between them. He felt coerced. If he didn't let Jordan take him that way, would Jordan think he wasn't serious about coming out? That wasn't fair.

Jordan rose and went into the bathroom. Rick heard the water run. Jordan came out and slipped on his briefs and jeans.

"Where are you going?"

"My room, to get dressed. I need to pack."

Heat rose in Rick's face. Jordan did this *every time*.

"Don't play martyr with me," Rick said. "You think this is hard for you? My whole life is about to change. The thing my mom wants most in the world is grandchildren, and I have to tell her I won't be able to give her that—at least not the way she always thought. After I come out to my friends, some of them won't be my friends anymore. And what sucks is, I don't know which ones it'll be." His face chilled. "Do you think Trent—"

"Trent won't give shit." Jordan sat on the bed and kissed him, tasting like toothpaste. "I'm sorry. I had you once and lost you—I can't go through that again."

"You didn't lose me. You've been in my heart all along." Rick kissed him deeply. "Come back to bed."

Jordan stripped and climbed under the covers. He wrapped his arms around Rick. They lay in silence a few minutes. Finally, Jordan said, "Sorry I freaked you out."

"The first time I bottom for you, it won't be to prove a point." Rick couldn't keep the anger out of his voice, didn't want to. He was used to being the asshole in the relationship—had been since he was six years old—but every once in a while, Jordan was the one who screwed up.

"I didn't mean it like that."

"The hell you didn't. You want me to prove I'm gay enough that you can trust me. Why isn't my word enough? The last time we were together, I was honest about wanting to explore my sexuality before making a commitment. I didn't lie to you so I could bone you."

"Getting my heart broken has been a trend for me lately."

"Don't compare me to your ex-boyfriends. You know I'm not like them."

"No—they couldn't have hurt me the way you could, because I never loved them like I love you."

Rick supposed that should make him feel warm inside, but it didn't. "Keep your shit with those guys out of this relationship. We've been friends too long. What is your actual fucking problem?"

Jordan outlined Rick's lips with his fingertip. With a smile, he leaned in for a kiss.

Rick met his lips, then pulled back. He studied Jordan's laughing expression. "What?"

"You. Even when you're pissed, I feel completely safe with you. And you feel safe with me."

Rick swallowed. "Haven't I always protected you?"

"Always."

"Then what are you afraid of?"

"That you don't know what you want. That you'll decide you like girls again."

"Jordy, I never liked girls in the first place."

"You've spent the past six years sleeping with them."

"But it never felt right. Even after I'd been with them for months, it felt like a one-night stand. Like it was just sex, with no attachment. I felt empty inside. With you, I feel complete."

Jordan snuggled against him, head on Rick's chest.

Rick stroked Jordan's hair. "You still don't seem happy."

"Still want to fuck you. Bummed that you don't want me to."

Rick's heart filled. He wouldn't bottom for Jordan to prove he was gay, but he would to get that sound of disappointment out of his voice. He wanted to make Jordan happy, to give him pleasure. Tightness snaked in his belly at the thought of Jordan wanting him that way.

"Never said I don't want you to."

Jordan rose onto his elbow and gazed into his eyes. "But you're not ready."

"I can't make any promises, but we can try."

"It won't work if you're not totally into it. I have a rule—no pain when bottoming. Which means you have to relax. Can you do that?"

Rick nodded. "Sure," he said, even though he didn't feel sure.

Jordan planted sweet kisses on his lips. "I'll be so gentle with you, babe. I've topped enough to know what I'm doing. Never had a virgin before, though." He grinned. "You know what this means? You were my first, and I'll be yours."

The thought made Rick stupidly happy. He remembered the first time he'd been inside Jordan that way, how Jordan had moaned and trembled beneath him. Suddenly, Rick wanted this very much.

He lifted his head and devoured Jordan's mouth. Jordy's fingers fumbled for the lube. He slid a finger inside, then another, stroking Rick's prostate. Heat built inside him, and his breathing came in uneven pants.

"Get on your knees," Jordan said. "It'll be easier."

Rick rolled over and drew his legs beneath him. He tried to turn off the chatter in his brain. Jordan's fingers entered him again—two, then three, stretching and lubricating him. Tingles of desire spread through him, but apprehension mixed with want, and his muscles clenched.

"Relax, babe." Jordan kissed the small of his back. "I can't do this if you're tense. I don't want to hurt you."

Rick took long, deep breaths to calm himself. He bore down, pushing back onto Jordy's fingers. He didn't want to chicken out too soon, or both he and Jordy would hesitate to try again.

"I'll go slowly at first," Jordan murmured, "until you get the hang of it. If at any point you want me to pull out, just say so."

"Okay."

Jordan withdrew his fingers and took a condom from the nightstand. Another moment, and the blunt head of Jordan's well-lubed cock found Rick's entrance. Rick inhaled, then slowly emptied his lungs. Gently, cautiously, Jordan leaned forward, the tip of his penis teasing him, making Rick's own cock stiffen.

Jordan's arm encircled Rick's waist. "Your natural inclination will be to clench, but try to resist it. Relax and breathe."

With his free hand, Jordan caressed Rick's thigh. His balls tightened. Jordan said, "Exhale for me."

Rick hadn't realized he was holding his breath. He let it out, and Jordan pressed forward, breaking through the tight circle of muscle.

He cried out at the pressure of it, then panted. Jordan pulled back and stroked the depression along Rick's spine, the touch soothing. Jordan said, "Deep breaths, babe."

Rick filled his lungs and then exhaled, pulling Jordan deeper inside. It was weird, but it was okay. While Rick focused on his breathing, his body adjusted to the new sensations, and the sense of invasion lessened. Soon, pressure built in his prostate, and his pleasure grew. He pushed back into Jordan's thrusts.

"Doing okay?" Jordan asked.

"Good."

He nipped Rick's ear. "That's my boy."

The words rolled over him and pooled in his solar plexus. "Yours."

The press of Jordan's hands on his hips warmed him. With no urgency in his rhythm, Jordan slid in deep, then drew out. The languid pace left Rick swearing and moaning, every stroke too much but not nearly enough.

"You feel so good, babe," Jordan murmured. "Don't want it to end. As long as I'm not hurting you."

"S'good."

Heat radiated through Rick's body, the unfamiliar sensations taking his desire to new heights. He'd never felt this vulnerable before, or this cherished. Jordan owned him, every inch of him, and he reveled in that belonging.

Rick's cock, dangling between him and the mattress, ached for touch. He fisted it, and Jordan asked, "Lube?"

"Yeah."

Jordan squeezed a dollop onto Rick's hand, and Rick stroked himself frantically. Jordan quickened his pace, pounding into him. The dual sensations on his cock and his prostate freed him from conscious thought, as if he were floating, in his body but somehow above it.

His shaft tightened. With a shattering groan, he spilled onto the mattress, and his ass clenched.

A few hard thrusts later, Jordan cried out. His spasms rumbled through Rick's body. When the shuddering stopped, his arms encircled Rick's waist, and he kissed the back of his neck.

Wrapping the condom in tissues, Jordan dropped it into the trashcan with a thud. He cleaned himself off, then wiped up the pool of semen on the bed.

Jordan rolled onto his back and looked into Rick's eyes. Rick smiled and kissed him.

They lay quietly, Rick with his head on Jordan's chest. He wondered if his world had shifted a little. He'd thought it would, but he didn't feel much different. Happier, maybe. Relieved to get it out of the way. Pleased to be able to give this gift to his lover.

And wondering why he'd waited so fucking long to try it.

Satisfaction settled over him, and he started to doze. Jordan's voice woke him. "Rick, say something. Please. I'm afraid I hurt you. I'm afraid you hated it."

Rick scooted up and laid his head on his pillow. He brought Jordan's hand to his lips and kissed it. "The next time, I want to do it face-to-face. So I can see it's you inside me."

Relief spread across Jordan's features. "You want to do it again?"

"Not all the time. But it can be part of our repertoire."

Jordan wrapped his arms around him. "You're mine now."

"I was yours before." Rick kissed the tip of Jordan's nose. "Ever since our first time together, you're what

I've fantasized about. Gradually, all my expectations of the future faded until the only dream left was you."

"Do you really think you're giving up everything else in your life for me?"

"Rationally, no. And I'm not coming out for you. I'm doing it for me."

"Good. Because if you're doing it for me, you'll resent me and eventually come to hate me."

Rick kissed his forehead. "Then it's good I waited until I was ready. And it's good your taste in boyfriends sucks. Where did you find those losers, anyway?"

"Gay men in their early twenties aren't generally into commitment."

"Lucky for me."

They met Cyn and Trent at a restaurant for brunch, this time taking separate cars. The hostess led them to the table where their friends were already seated, hands intertwined.

Rick's breath caught. Waking up next to Jordan, the puzzle pieces of their relationship finally falling into place, he'd half-forgotten Cyn and Trent's announcement from the night before. It felt more like a dream than reality.

As he approached the table, the sight of Cyn and Trent together irritated him like an ill-fitting suit. It itched and crawled over his skin. Which was stupid. He was happy with Jordan. He should be happy for them, too.

Still, his stomach hollowed out when he saw the expression on Cyn's face. She had never looked at him the way she was looking at Trent, eyes radiant, gaze locked with his.

*Don't be jealous. She's not yours—she never was.*

He swallowed. That old, stubborn dream refused to die. But maybe he was wrong to think it should. It was an important part of his past. Loving Cyn was one of the smartest things he'd ever done.

"Sorry," she said when she saw him, a blush creeping over her cheeks.

"Don't be." He pulled out the chair beside her.

Trent narrowed his brow, eyes turning to slits.

"Dude," Rick said, reproach in his voice, "we've been friends since middle school. I'm not going to touch your girlfriend."

"You haven't been able to keep your hands off her all weekend."

"I haven't had a reason to. If you guys are a thing now, I'll keep my distance."

The waitress brought them coffee and they looked at their menus. Trent continued to wear a sullen expression. Cyn whispered in his ear, and he gave her a crooked smile. "Seriously," she said to him. "This jealousy is left over from high school."

Rick's gut clenched. He looked into Trent's eyes. "Wait. Did you have a thing for Cyn in high school?"

Jordan laughed. "You are such an idiot."

Trent leaned toward him. "The entire time you were dating her."

He looked at Cyn, cheeks hot. "Did he make a move on you?"

"Never. He's a gentleman." She reached an arm around Trent's waist.

He kissed her forehead, then turned to Rick. "And I expect you to return the favor. Keep your hands off my girlfriend, even if you're just playing."

"If that's what you want. But I'm not a threat."

"Of course not. I trust Cyn."

"You can trust me, too."

Trent glared. "You wouldn't kick her out of bed."

"I would politely ask her to leave," Rick said.

"Bullshit."

"Excuse me," Cyn objected. "I'm right here."

"I'm seeing someone," Rick insisted.

Trent scowled. "You didn't mention that to your dad yesterday."

"I didn't want to say anything yet. You know how my mom is."

His stomach knotted. Whatever was going on with Trent, he'd feel better if he knew the truth. Rick didn't want jealousy over Cyn to come between them. Maybe it was just a habit Trent needed to unlearn, but that would be easier if he understood how little of a threat Rick really was.

"It's Jordy," Rick said, then sucked in a breath and bit his lip.

Trent scowled. "What's Jordy?"

"I'm seeing Jordy."

"I see him, too. He's right here at the table."

Jordan was turning red from choking back a laugh.

"I mean I'm dating him."

Silence. Again.

"You're dating Jordy?" Cyn asked. "Is that a joke?"

"Dude," Jordan said, "that has got to be the worst coming out speech ever."

Cyn looked back and forth between them. "What are you two talking about?"

He took her hand. "I'm gay. Well, sort of bi. But mostly gay."

"No. You're not." She crossed her arms. "You're taking this 'I'm not a threat' thing pretty far. Which is sweet of you, but totally implausible."

Jordan began laughing uncontrollably, and that's when the reality seemed to hit her. His gleeful reaction bore out the truth in a way Rick's words never could. She shrank back, ashen, then grabbed her coat and fled.

Rick and Trent rose at once. Rick held up his hand, and Trent nodded, sinking back into his seat while Rick went after her.

She stood in the parking lot by her rental car, back to him, a few flakes of snow in her hair. She turned as he approached. "You have got to be kidding. Were you with him while we were dating?"

"Of course not." Rick bit his lip, remembering the weekend at the cabin.

"You were!"

"No. It was after we agreed to see other people, although technically before we broke up…"

"That trip to the mountains. Shit, I knew something had happened there. You were different when you got back. Sure of yourself, when all summer you'd been struggling. You knew we needed to break up. You didn't want to hold on anymore."

"Even if I weren't gay, staying together after we left for college wouldn't have been good for us. I think you know that."

"You're gay? Not bi?"

"I'm no good with labels. I loved you, Cyn. In ways much deeper than physical attraction. I don't regret our time together." He squeezed her hand. "You taught me to French kiss."

"And gave you some damn fine blow jobs," she said in a low voice, "which you didn't appreciate."

"Maybe not as much as I should have."

He took her into his arms. She looked pretty and vulnerable, just as she always had. He leaned in to kiss her.

She pulled away and started to laugh. "Uck, we're like brother and sister! No wonder the sex was awful."

Rick scowled. "It wasn't that bad."

She grasped his forearm. "No, you're right, it wasn't. It's better that you were my first, than that loser I dated freshman year of college. You loved me. And you were good to me—just not as good as someone who was actually attracted to me would have been."

"Cyn, I was a kid. I didn't know what attraction was."

"Until you started seeing Jordan."

His cheeks warmed. "Yeah."

"Well, if you're going to be gay, I'm glad it's with him. I always felt guilty being with you around him, knowing he was in love with you."

"So we're cool?"

She took his hand. "Better than cool."

Jordan's gaze followed the waitress as she refilled the coffee cups at a nearby table. He should say *something* to Trent, but he had no idea what. He and Trent had hung out together in high school, but it wasn't like they ever talked about things that mattered. Rick had been the center of their circle, the glue that held them together.

Trent broke the silence. "So you and Rick."

"Yep."

"Didn't see that coming."

"Look, he needs your support. He acts strong, but he's worried you won't want to be friends anymore."

Jordan's cheeks warmed. He'd said too much, but he couldn't keep silent, not when Rick's happiness was at stake.

Trent stared. "Why would I stop being his friend?"

Jordan shrugged. "It happens."

"I didn't stop being your friend, did I?"

"Well…no."

Trent's face reddened. "I can't believe you two would think that of me."

"We didn't. He's not thinking rationally."

"I hope you don't expect me not to razz him. This is too good a chance to pass up."

Jordan shot him a look.

"Rick razzed you, remember? He called you fag all the time."

Jordan remembered. Hearing that word repeatedly from Rick had taken away its sting, until it sounded like a term of endearment.

Trent's gaze moved toward the window. "Who else has he told?"

"Just Kat."

"Wow." He sat back, brow furrowed. "In that case, I won't say anything. Jordy, you have to know, if I can do anything…I'm there, man. Rick's my bud."

Jordan knitted his brow. Trent must really have been freaking out to devolve into macho speak that way. But he would support Rick, and that's what mattered.

Cyn and Rick headed for the table hand-in-hand. Jordan exhaled.

Trent rose and hugged Cyn, kissing her cheek. "You okay?"

"I'm good."

Jordan thought they looked cute together until Cyn pulled out of the hug and thwacked Jordan on the back of his head. He rubbed the sting away, wondering what he'd done. *Oh yeah, I stole her boyfriend in high school.*

Still standing, Trent shook Rick's hand. "Dude, I'm there for you, no matter what."

Confusion crossed Rick's features, but he smiled. "Thanks, man. But look, my parents don't know yet. So can we keep it quiet for a while?"

Cyn nodded. "We've got plenty of experience keeping things from your parents." She shook her head. "I can't believe my ex dumped me for a guy."

"It wasn't like that," Rick argued.

Jordan sucked in his cheeks. It actually sort of *was* like that.

"That's okay," she said. "I should be able to get a book or two out of it."

"Cyn, I'm not out yet. You can't write about me—"

"It won't be about you. It'll be about a fictional character, like a cowboy on a ranch in Montana."

Jordan arched his brows. "Gay cowboys."

"Leather chaps and riding crops." She grinned.

Jordan nodded. "I would read that book."

# Epilogue

Rick set a cardboard box on the black granite countertop, which gleamed beneath the recessed lights illuminating the kitchen. The fragrance of tomatoes and basil from the red sauce simmering on the stove made his stomach rumble. Unpacking a few glasses, he opened the maple cabinet above the dishwasher. He peered inside, then looked over at Jordan, who was adding the top layer of noodles to the lasagna. "I thought you were going to make room for my stuff."

"That was before I saw your stuff." Jordan ladled the sauce onto the noodles. "It's crap."

"It's not all crap."

Jordan looked over. "Tweety Bird glasses?"

"Amanda picked those out."

"The woman who broke us up? And you brought them into my house."

Rick crossed his arms. "Like you don't have anything from past relationships."

Jordan sighed. He rinsed his hands and dried them on a thick black towel hanging from the oven handle. Stepping up next to Rick, he took down four green mugs crested with the Philadelphia Eagles insignia. "Damon gave me those. Now you've got some room for you non-Amanda inspired glassware. We'll put the mugs and Tweety glasses in a box for Goodwill."

Rick kissed him. "We should go shopping, buy some stuff that's ours together."

Jordan rested his forearms on Rick's shoulders "Maybe something to replace my grad-school-chic sofa."

"I was thinking a smaller ticket item."

"A new couch could be our Christmas present to each other."

Rick grinned. "I thought my dick would be my Christmas present to you."

"Then I'll have a full set, since I've already got you by the balls."

He nuzzled Jordan's neck and trailed kisses along the curve of his ear. "Let's get the lasagna in the oven, and I'll give you your Christmas present early."

"Are you going to put it in some wrapping paper?"

Rick's hands skimmed over Jordan's torso and squeezed his ass. "I was thinking we could forgo the wrapper."

Jordan pulled back, a slow smile breaking over his face. "You mean…"

"Mm-hmm."

Jordan moaned and ground against him. Working in tandem, they opened the door to the preheated oven and slid the lasagna inside without breaking contact.

They climbed the stairs to their bedroom. Rick fished through the nightstand drawer, mouth never leaving Jordan's. He pulled out the lube and tossed it onto the bed. The condoms he threw in the trash.

They were a couple, now and always. Whatever coming out would cost him, it was worth it. No more pretty girls who didn't excite him. No more horny losers trying to pick up Jordy in bars. Just the two of them, together, the way they were meant to be.

## THE END

# Book 3: Winning Jordan

# Chapter 1

## *2013*

Rick Ferguson gathered the bedcovers around him to ward off the December chill, dreading the ordeal looming over him. A dull ache gathered in his temples. He snuggled up close to Jordan Callahan, resting his head in the crook of Jordy's neck, seeking the comfort of his lover's touch. He wished their bodies weren't separated by boxer briefs and T-shirts, but he was too cold to strip them off.

Jordan's arm encompassed him. "Morning." He kissed Rick's cheek, stubble rubbing against stubble.

Rick loved the way that felt, the hard, masculine sensations of Jordan's body. "Morning."

"This is nice." Jordan pressed into him. "Waking up to you is still the best part of my day."

Happiness awoke in Rick's chest. "Mine, too."

Rick had moved in with Jordan a month earlier, after being best friends since childhood. He'd had a long struggle coming to terms with his sexuality, mostly dating women while pining after Jordan. The past few weeks had been the happiest of his life, but a storm cloud still hung over him. He had to tell his family the truth. He couldn't put it off any longer.

"I hate to say it," Jordan muttered in a throaty voice, "but we have to get up. Mom wants me in Chestnut Grove in time to get to Grandma's by noon."

Rick nodded. "Do you want to get up first?"

"No, because it takes you longer to get ready. With your primping and trying on three outfits—"

"All you have to do is step out of the shower, and you look perfect." Damn, the image that conjured, Jordan's lean, muscled body wet and glistening, dirty-blond hair slick and plastered to his neck, leaving plenty of access for kissing... "My hair is a disaster if I don't spend fifteen minutes gelling and drying and smoothing it—"

"Yes, but I love running my fingers through your dark curls."

Rick grunted. "Straight is better."

Jordan smirked and ground his erection into him. "But if you were straight, you wouldn't have me."

"I didn't mean it like that."

"Sure you did."

Rick lay flat on his back, splaying his arm out beside him. "Maybe a little."

"Stop worrying over nothing. Your parents aren't going to reject you because you tell them you're gay. You're not going to your execution. You're going to spend Christmas with your family."

"My mom will hate it."

"Your mom will get over it." Jordan leaned on his arm, facing him. "Ricky. Your parents are PFLAG members. When I came out, they were as supportive as my own family."

"This is different. I'm their son."

"You're right, it *is* different. They love you more than life. *Stop worrying.*"

In his head, Rick knew Jordan was right—but every time he thought about it, his gut tied up in knots. And not the simple knots like he'd learned in Cub Scouts. More like the ones for his Climbing merit badge, back when he wanted to make Eagle Scout—before they threw Jordy out for being gay, and Rick quit in disgust.

He pulled Jordy close. "I have to go a whole week sleeping without you."

"We could have avoided that if you weren't so set on waiting until *after* Christmas to come out to your parents."

"You know my mom. She spends 364 days a year planning for Christmas. On the twenty-sixth, she'll be shopping the sales for next year's decorations. I don't want to ruin the holiday for her."

Jordan kissed him. "Your parents will be fine."

"They'll be disappointed."

"Give them some credit."

"I've got Kat on my side, though," he said of his sister. "She's been sending me texts with pictures of hot guys attached. She thinks it's hysterical we have the same taste in men."

"The only man you're supposed to have a taste for is me," Jordan teased.

"In real life, you are."

"You mean you fantasize about other guys?" Jordan tickled him.

He squirmed and pulled away. "You're always there, too."

"Three-ways? That's what you're into?"

Rick's shoulders tensed. "It's not something I actually want to *do*. But don't forget, you're the only man I've been with. So I imagine what it would be like to get fucked by some big hairy guy while I'm sucking you off, or to fuck some hot twink while he sucks you off." He frowned. "That's okay, isn't it?"

"Whatever you fantasize about is fine."

He waggled his brows. "What do you fantasize about?"

Jordan chuckled. "Go take a shower, and I'll show you."

Rick threw off the covers and hopped out of bed. "I can do that." Heading toward the bathroom, he wiggled his hips and sang, "I'm bringing sexy back..."

"You're an asshole," Jordan called after him.

"And you love me for it."

The December sky was clear but the sun weak. Wind whipped across Rick's face as he stuffed a suitcase, belonging to his sister Kat, into the trunk of his car. The stone buildings of Lehigh University rose above the sidewalk, looking down on the steep valley below.

Kat slid into the backseat, behind Jordan, while Rick got into the driver's side.

"Good-bye, Lehigh," she said, as Rick pulled away from the curb in front of her dorm, "see you next month."

"You sound like you'll miss it," he said.

"You know, senior year. Nostalgia."

In the rearview mirror, he eyed her pretty face and smiled. Dark, shoulder-length wavy hair, dark eyes that matched his own. She and Jordan were the only two people in the world who truly understood him.

"So are you ready for this?" she asked him. "Your grand debut?"

Jordan chuckled. "Not even a little."

Rick gritted his teeth. "May as well get it over with."

"I keep telling him it's no big deal," Jordan said. "Your parents will be fine with it."

"Oh no, Mom will *freak*," Kat said with certainty in her voice. "It will blow her ordered universe to hell."

A weight dropped from Rick's chest into his stomach. "Thanks, Kat, that's just what I needed to hear."

In the mirror, her face scrunched into a scowl. "How is that your problem? Mom has an annoying habit of imposing her vision of the world on other people. You're not responsible for her delusions."

"You can't really call it a delusion when I've given her every reason to believe I'm straight."

"Loser." Jordan coughed the word.

Rick glanced over at him with an affectionate smile. "I guess I was the one who was deluded."

"Yeah, I've been meaning to ask you about that," Kat said. "Seeing as you've been dating women in a pretty serious way since you were fifteen."

"Sexuality is a fluid thing. There are people who can be attracted to both sexes but only fall in love with one sex or the other. That's me. I've dated some amazing women, but I've only ever been in love with Jordy."

"Aw, that's so sweet," Kat said. "Although I doubt your ex-girlfriends would agree."

"Cyn is cool with it."

Kat shrugged. "It's been five years since you dated Cynthia. Jessica won't be so understanding. You broke her heart."

His stomach tightened. He navigated the car downhill and around a sharp curve. "I didn't mean to."

"I know, Ricky," she said. "Things happen. It doesn't always mean someone is to blame."

"You sounded like you *were* blaming me."

"You wouldn't intentionally hurt anyone. I just wonder if...maybe you should have realized it a little sooner."

Jordan chuckled again.

"Will you stop?" Rick said to Jordy, unable to keep the irritation out of his voice. Kat and Jordan, with their binary sexual identities, couldn't understand the struggles he'd faced. "I need you on my side in this. You're supposed to be my partner now."

Jordan paled. He laid his hand on Rick's thigh and squeezed. "Sorry. You know I've got your back."

He stopped for a red light and looked around absently at the pizza shop and Puerto Rican grocery on the corner. "I hate this. I wouldn't have chosen to hurt anyone. I can't help who I am."

"There's nothing wrong with who you are," Kat said. "I'm sorry, Ricky. I didn't mean to upset you. Maybe Jordy should drive."

He took a deep breath. "I'm fine. I just want this week to be over."

Heading toward I-78, he wound the car through the streets of Bethlehem, Pennsylvania, the iconic star visible high on a hilltop. At night, it would light up over the city. Usually it gave him a sense of peace to see it. But at that moment, everything associated with Christmas made him sick to his stomach.

His relationship with his close-knit family was about to change. After this year, Christmas wouldn't be the same again. But he didn't know yet what that meant. He didn't know what loving Jordan would cost him.

# Chapter 2

Jordan dropped his bag in his old bedroom. It hadn't changed much since he was in high school: football trophies, art supplies, a poster of Pat Burrell from his days with the Phillies. A corkboard showed faded Polaroids, mostly of him and Rick in elementary school—birthday parties, Cub Scouts, school plays. They had so much history together.

Maybe no one else would have been as patient with Rick, waiting five years for him to figure out his sexuality, but for Jordan it had all been worth it. They were soul mates. And at twenty-three, they now had the rest of their lives to be together.

The three-bedroom ranch house he'd grown up in, built in the 1960s, still held vestiges of that era. As an architect, he hated the recessed sliding windows that gave the place an industrial feel. They had always seemed cold to him. But the rooms were spacious, and the kitchen large and open for that time period. His uncle on his father's side had helped his mom replace the shag carpeting and the harvest gold appliances when Jordan was a kid. It was a cozy, comfortable home, and his mom had worked hard to make it that way.

A pediatric nurse, she'd had a grueling schedule while Jordan was growing up, but she'd always made time for him. She wasn't a PTA mom like Rick's mother had been, but she'd never missed a school play or a football game. She was his biggest fan, and he was the center of her life.

Even now, she worried about him, especially since he seemed to attract guys who pretended to want monogamy while sleeping around behind his back. She'd be surprised about Rick, but relieved that Jordan was with someone who cared about his well-being. This past month, the evasive conversations with her had worn on him. He was looking forward to finally being open about the relationship.

He went back to the kitchen, where she was waiting. She'd apparently been to the salon since he'd seen her at Thanksgiving, the highlights in her blond hair lighter than before. He supposed that meant her natural color was turning grayer. He hated to think of her growing older, even if she was only forty-six.

He realized, with a sudden chill in his stomach, that she'd spent nearly half her life as a widow.

His father's plane had been shot down over Iraq during Desert Storm when Jordan was just a baby, and his mom had never remarried. She'd dated, but...he supposed the biggest reason she'd stayed single was for him. Maybe she hadn't brought a stepfather into his life partly because he was gay. *He'd* known it from the time he had a word to describe it, and *she'd* probably known even earlier.

She was involved with someone now, and they seemed pretty serious. With Jordan on his own, there was no need to protect him anymore. His stomach churned at the thought of what she'd given up for him.

But maybe it was worth it—Mike was a great guy, a cardiologist who clearly adored her. A widower with two grown kids, he was also a deacon at their church, a progressive Christian fellowship that cared more about feeding the hungry than about who their neighbors were sleeping with.

His mom looked over at him and smiled. "I swear, you get more handsome every time I see you." She approached and brushed imaginary lint from his sea-green sweater. "Are you dating anyone?"

He chewed his lip, unsure how to respond. "Yeah, I've been seeing someone for a few weeks." He gave her an enigmatic smile and hoped she would leave it at that for now.

"Not going to share the details? Okay—I'm sure you'll let me know if it gets serious. But it must cramp your style, sharing a place with Rick when you've got a new man in your life."

He bit the side of his tongue. "Hasn't been a problem so far." He didn't like deceiving her, but he couldn't really say anything more until Rick talked to his parents.

"You know, I hate to say it, but I was glad the two of you drifted apart in college. I never thought he was a good influence on you. I'm not thrilled that you've picked up that friendship again."

*Fuck.* This was going to be more difficult than he thought. "We never drifted apart. We were in constant contact, even if we were in different states. Besides, Rick isn't nine years old anymore. He's a responsible adult with a good job—"

"He's a homophobe."

Jordan stared at her. "What? No."

"When you first came out, he called you *fag* all the time."

Jordan rolled his eyes. "Mom...you have to understand Rick. Half the time, he's putting on a show. He used that word so I'd get used to it, and it wouldn't sting as much. And it worked, too. But if anyone *else* at school said that word to me, Rick was in their face about it. No one wanted Rick as their enemy. He was the most popular kid in class."

"Um, hmm." She didn't look convinced.

"I like living with Rick." Jordan's throat tightened and his eyes burned. His mother's disapproval of Rick had never bothered him before, but now it felt like a punch in the neck. She and Rick were the two most important people in his life. He wanted them to get along—it mattered to him.

"Jordy, look," she snapped, eyes flashing with anger, "I know you have special feelings for Rick, but he's straight. He will never return them. Instead of getting his own place, he's using you, moving into your townhouse and freeloading off you—"

"He's not freeloading. He's paying for all the utilities, and the groceries, too. It's an equitable arrangement, and it means I can afford to put money into retirement savings now." Frustration rose in his chest. This was what Jordan was reduced to, talking about finances because he couldn't tell his mom that he and Rick were in love.

He inhaled deeply, trying to get hold of his emotions. He hadn't felt this out of control since he walked in on his last boyfriend with another man. He'd always known that Rick wasn't his mom's favorite person, but he'd never seen her this way before. This wasn't just disapproval. She truly *disliked* him.

He rubbed his fingers across the countertop as if trying to erase those feelings. "Mom, just...please, try to keep an open mind. You haven't seen much of Rick since we left for college. He's not the dumb kid he used to be."

"I don't want him hurting you."

"He would never hurt me. He's my best friend. Always has been."

The plea in his voice had no effect. Her mouth a thin line, she got her coat and purse from the closet. "Ready to go to your grandmother's?"

"Sure," he said in a weak voice. *Now what?*

"Rick, could you set the table, dear?" his mother asked with a happy smile that evening as she took the roast from the oven. Kat was at the counter straining potatoes, mixer on hand. Surrounded by family, his mother was in her element.

"Sure." He got out the everyday dishes and stacked them on the table in the breakfast nook before getting the silverware.

His mother reached into the cabinet for a serving platter. "Have you talked to Jess lately?"

Rick stared. Kat grinned but said nothing.

"Why would I talk to Jess? We broke up four months ago. It did not end amicably. I'm surprised she didn't block me on Facebook."

"She's a lovely girl. I'm sure if you apologized for whatever you did—"

"I didn't do anything, except realize I'm not in love with her. I shouldn't have gotten involved with her in the first place. She was always more serious about me than I was about her."

His mother shook her head. "Young men don't understand the importance of settling down."

He breathed to calm the anger surging through his veins. "I understand the importance of being with the right person before making a lifetime commitment. Jessica wasn't it."

"The girls you've dated have all been wonderful— just the type a man should choose to make a life with. If none of them were right for you, I can't imagine what you're looking for."

"No, I'm sure you can't." He fought the urge to shatter her lovely stoneware dishes on the hardwood floor.

"Hey, guess what?" Kat said. "I got into Stanford Law."

Rick smiled, heart lifting. Not only because Kat was saving his ass, but because he was genuinely happy for her.

He went over and pulled her into a hug. "Congrats, sweetie."

Their mother huffed. "She is *not* going to Stanford."

Kat scowled. "Why not? Are you saying you and Dad won't pay for it?"

"Of course we'll pay for it. But why would you go to school in California, when Penn is so close?"

"Because Stanford is a better school."

"So Ivy League isn't good enough for you?"

Kat turned rigid and pulled away from Rick. She said to him, "You think you can handle mashing the potatoes?" before she rushed upstairs.

"Mom," Rick said. His mother didn't react. "Your daughter just told you she got into one of the most prestigious academic programs in the country. You can't try to be happy for her?"

"I should be happy that my only daughter wants to move to the other side of the country? That she can't wait to get away from me?"

"This isn't about you. It's about Kat and her career."

Footsteps on the basement stairs warned of his dad's approach. "Something smells good."

Tears filled his mother's eyes, and she headed toward the master bedroom in the back of the house.

His dad turned to him. "What did I miss?"

"Kat got into Stanford. Mom thinks she wants to move to California to get away from her."

"Oh, that," his dad said with a nod. "Well, I guess I can carve the roast if you don't mind finishing up the potatoes."

Rick smashed the potatoes with a fork and added a dollop of butter. "You don't think maybe you should talk to her?"

His dad chuckled. "I've been married to her for twenty-five years. I know better than to go near her when she's that upset. We'll finish up here, *then* I'll talk to her. And maybe you can talk to Kat."

Rick knocked on his sister's bedroom door. "Kitty-Kat," he said, calling her by her childhood nickname.

"It's open."

He went inside and found her sitting on the bed clutching a pillow to her chest, looking forlorn. He closed the door behind him.

"I'm sorry," he murmured, sitting beside her. "You saved my butt—"

"You'd think I'd know better by now, than to expect her to be proud of me. No matter what I do, it's never enough. And meanwhile, you can do no wrong in her eyes. Is it because you were born first? Because I'm a girl? What is the problem?"

He put his arm around her and pulled her close. "If it means anything, *I'm* proud of you."

"Thank you." She brushed away a tear.

"And anyway, in a few days, after I come out, you'll officially be her favorite child."

"No, she will be pissed at me because I knew before she did."

He sighed. "You're right. Sorry."

"And meanwhile, you'll be cool, like Anderson Cooper and Neil Patrick Harris."

He nodded. "Neil Patrick Harris is hot."

"I know, right? Have you seen the pictures of him with his partner and their kids? All my girly hormones just go nuts at that."

He got quiet a moment and brushed his hand over her hair. "Did you mean what you said a few weeks ago, about donating your eggs to Jordan and me?"

"Hell yes. I want that for you, Rick."

"It's a lot. Trusting us to raise a child that's biologically yours…"

"But I do trust you. Especially the combination of you two. You'll be great dads someday." She scowled. "We're not talking, like, right away, are we? I don't want to be on hormone therapy while I'm in law school. Like I'm not crazy enough already."

He chuckled. "No, I think we're looking at five years, minimum. And *you're* not the crazy one."

"Thank you. I needed to hear that."

Jordan sat on his bed dressed in flannel pants and a T-shirt, the only light coming from his cell phone and the next-door neighbor's red Christmas lights.

Rick picked up on the first ring. "Hey. I was just about to call you. Miss you like crazy. I don't even want to get into bed, it's so cold without you."

"You, too." Jordan's heart ached with love and longing. Rick's absence was a physical pain. "So how are things there?"

"Pretty much what you'd expect. Mom is driving Kat crazy, and trying to get me to reconcile with Jess. You?"

"Good. Grandma's doing fine. Mom and Mike are doing fine. It's just...well, my mom isn't happy about us living together."

Rick sighed. "I'm not surprised. She hates me."

"She, um...well, I always knew you got on her nerves, but..."

"No. She *hates* me."

"How did you know that and I didn't?"

"Because I'm the one she gives the icy stares to."

Jordan punched the center of his down pillow, both to fluff it and release his frustration. "Don't you think this is kind of a problem?"

"Why would it be any more of a problem now than it's always been? It's not like she can forbid you to see me."

"I guess not. I don't want her to hate you, though. You need to make nice with her. I mean, sincerely nice, not smooth salesman nice."

"I can try, but she won't trust it."

Jordan shook his head. "She's mad because you used to call me fag."

"That was eight years ago, Jordy. I was *fifteen*. Don't you think some of the onus is on her, to not hold a grudge against me for things I did as a kid?"

"She doesn't really know you as an adult."

"Then we need to change that."

Jordan flopped down on the bed. "It'll be better once we can stop hiding things."

"Soon. Three days."

"You're okay with it?"

Rick went silent a moment. "Kat reminded me of how much Mom likes Anderson Cooper. She thinks he's hot."

"He is hot."

"I mean, she's still going to freak. But maybe she won't hate me forever."

"She won't hate you." He rubbed his hand over the space beside him in bed. "I don't want to go to sleep without you."

"Me neither."

"Maybe we could talk until we fall asleep."

Rick's voice brightened. "Maybe you could send me a picture of your dick."

"You're such an asshole."

"Ooh, you could send me a picture of your asshole, too."

Jordan chuckled. "That is *not* happening. Good night, Ricky."

"Night, Jordy. Love you."

"Love you, too."

His heart hurt as he pushed the button to end the call. He lay on his side, holding his phone to his heart.

He thought back on all the nights Rick had spent in this room while they were growing up, the whispers and the shared secrets. Rick's spirit was in this room. As Jordan drifted off to sleep, a comfort settled over him. He refused to let worries for the future get in the way of their happiness today.

# Chapter 3

Christmas Eve for Rick meant extended family. Aunts, uncles, and cousins came and went all day, snacking on egg nog and angel-shaped sugar cookies. His mom still made the cookies the old-fashioned way, from scratch, rolling out the dough and using cookie cutters, topping them with sprinkles of red and green sugar crystals.

By late afternoon, everyone had gone except the grandparents. Rick was antsy because Jordan still hadn't dropped by. He understood that Jordy had family stuff to do, but Rick had never felt this kind of longing before, this acute *need* to be with someone. He hated himself for ever thinking that what he'd had with Cyn or Amanda or Jess could have been love. After years with them, he'd never experienced anything close to what he felt with Jordy after five weeks.

His phone beeped, the tone he used for texts from Jordy. A smile broke across his face when he read the words, *On my way.*

"Can't you young people ever turn off your phones?" his grampa asked. In his early seventies, his maternal grandfather was tall and trim but sat with a cane at his side, thanks to a war wound in Vietnam. His thinning hair was pure white, his face long and thin.

Rick bit his lip. "I was waiting for a message from my friend Jordan. He's on his way over."

His grampa nodded. "Is he the queer?"

"George!" his grandma scolded. "They prefer *gay*."

His grandmother was a petite, fidgety woman whose expression was generally one of worry. A mother of five, she'd never held a job, never learned to drive. Her family was her everything.

"Jordy's such a nice boy." His grandma straightened her skirt.

His grampa pulled a roll of peppermint Life Savers from his pocket. "Didn't say he wasn't. Haven't seen him in years, though." He popped a mint into his mouth.

Rick pursed his lips and drew in his shoulders. "He took summer classes so he could finish his bachelor's in architecture in three years, before getting his master's."

"So he's an architect?" Rick's grandma asked.

"Apprentice at a large firm. Wants to start his own business one day." Rick smiled at that thought. They could be partners, with Rick handling the sales end so Jordan could focus on the design.

His grampa wrinkled his brow. "Is he the one you're living with?"

"Um, yeah, I moved in with him when I relocated to Allentown."

"Aren't you worried people will think you're queer, too?"

Rick swallowed. "Jordy says life is too short to worry about what other people think."

"That's the damn truth," his nana said, entering from the kitchen with a glass of red wine in her hand.

"Rick's living with a queer," his grampa said.

His nana sat in a rocker and set down her wine on the end table. "I roomed with a lesbian in college. Who cares?"

"I'm sure Rick knows what he's doing," his grandma said. "Young people today, they don't care much about that sort of thing."

"No one cared when we were young, either," his grampa said. "We didn't talk about it. All this controversy started in the seventies with that Anita Bryant. Then AIDS happened, and ever since, people can't stop talking about it."

"Ugh." His nana adjusted her sweater. "Don't get me started on Anita Bryant."

At seventy-five, his nana had been a widow for fifteen years. A former schoolteacher, she now volunteered as a yoga instructor at a local senior center.

The doorbell rang, and Rick fought the urge to run to the foyer. Instead, he forced himself to walk at a leisurely pace. Jordy's image through the sidelights brought a smile to his face and a warm tickle to his stomach.

He opened the door, grabbed his lover by the collar of his parka, and hauled him inside. Rick said in Jordy's ear, "Fuck, I've missed you."

"You too." Jordan's blue eyes sparkled, his cheeks red from the cold.

Looking behind to ensure no one was watching him, Rick pulled Jordy into the adjacent den and shut the door.

He slanted his mouth across Jordy's frozen lips, breathing warmth into him. He pushed down the parka and drew Jordan's body against his own. "Need you." He pressed his forehead to Jordy's. "My grampa is being a prick. Called you a queer. Guess that's what he'll be calling me from now on."

"I've known your grampa a long time. He's not a bigot. He says that stuff to get a rise out of your grandma."

"And that makes him less of a prick?"

Jordy kissed him. "You are *irritable*. Keep it up and I'll have to force you to relax, like I did yesterday morning." He waggled his eyebrows.

His balls tightened. "Don't tease me. I get hard thinking about it, and my grandmothers are in the next room."

Jordy bit Rick's earlobe. "You turning into a bottom?"

"Like it both ways." Rick kissed his mouth. "Like it any way with you."

Jordy's fingers snaked through Rick's hair. Rick rested his forehead against the soft flesh of Jordy's neck.

"Love you. But I should go say hi to your family."

"Can't we stay here?"

Jordy kissed him. "Babe, stop torturing yourself. We could get this whole 'coming out' thing over with right now if we'd just walk in there holding hands."

"I could take you upstairs and fuck you instead."

"You need to spend time with your family. You see me every day."

"Can't get enough of you. Can never get enough."

"That's because we've only been living together a month. Six months from now, you'll be ready for a break."

"No." Rick suckled his ear. "Never."

"Come on." Jordan squeezed his arm. "Your family will wonder what's keeping us."

With slow steps, Rick led Jordan into the family room. His grandpa rose with the help of his cane and offered Jordan his hand. "It's great to see you, son. How long has it been?"

Jordan shook his hand warmly. "Too long. Sophomore year, maybe?"

"We understand you're an architect now," his grandma said.

"Yeah, I still can't believe they trust me to design buildings that won't fall down on people."

"Goodness! Have you ever had a building fall down?"

"He's joking, Grandma." Rick tried not to laugh. He loved her dearly, but irony was lost on her.

"Engineering is a science for a reason," his grampa said. "If you follow the rules, it works every time."

"Assuming the materials and the substrate are reliable, yeah," Jordan said.

"But he's an architect, not an engineer," Rick's grandma said.

"Engineering is a big part of architecture," Jordan said with such gentle patience that Rick wanted to kiss him. "That's one of the reasons I went into the field. I like the combination of science and art."

"Rick, why are you hovering?" his nana asked. "Sit down and relax."

He winced. "Yeah, okay."

The only available seat was next to her in front of the fireplace, a cushioned rocker that matched hers. It was set away from the other group of seats so Rick couldn't really mediate between his grandparents and Jordan. Not that he needed to. Jordan could handle himself.

"You're very fond of Jordan, aren't you," his nana said when he sat down.

His face heated. "He's my best friend. Always has been."

"And the two of you are living together now. How's that working out?"

"Fine, um...He's really easygoing and doesn't mind when I do dumb things. He calls me on it, and we work it out."

"When you were little, you were a natural-born troublemaker. But once you met Jordan, you always seemed to look to him for approval. He's a sensible young man with a good heart. Meeting him was probably the best thing that ever happened to you."

"I think so, too."

His nana rocked in silence a few moments. "You and Jessica, that's really over?"

"Uh, yeah."

"Your mom keeps bringing it up. You know, if you're seeing someone else, it might put her mind at ease."

Rick swallowed. *Oh, fuck.* Somehow, his nana knew.

"I'm gonna tell her. Day after Christmas. So we can get through the holiday in peace."

His nana grinned. "Your mom having a peaceful holiday—I'd like to see that. She could be on her deathbed, and she'd be telling everyone how to arrange the ornaments on the tree." She shook her head. "When your dad first brought her home, she was pretty and vivacious and talked a blue streak...your dad would just watch her with so much love in his eyes, he couldn't stop smiling. And I thought, what has that boy gotten himself into? She's a wonderful woman, the best wife and mother anyone could be—the best daughter-in-law, too. She makes me tired, though, worrying that some of the cookies came out of the oven broken...Kat and I ate the evidence. Problem solved."

He chuckled. "Kat must take after you."

"Possibly. You take after your mom."

"*I* do?"

"You worry about everyone's comfort the way she does. It's a lovely quality, Rick, as long as it doesn't get in the way of your happiness. You're not responsible for other people. They're responsible for themselves."

He nodded, trying to feel comforted by the words. But he couldn't. Knowing he was going to make his family unhappy was a hard burden to bear.

Once Jordan had chatted with Rick's family for about fifteen minutes, Rick decided it was time for them to spend some quality time together alone. Announcing they were going upstairs to watch the game, they went to Rick's room.

He closed and locked the door behind them, then dragged Jordan into a kiss, their bodies pressed hard together. He backed Jordan against the wall. Hands tore at clothes, heaping them into a commingled pile on the floor.

"TV," Jordan managed through bruised lips.

"Now?"

"Cover the noise. Bedsprings."

Dancing Jordan toward the mattress, Rick picked up the remote. He stopped at a channel with hot rods racing through red dirt, motors humming like bees. Perfect.

They burrowed under the blankets, quickly warming themselves against each other's bodies. Jordan's musky scent, so familiar, lulled Rick into a sense of contentment. His hands massaged hard biceps, lips suckled the flesh of a shoulder. "Need this," he moaned.

"Need to be quick. I have to be home by six-thirty so we can make it to my uncle's by seven."

"Quick is my specialty."

Jordan laughed. "Of course. How could I forget?"

Rick kissed his way down Jordan's body, stopping to give special attention to his nipples, then brushing his lips over the planes of muscle. Jordan's abs were the most beautiful he'd ever seen. He wanted to bounce things off them, but every time he suggested it, Jordan told him to stop being a dick.

He nuzzled the nest of Jordan's pubic hair, breathing him in, the urge to taste him overwhelming. His tongue circled Jordan's cap, inspiring a little moan that encouraged deeper exploration. Jordy was fully erect now, and all his coyness had fled. Hands threading through Rick's hair were gentle but firm.

"Babe," Jordan groaned, "oh, fuck, you're amazing at that."

Rick sucked and swirled his tongue, teasing the slit, outlining the head, tracing a vein down the shaft before deepthroating and swallowing to massage his lover's cock. Jordan thrust his hips, clearly wanting more but seeming to hold back. "Give me all of it," Rick said, voice humming around Jordan's cockhead, "fuck my face."

Jordan held Rick's head in place and pumped into him. Rick didn't mind the sore jaw or the trouble breathing, as long as it gave Jordan pleasure. He would do anything to make Jordan happy.

He felt the quickening in Jordy's cock just before he cried out and hot cum spurted into Rick's throat. He swallowed it down, sucking out every drop. As Jordan recovered from the high, his hand found Rick's cock, and Rick shivered. Heat swept over his body.

Jordan wasted no time. Rick's aching, throbbing dick required no foreplay. Jordan got down to it, sucking hard, his hot, wet mouth a piece of heaven. Rick grabbed a pillow and squeezed it to his chest, letting Jordan take total control of his pleasure.

The orgasm ripped out of him so hard he had to hold his arm over his mouth and bite down to keep from screaming. His body shook, and tears formed at the corners of his eyes. *This.* Enjoying this intimacy with Jordan was all he wanted for the rest of his life.

As they snuggled together, Rick felt boneless, spent, as if he'd lost his identity and become one with the universe through the union of their two souls. He never used to think about New Age shit like that, but since he'd been with Jordan, he thought about it all the time. He'd fallen into infinity, and Jordan was his soft landing.

His throat thickened with joy and sadness—joy because what he shared with Jordan was so perfect, sadness because they couldn't be together twenty-four hours a day through the holidays like a normal couple. He knew it was his choice, but still, he felt as if the world was forcing the choice on him. They couldn't just say they were in love. It would be an ordeal, no matter when or how Rick came out.

"You're too quiet," Jordan said. "What's wrong?"

"Nothing, really. I just feel like...I've waited so long for us to be together. I feel impatient for the rest of our lives to get here."

Jordan chuckled. "This is it, babe. We're living it. This is what the rest of our lives will be like. Although hopefully, this will be the last Christmas we'll have to sneak around for quick fucks while your grandparents are downstairs."

"Hopefully." He stroked Jordan's bare chest. "Maybe after your thing at your uncle's tonight, I can sneak over to your place to see you."

"By *see*, you mean *fuck*, right?"

"How did you know?"

"Pace yourself. We can be together anytime. We should both be focusing on family right now."

Rick's chest grew heavy. "You don't need me the way I do you."

"Of course I do. It's just different. I haven't spent the past five years having unsatisfying sex with women."

"You think I'm an idiot."

"No, I think sexuality is complicated." Jordan picked up a pillow and bopped him on the head. "Can we stop with the recriminations? We can't change the past. Let's focus on our future. Which, from where I'm sitting, looks pretty bright."

Rick thought so too, if only he could make it through this week. If his mother could be reduced to tears over his sister being accepted by Stanford Law, he could only imagine how she would react at learning her only son was gay.

# Chapter 4

Jordan refilled his coffee, breathing in the sweet aroma. The sound of the front door opening and closing reached his ears. It wasn't even seven—he hadn't expected his mother to come home from Mike's place this early. But then, she had to get the turkey in the oven, and dinner was at noon.

He looked over at Rick, not completely happy with the idea of his mother entering the kitchen to find him there. Not that it mattered, really. Jordan was a grown man who didn't need permission to bring a guest to his mother's house.

She strolled in through the dining room, dressed in jeans and a cotton sweater. She took off her white hooded overcoat and hugged him. "Merry Christmas."

He smiled and gave her a squeeze. "You too, Mom."

"Rick, Merry Christmas. I didn't expect to see you here." She headed to the coffee pot.

"Yeah, um," Jordan said, "you know it's our tradition to watch the *Christmas Story* marathon together. We just kind of conked out, so he spent the night."

"That's fine. I'm just surprised. I'd think you two would get enough of each other, living in the same house."

"Hard to believe Jordy puts up with me," Rick said.

Jordan's mother gave him an enigmatic smile.

"So how are things with you, Mrs. C.?"

"Good. I like the new practice I'm with." She stirred milk into her coffee. "No doctors with God complexes like the last place. How's your new job?"

"Glad to be out of the mountains, and closer to Jordan. It's less wear and tear on my thumbs, now that I'm not texting him a hundred times a day."

"You have been since we left Bethlehem," Jordan teased.

"That's temporary."

His mother shook her head. "You kids and your cell phones."

"It's different for you," Jordan said. "You're not allowed to turn on your phone at work. But for Rick, other than face-to-face meetings with customers, he can do almost his whole job from his phone."

"It's a brave, new world, Mrs. C."

"Yes, Rick, I'm aware of that. My generation invented it."

Jordan shook his head in exasperation. "What time is Mike coming over today?"

"Around eleven," his mom said

"Which reminds me," Rick said, "I should probably get home before my mom starts wondering where I am."

He squeezed Jordan's shoulder affectionately and gave him a bright smile. But it held no depth of emotion, and after the night they'd spent together, it made Jordan's heart hurt that they had to pretend to be friends.

"Merry Christmas, Mrs. C." Rick gave her a quick kiss on the cheek before leaving.

Jordan's eyes followed his car out of the driveway. His whole body ached at his absence.

"So Rick fell asleep in your bed last night?"

"It's no big deal, Mom."

"Maybe not for him, but it is for you. You feel more for him than friendship—I can see it in your face—and he's encouraging it. A real friend would be more careful than that."

Jordan gritted his teeth. *Twenty-four hours.* In one more day, Rick would come out, and he could tell his mother the truth.

"I don't have any illusions about Rick's feelings for me. He's my best friend, Mom."

"As long as it isn't one-sided."

"One-sided, how?"

She shrugged and sipped her coffee. "You're a generous person. Rick is self-centered, always has been."

"Not when it comes to me. He'd do anything for me. Literally *anything*."

She shook her head. "It worries me that you believe that."

He scowled. "Maybe it's an exaggeration, but not by much. Mom, you've seen him a couple of times a year since high school. It isn't fair to hold things against him that he did as a kid. Besides, even then, he was incredibly loyal. Remember how he quit scouting when they kicked me out? He'd been talking about how he was going to make Eagle Scout since second grade. He gave that up for *me*."

"His dad had a lot to do with that."

"I think it was the other way around. Mr. Ferguson would have stayed a Scoutmaster if Rick hadn't quit."

"That's not how I remember it."

"You didn't really know much about it." He struggled against the emotion building inside him. He didn't want to fight with his mom about this, but he needed to set the record straight. "You didn't see the expression on Rick's face when he first found out, or when he realized that no amount of appeals would change the outcome. He was more upset about it than I was. Maybe because I knew that if I came out, it would be the end of scouting for me. Rick had no idea. He couldn't comprehend how they could make a choice like that."

"After you came out, he was not a good friend to you."

"He was the best possible friend to me. He started dating Cynthia—so we didn't hang out together all the time like we used to—but that was just part of growing up."

"And because he didn't want anyone to think *he* was gay."

"Mom, he was fifteen. An organization he admired and felt a part of had just *rejected* me for being gay. So yeah, maybe he was wary about the possibility of facing that kind of discrimination, too, if people thought he was gay by association. But the guy had my back. He made sure I knew he wasn't going to treat me any differently, and he wouldn't let anyone else treat me differently, either."

She sighed. "Jordy, I didn't mean to upset you. I'm sorry, this is no conversation to have Christmas morning. I just worry about you—that's my job."

"You don't have to worry about Rick. Please trust my judgment on this. I know him better than anyone does."

"I suppose that's true. And this living situation won't last forever. You'll both start dating and want to settle down with other people..." Her voice trailed off as she opened the refrigerator door. "I bought us some cinnamon rolls to have for breakfast since they're your favorite. How about you start another pot of coffee while I pop these in the oven?"

He nodded and complied. No point in continuing this conversation until he could be honest with her. They'd keep covering the same territory, and she would feel deceived as it was.

As much as he hated to think it, he couldn't wait for Christmas Day to be over.

Rick snuck inside his parents' house, but his mother was already up making the stuffing for the twenty-pound turkey. She scowled at him. "Where did you go so early?"

"Fell asleep at Jordy's house. We were watching the *Christmas Story* marathon—"

"Oh." She giggled. "Fra-*gi*-le. Must be Italian." She dumped the chopped celery and onions into a pan of melted butter. "I remember when that movie first came out. It was an instant classic."

"Thirty-year anniversary this year."

He and Jordy had watched enough of the marathon to pick up that tidbit of information. He hoped it added authenticity to his story. When he'd learned Jordan's mom was spending the night at Mike's, he'd decided to spend Christmas Eve being naughty instead of nice. Nothing Santa brought could compare to the gifts his lover had given him. He'd happily settle for a lump of coal in his stocking.

He'd hoped to leave before Jordan's mom got home. Not that he didn't want to see her, but he didn't know what to *say* to her. Jordan wanted him to be sincere, but that was tough when she showed no desire to communicate with him at all.

He started the coffee since he knew his mother wanted some but would put all her energy into getting the bird into the oven first. She was very focused when it came to holiday preparations. She had a checklist in her mind and she followed it religiously.

Kat shuffled in wearing a fluffy white sweater over pajama pants and slippers. "Why are people up so early?" Her voice was gravelly, her eyes half-shut.

"Merry Christmas to you, too." He hugged her and planted a big kiss on her temple.

"Oh, yeah. Happy birthday, baby Jesus."

He chuckled and stroked her hair before she broke away. "So what is there to eat in this place?" she asked.

"Careful, you don't want to spoil your appetite."

"Mom. It's seven-thirty. Dinner is at one. I think I'll be okay." She took a vanilla yogurt and an orange out of the refrigerator. She set it on the table, then dragged Rick into the family room.

"So," she said in a low tone, "you spent the night at Jordan's? Sneaky."

"It's our first Christmas together as a couple. You can't fault us for wanting to wake up together Christmas morning."

"I don't fault you. I think it's adorable. Also, I'm jealous. Last summer, when you guys were playing one-

on-one in the driveway, and he took off his shirt... I
thought I would die from the sheer shining beauty of
it."

"I know, right?"

"So what is a hot guy like that doing, slumming with
a guy like you?"

"This may come as a surprise to you, but in some
circles, I'm considered good looking."

She shook her head. "Sorry, I just don't see it."

He grinned. "You know how Mom complains that
both of us look just like Dad?"

"Well I guess there is *something* of a resemblance,"
she conceded.

He hugged her. "I miss hanging out with you, Kat.
I've just moved to Bethlehem, and now you're moving
away in a few months."

"There are no law schools in the Lehigh Valley."

"You were accepted at Penn."

"*Et tu, Brute?*"

"I want you to be happy. I just wish you could be
happy here."

The coffee maker gurgled, signaling the end of the
cycle. He headed into the kitchen, Kat following.

"Anything I can do, Mom?" she asked.

"Well, I could have used some help chopping the
vegetables earlier, but that's all done now. The bird's
ready to go into the oven." She washed the stuffing
from her hands and dried them, then took the mug of
coffee with milk that Rick handed her. "Thank you,
dear. That's very thoughtful."

He put the roasting pan with the heavy stuffed
turkey into the oven, and she gave him a broad smile.
"Now that *that's* done," she said, "we can sit down and
enjoy our coffee."

"I could peel the potatoes," Kat said, "or the yams."

"It's too early. We can do that around ten. Come eat. Your yogurt is getting warm."

"I don't think my stomach can handle yogurt this morning," she said, putting the container back in the refrigerator. "I think I'll just take a shower."

"Katharine, for heaven's sake, have a cup of coffee and your orange with us."

"I'll eat later." She disappeared up the stairs.

His mother shook her head. "I'll never understand that girl."

"She's an introvert. Too much activity overwhelms her. Did you read that book *Quiet* she gave you?"

"I'm supposed to read a book by some doctor in order to understand my own daughter?"

"I don't think the author is actually a doctor—"

"Then what does she know?" His mother sighed. "I'm sorry, I didn't mean to snap. I just want this to be a nice Christmas, and Kat is already mad at me. I don't even know what I did."

Rick said nothing, determined to avoid getting into the middle of their issues.

After they finished their coffee, Rick headed upstairs to Kat's room and knocked on the door.

"It's open."

She lay on the bed staring at the ceiling, now dressed in gray slacks and a red sweater with a white lace collar.

He closed the door and sat on the bed beside her. "You okay?"

"She gets up at the ass-crack of dawn to make the stuffing, and then berates me for not being there to help her. She *knows* I hate to cook. Yet she keeps roping me into these domestic activities. I'm not the one who invited thirty people for dinner. If it were up to me, we'd have a potluck, or hire Jewish caterers. But no, Mom wouldn't think of it. She has to be the impeccable hostess because that feeds her ego. It's unreasonable to do all she does for the holiday, and she expects me to join her in her megalomania." She sat up. "But you see how grateful she was to you for making her a fucking cup of coffee."

"Kat, it's not a contest. She's upset, too. Can't you try to play nice with her today? Please, for me? I need her to be in a good mood tomorrow."

"Fine. I'll try." She laid her head on his shoulder. "Am I being a big baby about this?"

"Not exactly. The things you get upset about are definitely real. But you don't have to let them bother you so much."

"I know. She just pushes all my buttons."

"She created your buttons."

Kat chuckled. "Yes, she did." She looked up at him. "Do you have buttons?"

"Mine are different." He looked down. "I realized, talking to Dad at Thanksgiving, that a lot of my denial about my sexuality started when the Boy Scouts kicked Jordy out. The world didn't feel like a safe place to me after that."

"Aww." She squeezed his forearm.

"Maybe I'm just paranoid. All I know is, everything is going to change tomorrow, but I don't know *how*."

"Everything isn't going to change. *Some* things will—some for the worse, and some for the better. When you came out to me, it brought us closer, don't you think?"

"If by 'closer,' you mean that you text me more often, usually with dirty pictures attached—"

"They're not dirty. They're artistic. They're a celebration of the male form."

"That they are."

She hugged him again. "I'm glad that I have you. At least one person in the world understands me."

"Oh, I think Dad understands you. He just wishes you and Mom could get along."

Kat released him. "Ugh. I need to be nice to her today, don't I."

He shrugged. "She *is* under a lot of stress, making dinner for thirty people."

"Why would she want to make dinner for thirty people? Only an insane person would want to do that." She shook her head. "Sorry. I need to get out of that mindset."

"She does it because it's the one day all year the whole family gets together. You *love* that about Christmas."

"Yeah, I do. So I guess I should be more appreciative." She pointed a finger at him. "I'm not giving up on the idea of Jewish caterers, though."

He laughed. "Maybe next year."

Jordan put the cover on a stoneware dish of candied sweet potatoes to keep them warm. The electric knife whirred as Mike carved the turkey. The scent of sage and rosemary filled the air. The savory aroma heightened the gnawing in Jordan's stomach.

The two families sat with Mike at the head of the table. To one side were Jordan and his mom, to the other were Mike's grown children, Diana and Ben. They were both redheads, a trait they had apparently inherited from their mother. This was only their third Christmas since they'd lost her to a drunk driver, so they were still adjusting to new holiday traditions.

"Sweet potatoes, anyone?" Ben's wife Ashlee asked from the foot of the table, seeming eager to break the silence. Apparently the purpose of this small gathering was to see how the families blended, and so far, they didn't.

Jordan tried to put himself into the proper frame of mind. He looked around the table. Diana, a college junior, was super quiet. Her pale coloring—ivory skin, soft blue eyes, strawberry-blond hair—allowed her to blend into the background. She was the kind of girl that interfering matrons would describe as "pretty if only she'd smile more." He couldn't blame her for looking kind of lost, and not wanting to participate in this forced celebration.

Ben, a couple of years out of college, worked in the finance industry, as he described it. It was only after meeting him a few times that Jordan realized Ben was a bank teller. He either had an inflated view of himself or a narcissistic personality disorder. Jordan hadn't figured out which yet.

Ashlee seemed like the one person at the table Jordan could hold a tolerable conversation with. He was grateful they were seated together. Petite with waves of blond hair, she was talkative, pretty, and kind.

"Your mom says you've got some money to invest, now that you've got a roommate," she said.

He shook his head. "I can't believe she mentioned that to you."

"It may seem early since you just started working, but I really recommend talking to a financial advisor to start you off on the right track. I've got a couple of colleagues in Allentown I could recommend."

"To be honest, I'm hoping to start my own firm, so that's not a bad idea."

"Good! I'll write down some names for you. So this roommate, your mom says he's a high school friend?"

"We've been best friends since first grade."

"Oh, wow. She made it sound like he was just sort of crashing with you until he found a place."

"No. He's moved in permanently."

His mom broke in, "Then I hope you've got a written agreement with him about what his financial obligations are. I cosigned on your mortgage, so I know that place wasn't cheap."

"Jordy, did I ever tell you about my best friend from high school?" Mike asked. Jordan bristled. He liked Mike but hated when the man called him *Jordy*. That nickname was reserved for family and close friends, and Mike was neither—at least not yet.

"My best friend Pete," Mike began, "dropped out of college after freshman year. Flunked out would be a better word for it. He seemed to think he was there to party more than for academics, and his grades reflected it. He got a job selling cars, and he did all right. But whenever we'd go out for dinner or anything, he'd say, 'The doctor can pay for it,' when the check would come. Even when I was still a resident, working insane hours for shit pay. He resented the fact that I was a professional, and that my earning power was higher than his. But at the same time, he seemed to think it released him from any sort of reciprocity. When one person in a relationship is always giving, and the other is always taking, that's no way to live. Eventually, I had to let the friendship drop."

"I'm sorry to hear that, Mike," Jordan replied. "I'm fortunate that I don't have any friends who would use me like that. My friend Rick, for example, is the most generous person I know. When I complained a few weeks ago that the bedroom closet was too cramped, he paid for a designer to come in and build a custom closet system. I didn't even know he was doing it—he wanted to surprise me."

"That's kind of impulsive, don't you think?" his mother said. "What if you weren't happy with his choices?"

"Rick knows what I like." He cut a slice of white meat and stuffed it into his mouth. He was done with this conversation, and if occupying himself with chewing was the only way to get out of it, then that's what he would do.

# Chapter 5

The influx of relatives lifted Rick's spirits. He had coat duty, so that meant he got to welcome everyone as they arrived, wish them a Merry Christmas, and help them out of their hats and scarves before dumping the coats on his parents' king-sized bed. He was lucky to have all these cousins, aunts, and uncles in his life.

Kat, meanwhile, arranged the gifts under the twelve-foot tall tree that stood in the spacious, open foyer. It was decorated with white lights and red balls and a silver garland, but most festive were the wooden ornaments they had hand-painted as a family when he and Kat were children.

Against his mother's protests, the extended family had taken to the tradition of drawing names, but that still meant thirty-two gifts to unwrap, one at a time so everyone could ooh and ah. It was a long but joyful process, and Rick's favorite part of the holiday. The love that went into the gift selections was touching, and reminded him that not everyone had the abundance or the close-knit family he did.

Kat was in a better mood now that their aunts had taken over kitchen duty. She was laughing and whispering with their female cousins, getting caught up with the latest news.

"How can it be that a pretty girl like you doesn't have a boyfriend?" Uncle Scott, their dad's brother, greeted her, planting a kiss on her cheek.

"I'll be busy with law school for the next three years. I'm not looking for Mr. Right. I'm happy with Mr. Right Now."

"Katharine, you will give your father a heart attack," her mom called from the kitchen.

"You remember my friend Lexie, who dated the same guy all through college, then dumped him when she went to Duke Law? The poor guy had to be pumped full of anti-depressants and put on suicide watch. That's a much better choice, right?"

Her mother stepped into the foyer and glared at her. "When I was your age—"

"Erica, let it go," Aunt Pauline said, pushing a lock of straight, dark hair out of her eyes. A year younger than their mother, she was a juvenile court judge and basically didn't put up with shit from anyone. "When you were Kat's age, you'd been dating Steve for four years and would have followed him to the ends of the earth. Young women today are more career-focused. That's not a bad thing. For the first time in history, women coming out of advanced degree programs are making more money than their male counterparts. Kat has a bright future ahead of her. She doesn't need a steady boyfriend to make that happen."

"I got married straight out of college," said Aunt Torie, the youngest of the four sisters, sipping her white wine. "Look how happy that made me."

Rick couldn't remember her first husband. They'd divorced before he started kindergarten. He didn't know the details, but he knew they weren't pretty. She'd been married to her second husband for almost twenty years, and the guy clearly adored her. Some people, like Rick's parents, were ready for marriage at a young age. Some needed a little longer to figure it out or to find the right person. And there was nothing wrong with that.

If he and Jordan had dated all through college, as they'd tried to at first, would they have been happier? He liked the life they had together now, and he wouldn't change anything about the path that had led them to it, even the mistakes. It had been a long learning process, but maybe that's what Rick had needed, to be as confident as he was now.

His dad passed through on the way to the kitchen and put his arms around Rick's mom. "Are your sisters picking on you again, hon?"

"Always." She kissed him. "I'd still follow you to the ends of the earth."

"Please, no PDAs," Kat protested. "We have to eat soon."

And eat they did. Turkey, ham, stuffing, mashed potatoes, yams, gravy, cranberry sauce, green beans, corn, asparagus, dinner rolls, sweet cream butter. Rick allowed himself to indulge for just this one day.

"How's the new job going?" Uncle Scott asked.

"Good." Rick scooped a helping of yams onto his plate. "My boss has been welcoming, plus the office is ten minutes from the house…They've given me some of the accounts from the woman I'm replacing, so I'm not starting over from scratch, at least. Not that I mind working my butt off to get new clients. That's the most satisfying part of the job for me. But having old customers renew their contract, and just watching the money roll in, is good, too."

"I hope you won't get too settled there." His mother passed the rolls. "The regional headquarters is in Philly. That's where you want to be."

"I spent a year trying to get transferred to Allentown because I want to *work* in Allentown. That's my home now. Jordan and I love it there, or at least in Bethlehem, where we live. I can see myself putting down roots."

"You'll never make it higher than district manager if you stay in that office."

He shrugged. "I don't know that I'm going to stay with this company for the rest of my career. Jordan and I might go into business together. We've got complementary skills. If we work hard, we can make it happen."

She sawed into a chunk of dark meat and dipped it in gravy. "Friends becoming business partners is not always a smart move. A steady paycheck is important when you've got a family to support."

"Mom, I work on commission. I don't have a steady paycheck, anyway."

"But you're good at your job."

"I'm very good at my job. That doesn't mean I want to spend the rest of my life working for someone else."

"When you have kids—"

"What if he doesn't want kids?" Kat plopped some mashed potatoes onto her plate.

"How could you suggest such a thing? Of course he wants kids."

"No, you want grandchildren, and you just assume that Rick and I will oblige."

"Katharine!" his mom cried, eyes wide with shock and horror. "Are you saying you don't want children?"

"I'm saying you shouldn't make assumptions."

Rick shook his head. "Kat and I both want kids. She's just making a point."

His mom glared at her. "Why would you do that to me on Christmas?"

"Why are you telling Rick how to live his life?"

The signs of irritation on his mother's face briefly changed to deep hurt, but she covered quickly. "I'm not telling him how to live his life. I'm giving advice, based on my experience. That's my job as his mother."

"Will you two stop ganging up on your mom?" their dad ordered.

"Fine," Rick said. "But for the record, all I did was say I was going to live my life according to my choices. You guys can approve or disapprove, but you don't get a say anymore. You lost that right five years ago."

"Damn straight," Kat said.

"You better be quiet, missy," Rick said, "or you'll be putting *yourself* through law school."

"Are we done now?" Their mother massaged her temples. "I'm getting a headache."

Kat stood and walked up behind their mother's chair, draping her arms over their mother's shoulders and resting her cheek on her hair. "I'm sorry, Mommy. You know I love you more than anything."

Their mom clutched Kat's hands. "I love you, too, sweet girl."

"Thank you for making Christmas wonderful." Tears sparkled in Kat's eyes, and she sniffled.

"You're welcome, Kitty-Kat."

Kat managed to sit on her mother's lap and snuggle against her, even though Kat was now the taller woman.

Her mom stroked Kat's hair. "My beautiful girl. I'm amazed at the woman you've grown up to be. You've made me proud every day of your life."

"You've always taken such good care of us."

"It's a pleasure, sweetheart. But I *don't* try to tell you what to do. It's not wrong for me to voice my opinions, is it?"

"As long as they're just opinions."

"Of course they are. I support your choices no matter what. I trust your judgment."

Kat pulled back and scowled at her. "You do?"

"How can you question that? Your dad and I raised you to be independent thinkers."

"Then why do you get so mad at me when we disagree?"

"I don't get mad at you, sweetheart. I just worry. I've spent the past twenty-two years imagining all the bad things that could happen to you, so I could protect you from them. It's a hard habit to break."

Kat squeezed her one more time, then went back to her own seat.

It was sweet to see them getting along, but Rick knew it couldn't last. Even though everything his mother had said was true, things were changing. He didn't know where Kat would end up, but it wouldn't be in Pennsylvania, no matter how much the rest of the family wanted her there. She hated the cold and the snow. Even as a little kid, she spent snow days inside, reading and snuggled in a blanket next to the fire, rather than outside making snowmen.

This might be the last Christmas they all spent together like this. The realization hit him hard, like a weight crushing his chest. His family was already changing. Staying in the closet wouldn't keep that from happening. All the things about coming out that scared him were already unfolding. The family he'd grown up in wasn't the central focus of his life anymore. Jordan was, and the life they were building together. And as excited as he was about that future, it shattered him to think of the happy childhood he was leaving behind.

As the sun settled low in the sky, Rick stood at the window of his dad's study and gazed over the dry landscape, trees bare of leaves, the remnants of snow filling the hollows of the lawn.

The sound of footsteps on the hardwoods interrupted his melancholy. He turned. His father stopped and grinned. "There you are." His dad entered and closed the door behind him. "We're trying to get a foursome together for pinochle, but...Something wrong?" He turned on a table lamp, and it suffused the room with a yellow glow.

"Mom works so hard to keep the traditions alive...but it's over now, you know that, right? Kat and I are grown. We've got our own lives. Tradition won't keep us in these neat little roles you and Mom have carved out for us."

His father clamped his hand on Rick's shoulder. "Where's this coming from?"

"For over a year, I've been working to get transferred to Allentown. No sooner do I get there than Mom is talking about me moving to Philly, being regional manager…That's not what I want. It's like she hasn't been listening to anything I've said. Allentown isn't a stepping stone for me. It's home."

"I'm sure she didn't mean—"

"Dad, come on. She's been doing it my whole life. When I made the football team in high school, the first thing she did was talk about how proud she would be once I made first string. And once I did that, she started talking about my becoming captain. I'd never thought about becoming captain until she started pushing me. And I'm not saying it was bad. She's always pushed me to challenge myself, to reach for more. But I can't keep reaching for *her* dreams. I've got to reach for my own."

"She just wants what's best for you."

"But who is she to decide that? Did you see how disappointed she was when she found out that Jess has a boyfriend? I couldn't be more relieved, but Mom doesn't want to hear that. No matter how many times I tell her Jess and I were wrong for each other, she doesn't want to let it go."

"You can't hold that against her. She thought of Jess as a daughter."

"She shouldn't have done that. I didn't think of Jess as a wife."

"I know your mother can be pushy sometimes—"

"When I try living on my terms, I feel like I'm failing her. She'll never accept me for who I am."

His father's face reddened. "Your mother has been working for weeks to make today special for you and your sister, running herself ragged, for no other reason than to show how much she loves you. To show how special family is to her. How can you question her devotion?"

"She's weaving a web to lock us in. Most parents would be thrilled if their daughter was accepted at Stanford Law. Mom is doing everything she can to stop it."

"Can you blame her for not wanting Kat to move three thousand miles away?"

"Yes, Dad, I can. Because that's Kat's dream, and Mom is trying to take it away from her."

His dad scowled. "I don't think she wants to go to Stanford. I think she wants to go to Duke."

"Then why—"

"To soften the blow. If your mom is worried about Kat moving to California, she'll be relieved if Kat moves to North Carolina instead."

"Kat told you that?"

"No, but that's what I would do if I were her."

Rick shook his head, anger building in his chest at the way everyone in his family—including him—felt like they had to tiptoe around his mom to avoid upsetting her. He stormed past his father and pulled open the door. "I'm going out."

"Where?"

"I'm a grown man. I don't have to tell you where."

"Be careful. The snow melt on the road freezes after dark."

As if Rick needed to be reminded of that. As if he hadn't lived in the mountains for a year.

He grabbed his coat from the closet and headed out into the brisk air, needing Jordan in his arms, Jordan to clear the chaos from his mind.

Jordan entered his mom's kitchen. The counters were cleared and wiped, the stainless-steel sink gleaming. No remnant remained to hint at the dinner for six served earlier in the day.

Nothing but the pumpkin pie. Jordan took off the foil and cut himself a sliver, using the server to usher it onto a china dessert plate.

Ben, Mike's son, sauntered in and cut himself a big hunk of pie, not bothering with a plate and shoving it toward his mouth with his hands. Ben was about five-foot-nine with curly auburn hair and a pinched face. He might be called handsome by some standards, but to Jordan's eye, his features were lined and hardened by mean-spiritedness, by defensiveness that led to bullying out of a sense of insecurity.

"Good pie," Ben said as he chewed. "You're mom's a hell of a cook."

Jordan nodded. His mom could put on a spread for special occasions, but she disliked cooking. Mostly he'd grown up on pre-prepared meals. Her work as a nurse didn't leave much time for domesticity. Jordan had taken on some of the household chores and kept the place neat. At some point during his childhood, he had realized how hard it was for her, being a single mom. She'd put her life on hold for him, not dating until he was older. He was glad she had found Mike, even if his son was a prick.

Ben set his pie on a napkin and poured himself a glass of milk. He gulped down half of it. "So," he said to Jordan, "take it up the ass lately?"

"Thanks for the offer, but I'm in a relationship." Jordan watched Ben's face redden. "Unless you want to try a three-way. Or bring your wife along, and we'll make it four." He clapped Ben's shoulder, then took his plate into the living room where the rest of the group was chatting.

His phone beeped with a text from Rick. *On my way over.*

He couldn't help smiling at the words on his phone. He replied, *Good. Miss you. Ben's an asshole.*

Jordan was on his last bite of pie when the doorbell rang. "Sit," he said to his mother. "I'll get it."

He looked out the sidelights to see Rick shivering in his black wool coat and plaid scarf. A smile spread over Jordan's face, and the weight on his heart lifted. He hadn't realized until that moment how much he had missed Rick all day. Christmas meant spending the day with the people you love most in the world, and the person he loved most hadn't been there.

Jordan opened the door and pulled Rick inside. He looked around to make sure they couldn't be seen, then planted a kiss on those cold lips. "How was your day?"

"Sucked. Missed you."

Rick hung up his coat, then they joined the others in the living room. Jordan introduced him to Mike's family.

Rick looked Ben up and down. "Jordy mentioned you. You play hockey, right?"

"Yeah, for a local team."

"You're not like I pictured you. You're a little guy." Rick patted the top of Ben's head. "How much do you bench?"

"Uh, one-eighty, one-eighty-five."

"You'd never know it to look at Jordy, but he benches two-twenty-five. He does most of his reps at a lower weight so he doesn't bulk up. He's strong, though. I wouldn't want to have to fight him."

Jordan's mom scowled at him. "Why would Ben have to fight Jordan?"

"I didn't mean to imply that," Rick said. "Some people think gay men are easy targets. Jordan could hold his own in a fight, and he'd have me as backup."

"It's Christmas, Rick. Let's not talk about violence, shall we?"

"Sorry, Mrs. C. You're right."

"You know, Rick," Mike said, "her name is Mrs. Callahan. That's more respectful."

Rick stared, rubbing his hand over his fist. "You're right, Dr. Kovatch. My apologies." He turned to Jordan, eyes wide in a *what-the-fuck* look.

"Rick, I understand you're in sales," Ashlee said.

"My degree is in business. I might go for my MBA in the evenings once Jordan and I get settled. Lehigh's got a good program."

Ashlee nodded. "My boss has an MBA from Lehigh. I can give you her contact information if you'd like to ask her some questions."

"That would be great, thanks."

Jordan scowled at him. "You've never mentioned an MBA before."

He shrugged. "You've got a master's. My sister's going to law school. You know how competitive I am."

"How are you going to finance it?" Ashlee asked. "My bank has a competitive student loan program."

"My employer offers educational benefits. They pay a hundred percent, as long as you can use your degree at your job."

"Good deal," Ben said, apparently deciding that being nice to Rick was a better choice than an actual fistfight.

Jordan probed a little further. "When did you start with this MBA idea?"

He shrugged. "My mom and I were talking about how I might want something more stable than working on commission once I've got a family to support."

"So she suggested an MBA?"

"No, that was my idea. But she'll love it."

Jordan shook his head. "You are such a mama's boy."

Rick's eyes widened. "I am not!"

Jordan's mom laughed. "Oh, Ricky, that's the funniest thing I've heard all day."

# Chapter 6

Rick woke alone as the sun's first rays crept through the windows of his childhood bedroom. The place that once held the ultimate sense of security for him now filled him with apprehension. This day would be the watershed moment for him, the line of demarcation between childhood and adulthood. High school graduation, college graduation, his first real job—all had been stepping stones. But coming out as gay would be the moment he acted alone to choose what he wanted for himself, and not what his parents wanted for him.

He carried the sense of dread with him when he went downstairs for breakfast. Unlike Christmas morning, when they got up early and gathered in the kitchen in their pajamas, this morning everyone was showered and dressed. On the counter sat a slab of bacon, two cartons of eggs, the pancake griddle, and a bag of frozen hashed browns. His mom was going all out, as if they hadn't consumed three thousand calories the day before.

"We can't just have the eggs over easy?" Kat said. "You really need me to chop the peppers and mushrooms, and grate the cheese for omelets?"

"Vegetables make for a more balanced meal."

"If you're going for balanced, then this is too many carbs. Let's skip the pancakes."

"But your dad loves pancakes."

"Dad is almost fifty years old. He can do with fewer pancakes in his life."

Their mother rolled her eyes. "Fine."

Rick poured a cup of coffee and found his dad in the study. "You don't actually come in here to work, do you," he said as he sat.

His dad grinned. "This room is how I've stayed sane all these years."

Rick nodded. "They're getting along better today."

"Kat's putting in some effort, at least."

"Really? You're putting this all on Kat?"

"Not entirely. But your mother tries so hard, for very little reward. It breaks her heart." His dad sat forward. "When Kat says, 'I hate to cook,' what your mom hears is, 'I hate spending time with my mom in the kitchen.' Kat has never liked doing girly things. Remember when she turned thirteen, and your mom took her for her first manicure? Your mom thought that would make her feel grown-up. Instead, all she did was complain about it being a waste of time, and how she wanted to finish reading her Harry Potter book. She ended up ruining the manicure because she couldn't just keep her hands still for ten minutes."

"It was her birthday, not Mom's. Maybe Mom could try asking Kat what she wants, instead of making plans and getting disappointed when Kat doesn't want to go along with them."

"And maybe Kat could stop acting like every one of your mom's suggestions is designed to inconvenience her."

"Dad, you don't understand what it's like to be one of her kids. To have to listen to a constant running commentary on our lives. It's in my head now. I can't make a decision without worrying about how she'll react to it. I hate that."

"It's hard for her, too. You kids have been her whole life since the moment she got pregnant with you. She doesn't want to interfere, but she wants you close. And it hurts her that the two of you don't want that, too."

"That's not fair. We need to be able to make the best choices for our lives without worrying about mom's feelings."

His dad smirked. "Let me ask you a question. Why doesn't Kat want to go to law school at Penn?"

Rick's mouth popped open. He intuitively knew the answer to the question, but it never occurred to him that his parents did, too. Pain stabbed his heart. "Because she wants to get away from Mom."

"You think your mom doesn't understand that? You think it doesn't crush her?"

"If she could just let Kat be Kat—"

"She doesn't know how to get through to her. Every overture she makes toward her only daughter is rebuffed. Kat's got no excuse for that. She's not a teenager anymore."

"Mom treats her like one."

His dad scrubbed his face with his hands. "She sees you guys maybe once a month. Can't you just humor her? Let her mother you for a couple of days without getting so defensive?"

Rick tried to see the situation from his mother's point of view. He couldn't, not when he had so much else on his mind. Today, he had to stay focused on his own needs. He'd never get through it otherwise.

Forty-five minutes later, they sat down to a huge meal. The bacon smelled heavenly, and the omelets looked mouth-watering, but Rick's stomach was too fluttery for him to attempt more than hashed browns. Potatoes had always helped soothe his nausea when he was a kid.

Kat, seated next to him, kept reaching under the table to squeeze his hand. It helped to know he had her support. He had to get this over with. His mother, bless her interfering heart, gave him the perfect opening.

"Do you want me to come to Allentown one weekend to go house hunting with you?"

He scowled. "I…don't need a house. I'm living with Jordan."

"For now. But you can't stay with him indefinitely."

Rick bit his cheeks. He wasn't ready for this conversation. Once the words left his lips, he couldn't take them back.

"I see the way he looks at you," his mother scolded, "the way he's always looked at you. How is he going to feel when you bring a girl over? It's not fair to him."

His throat grew dry. He felt as if he'd lost the ability to speak. His heart rate had doubled, and it wasn't from the morning dose of caffeine. He *had* to say this. When he did, his whole world would change. His parents' world would change. But he had promised Jordy, and he owed it to himself.

"Mom, listen." He looked over at his father, who was pouring himself another mug of coffee. "Dad, you too. Come sit down. There's something I have to tell you."

"Rick..." His mother's face turned gray, and tears clouded her eyes. "Honey, are you sick?"

"No, Mom, I'm fine." He took her hand. "Sorry, I didn't mean to scare you. Everything is fine."

His dad sat down. "What is it, son?"

"It's complicated...or, well, it's not, really. It's just...I know you won't be happy about it, but I've been running from it for so long. I can't do it anymore."

Kat rubbed his arm, and tears stung his eyes. "I can't hurt another woman the way I did Jess, trying to be someone I'm not. It's not fair to her, and it's not fair to me. I deserve to be happy."

Kat moved her chair closer, and he clutched her arm. "Mom, I'm sorry. I know it's not what you want for me. Jordan and I aren't just roommates. We're a couple. For the first time, I'm happy—truly happy. Jordan and I belong together. We always have. It just took me a long time to realize it."

The mug in his father's hand hit the tabletop with a thump.

"I told myself I was bisexual, but I don't know if that's true. No woman has made me feel anything close to what Jordy makes me feel. I love him. I want to spend the rest of my life with him. That may be hard for you to hear, but it's not something I can change."

Tears formed in his mother's eyes. His father, looking stoic, stormed out of the house.

Rick leaned forward on his elbows and sank his face into his hands. He tried not to imagine what his father was thinking. It certainly couldn't be any worse than the fears that had haunted Rick ever since he and Jordan got together.

He looked up at his mother. "I'm sorry. I never wanted to disappoint you like this. I can't live a lie anymore. I can't live some pale version of life when Jordan fills every moment with color. He's my soul mate."

His mother was still, her eyes trained on her lap. "If you didn't love Jess, why did you stay with her so long? And Kristy and Amanda and Cynthia! How could you hurt those girls like that?"

"Because I didn't know. I was trying to figure out who I was. I like women. On some level, I'm attracted to them. But being with them, it just...it doesn't complete me. Jordy does."

"You don't seem gay."

"Why, because I'm not a stereotype?"

"I'm your mother. How could I not know?"

"*I* didn't know. When Jordy broke up with Damon...that's when I knew. I wasn't in love with Jess even after trying for a year. She's amazing. She deserves so much better than me. I hate that I hurt her. All I could think about was Jordy. He was available, and I had to have him."

"You're happy with this choice?"

"It isn't a choice. It's who I am."

She shook her head. "I don't mean being gay. I mean being with Jordy."

"Mom, he's half of me."

She shifted in her chair. "I suppose he is."

"Thank you. I'm sorry, I really am. I handled this badly. I wish I could take back all the years, all the pain I caused people. But honestly, I think I had to go through that to get here. To be certain, and to be okay with it. To be the man Jordy deserves."

"Of course."

His mother was staring out the window. He knew she wasn't really listening anymore. He rose and squeezed her shoulder, then went outside to find his father.

Rick found his dad in the tool shed, a large, open building behind the house. In addition to housing the lawn mower and the garden tools, it was a dry place to store the wood for the winter, to keep the fireplace going and save on heating bills.

Ax in hand, his dad was splitting wood. He looked over when Rick entered, then went back to what he was doing.

"Dad, let me do that."

"I'm not an old man. I'm forty-eight. You want to help? Stack that wood." He motioned toward the quartered logs lying about.

Silent, Rick arranged them carefully on the pile. It would be better to let his father speak when he was ready.

Finally, his father set down the ax. "How long have you known?"

"For a long time, I wasn't sure—"

"How long have you been attracted to men?"

Rick drew in his shoulders. This wasn't a comfortable conversation to have with anyone, least of all his father. "My feelings for Jordy started when I was eighteen."

"Good God, Rick! Five years? And you never once discussed it with me, asked for my advice. Did you think I would throw you out? Is that the man you think I am?"

Rick shrank from his father's anger. "I didn't want to disappoint you."

"You know what disappoints me? You broke Jess's heart. Your mom and I had started to think of her as a daughter. And you let us think that way. You let *her* think that way."

"I didn't know. I thought I was bi. Maybe I just wanted to be. Wanted to be the son you and mom expected."

"Rick, it's not a son's job to meet his parents' expectations. It's his job to be the best man he can be. And you failed."

Rick chewed his lips, blinking back tears.

"Fuck." His father shook his head, then threw his arms around Rick. "I'm sorry. That was an awful thing to say."

Rick's body heaved as sobs erupted from him, fueled by years of worry and grief and feeling not good enough. His father held him tight.

"Rick, I'm sorry. I'm proud of the man you've become. I know you didn't hurt Jess intentionally. If you were confused, you should have talked to me. I could have helped you through it."

He let his father's words sink in, then clutched him harder, all his fears gently flowing away.

"Why couldn't you trust me?" his father asked, a catch in his voice. "When Jordy came out, I stood up for him, wrote a long letter to the Boy Scouts, resigned as Scoutmaster when they wouldn't reinstate him. Did you think I was homophobic? That I would treat you differently?"

"It's not the same as with Jordy. I'm your son."

"I've always thought of Jordy like a son, too. And now I guess he really is."

Rick wiped his eyes on the sleeve of his jacket. His father was beaming.

"You're not upset?" Rick asked.

"I wish you could have been honest with me. But no, I'm not upset. You and Jordy." He shook his head. "That makes me happy."

Rick blinked. "Really?"

"You two are perfect for each other."

"We kinda are." Rick smiled, then shuffled his feet. "To be honest, I wanted to tell you. I've wanted to for a long time. But I wasn't ready to tell Mom, and I couldn't ask you to keep it from her. She's got this image she expects me to live up to—"

"Your mom sets the bar high for you because you rise to the occasion." His dad shook his head. "What a dumb shit you are. All your mom and I ever wanted was to encourage you. As a little boy, you were always a happy kid, content with the way things were. But you didn't have a lot of ambition. Your mom, in her subtle way, helped you set goals for yourself, and you always saw them through—you wanted to make us proud. You were externally motivated."

Rick nodded, unsure what to make of that.

"We learned early on that we couldn't do the same things with Kat, though. If we praised her for her performance at something, she got angry or stopped doing it. She was internally motivated and didn't want anyone else paying attention. That's why your mom feels comfortable telling Kat she doesn't want her to go to Stanford. Kat's going to do what she wants anyway. Whereas you would be torn up inside, because you didn't want to disappoint your mom."

Rick combed his fingers through his hair. *Wow.* That was his childhood in a nutshell, and it had been *conscious* on his parents' part.

"Do you think Mom will be able to accept that I'm with Jordan now?"

His father shrugged. "It'll take her some time to adjust. Hell, it'll take me some time to adjust." He creased his brow. "Yesterday, you said you wanted kids—"

"Kat's going to donate her eggs."

His dad stared. "Wow. That'll make your mom happy. So you and Kat have got this all worked out already?"

Rick winced.

"How long has she known?"

"A month, but don't tell Mom. Jordan wouldn't agree to a relationship unless I came out to at least one person who mattered."

"Good for Jordan." His dad chuckled. "Wait. The guy Jordan talked about at Thanksgiving, the guy who was closeted, that was you?"

"Um, yeah. It was a real kick in my butt." He drew his coat close against the cold. "It's better, right? That I'm out?"

"Of course. It's always better to be honest with us. We're your parents—we love you no matter what. Don't you know that by now?"

"I didn't think you'd stop loving me. I was afraid you'd be disappointed."

His dad laid his hands on Rick's shoulders. "What I want for you is what I've always wanted. A career that's meaningful, a partner who makes you happy, kids if you want them, enough money to be comfortable. You can have all that with Jordan. He's probably the only person who'll put up with you, anyway."

"I know, right?"

His dad patted his back. "We're good here. Go back into the house, talk to your mom. It's probably sunk in now, and she's moved on to the freaking out stage."

His mom was in the kitchen scrubbing the countertops, even though they were already sparkling.

"How did I not know?" she said when she saw him, a sob in her voice. "I'm supposed to know everything about you, and somehow I missed something that huge."

"I didn't want you to know. I've been actively hiding it because I wasn't sure it would lead to anything."

"Have you been tested?"

"Mom, come on. Think about that for a second. I tell you I'm gay, and you immediately assume I haven't been safe. Of course I have. Jordy has, too. But yes, we've both been tested, and we're both clean."

"Thank God."

"I just want you to know, this doesn't change anything. I still want to get married, settle down, have kids. Only it will be with Jordan, instead of a woman. Can you live with that?"

"I...well, of course I can. If that's what you want. I just don't understand *why*. You said you were bi— maybe you just haven't found the right woman."

"I used to think I was bi. I don't anymore. And even if I were, it doesn't matter. I've found the right *man*. I want to be with Jordan."

"But Rick, have you really thought about this? There's still such a stigma attached to it. Gay marriage isn't even legal in Pennsylvania."

"It's legal in *Utah* now. It'll be legal here soon enough."

She sighed. "I just worry about you."

"I've thought this through carefully. I understand what I'm getting into. Ultimately, I don't have a choice. I love Jordan. That's the beginning and end of it."

"It's a difficult path, Rick."

"I know that. He's worth it."

"Are you sure it isn't just—" She broke off, mouth pinched.

He drew his brow. "What?"

"Sexual."

He bit his cheeks. "It is in the sense that I don't want to be with a woman ever again."

"I don't understand that. All those pretty girls you dated..."

"Exactly. All those pretty girls. And yet, I'm with Jordan now. Doesn't that tell you something?"

"What if Jordan weren't an option? Would you be with another man?"

He shrugged. "I've never dated another man. I've thought about it, but never acted on those feelings. Jordy was the one I wanted."

"I just don't understand how you can change your mind like this."

"I didn't change my mind. Being with Jordan has helped me understand that I've never been in love with a woman, that I'm not capable of it. The intimate feelings I had for them weren't love. They never felt like enough, and now I understand why."

"Look, honey, you and Jordan have been friends so long, it's understandable that the relationship is easier for you than with someone else. But you haven't been a couple very long. Once you've been dating a while, you may find that it's just as difficult with him as it is with anyone else. I never felt like you really tried to fix the problems you had with Jess."

"The problem with Jess was that she wasn't Jordan. I don't love her—I never loved her. I'm not even attracted to her. Please try to understand that. For the first time in my life, I'm being true to who I am, and not who you want me to be. I deserve that. I deserve to be happy."

Anger flashed in her eyes. "This isn't about what I want. This is about what's best for you. Why do you and Kat think I'm manipulating you? I've lived longer, and I've experienced things you haven't. You should at least consider what I have to say."

"I've been living with this for five years. I've looked at it from every conceivable angle. I love Jordan, and I want to spend my life with him. And that's what I'm going to do."

Rick found Kat exactly where he expected her to be: in her room, working on her computer. She rose and hugged him. "How did it go with Dad?"

"Fine. He's pissed that I didn't tell him sooner, but he's cool with it."

"Mom doing any better?"

"She left for some retail therapy. I don't think it's quite sunk in yet—she still thinks I should date girls. She's got it in her head that I'm bi, and if I just work at it hard enough...Which is exactly what I've been doing for the past five years, and I'm done."

"From the things Cyn told me about the two of you...I think it's fair to say you were never bi. Bisexual men like vaginas."

His face warmed. "They're okay."

"They are not *okay*. They are fucking awesome."

He shrugged. "I'm lukewarm about them."

"That's because you're totally gay."

She mussed his hair, and he returned the favor. Soon, they were in a tickling fight, and fell onto the bed laughing.

Kat caught her breath and lay on her back. "Whatever I can do to help, I'm here."

"Just be nice to Mom."

"I'm trying really hard. I know she means well."

"She does, and this is a big thing to absorb, and you're going away to law school..." He pursed his lips. "Do you really want to go to Duke?"

"I've wanted to go to Duke since I was fourteen. The long summers, the mild winters...North Carolina sounds like heaven to me. And the Durham area has the highest percentage of PhDs per capita of anyplace in the country. My friend Lexie loves it there."

"And all this talk about Stanford..."

"Was a diversion."

He nodded. "So Dad was right."

"He usually is."

"The bastard." He sat up next to her. "I should go see Jordy. This is a big day for him, too. We don't have to hide anymore."

"You're coming out to the world?"

"Yep, and if they don't like it, they can kiss my ass."

Jordan's breakfast of fruit and cereal sat like a weight in his stomach as he placed his empty bowl into the dishwasher. His mom had spent the night at Mike's again, so he had the whole empty, silent house to himself to wait and brood.

The beep of his phone startled him. Rick's ringtone. He rushed to retrieve the message.

*Done. :) Dad's fine. Mom's freaking out but adjusting. Went shopping to console herself. I'm coming over to ravage you. <3*

Jordan breathed deep to calm himself, but he'd been waiting for this day too long. The desire to be with Rick clouded his brain. He watched out the window. When he saw the car, he smiled. Strange that Rick was driving his mom's car, but maybe she had taken his car shopping because it had a bigger trunk.

He stepped away from the window to avoid looking like a complete idiot. When the doorbell rang, he smoothed his hair and sweater, then opened it.

He blinked to see Rick's mom standing on the porch, her eyes steely. She put on a smile and said sweetly, "Jordan, honey, mind if I come in?"

He wasn't fooled. He stepped aside so she could enter, then took her coat, bracing for what was to come.

"Is your mother here?"

"No. Can I get you some coffee?"

"That would be lovely, if it's not too much trouble."

"The pot's still on." He poured the coffee into the first mug he could find, then added milk the way she liked it. He'd spent enough mornings in her house to know.

She thanked him as she took the mug, then sipped. She pursed her lips and spoke deliberately. "Jordan, I know that you love Rick. That you always have. But love means making sacrifices. You remember the time Rick fell off his bike when he was eight, and got sidewalk burn all down his leg? After I put peroxide on it, I made him get back on his bike, when all I wanted to do was hold him in my arms. I didn't want him to be afraid to ride again."

"You're a good mom, Mrs. F. No one would say otherwise."

"Thank you, dear, that's sweet, but it isn't my point. If you love Rick, you want the best for him. You understand as well as anyone the difficulties that life as a gay man brings. Do you want that for Rick? Wouldn't you spare him that if you could?"

"Mrs. Ferguson, I didn't turn Rick gay."

"No, of course not. But if he's bi—wouldn't he be happier with a woman?"

"He tried that, and it made him miserable. He's happy with me. Don't you want that for him?"

"Of course. If Jess wasn't the one, the solution isn't for him to turn to a man. It's to find the right woman."

"If you're asking me to bow out gracefully, that's not going to happen. Rick and I are building a life together. It's what we both want. I'm sorry if that makes you unhappy, but it's not going to change our decision."

"Don't be so sure of that."

"Mrs. F., I love you, you know that. But you really have two choices here. You can accept Rick for who he is and let him be happy with the life he's chosen. Or you can pressure him to be someone he's not, make him miserable, and lose his respect forever."

"You don't understand what he needs."

Jordan smirked. "I know exactly what he needs. Are you really going to ask him to choose between us? Because if you do, you'd better think seriously about the consequences. It's a battle you can't win."

"Rick won't turn his back on his family."

"It sounds like you're the one turning your back on him. Don't think for a moment he won't see it that way. He's been agonizing over this for weeks, worried that you would reject him. If you do that, you will lose him. Things will never be the same between you again."

She set down her mug. "I thought you were a better man than this. A better friend. You're so caught up in your own desires, you can't see what you're doing to Rick."

"This isn't my doing. Rick initiated the relationship. If you want to have this talk, have it with him. I won't play the heavy for you. I won't give up the best thing that ever happened to me because it makes you *uncomfortable*."

"This isn't about me. It's about Rick's happiness. He's been moping around since the moment he showed up—"

"Because he's been dreading coming out to you! And because he misses me. He's sent me hundreds of texts in the past three days. This has been agony for him. Please don't make it worse."

The doorbell chimed, and Jordan's head turned. He looked outside. It was Rick, and he was smiling.

Jordan let him in. No sooner did he cross the threshold than he plundered Jordan with a kiss.

Jordan wanted to melt into it, but instead, he stepped back. "Your mom didn't go shopping." He led him into the kitchen.

Rick scowled. "Mom?"

"Jordan and I have been talking."

Rick's happy expression shattered. "Unbelievable. You can't get *me* to end things with him, so you go behind my back and try to get him to do it?"

"I'm your mother. It's my job to protect you."

"That job ended five years ago. This is my choice, and I don't need protection from it."

"Rick." Jordan laid his hand on the small of Rick's back. Rick turned to him, the anger on his face dissolving into hurt. He crumbled into Jordan's arms.

"She's upset," Jordan murmured into his ear. "Give her space."

"Rick, I know you're angry with me now. But in time, you'll see that I'm right." She retrieved her coat and exited through the front door.

Rick held on to him. "I can't believe she tried to break us up."

"Now, what kind of boyfriend would I be if I let her come between us?"

Rick pulled away. "Is that what you think? That we're *boyfriends?*"

Jordan eyed him in confusion. "How do *you* think of us?"

"We're partners. We're soul mates. You're *not* just my boyfriend."

Jordan cradled Rick's face in his hands. "Of course. You're right." He drew him into a kiss, a proper one this time. Gradually, the tightness in Rick's body softened under Jordan's caresses. "You're mine," Jordan said against Rick's lips, "all mine."

Rick pressed against him. "Does your mom have any cooking oil?"

"You're a horny bastard. She could be back any minute now."

"Then maybe we should go to your room." Rick trailed his lips down Jordan's neck.

"I'm not sure it's such a great idea for us to be fucking when she gets home."

"Why not? It's the perfect way to tell her we're a couple."

Rick's hard, needy kisses silenced him. Sex was a terrible idea, but they both wanted it, and Rick probably needed it after the morning he'd had.

Rick groped at him, hands sliding underneath his sweater, coursing over the thin cotton fabric of his turtleneck. Deep kisses couldn't bring them close enough. Jordan missed their king-sized bed at home, where they could tunnel beneath the heavy covers, protected against the cold, their bodies joining as one—

The sound of the front door closing interrupted his thoughts. He turned and looked through the dining room to see the startled look on his mother's face.

Her wide eyes and open mouth quickly pinched into a scowl. "What in the actual hell?"

"Sorry, Mom. I wanted to tell you sooner, but I was waiting for Rick to come out to his parents—"

"Rick Ferguson, get the fuck away from my son."

Rick shrank from him. "Sorry, Mrs. C."

"It's Mrs. *Callahan*."

Jordan turned to Rick. "What are you apologizing for? You didn't do anything wrong."

Rick stared at the floor, looking tired, his body crumpling.

"Mom, look. I know you weren't expecting this, and I'm sorry you found out this way. Rick and I are in love—"

"Rick doesn't love anyone but himself." She shook her head. "This is just some experiment for him. He will break your heart."

"You don't know anything about this," Rick protested.

"I know about you. You've been a bad influence on Jordan his whole life."

"How have I been a bad influence? We both graduated in the top ten in our high school class. Jordy went on to get degrees from *two* Ivy League schools—"

"You've hurt him, and I won't let you do it again."

Jordan bristled. "Mom, you don't have any say in this. Rick and I live together, and we're very happy. Whatever problems you have with him, you need to work that out, because Rick is in my life to stay."

"I give it six months."

Jordan felt like a corkscrew was tearing into his chest and pulling out his heart. How could his mother have so little regard for his judgment? How could she actually wish for something that would break his heart?

"I may not have any control over what the two of you do in your house," she said, "but I do have control over my own. Rick isn't welcome here."

Jordan's jaw dropped. "What?"

"It's okay, Jordy, I'll go." Rick's voice was thin and tight.

"The fuck you will." He turned to his mother. "Think hard about this. If he goes, I go. And I'm not coming back without him."

"If that's the way you want it."

"This isn't what I want—it's what *you* want. I didn't say anything yesterday about your condescending boyfriend and his homophobic son. I endured that disaster for your sake. I expect the same consideration from you. Rick and I are a couple. You don't have to like it, but it's a fact."

"I will not stand here and be insulted in my own house." She stormed off into her bedroom and slammed the door.

Jordan could only shake his head.

"Told you she hates me."

"I'm gonna go pack. Think I can stay with you?"

Rick shrugged. "I don't know. My mom's crazy, too. Maybe Dad and Kat can talk some sense into her."

It had been a weird morning. Rick couldn't put it in any other terms—his emotions were ripped out of him and rolled flat. He could see them, but he couldn't feel them anymore.

Kat greeted him and Jordan in the foyer as soon as they entered the house. "What happened? Mom is in her bedroom crying. Dad's trying to get her to explain, but apparently she won't talk."

"Mom tried to get Jordan to break up with me."

Kat shook her head. "The fuck."

"Oh, but it gets better." He explained the situation with Mrs. Callahan. "So now, we're hoping Jordan can stay here."

Kat looked at him with sad eyes. "You don't suppose this has anything to do with menopause, do you? I don't want to go crazy when I turn fifty."

Jordan shoved his hands in his pockets. "I think Mike is a bad influence on my mom."

Rick chuckled.

"No, I mean it. He's kind of judgmental. And he raised a prick for a son. I know parents can't always help that, but even so."

Rick's dad came into the foyer, looking drawn. He hugged Rick, and then Jordan.

"I hope my being here isn't a problem," Jordan said.

"What? No," Rick's dad replied. "I'm glad you're here. Erica is having trouble adjusting, but she'll get there."

"How is she?" Kat asked.

"Right now, she thinks everyone is against her."

Rick barked out an ironic laugh.

"She really does want what's best for you, son. She's just not seeing things clearly right now. She's exhausted from yesterday, and thinks people don't appreciate how hard she works—which they don't."

"Then why does she keep doing it?" Kat asked.

"She's the glue that holds this family together."

Kat rolled her eyes. "I suppose."

A creaking resounded through the hallway, the opening of the master bedroom door. Rick clutched Jordan's hand, determined to hold on no matter what.

She shuffled into the foyer, eyes lighting up when they landed on Rick, but then darkening again when they made their way to Jordan.

"Jordy, honey, I don't think it's a good idea for you to be here right now."

"We're a couple now, Mom. Where I go, he goes."

"Rick, please don't argue with me about this. My nerves can't take it."

"I'm not arguing, I'm stating a fact. If Jordan leaves, I leave. It's your choice."

# Chapter 7

Jordan watched the countryside pass by as they approached the highway. When Rick turned onto Route 100, Jordan scowled and checked the compass. "You're heading south."

"Yep." Rick didn't elaborate.

"Home is north."

"We're not going home. I made reservations."

Jordan's heart rose like a balloon lifting into the atmosphere. "Where?"

"Baltimore. Inner Harbor."

Jordan drew his brow. He had been there once before and enjoyed it, but not in the middle of winter. "Any special reason?"

"You'll see when we get there."

Though tempted to push for more details, Jordan settled into the leather seat. Let Rick have his surprise. Jordan didn't have any plans for the next week, so why not? May as well embrace whatever romantic getaway Rick had planned.

He took out his smartphone and checked Facebook. His lips parted when he saw the number of notifications he had. Scrolling down to the first one, he found that Rick had changed his relationship status to *In a relationship with Jordan Callahan.*

"Dude! You came out on Facebook?"

"May as well get all the fun over with at once."

Jordan looked through the two dozen comments, most supportive, some shocked, some derisive, a couple hateful. No real surprise.

"So how many people called me a fag?" Rick feigned humor, but Jordan knew he was hurting.

"Just Bernstein so far. Janette Robinson quoted Deuteronomy and said she'd pray for you. Cyn's gushing about how happy she is for us. And here's one from your dad saying he loves us both, and we have his full support."

Rick nodded but stared straight ahead. "Nothing from Mom?"

"Not yet. Give her time."

"That's what I'm doing."

Jordan left a comment thanking everyone for their good wishes, then updated his own relationship status before putting his phone away.

He turned to Rick. "You did it."

"Yep."

"I'm proud of you."

"I'm proud of me, too." Rick gave him a little smile. "I realize that's dumb. After all this time in the closet—"

"It's not dumb. Coming out is hard. You start out life thinking people are basically good, and one by one, they disappoint you. When you come out, a whole bunch of people disappoint you at once. But then you meet more people, and you find out there are strangers who are incredibly generous and caring, more than you ever imagined. Hopefully, it balances out."

"It kills me that my mom is hurt by this, and at the same time, it makes me angry. It's like I'm doing something *to* her, like I'm an ungrateful son for being in love with you."

"It's a lot for her to take in."

"How can you be so patient with her? She kicked you out of her house."

"It's not about me. She sees me as a threat to your well-being. She thinks I'm the guy who seduced her straight son into a life of debauchery."

"Except I'm the one who did the seducing."

"I didn't put up much of a fight."

Rick chuckled. "That's true. And I hope you won't put up a fight later, because I have quite an evening planned."

Jordan opened the door to the hotel room and rolled his suitcase inside. He stopped short, eyes scanning the spacious interior. The king bed, topped with white linens, had a tall, dark wood headboard carved with a geometric design. A sitting area with two chairs and a small cocktail table backed the windows, which were draped with lace curtains.

"This place must have cost a fortune."

"Are you kidding? This is not a popular New Year's destination. They were practically giving the rooms away."

Jordan walked to the window. "Beautiful view of the harbor."

Rick walked up behind him, wrapping his arms around him and kissing his neck. "I made us dinner reservations for seven. So we can celebrate."

"Sounds nice." Jordan wasn't sure at first what they were celebrating. But then, Rick's coming out was a huge milestone for them, even if things hadn't gone as well as they had hoped.

Jordan looked out over the water at the boats floating on the bay. It really was gorgeous, especially now at sunset, with the sky pink and the city lights beginning to twinkle. From the warmth of their hotel room, it was an urban paradise.

Rick unzipped his suitcase. "I know we agreed not to buy Christmas presents for each other, because the new couch was our Christmas present. But I cheated."

Jordan frowned and shoved his hands into his pockets. "But I didn't get you anything."

"That's okay. I got something for both of us." He pulled out a blue velvet jeweler's box, flat and rectangular.

Jordan's cheeks heated. *What did Rick do?* As much as he was a horny bastard, he could be romantic when he tried. Jordan bit his lip to keep from smiling.

Rick opened the hinged box to reveal two pairs of gold rings. Each set included a plain band, and a matching one with a chevron design. Jordan stared at them, his throat thickening. Commitment rings? Was Rick ready for that so soon?

Then, Rick got down on one knee.

Jordan's hand covered his mouth to hold back the squeal that threatened to escape. Knees trembling, he forced himself to stay upright.

"Jordy, you're my best friend, my lover, my life, and I hope I can be yours." His voice quavered. "Will you marry me?"

Jordan's chest was so full it ached. This was so unexpected, but now, after everything, it seemed inevitable. After all the years of waiting, of wanting, this was exactly what was supposed to happen, at this exact moment in time.

He cradled Rick's cheek in his palm. "Of course I'll marry you. Nothing would make me happier." He swallowed. "But it's not legal in—"

Jordan drew a breath, his eyes feeling like toothpicks were propping them open. "We're in Maryland."

Rick stood, a huge grin sweeping across his face. With his free arm, he pulled Jordan in for a kiss. Jordan leaned against him. Tender lips suckled his own, but only for a moment.

Rick pulled back, then took out the yellow-gold chevron ring and placed it on Jordan's left hand.

Tears welled in Jordan's eyes. He swiped them away. "I'm such a girl."

"No," Rick said. "You're all man, and you're all mine."

Jordan took out the white-gold chevron ring and slid it onto Rick's finger. He set the box aside and pressed into Rick's body. "How long until we need to leave for the restaurant?"

"It's walking distance. We've got plenty of time to mess up that beautifully appointed king-sized bed."

They started with tender kisses as Rick backed Jordan into the mattress. They stripped off one another's clothes slowly, warm hands eager to find the skin beneath, to caress hard planes of muscle. Rick's lips tugged on Jordan's earlobe, and tingles radiated through Jordan's body. Breathlessly, he held Rick's mouth to his, devouring him, unable to get enough.

They slid under the covers, enveloped in each other's arms. As day turned to night, Jordan lay beneath

Rick's body, unable to tell where one ended and the other began. Emotions welled inside him, his heart fluttering like a bird's, happiness seeping through his body, warming him.

Rick's mouth explored his flesh, the curve of his neck, the hard ridge of his clavicle, the taut flats of his stomach. Jordan trembled. It was all too much, the feel of Rick's touch, the emotions quivering inside him. Almost too much happiness to endure.

Rick moved over him, their cocks rubbing together. Jordan moaned, his whole body rumbling with the pleasure of it. Hot skin on skin.

His senses came to life: the taste of Rick's kisses, the soft murmur of his breathing, the smell of his musk. Jordan reveled in it. He grabbed Rick's ass, not possessively, just enjoying the feel of their bodies together. There was no urgency to the touch, just this moment, and the satisfaction they gave each other.

Rick fisted their cocks together. The pleasure began low and built until it reached a screaming crescendo. Streams of cum shot from Jordan's body, coating his belly and his chest. Rick followed soon after. They dissolved in sweet kisses, coming down from the high, and lay silent, no need for words between them.

Minutes passed, or maybe it was an hour. Finally, Rick said, "We should get dressed for dinner."

They rose and showered. They put on their best outfits and headed out into the night.
The air was brisk but the stars bright. The bay sparkled with moonlight.

The waiter brought them surf and turf and champagne. For dessert, they ordered chocolate mousse and fed it to each other. They ambled back to the hotel with Jordan's hand in the crook of Rick's arm. He barely noticed the cold. Rick's love was the only warmth he needed.

Rick was flying. When he first bought the rings, he didn't have any plans to propose right away. He knew that he wanted to eventually, but he was in no rush.

When things went down with their parents the way they had, it just seemed like the right thing to do. He'd thought a bit about eloping, before he came out, as a contingency plan. But he wasn't sure he'd really go through with it.

When Jordan said yes, it was as if the world were vibrating in fresh new colors. As if he could see through new eyes, his powers of sight richer. Loving Jordan felt right, as if he'd always been meant for this life. How could he not have seen it sooner?

The champagne had gone to his head a little. He'd probably had more than he should. He felt giddy, his steps light. He wanted to scream his happiness to the world.

When they reached the hotel, they stopped at the bar. Rick ordered another bottle of champagne and offered glasses to strangers. He didn't remember when he had ever been so happy. Whatever was going on with his family, it would pass. But Jordan was his forever.

It almost seemed too good to be true. But Rick knew it was real, that this was his life now. He felt like the heavens had smiled on him, and he didn't deserve it. But he wasn't going to argue with it. He loved Jordan more than anyone else could, and he would make him happier.

Dance music filled the bar, and Rick couldn't sit still. He'd never felt so amped up. This was a new kind of happiness, a deeper one, a richer one. For too long, he'd lived a quiet version of life, and now he intended to live out loud.

"I think you've had enough champagne now," Jordan said. "I might have to get one of those luggage carts to wheel you upstairs."

"I haven't had that much. But I'll stop if you want me to."

"I just want us to have our wits about us tonight. I have big plans for us."

"I like the sound of that." Rick couldn't believe the way Jordan's words affected him. He was getting hard again. The sex that afternoon had been soul-wrenching and deeply satisfying. But now, he was in the mood for something raunchier.

They went upstairs. The long private ride on the elevator afforded them plenty of time for deep kisses. Once they made it to the room, though, Rick was done with romance.

He kicked the door closed and pressed Jordan to the wall. "My turn to top."

"Didn't realize we were keeping track."

"It's all I can think about, being inside you."

"Not complaining."

Their coats ended up in a pile. Jordan shuddered at the feral look gleaming in Rick's eyes. The tenderness had passed. With a low growl, Rick hauled him to the bed. "I need you out of those clothes and underneath me. Now."

Desire rippled through Jordan's body. The heat radiating from his lover, the spicy, masculine scent, shot a rush of blood straight to his cock.

Rick cupped Jordan's ass, massaging gently. "Want it hard and fast." He lifted Jordan's shirt off him, kissing his neck and nibbling his nipples. "Want you to ache when I'm done with you, so all day tomorrow you remember the feel of my cock."

Jordan moaned, balls tightening at the thought of Rick taking him and using him. "Do it, babe," he rasped. "Do it rough."

Their hands moved over each other, stripping off the rest of their clothes. Jordan leaned in for a kiss, but Rick grabbed his wrists. "No foreplay," Rick said in his ear. "I want you bent over the bed so I can fuck you until you scream."

Jordan's balls tightened, his erection lengthening. He didn't need foreplay. He'd had five years of it, waiting for them to be together. He was ready for whatever Rick had to give him.

Rick maneuvered him into position, holding him down with his body. A quick twist of his fingers slicked Jordan's hole, cold lube making his ass contract.

Jordan breathed and relaxed his muscles. Fingers pumped into him. "Hell, you're hot," Rick said. "Sorry, can't wait." The next moment, the head of Rick's cock was against his entrance. With a groan, Rick leaned forward. Jordan gasped at the burn, his body opening.

Rick entered him by millimeters, fingers curling in Jordan's hair. "Take it, bitch." The stretch was perfect, bringing him to the edge of pain without ever crossing that boundary. Rick might play rough, but Jordan knew he never wanted to hurt him.

Rick leaned over and whispered in his ear, "I want to hear you beg."

"More...please. You fuck me so good, babe. Yeah, like that."

"That's right, bitch, moan for me. Take it all."

*Yes, please, give it all to me.*

Once Rick was fully seated, he picked up the pace. Jordan could have wept with pleasure. The strokes against his prostate lit sparks behind his eyelids.

"This is mine," Rick said. "No one else will ever fuck this ass again."

"Yours, babe. Forever."

Rick slowed, and Jordan craned his neck to see what was wrong.

Rick pulled out. "Turn over. I want to see your face when you come."

Jordan complied. He rested his feet on the edge of the bed and scooted his ass forward.

Rick got out more lube and entered him again, forcing Jordan's legs wide. He grasped the back of Jordan's knees, owning him.

Rick pulled all the way out and shoved in hard again. Over and over, the punishing rhythm struck his prostate like lightning. He palmed Jordan's shaft and kissed his mouth. "You feel so damn good. Come in my hand."

Jordan was close but not there yet. "So good, babe."

Rick jerked him faster. "Come, damn it. Now!"

Jordan howled. The release took him by surprise and left him panting. Rick's face contorted as his own climax followed. He bit the inside of Jordan's thigh, then massaged the spot tenderly. He picked up a box of tissues and wiped the cum off his hand and Jordan's stomach.

Deep pleasure settled like a blanket on Jordan's body. Rick pulled out and rested his hands on Jordan's hips. "This ass was made for me."

"All yours."

Rick ran his hand down Jordan's arm. "You okay?"

"Fantastic." He nibbled his ear. "But I *will* feel that tomorrow."

"We'll let your sweet hole rest a while. Maybe tomorrow you can fuck *me*."

"More fucking?"

"Get used to it. This is what marriage to me is going to be like. Fucking morning, noon, and night."

"I can live with that."

They didn't bother cleaning up any further, just lay in that big bed letting sleep overtake them. Jordan managed to turn off the bedside lamp just before he slipped into unconsciousness.

Jordan woke the next morning to the sound of the shower running. He reached for Rick's side of the bed, the absence there sending a little jolt of pain into his heart. It felt like a rejection, although he knew it wasn't. When Rick woke up, he was either horny—in which case it was all Jordan could do to peel the guy off him—or he was all business, which meant cuddling wasn't on his agenda. The dichotomy had made Jordan feel used at first, but he knew there was no point wallowing in it. Rick had proven his love and devotion.

*We're getting married in four days.* The prospect still didn't seem real to him.

Jordan sauntered into the white marble bathroom, starting his morning routine while Rick showered. He listened to the sound of the water and pictured Rick's naked form inside. Water running over hard muscle and smooth, pale skin. His cock heated at the thought of it, but if he knew Rick, sex was not on the table this morning.

*Mmm, sex on the table.* He grinned.

The flow of water stopped, and Rick pushed open the shower curtain with a swish. "Morning, gorgeous." He ran a towel over his hair. "We should go to the courthouse first thing."

Jordan nodded. They had no time to waste. Given the 48-hour waiting period, they needed to get the marriage license before the weekend if they wanted to get married on New Year's Eve.

After a brief exchange of kisses, they switched places, and Jordan showered. When he went back into the bedroom, he found Rick dressed and standing at the window. Quickly slipping on his boxer briefs, he joined Rick there, sliding an arm around him.

"Pretty here," Rick said. "Depending on how long things take at the courthouse, maybe we could go to the aquarium afterward."

"Sounds nice." He kissed his cheek. "You doing okay?"

Rick sighed. "No. It'll be a while before I'm okay. It's just something we have to get through." He smiled. "On the upside, I get to marry you. So that's pretty awesome." He kissed him. "You talk to your mom yet?"

"Not since we left her house. She needs time to cool down." He hung his head. "It's strange to think of it as *her* house, after I grew up there. But if she's going to be that way about it, and make me feel like I'm not welcome to bring anyone I choose into it, then I guess it's not my home anymore. My home is with you."

Rick held his hand and stroked his palm. "That's not so terrible, is it?"

"Not at all. They shouldn't have made us choose."

"They're in shock. They'll get over it."

Jordan traced Rick's lips with a fingertip. "I've never seen you look so sad."

Rick smiled and wrapped his arms around Jordan's waist. "This is not a sad day. We're getting our marriage license." He patted Jordan's butt. "Now get dressed."

Jordan sat on a bench overlooking the harbor. Sun reflected off the water, and a cold breeze blew through his hair. The calls of seagulls sounded above.

He stared at the sheet of paper in his hand, from the City of Baltimore in the State of Maryland, allowing Jordan Sean Callahan to marry Richard Steven Ferguson.

Five years ago, it had been unthinkable that it would be this easy. Once they got to the front of the line, it had taken a couple of minutes, a few questions, some signatures, and they were done.

Rick put his arm around him, and they snuggled together for warmth. It was really too cold to keep sitting here, and they should store the certificate in the room for safe keeping, but Jordan wanted to savor the moment.

"You okay, babe?" Rick asked.

"I'm amazing." Jordan smiled at him, and Rick gave him a joyful laugh.

To save time, they went to the aquarium to get tickets. There was a one hour wait, so they walked back to the hotel, dropped off the certificate in their room, and went to the hotel restaurant for lunch.

They crossed the lobby and descended the few stairs into the sunken dining room, set with dark, heavy wooden tables. Gold brocade curtains framed the large windows that overlooked the harbor. The wait staff were dressed in black vests and bow ties.

While they waited for their food, Jordan checked Facebook to see what other comments Rick's coming out had inspired.

"Um, babe?" he said when he opened the app.

"Yeah?"

"Did you announce our engagement on Facebook before we told our families?"

"Oh, that. Yeah."

"Did you see how pissed Kat is?"

Rick chuckled. "I figured she would be."

Jordan laughed, and even to him the sound was hysterical and semi-deranged. The past two days had been surreal. He couldn't begin to process how disappointed he was with his mom, and it was worse for Rick. Yet he figured he owed his mom a phone call now, since he wanted her to hear the news from him before she heard it from someone else. She wasn't on Facebook, so it was possible that word hadn't gotten to her yet.

"I need to go call my mom. I'll be back in a minute or five."

Jordan took the elevator up to the room for privacy before dialing the number.

"Jordy, where are you?"

"Baltimore."

Silence. "Why are you in Baltimore?"

"Because Rick's mom thinks I turned him gay, so I'm not welcome in her house, either. Rick made us reservations at the Inner Harbor."

"Why Baltimore?"

"Because gay marriage is legal here."

She sputtered. "Jordan, you're not—"

"Yeah, we are. We're getting married on New Year's Eve. It's just a civil ceremony. Once it's legal in Pennsylvania, we'll have a big church wedding with all the family there. Okay?"

"No, not okay. Jordan, what are you thinking?"

He sank onto the orange couch and fiddled with the brochures scattered across the coffee table. "I'm thinking this is my life and my choice. If this is what we have to do to prove to our families that we're serious, then so be it."

"You're twenty-three years old!"

"You were twenty-two when you married Dad. Good thing, too, or I wouldn't be here."

"I'm just saying, honey, you have lots of time. You and Rick could live together for a year or so first, just to be sure—"

"I don't need a year to be sure." He hesitated a moment. "So you're coming around to the idea of Rick and me living together?"

"I wouldn't say that. But it's better than the two of you getting married."

"Better for who? For you?"

"Honey, you know how impulsive Rick is. How can you be sure he won't change his mind? Decide he's actually straight?"

Jordan let his mind wrap around that one a moment. "Mom, I'm not sure of much in this world, but I'm one hundred percent sure that Rick isn't straight. This wasn't some impulsive decision for him. He's spent five years figuring out what he wants, and he wants me. Every step of the way, he has pursued me, not the other way around. He loves me. I have every confidence in that. If I didn't, I wouldn't have agreed to marry him."

"Five years? Are you saying that you and Rick...?"

"We dated freshman year in college, but the distance made it difficult, and exclusivity didn't work out for us. After I broke up with Damon and he broke up with Jess a few months ago, we decided to give it another try."

"Why didn't I know about this?"

"Because Rick wasn't out."

"Jordan, you should have told me!"

"I wanted to. I couldn't, without betraying his confidence."

"I wish I'd known."

"Well, you know now. And when we have the church wedding, I hope you'll be there to give us your blessing."

"Of course I will be. You're my baby. I wouldn't miss your wedding for the world."

"Even if it's to Rick?"

"I still think it's a horrible mistake. But it's your mistake to make. I certainly can't stop you."

"Thanks for the vote of confidence, Mom." He grinned ironically.

"I trust you. I guess I have to leave this one up to you."

"He makes me happy."

"That's what matters most, I guess. As long as he keeps making you happy."

Jordan ended the call soon after and went back to the restaurant. The food was waiting. Rick hadn't touched his yet. It was a sweet gesture. Jordan wished his mom could see that side of him.

"Things okay with your mom?" Rick asked as Jordan sat.

"Yeah, we're good. She's not happy, but she's not crazed like yesterday. I think she realizes you're not as much of a threat as she thought."

Rick reached out and squeezed Jordan's hand under the table. "I should talk to her. Make her understand I love you as much as she does."

"That might help. It's the absence of information that's got her worried. She hasn't seen us together, so she doesn't know how right we are for each other. A lot of her opinions of you are based on misunderstandings."

"I can fix that."

"Remember what I said. Sincerity."

"I know. We'll work it out, Jordy. I know how much your mom means to you. I'll do whatever it takes to make things right."

"I know you will. Now we just need to work on *your* mom."

"Not yet. She needs time."

"Have you talked to Kat or your dad?"

"I'm not ready to do that yet."

"Babe, I know it's difficult, but they've been supportive through all of this."

"Yes, but they'll blame me for upsetting Mom, and I can't deal with that right now. Mom's upsetting herself. She's in the wrong, and I'm not talking to her again until she acknowledges that and apologizes."

"Okay." He sighed. "We should eat so we're not late for our entrance time at the aquarium."

"I'm not super hungry."

"Yes, you are. Your stomach's upset because of this situation with your mom. If you don't eat now, you'll be famished later. And I know how cranky you get when you haven't eaten."

"Yes, dear." He grinned and took a few tentative bites of his sandwich. Before long, he'd completely devoured it.

Jordan relaxed a little. Maybe Rick would be okay.

Rick stared into the tank of moon jellyfish. It was mesmerizing, watching them expand and contract their bodies to propel themselves through the water. For all their fragility, jellies had existed on the planet for half a billion years or more. He couldn't comprehend that time scale, but it amazed him to think about it.

He reached over and squeezed Jordan's hand. Seeing the tremendous variety of life at the aquarium had captured Rick's imagination and made him feel tied to the planet in a deeper way. The struggles he and Jordan were going through right now would pass. What mattered was the enduring love they shared.

A part of him couldn't believe it was real, that he and Jordan were truly together as a couple. His mind was still adjusting to the idea, and now they were getting married in four days. He didn't want to wait longer, though. Waiting might be the rational thing, but time wouldn't make a difference in his decision. It mattered very much to him that he and Jordan have the protections marriage offered. The hell he wanted the law to consider him Jordan's roommate.

A family walked up beside him, a couple with a little girl about four years old. She was dressed in a blue jumper and a purple overcoat, her black hair in pigtails. But instead of staring at the jellyfish, she was staring at him and Jordan. She pointed at them and said, in a soft voice, "Mommy!"

The woman, a blonde who looked to be in her late twenties, stooped down next to her. "Sweetheart, it's not polite to point."

"But why are they holding hands?"

"Alicia!" her father scolded. Dark-haired with a day's worth of stubble, he looked at Rick and Jordan through square-framed hipster glasses. "Sorry."

"No need to apologize." Jordan stooped down beside her and said, "We're holding hands because we're in love, and we're getting married next week."

"You're going to marry a man?" Amazement filled her voice. "Mommy, can they do that?"

"Um-hmm. Sometimes, the way God makes people, they fall in love with the same sex instead of the opposite sex. Do you know what that means?"

"Yeah. Daddy is the opposite sex."

"That's right. Mommy and Daddy are an opposite-sex couple, and these two nice men are a same-sex couple."

"And you're getting married?" Alicia asked Jordan.

"That's right. Next week."

"Congratulations," the mother said.

"Yeah, 'gratulation!" Alicia said.

"Thank you," Jordan said as he stood.

The father offered his hand to Rick. "All the best to you."

Rick shook it. "Thanks."

He and Jordan moved on to allow the family a clear view of the jellyfish tank. Rick wasn't sure what to make of the situation. Jordan had handled it well, and fortunately the parents were allies. But being a gay couple still made them conspicuous, and holding hands in public still came with risks.

He'd have to come to terms with that—whether it was better to live out and proud, or take the safer route. He and Jordan could hold their own one-on-one, but against a group, or someone armed, it would be a different story.

He looked over to see a wistful expression on Jordan's face. "You okay?"

"How cute was that little girl?"

"Pretty adorable."

Jordan smiled and tugged on Rick's shirt. "I can't wait to have kids with you."

"With Kat, you mean."

"No, I mean with you." Jordan crinkled his brow. "If you want to have one that's biologically yours, we can do that, too."

Rick shrugged. "If you had sisters, then yeah, I would. But you don't. Since Kat has offered—and she seems genuinely excited about it—I think that's the way to go. I won't love the baby any less because it's not biologically my child."

Jordan nodded. "We've got a few years to think about it. No need to decide anything now."

"You're so cute. You want a baby right away, don't you."

"It's not practical. We don't have any money, we don't have any space. Also, we should enjoy being a couple first. They're just so damn cute."

"Maybe we should avoid places where children congregate for a while."

Jordan chuckled. "Maybe."

"We could get a dog. A black lab."

"We live in a two-bedroom condo. How about a dachshund?"

"A wiener dog? You want to get a little wiener dog?"

"They're good dogs. They can cuddle up on the couch with us, and they keep the vermin away—"

"Fine." He shook his head and said under his breath, "I can't believe I'm agreeing to a wiener dog."

After the aquarium, they went back to the room to relax before dinner. They lay on the bed snuggled together, surrounded by pillows, checking their phones. Jordan changed his Facebook relationship status to *Engaged to Rick Ferguson*.

Unlike Rick, he didn't have his personal and professional accounts separate. Rick had a page where he communicated with clients, but his personal profile was pretty well locked down except to family and friends. Even so, the nasty comments were shocking— people who'd been nice to Jordan to his face, but who suddenly had a problem now that Rick was out. Jordan blocked four old high school friends. He couldn't say he was sorry to see them go.

More disturbing was the message from Kat. It was short and to the point: *WTF? This is how you announce your engagement to your family?* He could feel the hurt and disappointment in the words, and he knew Rick could, too.

He understood why Rick didn't want to talk to her. He was pissed, and even if Kat didn't deserve that from him, she was stuck in the middle. "You should call Kat."

"I don't want to talk to her."

"Just five minutes to clear the air. She deserves to know what's going on."

"Why don't *you* talk to her, then?" Rick said icily.

"Fine. I will."

Jordan rose and stepped out into the hallway. He remembered seeing a meeting room on their floor, and sure enough, it was empty. He stepped inside and pulled up Kat's number.

"Jordy, what the fuck?" she asked, voice frantic. "Rick announces his engagement on Facebook?"

"I know, he's an asshole, but he's pissed, Kat. He feels abandoned."

"Well, that's just stupid. He's the one who left. He should be here, working shit out."

"If you remember, we weren't welcome there, or at my mom's. Forgive us if we didn't want to spend all the vacation we'd saved all year holed up at the Hampton Inn in Chestnut Grove."

"So where are you, then? Did you go home?"

"We're in Baltimore."

She was silent a moment, then said, "Why are you in Bal..." Her voice trailed off, then came back with fervor. "Jordy! You can't do this. You can't elope."

A muffled "What!" in Mr. Ferguson's voice sounded in the background. After a slight rustling, he came on the phone. "Jordan. Son, this is getting out of hand. Rick hasn't returned any of my messages. He cannot get married without his mother there."

"If she wants any consideration from him, then she needs to apologize."

"She needs time—"

"She doesn't *have* time. We're getting married New Year's Eve. Gay marriage isn't legal in Pennsylvania, so we have to do this while we're here."

"Rick's first priority should be repairing the relationship with his mother."

"Rick is the victim in this situation. It's no wonder he's not returning your messages if you're blaming him."

"If he'd just given her time to adjust—"

"And what were we supposed to do in the meantime? She forced Rick to choose between herself and me. Rick chose me, and you chose her."

"She was upset."

"And you think Rick isn't upset? He was counting on you to have his back, but when it came down to it, you didn't."

"Jordy…"

"Mr. Ferguson, if you get your house in order, then maybe we can talk. But as long as you're siding with your wife, when she's acting as if Rick's relationship with me is a personal affront to her, then I'm afraid we have nothing to say."

He ended the call, shaking with anger. *Holy shit.* He'd never spoken to Rick's father that way before, never expected to, but the man was so deeply immersed in appeasing his wife that he couldn't see what it was doing to his son.

Jordan's phone rang, Kat's number, but he didn't want to take the call in case it was her father again. When he checked the message, Kat's choked voice pleaded with him not to let Rick get married without his family there. He texted her, reiterating what he'd told his own mother—that they'd have a church wedding later.

He went back to the room and crashed back down on the bed next to Rick. "What did she say?" he asked, voice thick with tension.

Jordan relayed the conversations he'd had with Kat and Mr. Ferguson. "I told him not to contact you until he's got things in order on his end, because you don't need that kind of stress."

Rick pulled him close. "Thank you for understanding."

Jordan pressed tender kisses into his cheek. "So for this wedding thing…" Jordan stroked Rick's hair. "Tuxes?"

"Yeah, I think we should. Maybe tomorrow we can look for a place to rent them?"

"Sounds like a plan." Jordan kissed him. "Anything else special you want to do?"

"Not really. I was thinking traditional vows unless you want to write our own."

"Traditional is good. Maybe we could have a spa day the day before—couples massage, mani/pedi's, facials…"

"That is the gayest thing I've ever heard. We should definitely do that."

Jordan drew him close and rubbed against him. "I can think of something gayer."

Rick grazed his lips along Jordan's jawline. "Yeah? What did you have in mind?"

"I want to be inside you, babe. So deep you forget everything but me."

Rick moaned. Their mouths found each other, and they stripped off their clothes amid hot, teasing kisses.

Naked beneath the sheet and heavy blankets, Rick said, "What is it with you wanting to top lately?"

"When you top, we go fast. When I top, we go slow. Are you complaining?"

"I'm just not used to it yet."

"Babe, if I ever hurt you—"

"It's not that, exactly. I'm still figuring out how to adjust. Once we get going, it's amazing."

Jordan kissed him tenderly, cheeks and lips and the hollow of his throat. "We don't have to do this. It's okay that you don't like to bottom as much as me."

"I'm not just doing this for you. I want it, too."

Jordan gave Rick a sultry smile, which said he wanted this more than he was letting on. Rick loved how Jordan took care of him, how they took care of each other. For the first time, he could show his soul without fear of rejection. Growing up, he'd felt like he was a bad kid, and if his parents really knew, they wouldn't love him anymore. Jordan knew everything and loved him in spite of his faults. Maybe even because of them. Because of everything they'd shared— everything they'd survived together.

Jordan's lips inched down his abs. The kisses were sweet, seductive, teasing. As if they had all night…which they did. If they missed dinner, they could order room service. Rick lay back and enjoyed the attention, knowing Jordan wanted nothing more than the pleasure of pleasing his lover.

Jordan's mouth reached the tip of Rick's cock, and Rick whimpered. Yeah, that was good. Just the soft flicking of tongue, the slide of lips down his shaft. He wove his fingers through Jordy's hair. "So hot, babe."

The tongue probed lower still, circling his balls, the hot, wet mouth sucking them in. Rick hummed a low note, then pulled a rapid breath.

Jordan cantered Rick's hips up and glided toward Rick's hole. With a whisper of a touch, Jordan rimmed him, darting in and out, up and around. Rick rocked toward him, wanting more, more. But Jordan tormented him with just the tip of his tongue until Rick was whimpering, mewling, pleading.

"Need you. Please. Fuck me."

Jordan got out the lube and slid a finger inside. His lips tantalized Rick's nipples, his hipbone, his cock. Rick melted into a pool of want. A second finger breached him, stretching the sensitive passage. Overwhelmed with sensation, the only coherent thought he could form was *yes, more.*

The addition of a third finger had him writhing off the bed, seeking his lover's touch and the delicious pressure on his gland. Kissing and nipping at his thigh, Jordan pulled out, then positioned himself over him. The head of the well-slicked cock breached Rick's opening, and he hissed at the burn. Jordan inched forward, drawing quick pants from Rick as he tried to adjust to the invasion. The steely prick sank deeper. Rick arched and cried out.

Jordan pulled back. "Bear down, babe. That's it. Tell me if you need me to stop."

His muscles loosened a little. "Don't want you to stop." Tears formed at the corners of his eyes.

"Exhale for me. Nice and slow." Balancing on one hand, Jordan stroked Rick's cock with the other. The thrumming heat distracted him, and soon he felt the glide against his prostate. Pleasure sparked through the pain.

He pushed toward Jordan until balls slapped his ass. He looked down and watched that thick, dusky cock reappear then disappear inside him. The decadent sight ratcheted up his excitement. Getting fucked. Being filled. Taking all Jordy had to offer.

With both hands on the mattress now, Jordy pumped him at a rate that kept him primed and on the edge.

"So good, babe. Now."

"Not yet." Jordy's voice was taut and strained. "Want you to remember this part. Not the pain."

Spurts of precum coated his belly. He fisted himself, spreading the natural lubricant over his shaft. Jordy's hand replaced his own, squeezing the base, stopping Rick from coming.

"No fair," Rick said.

"Go slow. Enjoy."

Their bodies rocked together. Each brush against his prostate took him to new heights. He cupped Jordan's ass, then slid a finger along the cleft, stroking the hole, the taint, the sensitive line between the balls. He couldn't get enough of Jordan, the hard muscle, the soft skin. He was glad they had stopped using condoms after they moved in together. Now, nothing came between them. Their bodies joined as one.

He grasped Jordan's hips to quicken the pace. Jordy gave a little grunt, then plowed into him. Rick cried out, in pleasure this time, his insides molten. Jordan's hard, insistent downward stroke on Rick's cock finished him off. His eyes rolled back from the rush of pleasure. Hot cum spurted on his chest and belly. The tight muscles of his ass clamped down and Jordan roared, body shuddering and collapsing on top of him.

Jordan's breath fell hot and heavy on Rick's shoulders. "You are an amazing fuck," he panted. "Ass so tight...It was okay, right? You'd tell me if it wasn't?"

Rick answered with a line of kisses along his jaw.

Jordan clutched his face. "Listen to me. I can live without fucking you. I can't live with hurting you."

"It was okay. I didn't realize how tense I was at first. It took a while to get good, but in the end, it was amazing."

"Okay. But I need you to be completely honest with me, okay? No hiding the truth to spare my feelings. I love bottoming, so if you don't want to, you don't have to, ever."

"I'll always be honest with you. I promise."

They cleaned up, then got back into bed and snuggled. Rick's ass still burned, but he liked the reminder that Jordy had been inside him.

It didn't feel real yet, his new life. More like an extended vacation, living with Jordy, fucking like bunnies. Maybe that was one reason why he'd felt the urge to propose so soon. He wanted that sense of permanence.

Ever since he'd come out—*was that just yesterday?*—he'd felt like he was on shifting ground. He didn't know where he stood with his parents. His dad was pissed, his mom was hurt. His foundation was rocking beneath him. That's what it took to be with the man he loved.

How was that fair? For years, he'd denied himself what he'd wanted, trying to create a "normal" life for himself. *His* normal was that he liked dick. So what? How was that anyone's business? It was just sex. Why did people care so much?

His mother was no bigot. She'd said a hundred times that Jordan was like a son to her. This should have been easy.

But nothing with his mother was easy. She didn't like surprises, and Rick had rocked her world. He knew he needed to be patient, knew this wasn't fair to her. But she wasn't being fair to him, either. He deserved a safe place to go, and that should have been with his parents.

The situation sucked, that was all. Emotions were high. Once things had calmed down, the situation with his family would get back to normal. Or, rather, find a new normal. One where Jordan was his husband.

*Holy. Shit.*

They were really fucking doing this.

The thought of it didn't scare him, just startled him a little. Two months ago, this wasn't exactly how he pictured himself spending New Year's Eve. Another night sipping cheap champagne, watching a stupid ball drop in Times Square—he hadn't imagined anything more exciting than that.

Instead, it would be the most important day of his life, the day he made a vow to his partner, the future father of his children.

Suddenly, this all seemed very real. It was exactly what Rick wanted, but it was scary at the same time. Or maybe that wasn't the right word. It was *momentous*.

Was he ready for this? Not just for sharing a home and a bed, but joining their finances, making a legal commitment to one another?

He rolled it over in his mind once more, and could honestly say that yes, he was ready. He was an adult now, and had become accustomed to making adult decisions. This was just one more. In fact, it was the easiest one so far, because it was Jordy, and they just fit.

He placed a kiss on top of his lover's head, stroking his hair. Pleasure settled on his belly. This was good and right. This was where he belonged.

For the rest of his life.

# Chapter 8

Jordan woke in the gray light of dawn. Weary from too little sleep, he rubbed his thumb against the ring on his finger. A smile crept over his lips, then faded as a pit formed in his stomach.

What were they doing?

By eloping like this, were they really just running away from their problems? If so, that was no way to start a marriage.

He held up his left hand and looked at the ring, new and gleaming. This was typical of Rick, making a grand, impulsive gesture to distract himself from his emotions. Could Jordan trust that Rick really wanted this?

He considered a moment. Rick must have bought the rings before Christmas—so at least he had put some thought into it. That did little to reassure Jordan. An engagement was one thing. Rushing into a ceremony without any friends or family present was something else entirely.

Beside him, the mattress dipped and the sheets rustled. He looked over, and Rick's eyes opened.

A wide grin broke across Rick's face. "Morning, gorgeous."

A tickle of excitement fluttered in his belly. Arms drew him close. Lips covered his, but he couldn't settle into the kiss. He laid his head on Rick's shoulder and intertwined their left hands. The two rings brushed together, one white gold, one yellow gold, with the arrow-shaped patterns fitting together like a jigsaw puzzle.

Jordan rolled onto his side and twisted his ring, then looked at Rick. "Are you sure about this?"

Rick scowled. "Aren't you?"

"That I want to marry you? Yeah. Not sure it's a good idea to rush into it."

The corners of Rick's mouth drooped. "This is what we both want. Why wait?"

Cold fingers gripped Jordan's heart and squeezed. He hated being the practical one—it didn't suit him. And he knew any negativity would chafe against Rick's already wounded psyche.

"We've been together six weeks."

"We've been together seventeen years."

Jordan grinned and shook his head. "Okay, but we've been a couple six weeks."

"Only because I was afraid to come out. I've been in love with you for five years. Maybe longer." Rick swept him into a kiss, and this time, he relaxed, letting Rick's love fill his heart.

"Whatever you need, babe," Jordan said in his ear. "Whatever you need to feel secure and happy, you tell me, okay?"

"I just want to marry you."

"Then we'll do that."

Rick turned quiet, thoughtful. Finally he said, "If you're not ready—"

"Babe, I'm more than ready. As long as you're sure."

"I've never been more sure of anything."

They spent the morning looking at tuxes. They finally selected charcoal gray with full tails. Rick looked so handsome in his, Jordan thought he would melt. He started getting excited about the ceremony, and all his doubts fell away. Rick seemed happy, joyful even. As if this was meant to be.

They took in the sights of the city, had crab cakes and clam chowder for lunch, did every kitschy touristy thing they could think of. The day was cold but clear, and they walked close together to keep warm.

But as night fell, Rick's mood changed. He seemed to be checking his phone a lot.

"Heard from your family?" Jordan asked once they were back in the hotel room.

"Got a voicemail from Kat," Rick said, his tone soft and melancholy.

"Why don't you talk to her?"

"I know what she'll say. She wants me to come home. She doesn't want us to get married, and I don't want to argue about it. I have to do this for me. I can't worry about my family right now."

Jordan had never seen him so edgy. The rift with his parents was eating away at him, even more than the nerves about the ceremony. Jordan understood Rick's single-mindedness, his desire to go through with the wedding before confronting his family about the situation. But it was tearing him apart, and Jordan hated to see that.

He placed a soothing kiss on Rick's cheek. Rick drew him close and just held him, breaths ragged.

"You won't relax until you talk to Kat," Jordan coaxed. "Make the call."

While Jordan reclined on the bed, Rick paced the room, cell phone pressed to his ear, stomach hollow as he waited for the sound of his sister's voice.

"Ricky, thank God. Are you okay?"

"I'm fine. How's Mom?" He fought to steady his voice. He could barely breathe for the knot in his throat.

"She'd be better if you were here."

"I think a little space now is best for both of us."

"We're not talking about a little space, Rick. You're getting married."

"It's just a civil ceremony. We'll have a big church wedding once it's legal in Pennsylvania."

"That could be years."

"Which is why I want to do this now. I want Jordy and me to have the same protections a straight couple would have."

"You couldn't have given Mom and Dad…I don't know, a week to get used to the idea? You drop this bomb on them, and then run?"

Anger burned in his stomach and spread to his chest. "That was Mom's choice. If Jordy isn't welcome in her home, then neither am I."

"She was upset."

"She tried to break Jordy and me up."

Kat sighed. "Look, I know she hurt you. But in her own twisted way, she was trying to protect you. She didn't understand the situation."

"She didn't try. I've been agonizing over this for five years—"

"And you didn't even give her five hours. That sucks, Rick."

"Look, I'm sorry, okay? I'm sorry she's upset. We'll stop by on New Year's Day, on the drive back to Allentown. We'll talk through it."

"After you and Jordy are married."

"Yes."

"Are you doing this—this wedding thing—to prove to Mom and Dad that you're serious?"

"Maybe a little. But I bought the rings a week ago. Now that Jordy and I are finally together, I don't want to wait anymore. I'm sick of hiding who I am. When we're sitting in the living room watching the game on New Year's Day, I want to be able to put my arm around him, like any other couple."

"You don't have to be married for that."

"I think I do, after my mother tried to *break us up*."

Her tone softened. "Boy, you can't just let that go, can you." Her ironic sense of humor broke through.

He let out a soft chuckle. It felt good to release some of the tension stored in his muscles. Kat might be upset with him, but she was on his side.

"Ricky." Her voice turned quiet. "I love you. I don't want to miss your wedding. Please."

Jordan watched Rick stuff his phone into his pocket. His harried expression had eased somewhat, but he still looked tired.

Rick flopped onto the couch. "I hate that my mom can't just accept this."

Jordan scowled. "I thought you talked to Kat."

"I did. My mom hasn't even tried to contact me."

"She loves you, Rick. No matter what."

"Jordy, you don't get it. She *doesn't* love me. She loves the image in her mind of some perfect son, but that's not me. It's never been. Maybe now she's finally realized I'm not the man she thought I was. Maybe who I am isn't someone she can love."

"That's complete bullshit."

"You know how she is. When we were ten, and we broke the Moroneys' window playing baseball, she convinced herself it was your fault. I'm the one who hit the ball, even after you warned me we were too close to the house. Yet the whole time Dad was yelling at me, she was murmuring under her breath, 'That Jordan Callahan, he's such a troublemaker.' You tell me, which of us is the troublemaker?"

"Definitely you. Just ask *my* mom."

"Have you talked to her lately?"

"Not since yesterday. But she's coming to terms with the whole thing. I think she'll be okay."

Rick put his feet up on the ottoman and stared at his shoes. "Sometimes I think you'd be better off without me."

"Don't say that." Jordan walked over and sat with Rick on the couch. "We're right together. You're my soul mate—we bring out the best in each other. You've always got my back."

Rick snuggled up against him. "I love you, Jordy. I will always love you. No man could love you more."

Emotion rushed through Jordan's chest. He hated to see Rick this upset. There had to be a way to fix this. He would find a way to fix this.

The next morning, Rick stood under the showerhead letting the hot water run over him. As he rinsed the shampoo from his hair, the sound of the shower door popping open caught his attention. A moment later, Jordan's warm kisses caressed his neck. He dried his eyes, grateful that the hotel room sported a two-person shower.

"I'm sorry things suck right now." Jordy reached for the body wash. "Let me help you relax. Turn around."

Rick's cock jumped. He wasn't sure what Jordan had in mind, but for the moment, he was willing to go with it. He faced the tile, gray porcelain accented with glass in burgundy and blue. Jordan rubbed the gel over Rick's shoulders, loosening the tight knots. "Feels good," he said.

"Just getting started." Jordan massaged Rick's neck, his fingers loosening the thick cords of muscle. His hands glided down Rick's spine, working the muscles on either side.

Moans escaped his throat. The strong hands on his body soothed him, replacing tension with a cool tingle. When Jordan got to the small of his back, Rick groaned, the pain in the stubborn knot easing as it gave way under his lover's ministrations.

"Feeling better?" Jordan murmured in his ear.
"Mmm."

Hands rolled the muscles of his ass cheeks. He loved the warm feeling, but anticipation tightened his stomach. In the corner of his eye, Jordan squeezed silicone-based lube onto his hand from the handy-dandy bottle they had stashed in the shower for just such an occasion.

Instinctively, he backed into the warmth of Jordan's hand on his crease, the lube coating him. His cock thickened, but his shoulders clenched.

Jordy tugged on Rick's ear with his teeth. "Hands against the wall."

The growl in Jordy's voice told Rick there was no point in arguing. Jordan was usually the more agreeable one, but he had a stubborn streak once he'd made up his mind.

Jordan's slick finger stroked Rick's entrance. Heat rushed through him. Jordan's touch felt like heaven, teasing the sensitive nerve endings. Rick wanted to please him, but... "Are you sure this will work, standing up?" He'd fucked Jordan this way, but Jordan was more used to bottoming than he was.

"We'll make it work. Trust me," Jordan plunged his fingers inside. "Don't tense, babe. Let all the stress leave your body. It's just you and me, and we're crazy happy together. The rest of the world doesn't exist."

Jordan's thrusts drove the tightness out of his muscles. He breathed slow and deep, letting the hot water ease the tension in his back. Jordy's fingers brushed against his prostate, and he moaned.

"That's it," Jordan murmured. "I'm going to drive all the way into you. We'll go as slow as you need to, but you *will* take it all. And I don't want you touching yourself. Your hands don't leave that wall."

Rick closed his eyes, pushing away thought and letting sensation fill him. He liked it when Jordy took control, and he could just *feel*. Those long strokes put him on edge and left him hungry for more.

He threw his head back. "Now, babe. Need it."

"Not until you're ready to beg."

Rick whimpered. Jordan's fingers pumped him fast. Rick's cock, full and needy, bobbed in response. "Please," he groaned.

"Please what?"

"Fuck me." Rick couldn't keep the urgency out of his voice. He pressed hard against Jordan's hand, taking as much as he could.

Jordan clasped his free arm around Rick's waist. He pulled out his fingers, lubed himself up, and pressed at Rick's hole. "I own you."

"Yes."

"Say it."

"I'm your bitch."

Jordan plunged into him, the head breaking through the circle of muscle. Rick gasped, then breathed out, pulling the length further inside.

"Shh," Jordan murmured in his ear. "It's okay, babe. I've got you. I'll go so slow. Relax and breathe. I won't hurt you."

The stretch and burn eased as Rick's muscles adjusted to the fullness. Damn, how did Jordan talk him into this? Make him beg?

Jordan eased back, then moved forward again by millimeters. The gentle motion on Rick's prostate made his toes curl. As his body relaxed, Jordan moved faster. Rick remembered why he had begged.

He reached for his cock, but Jordy grabbed his hand and placed it back against the wall.

"No fair," Rick complained.

"You'll go off too fast. Just enjoy the moment, babe. Don't be so goal-oriented." He pushed deeper.

Rick moaned. He felt impossibly full, but he knew Jordan had more to give him. He closed his eyes and breathed, letting his muscles go loose. Each time he exhaled, Jordan's cock buried itself further inside him.

"Almost there," Jordan said. "Push toward me."

Rick angled his ass backward, and Jordan's pelvis thrust into him. Jordan's rhythm sped up to an urgent pace. Pleasure built in Rick's gland, a burning hot and deep. His balls grew taut, and his neglected cock ached. "Please, Jordy. Touch me."

Jordan's still-slick hand curled around him. Rick felt like a geyser about to blow, all that stored energy needing an outlet. "Oh, fuck, yeah!"

"Not yet," Jordan warned. His hand squeezed but didn't stroke.

"More."

"Patience."

Jordan's breaths deepened. Rick thrust back to hurry his lover's orgasm. With their bodies in frantic motion, Rick felt the tension building in his cock. He pumped into Jordy's hand.

Jordan cried out and spilled inside him. Hot cum coated his insides. The sensation drove him over the edge, and he shot onto his belly, the wall, and Jordy's hand.

Jordy pulled out, then wrapped himself around Rick, pressing his chest against his lover's back. "Still can't believe I get to do that to you."

"I can't believe I let you." Rick turned and kissed him. "It's better when you take control...I can relax and do what you say."

A laugh rumbled in Jordy's throat. "I didn't realize you were the submissive type. We'll have to play the Prison Shower game more often."

"Ha-ha. I wasn't submissive a few days ago, when we played the Redneck and the Twink."

"I'm not a twink. I'm too bulky."

"You had more bulk when we played football. Now you're strong and well-defined, like Michelangelo's David." He ran his lips along Jordy's neck. "And all mine."

Happiness shone in Jordan's eyes. He cleaned them up, then placed a kiss on Rick's nose. "Love you. It'll all be okay, you know."

"Yeah," he replied, but he didn't believe it.

Rick straightened the tie of his tuxedo. In the mirror, Jordan appeared, standing behind him.

"Will you stop primping?" Jordan laid his hands on Rick's shoulders. "You look fine. You look fantastic. I can't wait to marry you."

The butterflies in Rick's stomach had morphed into hummingbirds, whirring and poking him with their beaks. But as nervous as he was, he was deliriously happy. His throat thickened. He wanted this, and everything inside him told him it was right.

A stretch limo carried them the few blocks to the courthouse. As they lingered outside the room where the ceremony would be held, Rick paced, the muscles in his neck tightening. He kept checking the time on his phone, but it didn't seem to move forward.

Waiting made everything worse. The magnitude of what they were doing grew more and more clear in his mind. He had no doubts about Jordy, but he wished—

The sound of laughter echoed through the hallway. *Strange.* It sounded like Kat. The thought lifted his spirits a moment, but then squeezed his heart in a sudden burst of pain. He missed her. He wanted her there.

Footsteps approached and rounded the corner. He trembled, and Jordan grabbed his shoulders to steady him. There she was, Kat in front, carrying balloons. Behind were his parents, followed by Mrs. Callahan and her boyfriend.

"How did you—"

Jordan just grinned.

Kat fell into his arms, and he squeezed her, happier in that moment than he had ever been. Next came his father, who clapped him on the back, mumbled some embarrassing words, and stepped aside.

His mother held back, then walked deliberately toward him.

"Mommy," he said, feeling like a little boy again.

She hugged him. "Oh, Rick."

His eyes misted. He searched for words, but they seemed unnecessary now. She was there. That was all that mattered.

"I wish you hadn't left," she said. "But I understand now why you felt you had to. I was wrong to interfere. All I want is for you to be happy. And if Jordan makes you happy, then I'm grateful you found each other."

"I'm sorry I disappointed you."

"You could never disappoint me. You and Kat are the best things that ever happened to me. Nothing you could say or do could ever stop me from loving you. If you committed murder, I would be at your trial every day supporting you, because you're my son. One day, when you have children of your own, you'll understand."

"You know they won't be mine," he said. "Not biologically."

"They'll be yours in every way that matters. Yours and Jordan's. You'll be brilliant parents."

He looked over to see Jordan holding his own mother's hands, the two of them smiling, light shining in their eyes. Jordan met his gaze, and time stopped again, but this time in a good way. For that moment at least, everything was perfect.

A door burst open, and a couple emerged, words of congratulations emanating from the room behind them. As they strolled away, a tall graying man stepped from the room and said, "Callahan and Ferguson. We're ready for you now."

A thrill rose in Rick's chest. He moved as if on autopilot. He did as he was told, and said what he was expected to say. When he recited his vows, he meant every word. But before he knew it, the crowd of them were ushered out of the room. After all, it was a busy day for weddings, and there was no time to dally.

He and Jordan tumbled into the back of the limo. Rick stared at him a moment, then laughed. Jordan joined him, a happy, giddy sound. "Holy shit," Rick said. "We're married."

"Husband and husband." Jordan's eyes twinkled. He looked ridiculously handsome in his tux. Rick was certain he was the luckiest man alive.

Their family met them back at the hotel, where Jordan had arranged an intimate luncheon for them in a private room. Rick's senses were overwhelmed, colors brighter, sounds richer, aromas more piquant. He could barely follow the conversation, but it didn't matter. The people he loved most in the world were there, and they were smiling.

## THE END

# About the Author

Andrea Dalling lives in the sexy Southeast, where the summers are hot and the romance hotter. She loves to torture her characters but eventually rewards them with a happily-ever-after. Married to her college sweetheart, she's an advocate for LGBT rights. When she's not writing, she enjoys gardening at her Raleigh home and scuba diving in the clear blue waters of the Caribbean.

# More Books by Andrea Dalling

*Handling Cynthia*, Book 2 in the *Ache of Desire* series:

Her dark fantasies could rekindle their romance, or shatter their last chance at love.

Cynthia Darlington won't let her dream guy walk away again. With their five-year class reunion coming up, she can't stop reliving the memory of Trent Weber's kiss—his strong hands possessing her, and her body yielding to his demanding touch. The call of her submissive nature confused her then, but now she understands. With Trent, she's willing to give in to her decadent fantasies, even if only for a weekend.

Trent can't resist the chance to see Cynthia, but he's not the love-sick kid he was. Watching her leave with barely a good-bye was enough humiliation for a lifetime. Yet one look at her now—her expression as sweet as ever, her body poured into a tight black dress—reignites his desire to master this self-assured, independent woman. A weekend of her submission isn't enough. This time, he's determined to win her heart.

This steamy BDSM romance novella is intended for a mature audience. It contains scenes of flirtation, hot kisses, seductive bowling, a spoiled sub, a demanding Dom, second thoughts, and second chances.

*Commanding the Billionaire*, Book 4 in the ***Ache of Desire*** series:

It takes a strong man to surrender to a dominant woman.

Bernadette Holt needs a sub who can handle a good spanking. At her five-year high school reunion, Max Martinov seems eager to be treated as her personal slave. The geek who once followed her like a puppy has grown into a successful entrepreneur and a sculpted hunk of man muscle. She doesn't do love, but his humble adoration could strip her to her core.

Max's genius has made him CEO of a billion-dollar tech company. Outside work, he wants someone else in charge. His power holds no sway with Bernadette—she wants him on his knees. He'll have to push past his limits, endure every humiliation, to penetrate her steely exterior and find her heart.

This steamy BDSM romance is for a mature audience. It contains scenes of pain and gentleness, sweet kisses, sensation toys, a well-equipped dungeon, a bossy Domme, and a confident sub who sometimes gets too toppy.